Midnight Clear:
A Holiday Anthology

by

Carmen Green
Monica Jackson
Leslie Esdaile
Gwynne Forster

Edited by Donna Hill

Genesis Press, Inc.

Indigo is an imprint of
Genesis Press, Inc.
315 3rd Ave. N.
Columbus, MS 39701

Midnight Clear: A Holiday Anthology

ISBN: 1-58571-039-3

Manufactured in the United States of America

First Edition

Midnight Clear: A Holiday Anthology

Angel's Legacy

By Carmen Green

*M*ost folks never heard of Mystic Ridge, and if truth be told we like it just like that. You can't find it on the map and if you drive too fast you'll likely go right by it. But if you make that turn, the one down by the lake, between the thicket of bushes and trees, you'll ease right on into Mystic.

Legend has it that Mystic Ridge been around since the beginning of time, that our ancient ancestors walked across these lands, swam in these waters, setting our course, defining our destiny. More than four hundred years ago, slaves found the route to Mystic and settled here, bringing their sorrows, joys, traditions, and hope. Some say the ancestors still live in the mountains, sit by the rivers and walk along the paths, watching over all who come here, casting their spells and making mischief. I believe it's true. There's something real special about this place. Real special. Some believe the stories, some don't. But I been 'round long enough to know they be true. Yessir. I'll never forget the winter that it snowed. First time in nearly five years. Yessir, all kinds of havoc unfolded in Mystic. Knew it was coming, too. If you want to set a spell, I'll tell you all about it.

You see, it all started with a big rumbling up in the sky, like it was going to open up. Oh, yeah, I remember that year...

Angel's Legacy

Queen Nefertiti glanced over at her esteemed queenly counterparts, Sheba and Dahia, and waited for them to join her.

"Queens," Nefertiti said, "Come. Time is of the essence. We must make a decision as to whom we will bestow the legacy of leadership, spirit and wisdom."

Dahia, who fought her last battle in 702 A.D., stalked toward Nefertiti, agile as the fiercest lion of her day.

How different we all are, Nefertiti thought. While she was tall, slightly sun-kissed and preferred silk to lamb's wool, Dahia's color resembled the deepest shade of earth. And Dahia preferred her metal breastplate above any fine fabric.

Sheba, on the other hand, was a natural woman. Adorned with rings on her ears, neck, and arms, she possessed the stride of a goddess with her beauty further enhanced by the pride she took in being a woman.

Quite an odd group, Nefertiti thought, as the metal of Dahia's breastplate caught on a ray of heaven's light.

Sheba reached Nefertiti's side and adopted her at-ease stance.

"We must succeed this time," Dahia commanded. "Our future depends on it. Sheba! Have you narrowed down the selections?"

Makeda, the Queen of Sheba, considered Dahia with

an arched brow and a gentle but firm tone. "Calm yourself, sister. You are no longer on the battlefields of Aures
issuing orders to your men. Yes, I have done my job. Sit.
I am ready."

Queen Nefertiti, known for her beauty and intelligence, waited for the queens to gather around before
grasping their hands.

The resistance was real as Dahia, who had slain men
with those hands in her effort to save Africa from Arab
invasion, struggled with the notion that her hands were
needed for another type of battle.

Sheba, as exquisite as her name, struggled less, but
Nefertiti could see the wariness in her eyes.

"Give us her name," Nefertiti said to Sheba.

"Our chosen one is Angelina Snowden."

Dahia tugged to get free but was unsuccessful. She
stopped for a moment. "Did we not try with her mother,
Ruth Snowden?"

"Correct." Sheba's self-assurance was unconvincing
to the warrior priestess.

"Then why try again with the descendant of a failure?"

"Have we not all failed at one time or another? I fell
from my husband's grace before his death. You, Dahia,
were slain on the battlefields of your beloved country,
and Sheba bore David by a King she did not marry."

Sheba drew herself up. "That is a regret I care not to
discuss." Nefertiti didn't intend to engage that discussion
either. Sheba could go on and on about Solomon.

"We are here to instill the legacy," Nefertiti said. They
each turned to view moments of Angel's life. But it was-
n't birthday parties they watched. They studied her
fights, tests of her character, moments of failures.

"She's the one." Sheba saw Angel's future sons and
smiled. "So like my David. Strong. Men of God."

Dahia saw her strength. "She will fight for her land
and her family."

Nefertiti saw her wisdom. "Although beautiful, she will not rely on looks to enhance her success. She is smart. She has spirit. She is the chosen one. This legacy belongs to Angel."

Images flashed of a young Angel's numerous spankings for displays of stubbornness. A tear streaked her cocoa brown face as her father whipped her.

"Look at her," Dahia said in a hushed tone. "She is a warrior. He cannot break her spirit."

Nefertiti applied gentle pressure to Dahia's hand. "She survived. Look at her. She is love." They watched as the young Angel grew into womanhood and experienced her first love. They watched her fall in love and viewed her making love.

Sheba cocked her head. "They still do that? Solomon and I invented that move."

The queens smiled, indulging Sheba's fantasy. They each had invented moves of their own. Sheba continued. "She has traveled the world and has seen the atrocities perpetuated against our people and experienced the breakdown of our own self love. Yet, she is not bitter. Angel is the chosen one. Nefertiti?"

"Yes, dear one?"

"What say you?"

Nefertiti regarded her counterparts. "We have chosen in the past and failed. The legacy must be instilled before the turn of the millennium. The woman chosen will be responsible for restoring wisdom, leadership and spirit to the people of African descent. If the legacy is not instilled, our race will never know true unity. Angelina Snowden is our last chance. The Kings have chosen another male who will mate and marry Angelina. But they must mate and marry while in love, queens, or we have lost our opportunity. If we are of one accord, then let us link fingers, palm to palm where the lifelines meet and cast down the legacy."

Nefertiti held up her left hand and linked with Dahia's right. Sheba's right linked with Dahia's left and Sheba's left linked with Nefertiti's right. The circle was complete. The whispered prayers in the native language of each rose into a swell of adulation, hope and praise.

Power emanated from the trio, and from the soles of their feet to the tips of their hair, each shook with the pride of their African heritage. Nefertiti moved first, bringing her and Dahia's hands into the center of the group. They clasped together in a show of solidarity and spoke in unison.

"Father, you ordained us queens, but it is you we give the honor and praise. We are one in the spirit, one in you and we pass on our ordination to another of your children. Angel," they said in unison, "is the chosen one. We give her what you gave to us."

"Spirit," said Dahia.

"Wisdom," said Nefertiti.

"Leadership," said Sheba.

"Love," they said in unison. "We pass it on."

Tingles passed among the three and each opened her eyes to view Angel traveling in her car on a long dark stretch of road.

Her car jolted suddenly and came to an abrupt stop. Each held her breath. Then the car started to move again. And they breathed a collective sigh of relief.

Dahia and Sheba rose from their kneeleing position and watched Angel as she drove into her hometown of Mystic Ridge, Maryland.

"She's got it," Sheba said.

Dahia harrumphed. "Let's see what she will do with it."

"Angel will succeed," Nefertiti predicted, still on her knees, her hands clasped. She whispered a fervent prayer and joined the other two as the waiting began.

Chapter One

The long, dark desolate road snaked ahead of Angelina Snowden, winding her closer to her hometown of Mystic Ridge, Maryland.

She pushed back strands of her spiral-curled hair and guided her brand new candy-apple red BMW convertible through the clear night, keeping one eye on the road and the other on the hand held CD player remote.

The car had been an unmitigated indulgence when, she, as the first black executive for the Crown Company, had won the Dyer account, and it served as a reminder as to why she'd driven nearly two thousand miles from Los Angeles to Mystic Ridge.

Convincing the powers that be of the four hundred-year-old town that change is good would take some doing, but who better than she to do it? The Dyer Corporation was known for reviving the economy of small towns and according to her mother and other locals, Mystic Ridge was ripe for change.

Tall smoky columns of fog appeared suddenly and stretched toward the dark sky. The long white swirling pillars surrounded the car and it rocked as she drove deeper into the smoke screen.

Easing off the accelerator, Angel let her imagination run away for a moment and gave in to the first question that entered her mind: What lay behind this great white gateway?

Nothing in her life had ever been so. . . Mystical before.

She chuckled at the irony but caught her breath as her body started to tingle, going hot and cold in a full body flush.

Suddenly the car shook violently, casting her sideways.

In an act driven by instinct, she grabbed the steering wheel, planted both feet on the brakes and brought the vehicle to a screeching halt. Angel's heart raced, her palms sweat and her body shivered as her breath came in drawn-out gasps.

She opened her eyes to see a navy blue sky, dotted with glistening stars and a luminescent crescent moon.

The clouds were gone, the pillars of fog nonexistent. The flush that had flooded her body with sensation had been replaced by a warm sunk-in-the-tub feeling.

What had just happened?

Angel looked at herself in the rearview mirror.

Nothing was different. She didn't have any strange markings to indicate she was a case for the "X-Files", nor had she entered a new "Stargate" dimension.

She was on the highway, twenty-five miles from her mother and step-father's house——at a complete standstill.

White headlights on the other side of the tree-lined barrier continued to flow, but no car had come near her in the past half-hour. Angel decided not to chance fate or her safety and got underway.

After a few miles of riding in tense silence, she decided the car had malfunctioned and needed to be reprogrammed. The dealer would fix it when she got back to L.A.

Reassured, she pressed the gas pedal.

An ethereal voice, strong and distinct filled the car. "You are the chosen one."

Stomping on the brakes, Angel jumped from the vehicle, her mouth open in a frightened scream.

Who was speaking?

She grabbed her face, looking around for rescue, or any living soul to verify what she'd just experienced.

No one came. Minutes passed as she fought to regain control of herself. In the night air, her breath puffed a small cloud and her ringlet curls flapped into her eyes.

Angel stared at her car.

The driver side door gaped open and the bell dinged intermittent warnings. This is insane, she told herself repeatedly. I'm in the middle of the road, scared because my car talked.

Who'd believe me?

Suddenly the weight of all that had happened rushed over her and she promised herself to never repeat this incident to another living soul. Not even her mother who used to tell the most bizarre stories about. . .Angel swallowed. Being chosen.

People in Mystic Ridge chalked up her mother's tales to a 'rough time' when her first husband was killed in Viet Nam, but Angel sensed what they said behind closed doors before she'd married Luther.

Angel knew if she told anyone what had happened, her credibility would be shot and she'd never convince the town folk to allow Dyer to build a large variety store in Mystic Ridge.

Gathering her courage, she took tentative steps past the rear bumper and finally slid her foot, then the rest of her body into the car.

Familiar music from Yolanda Adams's CD began to play and Angel tried to swallow in her dry throat. I knew I should have flown. Twenty-four hours on the road would make anybody hallucinate.

A feeling of calm stole over her, washing away her fear.

Angel put the pedal to the floor and sped the last twenty miles to her mother's house.

"Why did you do that?" Sheba demanded of Dahia. "You intentionally tried to scare her."

Dahia looked unconcerned as she put her fists on her hips and planted her feet in a wide stance. "A warrior priestess should be challenged."

"This is the year 2000. She is not a warrior priestess. She is a modern woman challenged with saving a race. Do not spook her again."

Dahia advanced, her expression provoking. "And what will you do if I do?"

Sheba tilted her head to the side, her gaze no less challenging. "I will command the locust to invade your chambers and eat your eyes out while you sleep. Once they gain entry, they will suck on your capillaries, and eventually chew out your heart. When God sees you again, you will be an eyeless, heartless old woman who—" Sheba stared at her counterpart, "has rust on her breastplate."

Dahia grabbed the metal at her chest and staggered back.

Smug, Sheba walked away.

"Are you two finished?" Nefertiti asked, biting back a laugh at Dahia's drained expression.

"I am done," Sheba said confidently.

"You are insane. That is what you are." Dahia joined the ladies as they watched the reunion of Angel and her family.

"Behave, queens," Nefertiti said. "Our purpose is

higher than tests." She gave Dahia a stern look, then shifted her gaze to Sheba. "And control. Peter and Angel will meet soon. The real work has yet to begin. We must remain of one accord. Agreed?"

Dahia's chin lifted and Sheba slanted a compromising gaze at her rival. "Agreed. But she must control herself."

"I am the queen of ten thousand men!"

"Dahia!" Nefertiti could feel her patience wearing thin.

"Fine," Dahia finally conceded. "I am bored."

All three focused their attention on Angel and finally caught a glimpse of Peter.

"He's handsome," Sheba said with the heat of a woman who still desired after one hundred thousand years.

Dahia cast a knowing look at her. "He is quite a man. The kings have chosen well. Shall we begin our counsel?"

All three reclined on lounging clouds and awaited the reunion of Peter and Angel.

Chapter Two

*P*eter Richland strolled along Main Street's planked walkway, absorbing bits of life in the town that had been his home since his birth.

The weather was sunny and warm for the early November morning, and his shadow rolled across the weathered wooden sidewalk as he passed the Apothecary, Meadows Hardware store, Franklin's Antique Shop and Bunny's Beauty Salon.

Peter cast his gaze skyward when a flock of ducks flew overhead in a perfect V formation. From the park, children's voices floated toward him on a breeze, and based on the excitement level, he knew the elders had their hands full.

He took a moment and closed his eyes against the sunshine.

Wheat, yeast, butter, and spices scented the fall air and made his mouth water, while catapulting him on a dipping wave of nostalgia.

The pace and smell and feel—this was Mystic Ridge. Quiet, fragrant and unchanged by time, yet modern enough to stay afloat in the techno-crazy world.

Crossing the street, he headed toward the fourth generation owned Clay general store and slowed as Miss Lula Mae Clay stepped from the archway with her straw broom. When he was a child, he used to be scared out of his wits because Miss Lula Mae could make a pit bull cower. She still possessed that ability, but Peter was grown now, and they'd developed a mutual respect. Her daughter Maureen and her husband Will ran the store now, but Miss Lula Mae still came to work every day.

"Mornin', Miss Lula Mae. Beautiful day, isn't it?"

She arched her ninety-year-old eyes up to the sky and squinted. "The sun ain't been this bright since 1933. Course with it being the Great Depression and all, nobody but us po' folk noticed the sun at all. Just a regular day to us."

He chuckled, but didn't doubt her word.

She swatted at the dirt. "Heard a bit o' news, Petey."

Peter leaned against an old Ford truck parked diagonally in front of the store, and settled in for a spell.

"Care to share?" He expected to hear about her great-granddaughter Linda's latest pregnancy but the news had already spread. Darlene at the Apothecary had shared that little nugget of information about fifteen minutes ago. Still, he waited with polite interest. As the town council president, he was expected to listen and know the happenings in each of their lives.

Lula Mae swept vigorously for a moment then stopped just as abruptly. "Angelina Snowden done hit home. Arrived in the middle of the night. Her mama was up early buying some shrimp and fifty pounds of crabs."

Peter's heart hammered against his ribs and he wiped his mouth. "Shrimp, huh," he managed to say, his mind reeling.

Ruth's gumbo was renowned in these parts but when her daughter, Angelina, left fifteen years ago, so had Ruth's desire to cook.

A greater question pressed in on him and he let it flourish. What was Angelina doing home, and why hadn't he heard about it until after she'd arrived?

"Course Ruth and Luther are planning a welcome home party at their farm tonight."

"What time?" he said blandly, not knowing why he asked such an inane question.

"Same time as always, son. Dusk. Weren't you two thinking of jumping the broom at one time?"

Peter inhaled and let it out slowly. So this is what having Angelina home would do. Dredge up the painful past.

"We were young and foolish."

Lula Mae giggled like a schoolgirl. "Those were the best of times." Her voice softened. "You need to go and show her what she missed out on. Young, strapping buck such as yourself. It's her loss, Petey."

The vote bolstered his confidence and confirmed his good sense. He and Angelina were old history. She'd left town a lifetime ago and had never looked back. But memories of her lingered like the sweet taste of cranberry tea. "I expect they can have a party without me, Miss Lula Mae. I have lots of town business to attend to."

Peter didn't ever compare himself to others, but he imagined the type of man Angelina would now be attracted to.

Probably some Ivy League, loafer-wearing brotha who wouldn't know a wheelbarrow from a tractor.

She was a corporate professional who undoubtedly earned good money and had a lot to show for her hard work. She probably made as much as ten of the citizens of Mystic Ridge put together. He was no closer to corporate America than he was to becoming the Mayor of Saturn. Sure he ran Mystic Ridge, but his suit of armor was dusty jeans, not hundred dollar suits. "I won't have time to stop by."

Lula Mae swatted him with the broom. "You know what they say about he that protests too much. The day you ain't got time to visit old friends and see what brought them home, is the day this town begins to die. If you don't go, how will I know what went on, Petey? I can't get around like I used to and if I do go, they sho' don't want me to show my knees and start dancing. Naw, they don't."

The image made him chuckle. Pulled by an unknown lure, he felt himself changing his mind. Peter grappled with his indecision. This was a first. He always made decisions and stuck with them, but even as he wanted to resist, he heard himself say, "All right. I'll go. Just for you."

Miss Lula Mae hugged his frame, although he towered a half dozen inches over the woman who used to stand a statuesque five foot ten. How could he deny this sweet old lady? Miss Lula Mae represented the essence of Mystic Ridge and he couldn't let her down. Could he? "I'll have a full report on Monday."

"You do that. And pass along my respects. I got to get back inside and take my nap. The chil'ren will be home from school in a few hours. I got to have my wits about me to deal with that lot."

"Have a good one."

Lula Mae passed Maureen, who stopped shelving bottles of syrup bearing Mystic Ridge's name, to wave at him.

Peter continued on his daily stroll and heard the news again and again. Angelina Snowden was back.

Back in his office, his first cousin and secretary, Brenda, stuck her head in his doorway. Brenda was one of those relatives people used one word to describe. Different. Her most recent thing was to shave her head completely bald. She had slightly bugged eyes, which were further enhanced by the roundness of her head.

Peter just looked at her and prepared to be swept away by her fast-talking mouth.

"Did you hear? Angelina Snowden is back. I wonder why she's here? Been so long since I last saw her." She tugged the tire around her waist. "I hope she got fat like the rest of us. Do you suppose something is wrong with Ruth? Maybe Angelina is the one sick."

Peter massaged his sun-bronzed forehead. "Don't you have anything else to do besides mind Ruth's business?"

Brenda eyed him strangely. "When aren't you up for town gossip? Honey, for your information, I have plenty to do. Ruth is having a party for Angelina and I'm going. Can I leave? Nobody is coming to see you."

"What's that supposed to mean?" Affronted, he lined up his Bic pens then straightened his Post-it note pads. In truth, today was slow, but there was always something to do. He pulled out a stack of invoices. These had to be approved, signed and mailed.

"Peter, quit fooling yourself. This ain't Alexandria or Wilmington. The only people that called today were Charlotte and Rudy from the edge of town and they wanted to complain about the stop sign you told Oscar to put up near their road. They said nobody comes out that way so why have a sign." She twirled her finger in the air. "Whoop-dee do."

Peter rubbed his cap from his head. "Did you say you were leaving?"

"I sure did. You coming to Ruth's?" Brenda talked while she packed her satchel with her lunch containers. "Let the past go and come see Angelina. It's been a long time. Do you think one of them is sick?"

Ruth wasn't sick. He'd just seen her about a week ago at Clay's. "No, I think she's just home to visit her mother."

"Well, my second cousin Bertha on my father's side thinks you're cute."

Bertha was six feet four and wore more hair on her face than he. "How fast are you leaving?"

Brenda grabbed her bag and gave her head a

resigned shake. "You're alone because you've got a dry personality, Peter." With affection in her voice she said, "See you tomorrow."

Brenda's car rumbled to a start and faded in the distance.

Thankful for the silence, Peter gave her words serious consideration.

Did he indeed have a dry personality? Is that why he and Angelina never hooked up? Is that why he at thirty-three wasn't married when all his brothers and male cousins were in meaningful relationships? Had his supposed personality flaw kept him from experiencing the joy of having a family of his own?

Peter tried to laugh at the insecure notions. His voice cracked and he injected some bass until the laughter bloomed full and rich. Much better. I'm not married because I'm not ready to be married.

He finished the invoices and dragged out some zoning requests and didn't resurface until after the sun had set.

The party was in full swing by now.

He tried not to think about what Angelina would look like, but he couldn't help it.

She had been gorgeous as a young woman; she could only be extraordinary now. His body stirred at the memories of him and Angelina together. They'd managed to balance wit with intelligence and pleasure with control. They'd often refrained from fulfilling the desires of their flesh, but...

Sometimes, Angelina just made him so hot, his craving for her had to be sated. He wondered if they would still generate such heat.

Peter looked down at the zoning requests and shoved them back in the drawer. There was only one way to find out.

Chapter Three

Angel quietly closed the front door of her mother's plantation style home, headed around the wrap-around porch and toward the back swing. In search of solitude, she ducked past an open window where her step-father Luther and aunt Dolly sat talking and eating.

The reunion had been a nice idea, but even as her mother had paraded endless relatives past her, and she'd become reacquainted with friends she hadn't seen in years, Angel found herself looking for the one person who hadn't come.

Settling on the swing, she shoved into a gentle wind, leaned back and let the cool breeze nip at her disappointment.

Since arriving home, life as she'd known it had ceased to exist. Almost immediately, she found herself letting go of the intense California pace for the leisurely flow that was vintage Mystic Ridge.

Angel closed her eyes and let the swing sway in weightless motion. The spicy fragrant air, the people—this was Mystic Ridge. It felt good to be home.

The scent of man and musk greeted her and her stomach jumped at the familiarity. He was here. Finally.

Two hands slid up her shoulders, nudged and sent the

swing into a gentle rhythm. Excitement curled through her veins and raced toward her head.

"Welcome home."

Peter's deep voice caressed her and warmed the cool breeze.

"Peter Richland." Angel wished she hadn't whispered his name so softly. She sounded as if she had been waiting for him. "What a surprise."

He stopped the swing, and came around.

Unable to find the strength to stand, Angel pushed back on her heels and looked up. So he'd known where she'd been all along. Her roiling emotions vacillated between flattery and disappointment. Why hadn't he come around sooner?

"They teach you that in California?" Again the deep texture of his voice rolled over her like warm butter on a hot roll.

"What?"

"To lie to old friends."

An argument as dusty and old as the ground beneath her feet resurfaced and Angel wondered where Peter was going. Surely he'd gotten over her leaving Mystic Ridge for a better life. "Don't be ridiculous." To establish more even footing, she found her professional voice. "How are you, Peter?"

He gazed into her eyes, his expression serious. "How do I look?"

"Healthy. Strong." Sexy. "Good."

He stooped his tall frame down in front of her. "What was that glint in your eyes before you said good?"

Angel averted her gaze so the truth wouldn't spill from her lips. "Nothing."

"You were never shy, Angelina. You always spoke your mind. Every thought. Every idea. Always the truth." His voice dipped low. "Is lying an institution on the West Coast or can you buy a video and learn like that Tae-bo?"

She must have looked surprised because he said, "We
do get cable in these parts."

Angel laughed at herself, at him. "Of course not." He
was pushing to know who she was, searching to see if
there was any resemblance to the woman who'd left so
long ago. She wanted to say she was the same, but held
back. Peter had no right to be so familiar with her. Other
men had tried and failed. And as much as Peter tried to
regain ground, she resisted.

Only his voice stroked her, filled her up with seductive
memories of the past and romanticized their youth. Her
body fairly hummed and all she could imagine was for
him to hold her and never let her go.

The thought scared her.

That thought was a 'marry me' thought. And Angel
would never do that. The path was littered with men
who'd asked and been rejected.

California was scarce on men who sought the truth.
Between the ego-fragile actors, the wannabes, the men
who shunned "the business" and the boys from the val-
ley, few had ever wanted to keep it real.

But Peter was real. His denim shirt hugged a six pack
of muscles that her hands itched to remember. Long
legs were tucked into worn jeans, his feet pressed into
broken-in boots.

On his head he wore a newer version of the high
school's baseball cap, and where he once wore glasses,
dark brown orbs looked clear into her. His hands
teetered inches from her waist and his mouth—Angel
recalled how it felt to the touch.

"Tell me." He spoke slowly. "Your thought between
strong and good."

He still hadn't touched her and she yearned for it.

"Are you married, Peter?" In her heart she prayed she
wouldn't crumble to pieces with his answer.

"No." Emphatic. Direct. The same Peter.

His finger touched her breastbone. Angel stood as if under the influence of a powerful magnet. The swing's linked chain lined her spine and she answered him. "Sexy."

He answered with a pleased chuckle that made her day.

Peter moved to embrace her.

Angel felt his power, his strength, the safety he offered and let herself lean into him. Her body shook as she vowed to hug him and let him go, because she knew what touching him would do. Remind her of the last time he'd held her. Been over her. Inside her. Beneath her.

His arms glided slowly around her back and he seemed to lift her off her feet as he brought her closer. They hovered, until she felt the muscles in his arms contract.

Angel closed her eyes.

And he squeezed.

A thousand points of light burst in her head. In her heart she commanded time to stand still. The moans of the cattle in the distant fields ceased and the insects hushed.

Angel listened to Peter's strong, steady heartbeat and felt hers slow to meet the pace. They stayed this way for what seemed an eternity.

"Welcome home, Angelina."

"Thank you. Call me Angel."

Like a stalled carousel infused with a jolt of electricity, reality lurched into their world. One by one, the sounds of bugs, animals, music from the house and voices filtered through the haze of their reunion.

Peter stepped back as if he just remembered an important obligation. His eyes held a distant curiosity and his arms fell to his side. "Angel? When did that happen?"

Wary of his reaction to her new self, Angel clasped her

hands together and stepped back. "It's just one of those things. Angelina can be such a mouthful."

"No one around here ever had a problem with it."

So this was it. Her leaving would stand between them. She'd come back stronger, and more confident than the person that had left, but obviously Peter couldn't handle it.

"I'm still me."

His gaze took in the mass of ringlet curls, her designer clothes and the choker around her neck and Angel could just imagine his thoughts.

He nodded as if in acquiescence. "So, what brings you home?"

Careful, she warned herself. Peter was a man who needed time to adjust to change. Angel could tell that from the way he looked at her. She pushed a curl behind her ear.

"I came home to see my mom and Luther." They took leisurely steps back toward the house. Now that wasn't a lie. "And do a bit of business in Maryland."

"Ah," he nodded. His voice slid into the night. "How long are you staying?"

Their eyes met. A hundred unspoken questions filled the space between them, but Angel couldn't bring herself to move away. It felt good to be in his presence and she answered as truthfully as she could. "Until my work is done."

"So you just came home to take care of some business and see your folks. Nothing to rush back to?"

"I beg your pardon?"

He shrugged. "You might have a dog or a cat or a tiger." Angel started to laugh. "I don't know," he said. "Or you might have somebody."

She pulled her top lip between her teeth and moistened her lips. "No tigers allowed in my county. I don't have dogs or," she hesitated and watched him draw in a deep breath. She smiled slowly. "Cats."

Their right feet hit the bottom stair at the same time. "If I didn't know better, Peter Richland, I'd think you wanted to know if I were involved."

Angel put her hand on the beveled white post and swung to face him. "What I can't imagine is why that would be of interest to you."

"A man can't satisfy his curiosity?"

"Most definitely." She leaned against the post, curious about him, too. How had he managed to stay single? Why hadn't life changed him? Why had he stayed in Mystic Ridge?

She knew that his job as the town council president held the prestige afforded to the Mayor of a larger city.

Peter made the decisions here and his opinion was sought after and well-respected. She knew in order to bring a company the size of a Mall-mart into the area, she'd have to go through him, but she wanted to get a feel for the town and the people on her own. The time would come when they would sit across from each other in a boardroom, but tonight they might as well have been eighteen again. Keep it light, she told herself.

Angel crossed her arms and answered him. "Well, old friend, I'm single. So——"

He pulled her by her crossed arms until his mouth was inches from hers. "Well then, old friend. Let me give you a proper welcome home."

Peter's mouth covered hers in a sensual meeting that sent a bolt of pleasure rocketing through her.

In an instant of blind pleasure, she opened her mouth. . . and met cool air.

He was gone.

Angel opened her eyes. The bright light from the porch blinded her briefly. Her chin fell to her chest. It was just a friendly kiss. Embarrassed, she covered her mouth and dried her lips.

"Coming in?" Peter said.

Angel couldn't meet his gaze as she stepped past him and walked into the house. "You'll pay for that—old friend," she said under her breath as her relatives greeted him with raucous hellos.

They accepted beers from her cousin. Then Peter slid his index finger down her shoulder blade.

Angel pivoted, knowing his touch anywhere. He tapped his can with hers. "Looking forward to it."

Chapter Four

Dahia whooped and tossed Sheba into the air. They hugged like sisters, then realized what they were doing and snapped apart. Sheba shifted the fabric around her legs and shoved her chin into the air. "You're insane. I do not know what has come over you."

Dahia danced by, her eyes glittering like African gold. "Our job is done. They have kissed. Now I can receive the final crown."

Nefertiti shot Sheba a warning glance, and Dahia's eyes turned into a sparkling obsidian. "Queen Dahia," Nefertiti said. The woman whirled around, her spine ramrod straight. "Look at the lifeline on your palm. Is it not faint like mine? Like Sheba's?"

"It is not!" she declared, staring at her hand. She closed it into a tight fist. "Mine is dark like the earth's richest soil."

"Mine, too, is dark," Sheba said. Surprised, Nefertiti stood, looked into Dahia's then Sheba's extended hand.

Dahia's hand looked as if the bark of an oak had been etched into it. Sheba's was more the color of clay.

Nefertiti unfurled her fingers and stared at her palm. The color of sand.

"Look, sisters," she exclaimed, excited. "We are making a difference. It is working."

"Working? It is done. We are done. Are we not?" Dahia said, suddenly unsure.

Sheba examined their palms and touched the center. "Storm clouds are rising. Dahia, you are the warrior priestess. Angelina is approaching her fiercest battle. Will she survive?"

The priestess was able to view flashes of peril ahead. "She will be wounded," she said gravely. "But she will survive."

They turned to view Angel as she walked through town, reacquainting herself with the people. After acquiring two parcels of land from gentlemen at the retirement home, she stopped at the daycare and spoke to the elderly. Soaked up their wisdom, shared her youth.

As the day shifted towards afternoon, her steps slowed, her shoulders heavy, her thoughts jumbled. She'd learned much about Mystic Ridge, her hometown. It was the same, yet different.

The queens felt the draw on her strength.

Without words they linked arms, stood shoulder to shoulder and infused their energy into Angel.

As her stride ate up the wooden sidewalks, her head arched toward the sun. "She can feel us. Go forth and conquer, priestess," Dahia said strongly.

Angel jogged toward her car, confidence replacing her worry.

Nefertiti clapped her hands and smiled.

Peter sat across from Roy Cochran, the only real estate agent within four counties, and tried to look interested while Roy expounded on the health of his livestock.

But Peter's eyes kept closing and each time they did, he saw Angelina. Beautiful, sexy Angelina. Desire heat-

ed his blood to a simmer and made him adjust, not for
the first time, in his seat.

Roy misinterpreted the movement and hurried along.
"I know you're a busy man, but the reason I stopped by
was to tell you that somebody has bought up about seventy-five acres of land that comprise the south bank."

Surprised, Peter sat up. The land known as the south
bank represented Mystic Ridge's beginning. It had been
built by runaway and freed slaves four hundred years
ago.

By way of compensation, each of the original families
in Mystic Ridge owned five acres of the south bank and
had agreed to never sell the land so that it would be a
legacy for future generations. The fact that strangers
owned it alarmed him.

"How much did you say is gone?"

"About seventy-five of the three hundred acres." Roy
sat forward. "Joe and Lacy Jordan called and mentioned
that some surveyors from Baltimore stopped by the truck
stop and said they were working on some land called the
south bank. Lacy got right on the phone and called me
and I came by to see you."

Peter nodded his appreciation. "You did the right
thing. But if you didn't handle the deals, how is it gone?"

Roy scratched his grizzly whiskers with thick fingers.

"Apparently somebody has been paying the taxes on
land that was forgotten about when some of the old folks
died. Recently the papers were filed in Baltimore and the
property converted to a company's name." He dug into
his breast pocket. "The Dyer Corporation."

Peter scratched down the ominous sounding name.
Big companies were always trying to encroach upon the
tranquillity of Mystic Ridge. Years ago it had been condo
developers and before that homey B&B's.

It seems hardworking city folk needed a place to rest
on the weekend and with Mystic Ridge being four hours

between two major cities, many thought it a perfect place to escape—with a few minor improvements.

Most of Mystic Ridge's citizens liked the tourism dollars, but they wanted people to enjoy Mystic Ridge just as it was. Peter cringed every time he thought of what had become of Savannah, Georgia. That land had once been home to settlers and now was one of the biggest tourist attractions in Georgia. Only it wasn't the native Blacks that were rich. They'd sold land to developers dirt cheap and now worked on land they once owned.

Seventy-five acres of the south bank was significant. He tried not to convey his alarm and opted for damage control.

"Roy, are the purchased sections connected?"

The older man shook his head. "But there's a possibility that they could be. Lula Mae Clay owns one piece, your daddy owns another and about five separate pieces are owned by some of the old folks in Tracey's Retirement Home. All told, they need about seven more pieces to connect what they've got."

"That's good news. Whoever is buying can be stopped. They seem to have gotten the easiest lots first. But the rest of us won't sell." Peter grabbed his baseball cap and he and Roy shrugged into winter jackets.

Brenda had already gone to lunch and Peter didn't expect her back for another hour. He decided to take his daily walk and figure out how to handle this latest development.

His breath huffed in front of him and he slowed his stride to accommodate Roy's slower pace. "Peter, would it be so bad for a business to come in?"

"Not if it were the right one."

"What's right in your mind?"

Peter shook his head. "My preference is for Mystic Ridge to remain a small town where the people know their neighbors and look out for one another. Towns like ours that grow too fast, invite trouble. We don't have the resources to fight drugs and crime. We don't have to worry about locking our doors, and if we forget, we're not worried.

"Our town has the lowest divorce rate in the state because we know the meaning of family. I won't jeopardize all that we've built. Believe me, Roy, Mystic Ridge is fine just the way it is."

When Roy continued his silent contemplation, Peter pressed on. "Do you want pollution and crime to invade your life?" Peter urged Roy to look at the mountains. "Do you want all this to disappear? The peace? The hominess? That's what would happen. Trust me," he said, determined to make his longtime family friend understand. "You don't want that."

Roy hooked his hands together behind his back. "No, I don't. But my son and daughter-in-law can't stay in Mystic Ridge without having jobs that will support the life they deserve. They've got degrees in marketing. What can they do here?"

Aware of the flat economy and lack of jobs, Peter nodded his head in agreement. "True, Mystic Ridge isn't Baltimore or D.C., but I promise you, whatever company is buying up that much land will destroy this town. I can't let that happen. I'll do some research on them today and by this evening I should have a clear picture of what they want."

They stopped in front of Roy's office and the man's eyes were sad. His gaze roamed over the cream stucco building before meeting Peter's.

"Junior and Sharon are all Muriel and I have left. If they leave, we're going with them. I don't know too many of us old folks who don't want to be around their grand kids. If a company is interested, we should listen. Think about it, Peter."

Roy clapped him on the shoulder and Peter considered his words as he stopped at Bunny's hair salon. He greeted the ladies, ranging in age from eighteen to eighty, and guided them into a conversation about the economy. The spirited conversation gave him insight to everyone's feelings, but the consensus was that they were satisfied with Mystic Ridge's present state.

After a brief stop at the daycare and the Apothecary, Peter continued on his stroll to Clay's General store. Maureen stepped from the aisles and greeted him with a big smile. "Peter. Good to see you."

"Thanks, Maureen." He removed his hat. "Miss Lula Mae up?"

"No, she's down for a nap with little Will. I think she sleeps longer than he does most days. Anything I can do for you?"

After listening to the ladies at the salon, Peter didn't want to start a four-alarm talk-fest about the south bank, so he backed toward the door. "Thanks, but no. I'll see Miss Lula Mae tomorrow."

"All right then."

He stepped outside, when struck with a thought. "Can I borrow your phone, Maureen?"

She walked behind the register and handed him the cordless. "Help yourself. I'm running to the back for a second. Just leave it on the counter when you're done."

Peter dialed Lacy at the truck stop. When he finished, he hung up and strode back to his office and hopped into his truck.

It seems that someone other than the surveyors were interested in the grassy lands that made up the south bank.

Lacy had just given Angelina Snowden a large cup of coffee and short cut directions.

Chapter Five

Angel stepped from her car and drank in the sight of the lush fields that spanned for miles, rich and vibrant under the native sun.

Birds cawed overhead, dipping and swirling in the magnificent daylight. She shielded her eyes with her hand and executed a deliberate three-hundred-sixty-degree turn.

Everywhere she looked, she noticed pearls of the earth's beauty. A duck tucked his neck and dove in for a landing. A raccoon scuttled along the bank of trees. A family of deer darted into the brush.

The south bank had changed in fifteen years. When she had last visited, cars could proceed only so far on the gravel roads. Now paved roads led the way and as she followed the precise directions through unfamiliar woods, she heard the lap of water. Nostalgia stole over her.

Peter brought her here once to Point Royal Lake. Just thinking of him gave rise to guilty feelings. He deserved to know the real reason why she'd come home.

She strolled the edge of the body of water, reacquainting herself, then stooped and gathered a handful of pebbles. One at a time, she tossed them into the lake, each ripple finding its way back to her.

*You are the pebble and all that you do will touch oth-
ers, and you will be blessed.*

It was the same voice from the car, only Angel wasn't
afraid. A strong sense of responsibility overcame her
and she wrapped her arms around herself and twisted in
the cool breeze. If she ever questioned why she'd come
home, she had her answer. Mystic Ridge needed her.
Just as she needed to connect with the people she and
Peter once were.

When they'd come to Point Royal, they'd been full of
youthful ideals. They'd planned a future at this lake and
she smiled as she remembered their brazen thirst for life.

But the very ideas that brought them together had torn
them apart. Peter wouldn't consider making a life outside of Mystic Ridge. And she couldn't reconcile that
Mystic Ridge was the only choice for life.

Dreams had pushed her to leave and saw her through
six years of UC Berkeley. Master's degree in hand, she'd
paved her way in the world until she was at this lake-
side—right back home.

Angel shook her head.

Behind her trees rustled, and she turned in time to see
Peter burst through a patch of dense foliage.
Surprised,her heartbeat increased and she fought off a
welcoming smile. He deserved to know the truth. She
couldn't deny him that.

His arms were laden with a patchwork quilt and a
thermos.

Glory, he looked handsome. Taller than the average
man, he couldn't help but grab attention. Crayola brown,
with a serious face he'd earned from his daddy, he
squinted at the eastern sun and adjusted his baseball
cap.

He took his time joining her and Angel felt herself waiting for him to grace her with a word. "Angelina."

Uh-oh. "Peter Dawson Homer Richland."

His head whipped sideways. "Don't call me that. You know I hate that name."

"Call me Angel." He looked as if he would protest. "A compromise works best if both parties agree."

Angel kicked at some rocks and closed her eyes on a burst of cool air. "How did you know I was here?"

"Mystic is small. Lacy told me. The temperature is changing and here you are in the woods, at the lake, in high heels, unprepared," he scolded.

"Aw. You care."

He shrugged off her sarcasm.

"Joke if you want, but I'll bet you couldn't find your way back to your car if I laid a hundred dollars in your hand."

She accepted the challenge and pointed in one direction, turned, and pointed over her shoulder. Suddenly the woods all looked alike. "Well. . .I'd have found it eventually."

"If the bears didn't find you first."

She gave him a disbelieving look. "I don't scare that easily." To prove her point, she let him walk a few yards away before she followed and sat on the blankets he'd laid down. Angel took a grateful sip of hot coffee.

Resting his elbow on his propped up knee, he pulled blades of grass from the ground, tore them into strands and pointed straight ahead.

At the far end of the lake, two deer broke from the forest, sipped water then abruptly lifted their heads to view them. Angel felt the scrutiny from all the locals. The deer turned and ran. Peter stayed and gave her a look she couldn't avoid any longer.

"Mystic Ridge," he began, "is Maryland's mistress. She's the best kept, most seductive secret the state has ever had."

"Secrets are almost always revealed."

He shook his head. "The beauty of our town is that we're forgettable. For four hundred years we've man-

aged to keep out people who want to hurt us. Change
us. Strip the innocence under the guise of 'helping us
advance.' Shame, isn't it?"

She felt as if she'd been punched in the stomach.
"What," she whispered.

"That outsiders, people who haven't ever loved this
town the way I love it, think they know what's best."

Angel thought of all the small town jokes she'd fielded
in L.A. because of her accent. How during her first years
at Berkeley she'd worked hard to smooth it out, make it
twang less. How over time, she'd become less the butt
of jokes, and more the perpetrator.

"I love it, too, Peter," she said, but felt the words fall
from her mouth and shatter like panes of glass. Had she
really changed? When had her resentment for the livestock, and dirt, and one stoplight town turned to love?
Confused, Angel didn't know.

And until she knew, she couldn't perpetuate a false-
hood. She'd already lied enough. Tonight when he
came to her step-father's meeting, he'd know why she
was home. The whole town would and from then on
things would be different.

Deep in her own thoughts, she was startled when she
felt Peter behind her. His long legs snuggled up beside
hers and he embraced her. Warmth emanated from him
and penetrated through her back. "I'm glad to hear that.
Maybe you'll find lots of reasons to stay."

Even as wanting rocked her system, she couldn't give
in. Stay? Staying in Mystic Ridge would mean abandoning all she'd worked for. No matter how much she
wanted to share Peter's warmth, she could only pray that
when it was time for her to go, there wouldn't be any
emotional hang-ups.

"The last time we were here was pretty special," he
said.

"That's because you thought you were getting some,"

she reminded him.

"And I didn't?"

Her cheeks grew hot. She closed her eyes, glad he couldn't see her face. "You tried," she conceded.

"Tried, hmm. Let me test my thirty-two-year-old memory."

His hands slipped beneath her wool jacket and found the softness of her poplin shirt. They moved in gentle strokes across her belly, settling her back against him.

Low and easy, he started to speak. "We came up here one August night, the heat hanging thick in the air. I laid down one of Ruth's soft patchwork quilts and lowered you beside me. You looked so expectant and shy and I felt your innocence. I knew the night was special for us and I wanted to give you the very best I could."

She rocked gently on the cadence of his voice. She felt the heat now, remembered it from way back when.

"You wore the prettiest pink top with these tiny pearl buttons and I took my time releasing each one. I needed to see you. Had to. You were beautiful." His lips touched her behind her ear. "You're more beautiful now. With each button, I saw your skin, wanted to touch it. Feel its softness beneath my fingertips. Like now."

"Yes."

He pulled the long zipper that started at the neck, and in a lazy motion, opened her to his exploration.

He didn't reach for her breasts although they strained for his touch. His fingers found her neck, tipped her head to lean on his shoulder. Angel released the last of her reserve and rested against him.

"Your bra was stark white against your skin and I pulled it down one shoulder and up on the other." His laughter was full of anything but humor. "Didn't know what I was doing. Just wanted to touch you."

Her bra snapped open on her back.

"Figured out finesse, I see," she sighed.

His large hands covered the slopes, her nipple caught between his middle and ring finger. The pressure was enough to make her moan aloud. "It was worth it to feel you like this."

They stayed this way, him stroking her breasts, making her hot in the confines of the old quilt.

Touching her breasts was safe. But she wanted to hear the rest. "Tell me, Peter."

"I couldn't stop with just touching your breasts, tasting them. I had to know your hidden treasures." His hand touched her belly. Searched lower. "You had on these blue shorts with this ruffle around the legs. Never seen anything sexier than that in my young life."

"Really," she said, feeling his hand snake slowly towards her center. Her breathing shallowed. She anticipated. Hoped. Prayed.

He touched.

Her heart sang.

"The shorts were gone and the white panties disappeared. There you were. Naked before me. I wanted to see pleasure in your eyes." His hand cupped her at the apex of her body and she pushed into his chest and lifted her hips. Through her panties his thumb played her like she were the string on a precious violin. Her body had its own music and it felt sweet with Peter as its maestro.

"I laid you down and went on a search to find every curve, bend and fold that would bring you pleasure. Make you feel good, special."

She pulled air deep into her lungs. Teetering on the edge. If only. . .he would let her go over.

Needing to, she lifted her hips and for a second she was airborne.

Then lying beneath him.

His breath touched her cheeks, her lips. "I want you."

The length of him pressed into her and she moved not

to tease, but to satisfy. "No protection."

"Next time," he said, lifting her butt into his hands and rocking himself against her until the bright blue sky shattered into a million drops of silver stars.

His coat was still on. Hers gaped open.

Her body tingled in the wind.

His manhood stood prominent against his jeans.

"Peter," she whispered. Her body trembled.

"You said my name just like that the last time." He caught the tip of her nose between his teeth.

Angel closed her eyes. He'd see the truth. Truth and betrayal couldn't co-exist. "You're embarrassing me."

"Don't be. It's just me. Peter."

His mouth descended toward hers. Discouraging him was an option, but anticipation rose and Angel couldn't fight it. She wanted his kiss as much as she wanted her next breath.

His gaze flicked over her. Then his mouth covered hers, knowing the valleys and plains, staking chartered territory. His tongue lined her lips and she parted, tasting him with fervor and longing.

Shudders of pleasure zinged through her and Angel sank deeper into his kiss. But guilt sneaked in. Stole the joy, tarnished the passion and usurped her desire.

Sadness rushed in and her mouth slid from his. She buried her face in his collar. She was using him. Misleading him.

He must have sensed her emotional withdrawal. "Don't ever tell me you're sorry this happened. We're not children. I want you. All the way. Remember that." He pushed to his feet and the cold rushed in and enveloped her. He gave her a hand up. "One day at a time."

"Right."

"We'd better get back. I've still got a couple of hours work to finish."

Work. Yes. The reason why I'm home in the first

place.   "I do, too."

He helped her rearrange her clothes, gathered the blanket and she the coffee.

Angel followed him through the woods, glad to concentrate on the rough terrain.

Ten minutes later, she slid into her car. "Thank you for," she searched for the right words, "coming to see me."

He leaned on the door and kissed her hard. As a reminder.

Then he stepped back. Looked directly into her eyes.

"Would you know anything about surveyors up in these parts?"

Her heart raced so fast, she became lightheaded. What had Dyer done? No surveyors were supposed to be up here until the last parcel of land was secured. Had they gone behind her back? No, they trusted her to do her job. Perhaps one of the families wanted to get their property staked.

She shook her head and squeezed her eyes shut in a silent prayer.

"What's the matter?" he said.

"I-I haven't eaten."

"See you later?" His eyes conveyed interest and longing.

"I have a thing tonight at my parents home."

Peter nodded. "L.A. talk is interesting. A thing." He shrugged, his grin seducing her sinning soul. "Luther invited me over, too. I'll see you there." He caressed the car's bright red finish. "And maybe afterwards."

Her breath caught in her throat. "Yeah. Maybe."

"Follow me. I want to make sure you and your fancy car make it back safely."

His truck rumbled to life and she trailed him back to Mystic Ridge. He cast a hearty wave when she veered right at the fork leading to her mother's house.

How deceitful have I become? Has L.A. turned me into a pathological liar, or do I lie for sport?

Grateful her mother was gone, Angel climbed into a hot bath, but couldn't soak away the guilt of knowing how hurt Peter would be later tonight.

Chapter Six

The engine on Peter's truck sputtered and the car shut down. Steering to the dusty shoulder, he turned the key. *Click.* The battery was dead.

He got out on the road, figuring the distance to Luther and Ruth's house, and completed the mile trek in just under fifteen minutes.

Angel's car was parked on the grass some distance from the house, leaving room for all the familiar vehicles. Looked like the whole town council was there.

Pushing the handle on the front door, he let himself in and was greeted with friendly hellos.

Ruth came and hooked arms with him. "I didn't hear you pull up."

"My battery died a mile up the road." He grinned down at her. "You sure have perked up since Angelina——Angel got home."

"She gives me a reason to smile."

"Looks good on you. Where's everybody?"

"Out back. I'll take you. It's not often I get to hold hands with a handsome young man."

"Ruth," he chided with a big smile. "You're making me blush."

The familiar rooms teemed with life and he felt a sense of peacefulness. He would always remember coming to the Snowden's house. The couple used to host lavish parties for employees of the Snowden Glass Company, one of the town's largest employers.

As a summer intern, he'd reported directly to Luther and learned the finer points of leadership and balancing good business sense with politics.

Many nights he'd eaten at their table and sat on their porch. And under a full moon, he'd romanced their daughter and fallen in love.

The Snowdens had been good for Mystic Ridge. It pleased him to see the family together again.

Peter kept an eye out for Angelina, but didn't see her. "Looks like you have a house full. What's going on?"

"You know Luther. Always has—"

"Something to say," they finished together and laughed.

Ruth patted his hand and guided him toward the back porch where the men had gathered. "Why don't you go on out. I'll get you something cold to drink."

He wanted to ask her why her smile seemed forced, but instead stepped onto the deck where men smoked cigars, lounged in wooden rocking chairs, sharing laughter and the fading sun.

The smell of grilled food reminded him that he'd missed dinner, but he'd grab a plate later.

He headed toward his father who stood in the corner talking to Luther, and accepted the cold beer from Ruth.

"Dad, I didn't know you'd be here."

"I got to get out sometimes."

"You're on the lake eighteen hours a day. That's not out enough?"

His father, Peter Sr., looked at Luther. "This boy thinks he knows everything."

Fondness radiated from Luther's eyes. "He ought to. We trust our town in his hands."

"That we do."

Feminine laughter made the trio turn. Angel had

approached from behind and Peter stepped aside to give her room. He'd taken a swallow of beer and felt it go down as slow as it took for his eyes to take her all in.

Her long legs were clad in dark tights that ended in a beige skirt. A beaded belt hung from the waist and he resisted the urge to tug it. A long-sleeved pristine white T-shirt nestled her chest, covered slightly by a black quilted vest. "You do what?" Angel asked.

Luther pressed his lips to Angelina's forehead. "We trust Peter with our town."

Her head dipped and she nodded, a strained smile on her lips. She was worried, Peter knew intuitively, pleased that he could still read more than one of her emotions after all this time.

"How does everything look to you, Angel?"

She hesitated and Peter stiffened wanting her to love Mystic Ridge or at least not tear it down.

"Everything looks. . .smaller. I feel like I've grown taller in a doll house." She angled to look at him, holding back curls. "I didn't realize how good it would feel to be with family and friends." Her eyes never left Peter's.

"Well, we're glad you're back, too," Luther said. "We'd better get started. The night promises to be long."

When Luther disappeared into the house, Peter gave Angelina his full attention. "Any idea what he's talking about?" A distinct feeling of discomfort stole over him when she waved a hand in front of her.

"You know Luther. He doesn't like to have his light stolen. Let's just hang out until he's ready."

The suggestion conjured up so many images, Peter couldn't help leaning close to her. A soft citrus scent floated on a breeze toward him as she leaned on the railing, overlooking rolling pastures. "I meant what I said, Peter. It's good to be back home."

"Are you ready to tell me what brought you back?"

"I came home to help—"

Luther's voice cut her off. "Will everyone come inside? It's time to get started."

Angel's eyes filled with a mixture of hope and reserve. She had clasped her hands together and Peter took one in his. She looked down at his fingers pressed to her palm. "I want to see you afterwards."

"Peter, I don't know."

"I know."

Concession lit the dark orbs behind the yellow shades. "Okay, we'll talk."

The men brought in chairs so everyone could sit together in the living room. About fifteen of Mystic Ridge's influential families were present as well as council members and neighbors.

Peter settled down on the overstuffed sofa and made room for Angel, but she stood by her mother in the doorway just behind Luther's shoulder.

"Friends," Luther began. "I asked you to come here today because what I do will affect you. I came to this town twenty-two years ago and fell in love. With the town, and especially the people. I met a beautiful woman who stole my heart. We got married and I opened my family's Irish glass-making business, and as they say, the rest is history.

"Our life wasn't always easy. We took a lot of heat being an interracial couple, but we made it. She stood by me during the tough years and now it's time for me to give her my undivided attention. I'm stepping down from the helm of Snowden Glass and—" he looked down, suddenly emotional "—closing its doors."

A shock wave hit Peter with the force of a lightning bolt. How would the town survive? Snowden Glass was one of the biggest employers.

Why hadn't Angel mentioned Luther's retirement this afternoon? She'd seemed distracted, but he'd chalked it up to her being in the woods with her ex-boyfriend who was doing his best to make a move on her. Instead of taking care of town business and knowing this was about to occur, his mind and body had been preoccupied. Anger and disappointment shot through him.

"Why do you have to close down?" Bunny asked. "Can't you get another president?"

"We aren't competitive anymore. The younger companies are doing things better and faster. Most of their business outside of manufacturing is web based. Unfortunately, the problem is two-fold. We aren't competitive and the cost of doing business from current resources is prohibitive."

Maureen Clay spoke up. "We do great with the specialty bottles. Can't you keep that division open?"

"It's a matter of supply and demand. We just don't get enough orders."

"How soon?" she asked.

"Two months."

Suddenly, everyone started to talk at once. "What are we going to do?"

"We'll have to move."

"Give up my land," snorted Jesse Transom, great grandson to one of Mystic Ridge's first settlement families. "No way. I was here before Mr. Moneybags showed up and I'll be here after."

"Peter?"

"Peter?"

The sound of his name filled his head and Peter wished he'd worn his glasses. At least he'd have something to do with his hands. He dragged his gaze away from Angelina and started to stand, when she spoke up.

"I'd like to throw something out." Everyone sensed the tension. Felt his anger mingle with theirs. They hushed. "If you don't mind."

"What is it, Angelina?" Peter's father said.

She looked directly at Peter. "I mighty be able to offer

a solution."

He lowered himself to his seat. "You have a captive audience."

Her voice shook but grew stronger as she talked.

"I know how much Snowden Glass has meant to Mystic Ridge. I've watched my step-father and my mother dedicate their lives to making it a success. I didn't know before I returned home that this was going to happen, but where there is an ending, there is a beginning. The company I work for loves to do business with small towns."

Interested eyes turned Angelina's way and the weight of anger dissipated into a desperate-like fungus. Panicked eyes darted between them.

"Who is this and where do we sign up," said Bunny.

Invisible red flags flew up, but Peter chose to pick his moment. "What company is this?"

"The Dyer Corporation," Angel said calmly. "They build shopping complexes."

The women in the group whispered excitedly. But Peter zeroed in on what she wasn't saying. "Shopping complexes," he said ruefully. "I seem to recall reading somewhere——" Angel tried to cut him off, but Peter wouldn't be railroaded. "Dyer owns——"

"Mall-Mart," they said in unison.

Peter spoke as if they were the only two in the room. "Dyer is the company that bought up land in the south bank. This morning surveyors went out and marked their land from ours."

He now had everyone's attention. Ray Cochran hung his head while Maureen Clay's and Bunny's mouth gaped. Everyone else sat in stony silence.

"Congratulations. Someone has just put a price on our heritage. Is that what you want?" One by one, heads shook.

"Sorry, Angel. No deal. Mystic Ridge isn't for sale."

Chapter Seven

Peter's proclamation jabbed a hole in her carefully planned proposal and deflated Angel's enthusiasm. His words were filled with hurt, anger and resolve. He'd go to his grave trying to protect the town and the people who entrusted their well-being in his hands. Instead of being angry about his opposition, Angel reached out to him.

"You're right. Mystic Ridge isn't for sale."

"What?" he cried in disbelief. "You're agreeing with me?"

"Yes." Glances volleyed between them.

He laughed, one hand on his hip, the other stroking his upper lip. "Why do I smell a dead fish?"

"Come on now, son. She said you were right. You don't have to treat Angelina this way."

She briefly met Peter Sr.'s gaze then returned to look at his son. She read not only disbelief, but distrust. Guilt gripped her. "No, Mr. Richland. Peter is entitled to his opinion. I agree Mystic Ridge isn't for sale, but this town needs a business so that we don't go under. I have a company that's interested in making this town successful."

"We?" Peter said. "You're back home for the first time in fifteen years and you expect us to believe that you have our best interest at heart?"

"I can see why some of you might have reservations." A growing murmur began to swell. "But I believe you said the operative word. Home. Mystic Ridge will always be my home. I want to see it survive."

"By selling off pieces of sacred land," Jesse Transom said matter-of-factly. He rose, leaning heavily on his cane and headed for the door. "That land has been ours since the first slaves walked out of the south. I won't stand by and let it be desecrated by strangers."

Several of the older folks followed him out the door. The rest looked scared.

Roy Cochran leaned forward, elbows on his knees. "Don't let them bother you," he reassured. "They're old and don't want change to leave them behind." He smoothed his salt and pepper hair. "I don't either. But the fact remains if this hadn't happened now, it would have happened later. My son and daughter-in-law can't find jobs around here. If Muriel and I pack up and go with them, what does the south bank mean to me?"

Angel hated the position Dyer had put her in. They'd compromised the delicate balance of this mission and were not allowing her to do her job. The support several locals gave fueled her desire to see this deal through to fruition. Roy gave her a thumbs up and Angel grasped at his overture. "Thank you for the vote of confidence."

Peter quickly jumped in. "No disrespect intended," he said to Luther, "but this town was surviving before Snowden Glass. We can again, if necessary."

"Now, Peter are you saying you won't even consider hearing a proposal by Dyer?" Bunny said.

Stormy eyes glanced around as he struggled for the right words. "I would consider it if they'd approached us in the right way. Buying land from under our noses is underhanded. There's no telling what else will happen. We have two months. I don't see why we can't look into

various opportunities instead of immediately jumping into
the first one that comes our way."

"I agree," Angel said, "but this is a great opportunity
and I'd hate to see Mystic Ridge lose out."

Their gazes penetrated Angel and she felt as if she
were in a room full of hot air.

"You agree," Peter reiterated.

"Yes. I can straighten out the land situation and give
you as much information as you need. I have charts and
facts and demographics, facts from other cities this size
and later this week I should receive a detailed analysis
from their local officials."

Maureen stood and gathered her purse. "Peter, I think
you should review all the information before you dismiss
this out of hand. As a member of the town council, I vote
that you two work together and present us with a proposal."

Peter's father stood, as did other council members.
"All in favor of Peter and Angel working this into something we can understand say 'aye'."

"Aye's" resounded.

"Opposed?" He waited a second. "The 'Aye's' have
it."

A slow procession filed between them, Peter on one
side and Angel on the other.

Relieved the idea hadn't been shot down completely,
Angel wondered if working so closely with Peter was the
best course of action. Although he probably hated her
now and would find her betrayal unforgivable, ever since
she had seen him, they could hardly keep their hands off
each other.

She stepped aside as her parents accepted hugs and
quiet congratulations until finally, the house was quiet.

Luther studied the couple and grabbed his wife's
hand.

"Ruth, let's go out back and see the—trees."

Her mother laughed as she walked with her husband. "Honey, just say you want to be alone with me. . ."

Their voices faded and Angel turned to Peter. His face was taut, his eyes narrowed. His mouth had turned upside down and anger drifted off him in waves.

"What was this afternoon about?" he demanded.

She'd asked herself that very question a thousand times but couldn't form a coherent answer. An unknown force seemed to have taken hold of her emotions and wrapped them around Peter. She'd thought of nothing else all day.

"Did you come home thinking you could romance your high school sweetheart into getting what you wanted?"

Angel shook her head, speechless. She should have known this would hurt. That he'd think this way. In fact, she felt the opposite of manipulative. They shared a unique harmony that couldn't be described with words. She felt it now, even as his anger invaded every cell in her body.

This couldn't be love, she thought as her skin prickled and her stomach jumped. Love wasn't supposed to hurt this deep and make her want to fall over herself apologizing.

Angel opened her mouth to speak and he stepped forward expectant. "What, then, Angelina?" His bark of laughter tore at her heart. "I know how you see me now. I'm just a country boy living in a backwards, one-horse town who never made it out of the boondocks." He shrugged his acceptance. "But I love this town and I'll protect it from everyone," his voice lowered. "Even you. Go back to California. You're not one of us anymore."

Peter started for the door, the bright overhead light stark against his retreating back. She didn't want him to go. Didn't want him to leave on these terms. This afternoon had been special. But she had a job to do. And so did he.

She spoke up, her voice displaying none of her inner struggle. "I'm not leaving, so get that out of your head. If you take your job so seriously, why aren't you listening to what your constituents have to say? You remember the other twenty-five thousand or so people with Mystic Ridge on their birth certificates, including me. You can't make me or invite me or tell me to leave. I have a job to do."

"So do I."

At a loss, she shook her head saying, "Did you invent the saying 'My way or the highway'?'"

His hand stopped on the door. He stood between the frame and freedom and gazed at her. "You don't get it, do you?"

Angel planted her hands on her hips. "I get it, all right. I get the fact that you're running from change. You're giving people a false sense of security if you lead them to believe they can keep the outside world at bay forever. Instead of embracing opinions, you shut out any that don't mirror yours. I never thought I'd say this, but you're a Type A, ego-maniacal man who would lead his people to extinction rather than listen to a voice that isn't your own."

He smacked his palm with his fist. "Mystic Ridge is four hundred years old. This town has been through and survived change. But do we have to jump at every opportunity that looks like gold? No! This town is too important. Outsiders wouldn't understand."

She stepped back affronted. "That seems to be your claim to fame. I made it out and did something for myself."

His sobering gaze filled her with longing and his anger suddenly subsided. "I'm proud of you," he said.

She stepped forward and grabbed his hands. "I know you are. Please, Peter. Listen to the ideas I have and let me show you how I can help our town."

He turned her hands over and grazed his fingers over her manicured nails. Angel drew them back, knowing he struggled with her L.A. image. "Why do you care? You don't live here. Your parents are going to be traveling. So what's your vested interest?"

Angel brought her hand to her heart. "I care. Mystic Ridge is my home. My roots run deep here."

He gave a disbelieving snort and stepped onto the porch. "You care enough to represent a company who could care less about your roots, except to buy them at the lowest price. Your type of caring is more than we need. Thanks anyway."

He bounded down the steps and started slowly up the winding walkway. The automatic lights attached to the carport flickered on and gave him guidance as he headed toward the grassy knoll.

Angel stood on the porch too. "Where's your truck?"

He shoved his hands deep into his pockets, still walking. "A mile back."

Angel took the stairs one at a time, unable to give up. "What's wrong with it?"

"Dead battery. Go home, Angelina."

"Go home, Angelina," she mimicked. "I'm grown. I can walk beside you if I feel like it."

"No."

"No," she mimicked again.

"Angelina."

"Angelina."

"Hardly the mature woman I expected."

Angel scooped up some dead acorns and pelted him with them. "I'm not scared, you are."

"Angel," he warned.

She threw the last one, then bolted.

Peter caught her within seconds and had her arms pinned to her sides. "You never knew when to stop playing games," he said, his body stiff against hers.

Their breath puffed little white clouds. "This isn't a game to me. Give me a chance. One week to show you the potential of this company. One chance is all I ask."

"A chance to get everyone's hopes up and dash them when this doesn't come through? A chance to divide the town and make us enemies? I can't allow that to happen."

"I promise—"

"To love, honor and cherish—" he supplied.

At her questioning look, he said, "That's what it's going to take. Promise me you won't promise anything you can't deliver and I'll give you one week of my time. You don't have the power to do that, do you, Angel? Mystic Ridge is special. We have our quirks and our faults, but they're unique to us." He let her go, brushed his hands along her arms. "If you only saw Mystic Ridge through my eyes you'd understand."

"Deal."

His wistful expression closed. "Deal what? Oh, no. I'm a busy man and I don't want to hear you preaching to me about your project."

Angel rubbed the cold air that dusted her arms. "Come on. You were always, if nothing else, fair."

He looked doubtful, like a man with the weight of the world on his shoulders. Angel wanted to smooth the worry lines from his forehead and tell him everything would be all right. But she couldn't. She'd compromised herself and him once today. Another time could have far reaching consequences.

"What did today mean?"

"I wanted to call this afternoon a mistake, Peter. It wasn't. But it can't happen again."

She struggled to speak while fighting the urge to give in to her riotous emotions. "I don't want you to think I'm trying to manipulate you with sex." He closed the distance between them. "We share something. A special bond that has surpassed time and distance. But—"

Serious eyes regarded her. "Can't happen again."

"So we have a deal, right?"

"Deal."

Angel touched his arms briefly. "Good. "I'll drive you home before we freeze to death."

"In that little bucket of tin?"

"Does zero to sixty in four point five seconds."

"Really," he said, male appreciation overriding his own objection.

Angel tossed the keys and gave him a wide berth. She didn't look over her shoulder, just hoped he'd follow.

She waited at the car and was pleased when he opened the passenger door for her.

Chapter Eight

Monday morning arrived bringing blustery winds, freezing pipes, and reserved moods. As it was, the parking lot of his office was full of people who'd heard the grapevine gossip.

Immediately, Peter regretted his hasty decision to accept a ride from Angel this morning. On the surface all was normal, but to most of the men and women watching her park the car, he looked like he was in bed with the enemy.

Before the car had fully stopped, Peter had the door open, his heeled boot digging into the gravel. Angel braked and Peter indicated with a jerk of his thumb. "Park in visitors."

She glanced out as he hefted himself up.

"Peter?"

He had to stoop to see inside the car. "Yep?"

"That says Visitor parking, five minutes. Will I get towed?"

"Let's see, Angel. My father owns the tow truck. I think you're pretty safe."

Seeing her surprise, he backpedaled. "Sorry. That wasn't called for."

He couldn't keep his eyes from straying to her chocolate colored turtle neck, black vest over denim jeans.

She'd piled her hair on top of her head in a loose band
and had traded her yellow shades for black rimmed
glasses that looked useless except to make her more
beautiful.

"Lots of people to see you, huh?"

He glanced out the windshield. "Promises to be a full
day. I'd better go."

"Meet you inside," she called cheerfully, but he closed
the door firmly. Being with Angel made him want to relax
and share the inconsequential events of his day.

Focus, he told himself and strode up to several families that greeted him with grave stares. "Mornin'. How
long have you folks been waiting?" he said to pregnant
Linda Clay Emerson, LulaMae's great granddaughter.

"Just awhile. Came to talk to you 'bout something."

He clasped her hand and shared his strength as she
waddled up the stairs.

Inside, he eased her into Brenda's chair and looked
around for his secretary. Nowhere in sight and the rooms
were ice cold. He swore silently, stripped off his wool
jacket and tucked it around Linda's legs. He could see
his breath even inside the building.

The door opened behind them, letting in a full gust of
cold wind.

He looked into Linda's friendly eyes. "Don't get this
kind of treatment at home, Peter. Kinda nice. Thanks."

"Well don't get too used to it," her husband Sherman
said from behind. He came over and kissed Linda on the
forehead and shook Peter's hand.

Peter adjusted the thermostat and joined the couple.
"What you lookin' at, Sherm? You want the shirt off my
back?"

"That piece of rat's nest? How long you had that?
Since high school?"

"Probably, good friend." The familiarity eased tension
and Peter knew Sherman would hear him out before

drawing any conclusions. "Lot of people still outside?"

Sherman nodded. "Yep. Might as well let us all in. We all want to know the same thing."

Angel walked in laden with bags followed by the Terry, Hodges, Jackson and Henry families. A few stragglers eased in seeking truth and warmth.

"Everybody, go into the big room over there. I promise the heat will kick on in a minute." Peter took the paper satchels from Angel's arms and put them in the kitchenette. The noise outside the tiny alcove rose as people talked weather and the impending holidays. The undercurrent of worry was about jobs and the future.

"What's all this?"

"Just a few snacks and drinks to make everyone comfortable." Angel bent down and started opening cabinets. "Coffee-maker?"

Focused on her assured movements, he almost missed her question then pointed to the counter. "Kettle. That's the best I've got. I'd better get this impromptu meeting started. Can you handle this?"

"No problem." She opened a box and pulled out a batch of homemade sticky buns. "Delicious," he exclaimed in a hushed tone. Peter popped one into his mouth and savored the flavor of Mystic Ridge's homemade bread and syrup confection. "Bribery isn't going to work."

Angel's serene smile kicked his libido. She wiped his mouth with the tip of her finger.

"I never thought it would. I'll be there in two shakes."

Peter solicited Sherman's help, rounded up chairs and filled the boardroom with as many people as the room could hold. Some of them had traveled many miles, and he didn't want to turn them away without giving them the answers they deserved.

He settled the children in Brenda's office with a box of sticky buns, and plugged in her portable TV so they could watch the purple dinosaur prance around. For some who lived high in the mountains, this was their first glimpse of TV since visiting the local pediatrician once a year.

Peter entered the boardroom and looked at the folks that depended upon him. He stood against the wall and gestured for an older gentleman to take his seat.

"Let me just start by saying I know why you've come and I know you want answers."

Angel slipped into the room with steaming cups of coffee and a platter of fresh buns. Eager eyes devoured the food and happy hands made quick selections. When she received a disappointed look from those that didn't receive any, she smiled reassuringly.

"Don't worry, I've got lots more." She turned her seductive smile on Peter. "I didn't mean to interrupt. Please, go ahead."

But from the gracious and thankful looks she received, he knew he wouldn't have their attention until everyone had been served. Peter headed toward the door. "I'll help so we can get on with the discussion."

In her comfortable clothes, Angel didn't stand out against the worn overalls that was pretty much the dress code of Mystic Ridge citizens.

They worked side by side for a few seconds and as she hoisted a tray onto her palm and fingered the other one into her hand, she glanced up and met his gaze. "What?"

"Homemade sticky buns and coffee are not going to sway my decision."

"I know."

Taken aback by her abrupt no-nonsense response, he didn't have a witty comeback. "Just so you know."

"I believe I said I did."

He wanted to say how much he appreciated her help, but thought better of it. Her help would likely destroy Mystic Ridge.

"Let's get this over with. I don't have all day."

"After you," she said and swung the trays shoulder high.

Angel's calm disarmed him and he returned to the room with a full coffeepot.

After dispensing the refreshments, Angel assumed a post in the back of the room. Good. Out of the way.

"Folks, I know you've come because word has spread that Snowden Glass is closing," Peter began.

Several people around Angel offered her a hand pat of sympathy, which annoyed Peter. That wasn't supposed to be a pity party. He was ready to expound upon the argument that Mystic Ridge didn't need the Dyer Corporation. He wanted to share with citizens how they could make it on their own. But with Angel, his nemesis, garnering support, he had to change tactics. Peter regained their attention when he loudly cleared his throat.

"What you've heard is true. Snowden Glass is clos-ing. But we will survive. And not necessarily because we embrace a new corporation. Mystic Ridgeians are strong. This town was built on the backs of freed slaves without commerce from the outside."

"Are you saying we should be thankful we're about to lose our jobs and glad our children will have no other choice but to be farmers? I don't want that for them. Farming is a hard life."

Angry stares and restless movements expressed their discomfort. Heat grew on the inside of his collar. "Not at all," Peter said. "I'm suggesting that we band together before settling for the first company that offers to build here."

"Tell us about the offer. Who is it?" Sherman wanted to know.

"The Dyer Corporation." Angel spoke up then fell silent.

"Give us as much information as you have."

Peter reluctantly nodded his head.

"Dyer builds large variety stores that have everything from clothes to jewelry to food. It's an all-inclusive shopping experience that has been successful in fourteen other cities."

"Woo-oow," said the women in the room.

Peter stared at the back of everyone's head and wondered when he'd lost control.

"Just a minute, Angelina."

Everyone turned to him. "I don't want to get into the details until we have all the facts. Besides, before it can be brought up before a committee, the board members have to discuss whether they believe the company is good for the entire town as well as the ramifications to the state."

Not a single person moved.

Angel filled the silence. "It seems only fair to let everyone know where we are."

Many of them agreed. "Yeah. We're always the last to know."

Angel gave details about her hopes for Dyer and what they'd been able to accomplish with other small cities.

She spoke in a language they understood but even as she gave them information, she was careful not to raise false hopes. Peter found himself listening, wanting to know more.

When Angel finished talking, people were shocked at the financial possibilities. They could be managers, and work regular hours. The earning potential seemed endless and it was hard for Peter not to allow himself to hope what tax revenue would do for the town.

"This is just talk and supposition," he added, deflating the thin layer of hope many had. "Come to the meeting if you can next Wednesday night. We'll know a lot more then."

"Try to see the forest through the trees, Peter," Linda said. "We need a business to save Mystic Ridge. They might not have approached us the right way, but we have you and Angel to protect us. Think about it." She pushed slowly to her feet. "All right, everybody. Let's let them get to work."

When everyone filed out of the office and to their respective cars, Peter noticed the flashing light on the phone and answered the messages. Brenda had called, explaining she was sick and couldn't make it in. He smirked. She'd be disappointed she'd missed all the fun.

He hurried through the rest of the messages, all from concerned people wondering what the next move was.

Peter wished he knew. He didn't like Dyer's approach and didn't trust them. One thing he'd learned was to follow his instincts. But beyond the money and growth potential, he saw the new schools and hospitals that could be built. He saw paved and not gravel roads. He saw a town teeming with renewal, spirit and life. Rising, he walked back into the conference room.

Angel was cleaning up and didn't say a word as he filled the sink with platters and empty cups.

They worked side-by-side, Angel washing, him drying. The scene was almost too domestic. Angel, elbow deep in soapsuds, him coming up behind her for a free feel.

Peter put the breaks on his thoughts, like a race car driver with a warning flag. "Do you agree with Linda?" he finally asked, Ruth's glass platter tight in his hands.

Angel looked at him with the eyes of an angel. "About you not seeing the forest through the trees?"

Impatient, he stared at her. "Why are you making me work so hard? Yes."

"You have foresight and you have great instincts, but in this particular instance, you're operating on an emotional level that can be or will be a hindrance in the future." She dried her hands on a cloth and extricated the platter from his hands. "I'm not the enemy, Peter."

"Never said you were."

Angel packed the plate in a special-made vinyl container. She moved throughout his space with confidence and ease. He leaned against the sink, drawing the dishtowel across another plate and wondered how long it would be before she took it and dried it to her satisfaction. Self-assurance radiated from her, making her sparkle.

For a second his thoughts returned to the meeting and his unusual level of annoyance. Then he realized why. She'd charmed them.

Angel was a real beauty. The kind of woman other women wanted to emulate, from her hair to her style of dress. But that hadn't been what had impressed the people today. Her face had been void of make-up, her hair style simple, her clothes generic. But her voice and her words had held them captive, offering them hope in a time of trouble. Even he couldn't be sure he'd given them that.

"Did you ever consider how many jobs this opportunity could bring to Mystic Ridge?"

"Probably thousands." Even as he wanted to reject the possibilities, Peter had to know what he was in for.

She shrugged. "Maybe not that many initially, but eventually it could. Ever consider what that type of commerce could do for the economy?"

"Generate thousands?"

"Hundreds of thousands."

"Impressive."

She turned to see if he was patronizing her and Peter laid the plate on the table.

"What is it, Peter?"

"Do you ever wonder why I stayed in Mystic Ridge?"

Their eyes locked and she moved slowly to the table and sat. He stayed against the sink, grateful for the distance.

"Yes. Every day since I've been home. I've wondered."

"Because there was nobody like me. That gives legs
to your ego-maniacal comment, doesn't it?"

She graced him with a self-deprecating smile.

"Look around you. The town is getting old. The members are retiring, moving, dying off one at a time. I've
eulogized so many, I sometimes fear I'm boring everyone
with the same stories. After college I never intended to
stay. I came home to check on my mother and father and
when I walked into their house, they were old. It's like for
every year it took me to get my degrees, they'd aged ten.
At the time Seymour Plunkett was the council president
and while I was home, he died."

"How awful."

"You know how Mystic Ridge is. We shut down for the
funeral and I agreed to help his wife get his paperwork
into a manner she could understand. Next thing you
know, I'm sitting in on meetings for my father and one
day I look up, and I'm the president."

"Did you ever want to leave?"

He nodded, pursed his lips. "Sure, lots of times. But
it became more a passing fancy rather than a goal. After
a while, I stopped thinking about it."

"Would you ever?"

He laid his hands on the table and drew back. "Never
had a reason good enough to."

"If you found the right girl?" she sounded shy, but her
eyes conveyed her desire for an answer.

"Maybe."

"Have you ever. . .found her?"

"I thought I had—once. But it didn't work out. So I
guess the answer is no."

Angel nodded, seemingly satisfied. She reached out
and laid her hand on top of his. Warmth worked its way

to his fingers and up his arms. A lightness invaded his head and if she were not in his presence, Peter would have shut his eyes and reveled in the spirit of her touch.

As it was now, he couldn't tear his gaze away. She tilted her head, her eyes soft. "I came back with certain expectations of the town and they were all blown to bits. You've done an excellent job. You were chosen, Peter."

As if burned, Angel jerked her hands away and pushed to her feet.

He stood too, wanting to go to her, misunderstanding her resistance to the unusual but heady power that connected them.

"Oh my, I never thought—"

"What, Angel?"

She waved her hand and backed toward the hallway leading to the front of the office. "Nothing. I need to make a couple of private phone calls." She swallowed. "Is there one available?"

Peter felt strange looking at her so closely, but she'd been affected as well. She'd insisted on the rule of non-involvement, and while he thought it prudent, his body and mind told him different. "You can use my office."

"I just need to get my briefcase from the car and I'll be right back."

Hurrying up the hallway, Angel's boots clicked in decisive steps. Even in her confusion, she sounded self-assured.

Clearing off his desk, Peter gathered his Rolodex and laptop. No matter Angel's job, if he were going to save Mystic Ridge it had to start with calls to the remaining landowners in the south bank. It seemed folks needed a reminder as to why owning that property was so important.

Chapter Nine

Frigid air chilled Angel's skin, but not enough to cool her own self-directed disbelief. A few more seconds in Peter's presence and she'd have blurted the bizarre tale of her car talking. The word 'chosen' rattled around in her brain. You are the chosen one.

The words had been spoken as if they were meant for her, and now she'd said them to him. She took a moment to indulge the absurdity of it all. What if they had been meant for her?

What had she been chosen for?

Yes, Peter was the perfect man to lead Mystic Ridge into the twenty-first century. He possessed deep convictions, but balanced his strength with sensitivity. Her words to him made sense.

But why me? I'm regular, she argued with herself.

Angel pulled down the skin under her eyes and stared at herself in the rearview mirror. Letting go of her face, her features returned to normal. But her heart hadn't been normal since she'd pulled into town two weeks ago.

She felt as if she were pushing herself up a steep hill with no supports to latch onto and no net to catch her if she fell. Cold, she blew into her hands and considered starting her car, hitting the highway and not looking back. But what would that accomplish? For the second time in her life she'd be running from feelings that scared her.

Her feelings for Peter were intense. Even after fifteen years. She groaned aloud. What am I doing? Am I doing the right thing for the people of this town? Yes! The answer pressed in on her, leaving no alternative but to believe.

Relieved, she grabbed the door handle, startled as Peter stood there, concern bright in his eyes. "Considering an escape route?" he said, eyeing the Atlas she'd pulled onto her lap.

"Not leaving until my job is done."

"You're leaving town right after that, huh?"

"I've got a job waiting," she said with little conviction. She cleared her throat and looked away.

"That's important."

"Yes, it is." Suddenly Angel wished he'd say the words that hung thick like humidity in the air. She wanted to tell him she didn't have a reason to stay in Mystic Ridge. Her parents had recently bought a RV and were planning vacations—without her.

She wanted to tell him that whatever connected them, was so strong she couldn't sleep at night for wanting to be near him. But Peter stood silently. Emotionless, stoic and strong. As much as a part of her wanted to, she couldn't love him. He'd break her heart. He'd already done it once when he refused to leave Mystic Ridge fifteen years ago.

Peter stuck out his hand and she reached for it. "You'd better get inside. I won't have sympathy even if you end up with a touch of frostbite."

She got out of her car, laptop in hand and Peter draped a thick wool sweater, several sizes too big, over her shoulders.

"Ever heard of a coat?" He shoved his hands in his pockets as they walked back up the stairs.

"Zip it, smarty."

He held the door for her. "That mouth is dangerous. Use my office. It's ready."

At Brenda's desk, Angel put down the laptop and shrugged off the sweater. She held it out to him, missing the heat, yearning for his touch. To touch him would take so little effort, but she made herself stand still. "Thank you. I'm warm now."

"Really?" He grabbed the wool, then discarded it with a flick of his wrist. Peter stood so close, they shared one breath, then two. "Sure you couldn't get any warmer?"

"Probably."

"But you don't want to."

"Peter, we're not on the same side. I don't want you to hate me when this is over."

"Could never hate you." Her gaze flickered to his. Peter's eyes were hooded, his stance casual, the heat emanating from his body anything but. He reached up, fingered a curl, twining it, guiding her forward until they were chest to chest.

"This is dangerous," she whispered. "Don't know if I can keep things separate."

He smoothed back the mass of curls and smiled gently when they popped back at him. "Me either. One day this will be dealt with."

She gazed up at him. "I know."

"Could have serious consequences."

Angel nodded, not trusting her voice.

Peter stepped back. "The office is yours. In about an hour, we'll head out."

Pulling in a hearty breath, she tried to act as if her emotions weren't the object in a crazy ping-pong game. "Where will we start?"

"You'll see. One hour." He ducked out and headed toward the kitchen.

Sitting behind his desk, Angel plugged in the computer and answered e-mail. The partner she worked with at

Dyer had left several messages and she called him first.

"Bryce, Angel Snowden. By any chance have you sent surveyors out here?"

"Sure have, Angie." Bryce's quick rush of words filled every empty space. "Look, you've been there a week. Have you got the other parcels secured? Tell you what. Are you near a fax machine? Send those documents on over and I can have the boys back out there as early as tomorrow."

"Hold on a second," she said, trying to slow him down. Unease settled around her and she suddenly couldn't tell him about the three parcels she'd already acquired. It seemed wrong to give Bryce that information. "According to my notes, we were just in the acquisition stage. This hasn't even gone through all the channels yet. Much less to the point of hiring surveyors. I mean," she laughed, "this could all fall apart, and then what?"

"This can't fall apart. Angie, have you got the land secured?"

"No," she lied, stunned that he'd gone behind her back. What else had been done since she'd been away from the office? At that very moment she understood Peter's resistance in wanting to do business with Dyer.

A long pause stretched into an uncomfortable silence.

"Bryce, the people are reluctant to sell family land, and understandably so. We need time to work on them."

"What have you been doing?' His voice rang with thinly veiled contempt. "You've had plenty of time."

She drew her hands through her curls and massaged her scalp. A monster headache was on the way as she stalled him. "Don't worry. I'm meeting with some people who I believe will donate their land. I hope to have several parcels before the end of the week."

Angel imagined Bryce in his usual state. Blond hair spiked, sky blue shades over his blue eyes, feet on his desk.

"Define several, Angie. Mall-mart is ready and waiting for the green light. We'll have bulldozers in there before you can say commission check! Come on, girl. Get-it-to-ge-ther! How many can we count on by the end of this week? Five or six? That's all we need. Those other hillbillies will sell when they see there's no hope."

Images flashed in her mind of Linda and Sherman, Jesse Transom and Peter. LulaMae Clay! The callous way Bryce spoke of them chilled her blood.

"Bryce! Don't you say one more disrespectful thing about these people again. We're partners on this project, but don't think I won't demand that you be removed. Is that understood?"

Angel could only imagine what was going through his little pea brain, but she didn't care.

"Sure, Angie," he replied, conciliatory. "I'm just anxious to get this underway."

"Is that all?" Angel demanded.

"We need the zoning requests. That rinky—sorry, town council president has been sitting on them for months now."

"He has?" she said surprised Peter hadn't mentioned them. Maybe he knew more than he was letting on.

"Don't tell him they're for us or he'll drag his feet into eternity." His tone dipped. "How is it, Angie? Is it just killing you to be in that one-horse town?" Though he tried to sound sympathetic, he failed miserably.

"I'm fine, Bryce."

"A lot hinges on securing this land," he continued. "You know this south bank was grand-fathered to these people by some ancient governor and can't be developed except as a whole. Essentially, if we don't have an entire chunk, it's worthless. Do your job, Angie, and call me at the end of the week."

"My name is An—"

The phone clicked in her ear. She prepared to hang

up when her voice mail beeped and indicated another message had been left.

The company's vice-president wanted her to locate a new headquarters for a dessert company in the Maryland area. Did she have any suggestions?

"No," she answered aloud, rubbing her fingers over her forehead as sites came to mind. She dialed his number, praying to leave a message, but he picked up on the second ring.

"John? Angel Snowden."

"Great hearing your voice, stranger. How goes it?"

"Busy and I've only got a minute. I've got a couple of sites for the dessert company. Got a pen?"

"Shoot."

Angel quickly listed the sites and gave an update on the status of the Mall-mart account. She debated asking for Bryce to be reassigned, but decided against it. He was a good partner, who was entitled to make one mistake.

"Anything else," John said after she completed the report.

"No, except if you're interested in buying a glass company, I know where you can get one cheap."

"What kind of glass? Windows?"

"No. Mostly bottles for product." Why had she mentioned this? Luther was closing, not selling. "John, forget I mentioned it. I'd better run."

"Why close the company when you can run it? Ever consider it?"

She shook her head. "You'd never let me go. Who'd bring you treats?"

"Got a point there," he said slowly. "You sure you're okay?"

Angel smiled. John and his wife Francine had been so good to her. Like second parents since she joined the company five months ago, they'd developed a unique closeness. Nearing retirement age, John wanted her to take his job once he left and Angel aspired to one day rule the roost.

If John were asking her if she were okay, she must sound pretty bad. She mentally kicked her mood up a notch and put some cheer into her voice.

"Everything's fine. I'd better run. Kiss Francine for me."

"You got it, kiddo. Hey, one last thing."

"Yeah?"

"What's the local specialty? Anything to eat?"

Angel smiled. She'd never met a man who loved sweets as much as John. "Let's see. Oh, how about a case of Mystic Ridge's homemade, manufactured and bottled syrup? This stuff is delicious. In fact, the bottles come from my step-father's factory."

"Great! Take care and call soon."

Opening her laptop, Angel lost herself in answering e-mail and didn't look up until a discreet knock sounded at the door.

Peter poked his head in. "You about ready?"

More e-mail waited, but she needed to focus on her job and get more parcels of land. Then this deal would be secure. "Sure am. Get much done?" she asked, as she stood and stretched.

Peter watched her, interest written all over his face. "Some," he said in a guarded tone.

"You received zoning requests regarding the south bank. What did you do with them?" she asked, afraid he'd already made the decision to deny them.

"We have an agreement, Angel. I intend to abide by it."

She zipped her computer into the leather case and lifted it off the desk. Coming around she prepared to pass, but he took the computer from her hand and stepped back into the doorway.

"Doesn't have to be this way. You could see things my way and make it easy on yourself."

He threw his head back and laughed. "I'm up for anything you can throw my way." Now this was the Peter she remembered. When they were kids, they'd found so much to laugh about.

Since she'd returned, she'd missed his insatiable sense of humor. He was so serious now.

Things must have changed when he took over the town. Perhaps he was living an unfulfilled existence because of the noble spirit that ran through his veins. More than ever she wanted him to be happy.

"What's first on your agenda?" She passed him and he reached around her. For an instant Angel thought he was going to wrap her in his arms. Instead he flipped the light switch, casting the room into semi-darkness.

"First thing is my truck. My father's got it at the garage and said he would have the battery in this morning."

Angel checked her watch and nodded. "No problem. And after that?"

"We hang out."

"Ooo-kay." She followed him through the office and watched as he juggled her laptop and the vinyl covered bag of platters.

"Let me help you." Angel took the vinyl bag of plates and was grateful they hadn't touched. They seemed to possess a connection because every time he touched her, she felt that warm-in-the-tub-feeling.

Angel gasped and brought her hand to her throat. Just like in the car. It felt right.

"You okay?" he said from behind her. "Angel?"

"Fine." She patted her warm cheeks. "I know this is going to sound funny, but something weird happened to... a friend awhile back and it just came to mind."

He guided her outside and when she strutted to the driver's door, he looked offended.

Snow would fall in Mystic Ridge before she asked him to drive her car again, and everyone knew it hadn't snowed in the small town in over five years. Angel flipped her hand in an offhand manner. "One day she was alone in her car and she said it talked."

"What did it say?" he said without a hint of a smile.

She debated telling him for fear she'd reveal herself as the "friend." But he seemed to be listening with only half an ear. His gaze roamed the streets as she pulled out of the lot.

"Wait a sec," he said, hopped out to move some garbage cans onto the curb, then got back in. "All right. So go ahead with your story."

"She said it said something about her being chosen."

He stared right into her soul. So much for him not being interested. "To do what?"

"She doesn't know."

"Maybe to lead. Maybe to deliver a message. Everyone has a purpose here on earth and sometimes it's just enough to know God put you here to serve." He spoke with such reassurance, suddenly the experience didn't seem so weird.

Angel drove through the town that had been built like rings on a tree. All the businesses started in the center and rotated out until they met farmland and miles of nothing but trees.

Beautiful even in the winter, the bare tree branches had been strung with white Christmas lights, and happy black elves painted on the doors of the local businesses.

They cruised twinkling Main Street and waved to people as they passed. Peter assisted her failing memory with reminders of each person's family, and updated her on the latest happenings in their lives.

When Peter directed her to the Apothecary to pick up a prescription for his father, Angel felt like Junior Miss Mystic Ridge, the way everyone carried on about her coming home, and her success in California. Obviously her mother and Luther bragged regularly.

The special feelings didn't dissipate when Peter whisked her back into the car when some teenage boys tried to pick her up.

"They want the car, not me," she said, flattered by their attention and even more by Peter's jealousy.

"Making it with a beautiful woman who owns a car is a dream come true for these boys. Don't smile. You're encouraging them."

She waved and winked, causing them to follow along the planked sidewalk until Angel drove through the intersection. "They're kind of cute."

"Cradle robbing?"

She smirked at his jealous streak. "Hardly," she said breezily. "You're a day past dirt so I wouldn't hate on anyone." He chuckled with her.

Richland Automotives was on the next block and Angel turned right and pulled in behind the senior Richland's truck.

Clothed in a one-piece workman's uniform, Mr. Richland pumped gas into the truck in front of her, collected his money and waved them ahead. Angel put down her window and got a full blast of cold air in the face.

"How are you two doing today? Gettin' along?"

Angel laughed. "Of course."

Peter snorted at his father's comment and gestured toward the garage. "Where's Sherman? I thought he was on today."

"You know Linda's going to drop that baby any day. Every time I turn around she's calling, thinking it's time. Women," he said, slightly exasperated.

"My truck ready?"

Mr. Richland took a rag from his pocket and rubbed bugs from the windshield. "Naw, your truck ain't ready. I

told you to bring it in for a tune-up last month and you
didn't, so I got it in the garage gettin' fixed right."

"Dad, I need my truck."

"Why? Seems to me you got a pretty good situation
right here."

"I can't rely on Angel to drive me around town. Give
me your keys. I'll take your truck until mine is fixed."

"Think again. You can't borrow my truck."

Angel couldn't suppress her smile any longer. Nothing
had changed. Peter and his father had always bickered
but the love between the two ran deeper than the sea.
Especially since Mrs. Richland had died so early in
Peter's life.

"Why can't I borrow your truck? If I recall, I bought you
that truck."

Mr. Richland slapped his thigh with the rag and stuffed
in back into his pocket. "You bought it, but you don't own
it."

"Dad—"

"Angel, you don't mind riding Peter around until I can
fix his truck, do you?"

"When will it be done?"

"Wednesday."

"Wednesday!" they exclaimed at the same time.

"Afternoon," he said, flexing his thick fingers.

"That's over a week. What are you doing to it?
Rebuilding the thing from the inside out?"

Mr. Richland waved to the occupant of the blue
Pontiac Grand Am that had pulled in behind them. "You
ain't a paying customer, son. I got to take care of people
who got money," he said and went to greet his customer.
He walked around the rear bumper and turned up at
Peter's window.

"What now? You want to reupholster the seats while
you're at it?"

"Give me my prescriptions before I decide to put monster wheels on it." He received the bag and with surprising quickness, pinched Peter's cheek, then went back to his customer.

Angel howled at Peter's embarrassed expression. He soon joined her but kept shaking his head.

"Where to?" she asked.

"Rural route 7 is where we'll begin. That man drives me crazy," he said with such a touch of affection she reached out and patted his hand.

"He means well. Just think. you'll have a brand new truck next week."

"You don't have to chauffeur me around. I can borrow Sherman's old Tempo. I don't want to put you out."

She shook her head, drawing back her hand. It tingled as threads of awareness shot to the center of her body. Her breath caught as she tried to out-wait the thrumming between her thighs.

"It's not a problem. We vowed to see Mystic Ridge your way, so it doesn't really matter who drives. Right?"

He rolled up his window and sat back. "I guess not, but it just doesn't feel right."

"What?"

"You driving me around."

Angel stared out the windshield, the car dipping into the holes in the gravel road that represented the rural route. It was about to snow. "Do you want to drive?"

He shrugged, sounding casual. "It only seems right."

"Fine." Angel pulled over and pushed back the seat. He seemed happy behind the wheel even if his knees were drawn up to the dash.

"Go easy. My car has never seen roads like this before. We're completely at your mercy."

"Never tell a man you're at his mercy," his voice rubbed her like strong but gentle hands. Excitement burned her belly and anticipation made her look at him from the corner of her eye.

"Why?"

"It's an invitation too hard to resist. Believe me."

The thrumming increased. Angel drew her knees together and squeezed.

Time was closing in, Dahia knew, and Angel needed a boost. She heard Angel's thoughts and felt her attraction to Peter, but at this pace they wouldn't get married before 2002. She glanced over her shoulder at Nefertiti and Sheba who were in quiet conference with God and focused her attention on Angel.

For them, she said to herself, I will help Angel.

She began her council with Angel's heart. "Open you reyes. God gave them to you to see. Close your mouth, for if you are speaking you cannot hear. Listen with your heart. It hears what your ears cannot. Succeed! You are the best of us all."

Rain drops dappled the glass on the front of the rolling contraption and Angel and Peter drove on.

Chapter Ten

Lead seemed to fill Angel's shoes and her legs felt as if they were made of rubber. Her face burned from being in the harsh winter sun and her jaws hurt from smiling.

Angel climbed out of bed on the ninth day of seeing Mystic Peter's way and wanted to collapse. For over a week, he'd taken her to the most remote corners of Mystic, parts she'd never known existed.

They'd met farmers, cattlemen, cowboys and modern day shepherds. In some places there was no running water and in others, the locations were so remote, the people didn't come to town in the winter.

Peter knew them by name, their children and even their animals. He knew of their struggles and never showed up empty-handed.

In a twenty-pound back pack, Angel carried food and bottles of medicine, while Peter carried the other two. No matter where they turned up, everyone was grateful to see him, and never sent him home without something for him or his father or Brenda.

During the course of the visit, the subject of the south bank would come up and everyone had different opinions. Many didn't want anyone to come in and take over their town. Most lived by the land and didn't want it destroyed. But there were some who welcomed change and wished them the best.

Angel sat quietly most of the time watching and absorbing. She wanted to explain Dyer's position, but after hearing the initial reactions, found it more prudent to listen.

She saw things, felt emotions she'd never had before and allowed herself to simply absorb.

When Peter introduced her, everyone spoke highly of her step-father and mother, and their sincerity was something new to Angel. She'd been away so long, she didn't identify with Snowden Glass. That was her step-father's enterprise. But seeing the impact on the town made her realize how much of a loss it would be and reconfirmed her belief that her ideas could help.

Stepping gingerly into the shower, she groaned when the massage sprayer soothed her aching muscles. Tomorrow night was the town meeting and it promised to be a doozy. She needed all of her strength.

Pulling on loose cotton pants and a warm sweater, Angel sank onto the kitchen chair and looked at her bare piece of toast. She dribbled out a bit of syrup, started to eat and turned her attention to her e-mail.

Fourteen were labeled 'analysis' and she downloaded each one, then printed.

Noticing the empty plate, she popped more bread into the toaster, then added syrup. She nibbled at the toast and sat down, licking her finger for a wayward drip. Somebody ought to market this stuff. It was delicious.

Her stomach grumbled for more, but Angel took the syrup and bread and shoved it all in the refrigerator. Out of sight, out of mind.

Gathering the reports, she glanced through, liking what she saw.

A knock at the door brought her attention up and she could see Peter's large frame through the clear paned glass.

Her heartbeat quickened and she took a swallow of lukewarm tea. For the past nine days, she'd been in firm control of her libido, but she had to work hard to keep her guard up. Today would require extra strength. Being together so much, they'd grown closer than she thought possible.

Tossing the briefcase and reports onto the dining room table she hurried to the door and opened it.

"Hey you," he said, stepping in to the kitchen. "You look warm," and after giving her a second glance, "and happy."

Angel couldn't keep a smile from her lips. "I am. Care for some breakfast?"

He shrugged out of his wool jacket. "Sure. What you got cooking?"

They both turned to the spotless daisy covered kitchen and chuckled. "Nothing. But I can fix you something. Won't take but a minute."

"Where's your mother and Luther?"

"She convinced him to take her to D.C. for some shopping. You'll see them tomorrow at the meeting."

She cleared the table of her computer and printer.

"You wouldn't believe I'd been gone fifteen years," she said, coming back into the kitchen. "My room looks like I never left."

Seeing Peter in her mother's kitchen reminded Angel of long ago days when he used to come over and they'd study together.

Suddenly she felt nervous, as if something was about to happen. He watched her with curious eyes. "What are you looking at?" she said.

"Can't look at something pretty?" he said smoothly.

"Mmm, compliments. You must be hungry. What do you want to eat?"

"What do you have?"

Angel's muscles screamed in protest as she pulled Canadian bacon, eggs, cheese and a bag of oranges from the crisper. "I've got enough for a good old fashioned breakfast." She unloaded everything on the table. "Or an omelet with freshly squeezed orange juice. I figured we'd eat then go and do whatever you do on a Tuesday."

"I don't want an omelet."

Her head snapped up. "Okay. You want just eggs and grits? I know mother has something in here you like. Don't tell me your taste has changed that—" She stopped mid-sentence and turned to him. A flush of desire hit her suddenly. "What do you want?" she asked, her breath growing shallow in the heat of his gaze.

"You know what I want." His legs were braced open, his arm leaning casually on the table.

Angel looked over the sink and into the backyard. Cold wind whipped around leaves and twigs, but inside the house the temperature had shot through the roof. She took a step toward him. "You want me?"

"Yes."

Joy leapt in her chest and she fought a smile. "Now?"

"Now."

"What happens after that, Peter? How do we move on? We live a country apart—"

"And tonight," he said.

Her objections fizzled. "And?" she swiped at a stray curl.

"Tomorrow."

She moved a step closer. "You work tomorrow."

"I'm sick tomorrow."

"Oh."

"Take off that sweater."

She laughed, suddenly nervous. "Here? In the kitchen?"

"I want to see you." The simple request was filled with

such yearning, her heart swelled.

Crossing her hands, she pulled the hem over her head and tugged until free of the garment. It stirred the air on its way to the floor. Her stomach was no longer pancake-flat, but she tingled at his appreciative gaze.

Angel hooked her fingers into her waistband and gave him a questioning look. His gaze moved from her hands to her eyes. She licked her lips and said, "Do you have protection?"

Peter smiled and with agonizing slowness, stretched out long legs, reached into his right pants pocket and withdrew a handful of condoms.

Angel unzipped.

He reached into his left pocket and withdrew another handful of condoms.

She let the pants slip down her legs and stepped from them.

When he reached for his back pocket, she knew she was in for a long day and night.

She walked toward Peter and lifted his face in her hands. She wanted to say what lay on her heart, but her emotions were in a jumble. Instead she kissed him, tasting him as if for the first time. His lips were firm, but gentle, moist and thick, moving with her mouth in a steady beat of loving. His tongue sought hers first, tentatively seeking it for a pleasurable tango.

His broad hands cupped her mid-thigh and leisurely slid up. When his fingers squeezed her butt, Angel broke the kiss to share a breath with him. Her eyelids lifted enough to see desire bright in his eyes. "Peter?" she said, as his fingers hooked the band of her Victoria's Secret panties and pulled them part of the way down.

"Yes?" He cupped her ass and squeezed.

The onset of a climax started to roll through her body. "I want you now."

He picked her up and Angel had just enough time to

grab a handful of condoms before his mouth locked on
hers and they stumbled into her room and onto her bed.

In a deft move, he tugged her panties off as Angel
pushed at his sweater and jeans. Skin to smooth skin, a
thin barrier separating their most intimate parts, Peter
pulled her astride him and impaled her, sending her over
again.

The thrill of climaxing didn't completely ebb as they
established an aggressive pump and thrusting motion
that had the bed knocking against the wall. Angel didn't
care if they shook the house down. She only wanted to
be with Peter and give him all that was inside of her.

Their mouths met, wide and hot, moving to satisfy the
insatiable. He held her with his arms wrapped in hers,
his hands gripping her backside, his manhood to the hilt
when a growl tore from his chest.

With all his might Peter pulled her to him, his teeth
grazed her collarbone, and he burst inside of her.

Chapter Eleven

Peter held onto to Angel as if his life depended upon it. He didn't care that he vowed to leave her alone and to handle their situation as he would with any professional. All those plans were shot to hell. How could he keep her with him?

This business had to work. But he didn't want to think of that now with her in his lap, naked, warm, wanting him. He'd never felt better in his life.

Angel felt good. She was so soft, but he wondered about her heart. She had things waiting for her back in California, but he wanted her here in Mystic Ridge. Would that be enough?

Her head rested against his shoulder, her arms around his back. "I think you just tried to kill me."

He laughed, holding her closer. "Well, thank you, Ms. Snowden, I've never been paid such a high compliment."

She moved and her perspiration slick breasts drew a path up his chest. Peter groaned and looked into sexy eyes.

"Your eyes say so much more than your mouth ever did. I don't know if I can—"

"Don't say it. Not now, Angel. We're both adults. We can both have our own agendas and still find a way to make this work."

She pressed her mouth to his, her lips full of affection and tenderness. This was not a kiss good-bye, but one of beginnings. He accepted it, the passion behind it sweeping him into a feeling of well-being.

Her thumbs grazed his cheeks as her forehead rested on his. "I've wanted this for a long time, but I don't want to mess it up."

His body stirred and he laid her down gently. "You can't. We're in this until we decide otherwise."

"Is that it, Peter? 'Otherwise' decides our future?"

"We do, Angel. You know that." He touched her chest, drawing his finger slowly down the center of her body.

Angel tried to keep her wits about her, but his fingers were driving her closer to ecstasy and further from a level head. She gladly made the leap into pure joy.

After the sun had sunk for the night, Angel and Peter left the room and had their long forgotten breakfast. He watched her constantly, never having seen anyone so sexy.

Clad in a T-shirt and boxer pajama bottoms, she cooked and cleaned the kitchen while he read Dyer's prospectus. She held her breath as he slowly turned the pages of data she'd memorized months ago.

When he finally looked up she gazed at him expectantly.

"So?"

"Impressive."

A sigh of relief flew from her lips and she clapped her hands. "I knew you'd think so. I was thinking we could visit towns where there are Mall-mart stores and perhaps see how they operate on a day-to-day basis. That would raise your level of assurance and show you how this whole concept can work. I don't want there to be a shadow of a doubt. Anywhere."

"I never doubted you."

Angel sat at the corner of the table. "Never once?"

He shook his head. "I tried to test you at every phase and you never complained. Not once."

Angel folded the dish towel she'd been holding and placed it on the table. "You tested me? How?"

"I took you every place I thought a city girl might hate. I took you places some aren't proud of. The farms, the mountains, the valleys. You saw what I see. The poor Mystic Ridge. The part I want to help, but can't because that's their life."

"Oh, Peter," she sighed, understanding.

"I know you wonder why I stay. I belong here. I love it here. The good and the bad. The poor and the wealthy. The one stop light and the stop sign nobody wants."

She giggled. "Yeah, that did cause a flap. I like it here, too. I never saw this side of Mystic Ridge before. I guess I was so busy wanting to get out and see the world, I didn't see what was around me."

"And?"

She covered his hand. "I see it now and I want to help. Dyer will hire at least five hundred employees and offer jobs from builders to clerks to managers. This is an awesome opportunity."

Peter took her hand and caressed it. "I wasn't convinced before, but I am now."

Angel flew into his arms. "Thank you," she whispered. "You won't regret this."

"It's not for me," he said gruffly. "It's for Mystic Ridge. But I'm no longer the one you have to convince. There's a town of people and half of them don't want this type of change. I don't like the way the company went about getting the land and I plan to make sure nothing like that happens again. But that doesn't mean they don't have my approval."

"Thank you. Thank you." She kissed his lips, wishing

they could share this type of bliss forever. The idea didn't even scare her anymore. Angel smiled against his
mouth. "Come back to bed with me."

"My pleasure."

She took his hand, led him to her room and closed the
door.

Nefertiti, Dahia and Sheba watched over the couple
with joyous smiles on their faces.

Dahia moved first, extending her palm. The lifeline
was eel black and deep. Nefertiti extended hers and
smiled her satisfaction. Nervous, Sheba extended her
hand and wanted to collapse in tears. Her lifeline was
still sandy brown.

To her surprise, Dahia came and gave her a sad
pounding on the shoulder.

Somehow Angel wasn't where she needed to be and
time was running out. "Where have we failed her?"
Sheba demanded, afraid she had not only chosen
wrong, but not fully blessed Angel with the skills needed
to instill knowledge and truth. "This is my fault."

"This is not your fault. Angel must be in love, and possess all the skills to instill the legacy. We have time, but
I admit she needs a nudge," Nefertiti said. "What about
her mother? Ruth was intelligent and perhaps she would
have succeeded had her husband not been killed in that
war."

"That is true. He was quite a fighter. Those types
always did attract me."

Sheba and Nefertiti looked at Dahia shocked. "What?
I cannot like a man?"

"I thought you only liked them for gouging lamb from
your teeth with the tips of their heads," Nefertiti said.
"Unless there is a good battle going on."

"Oh, they are worth so much more than that," Dahia
said, unexpectedly.

They both looked at her and giggled, but then their

laughter drifted off as they looked at Angel.

"She is about to experience a fall she might never recover from. How can we prepare her for this challenge? Prove that this test and love can co-exist?" Dahia said, sounding weary.

Nefertiti reached out for their hands and they locked.

"Our strength, our power, our love will be her guiding force. She will feel us in her soul and she will do the right thing. She is the chosen one."

Lightning flashed across the heavens and the queens prayed, infusing love into the thunderbolts and sent them rocketing to Angel's heart.

Chapter Eleven

Peter left Angel in the late morning hours on Wednesday. He'd stayed with her nestled in their den of happiness and she was glad they'd been together. It wasn't just that he was a fantastic lover. Peter made her feel a wholeness she hadn't ever felt before.

Her parents had decided to visit some relatives in the Virginia area and wouldn't be back until right before the meeting. Angel had taken advantage of their absence and thoroughly enjoyed Peter's company. She let him out the door with a toe-curling kiss, and decided to spend the day working on her pitch for Mall-mart.

The town council would have plenty of data to make a sound decision. She loved Mystic Ridge and wanted her place of birth to be a place of pride and joy for generations to come.

Stopping in her tracks, Angel felt the first swell of love and let the odd feeling overtake her.

What am I saying? She sank onto a kitchen chair. Sure I love this town, but do I want to stay?

The thoughts didn't shock or repulse her. In fact, she felt lighter and happier than she had in a long time.

She looked around the kitchen and decided to clean up first, answer e-mail then write up her report. Given that the sun went down early, the meeting was scheduled for six o'clock. That would allow enough time to go to town and use the copy machine if necessary and then enjoy the afternoon.

Getting down to business, Angel had the house sparkling in two hours.

Showered and dressed, she gathered boxes of paperwork and set them out making sixteen sets of individual packets of information. In each she included photographs of other locations and color photos of what the property would look like.

Proud of the projection information regarding jobs, she placed a sheet on each packet and filled in the folders with other pertinent information. In an hour she was done and stuffed them into manila folders and back into the box, which she dragged to the porch. Peter still had her car and they had grown accustomed to traveling together. He was supposed to pick her up at five-thirty.

The sky threatened a snowstorm but she prayed it would hold off until Christmas night, only a month away.

This past week she'd driven through the festive town marked with holly and silver garlands. The air was frigid on days, but it helped bolster the holiday spirit.

Though everyone was worried about Snowden Glass closing down, they didn't stop being cheerful and willing to express their glee with the holiday.

Mystic Ridge was so different from California. The seasons changed here and even though spring was months away, a sense of renewal was in the air. Over the past weeks, the citizens had shown her more love and acceptance than she had ever felt in L.A.

Maybe I am just a country girl, she thought as she wiped the counters in her mother and stepfather's kitchen and walked into the deep pantry and looked for a snack. Her eyes came to rest on a bottle of syrup and she fingered the special design with a wave of sadness.

With Snowden Glass closing, this would end too.

Angel closed the door and with it the sad feelings.

Something better was around the corner and she headed into the dining room to get the remainder of her paperwork.

Angel reread each analysis for a second time and couldn't believe her eyes. If Peter ever saw these reports, he'd never agree to allow Mall-mart anywhere near Mystic Ridge.

Detailed information of environmental hazards, waste disposal, unfair hiring practices, increased crime and drug use, and stress on town's resources highlighted each report.

What had she done?

In fifteen minutes, Peter was supposed to pick her up and what was she going to say? I've made a terrible mistake and I'm sorry?

The ringing phone cut into her thoughts. "Angie, baby. It's Bryce. So, what do you have good to tell me?"

"Did you read the reports from the markets we've already moved Mall-mart into?"

"I read them." He sounded confused. "How did you get those? I put them on your desk and was planning to mail them uh, next week."

"John sent them to me. You weren't ever going to let me see these! Bryce, I can't believe you. This isn't going to work. We can't mislead these people into believing this is for their own good. This will destroy Mystic Ridge."

"What will it do to your career, Angie? You ever thought of that? I swear, you sentimental types make my butt hurt. Save the whales. Don't run over the manatee. Grow up, Angie. This is the real world. Join it or stay stuck in your one horse town. I don't care, but you're not going to ruin this sweet-ass commission for me. This is my career, too." He made gurgling noises, then hung up.

The warning sound indicating the phone was off the hook signaled the end of Angel's dream. Sadness and shame worked through her bones making her feel a weariness she'd never felt before. She blamed herself for not knowing the results and for raising the hopes of people she now must let down. It didn't matter that she'd inherited this project when she came on board with the company. She'd brought them to Mystic Ridge and if the town suffered it would be her fault. There was only one thing to do.

Picking up the phone, she dialed and before she could change her mind, she resigned.

When Angel heard a car pull up outside, she grabbed the reports and hurried out the door.

Weighed down with the box, she grabbed the handle of her car door and hopped in. "I've got to tell you something—whoa. You're not Peter."

"Sherman," he said by way of introduction. "We've met. Peter had to get over to the gymnasium and set up some chairs, so I'm filling in."

"Doesn't he have a cell phone? I really need to get in contact with him." Sherman looked at her with patient eyes. "It's vital that I speak with him right away."

He held up his hands seemingly used to hysterical women.

"He has a cell phone, but, no, you can't call him."

"Why not?"

"His cell phone is right here."

Angel muttered an unladylike oath under her breath and she sat back. "I just need to see him before we get started. Can we hurry?"

"He told me to make sure you were taken care of. If you want to get there early, I'm your man. Fasten your seat belt," he said. "I always wanted to drive one of these things fast."

Angel appreciated the glow in his eyes. "Let's see how fast you can make it go."

Thick gray clouds poured great sheets of water from the sky, but that didn't deter nearly every citizen of Mystic Ridge from filling the high school's gymnasium.

This coming together was an event.

The atmosphere was jovial, but most were interested in what was going to happen, rather than say that a change was about to occur.

Angel looked for Peter in the crowd, but couldn't find him. She wanted to scream his name and have him appear at her side, but couldn't without alarming everyone present. So she rushed through the crowd staring into faces until the town council, minus Peter, took their places behind long tables.

Angel took a seat. She had no choice but to tell the truth when the time came.

The cheerleaders had just performed and the band finished up a selection when Peter approached the microphone.

He looked so handsome standing there in black jeans, a brown sweater and a sparkle in his eye. She wanted to rush up to him and tell him he was right and she wrong. But the crowd was immense and she just couldn't add another humiliation to her growing list.

Peter took care of all the other town business and then got to her. Sherman wheeled in a projector and everyone clapped enthusiastically when Peter called her name.

Angel got to her feet, the pit of her stomach down around her ankles. She went through with her presentation and received hearty applause. "But I'm not done," she said and took a sip of water. "There's another side."

She looked into Peter's eyes and felt sadness for what she'd lost and for how she'd made him feel. But the truth was the truth and they deserved to hear it from her.

"Crime in ten of the fourteen cities has increased thir-ty-four percent. Cities suffer traffic jams when they never used to, and four of the cities report a seventeen percent increase in drug use.

"With the seventy-five families they reportedly bring in, only one in four of those have ever lived in a small town. They stay approximately two years and then move on. This has raised taxes for local homeowners nearly forty-four percent." She pointed to the graph. "This level here, is where Mall-mart pulls their managers." She shook her head. "Not from the locals."

"What about marketing?" Roy Cochran's daughter-in-law asked.

"They have a corporate office in Georgia and based on their past record, they don't generally hire anyone from the outside. Our citizens will be relied upon to pro-vide clerical staff, builders and other—as they put it 'non-essential' staff."

A disappointed murmur filtered throughout the crowd. "There's more." By the time she finished talking, she could have heard a pin drop.

Angel didn't know what she expected, but it wasn't absolute and utter silence. Everyone stared at her wide-eyed yet accepting the truth. She stood at the micro-phone surrounded on every side by people she'd been reunited with and loved, and felt wholly responsible for them being there.

She raised the report in her other hand. "This will not save us. We can only save ourselves. Mystic Ridge has so much to offer herself and I don't believe I took the time to look at its beauty and simplicity before trying to change it. The south bank can only be developed as a whole. Dyer doesn't own enough of the land to do anything with it." The murmur turned to relieved sighs. "This can end here and now. I'm sorry," she said finally.

"You did what you thought best," Maureen Clay said from behind the long table where the council members sat. "You got us rejuvenated and looking at our future. And in the end, you came forward and told us the truth. That's all we can ask for."

Angel thanked them for their support and took her seat, waiting until she could pack her car and leave.

As much as she wanted to stay in Mystic Ridge, she didn't know what she had to offer now. She couldn't not work. That wasn't an option, besides she had bills to pay. And what was there to do in Mystic Ridge? Adding herself to the unemployment statistics just didn't seem fair.

Tears burned behind her eyes, but she would not let them fall even as the crowd applauded her effort and many came to shake her hand. This didn't work out, but something else would, she told herself.

Keeping her gaze off Peter, she sat through his short speech to rally the citizens, and his good wishes for a happy holiday. He promised them he'd find a solution by the first of the year and when Angel looked up, hope shined in his eyes.

They ended with Reverend Benson giving the benediction and the meeting was adjourned.

The gymnasium emptied and the men and kids stacked chairs, while the women packed food and exchanged small gifts. Toddlers lay sleeping in the corner on quilted blankets. A few kept up a crying harmony, and those able to walk were watched by the elders who sat in a circle of canes and stocking feet.

Angel loved it. This was home. No matter what, Mystic Ridge would always be home.

Peter worked with the men stacking chairs and with his gentle manner, offered advice to several of the teens. He looked so handsome in the midst of his followers, he was the chosen one for a reason.

She had to see him, talk to him to apologize for what she'd put him through, but Angel didn't know if she could without crying.

"If you love him, tell him so," her mother said gently.

Angel was startled and surprised to see her mother and Luther. "Mom, Dad. I'm so glad to see you."

Her mother's eyes filled and Luther embraced her and gave her a wet kiss on the cheek. "I love you," she whispered in his ear.

"I've always known," he said emotional. "We want you to stay, Angel."

She shook her head and her father took her face in his hands. "Don't just stay for us. Stay because you want to."

"I have to face him and apologize for what I've done. I believed the Dyer Corporation could help Mystic Ridge. Even when Peter objected, I pushed. Once I say what I need to, I have to go."

"You don't have to go," her mother said gently as Peter and the teens pushed dust mops across the gym floor. "You were chosen for Mystic Ridge. We still need you, Angel. You're our bright star. Admission of a mistake shows honor, strength and intelligence. I've never seen you back down. Don't start now. We're going home. I want to see you tomorrow."

"Mother—"

"Goodnight, child of mine."

They passed Peter who seemed intent only on her. He took her hand and led her from the building and helped her into her car. The car hummed and the wipers beat a steady rhythm as they cleared white snowflakes from the windshield.

Angel felt Peter's intensity and didn't know how to respond to it. She wanted to say the words in her heart, but her mouth couldn't speak them.

Everything in her body said 'tell him you love him,' but

she couldn't. Couldn't risk his rejection.

She closed her eyes wondering where they were going, but not anxious to end their last evening together. When the car stopped, they were at the top of a hill, a wood cabin before them.

"Where are we?"

"My house."

"Peter, I'm sorry. I—" her voice broke. "I just want to go home."

"Come inside for a minute, please. We need to say some things."

She looked at him, but didn't want to fight. She got out of the car and followed him inside. He flipped a switch and flooded the downstairs with light. In the weeks since she'd been home, Angel had never been to his home.

The log cabin was absolutely beautiful. A large stone fireplace dominated the living room with a staircase against the wall. It led up to a large king-size bedroom that could have been made especially for him.

A bathroom sat off the room as well as a closet and hot tub. She looked up. "You have a very nice home."

"Thank you. Let me show you the downstairs."

Two additional bedrooms were off the kitchen and dining room, and large glass doors looked over the mountainside.

Rain and snow pattered against the roof and water ran down the outside windows insulating them from any disturbance.

Angel walked back toward the dining room where Peter stood in the center of the floor. "Why did you bring me here?"

"I wanted you to see my home. I want you to know that you'd be happy here. With me."

She attempted to talk and her voice cracked. "I can't stay. I failed you and Mystic Ridge."

"You are the most admired woman this town has ever

had. Not only did you single-handedly try to effect change, but you saved us from situations that would have hurt us."

He took her hand and led her to the sofa. She looked at her hand locked in his and wanted this moment to last forever.

"We have simple needs, Angel. Mall-mart is too lofty for us, but keeping Snowden Glass open, isn't."

"My father said that," she whispered.

"It seems a man named John thinks so too. At least according to his phone call a while ago."

She smiled through her tears. "My ex-boss."

"From the way it sounds, he has some ideas."

She grasped his hand in hers. "John would."

"In Mystic Ridge," Peter said, "we don't remember old fights and we don't hold grudges. Life is as it is, but you're a part of this town. And me."

"Peter, I nearly destroyed part of our legacy. I acquired land for the Dyer Corporation and was prepared to turn it over to them. How can you forgive me?"

"You didn't, did you?"

"No. I couldn't."

"Then there's nothing to forgive. I love you. You have a much bigger legacy to instill and you started tonight when you admitted you'd made a mistake."

Tears of joy trickled down her cheeks. "I'll get the land back. I promise. Oh, goodness. I quit my job today. What—" She smiled through her tears. "What are you smiling at?"

"You are a courageous, strong woman full of integrity and wisdom and immense strength. I love you very much. Stay," he said.

Angel felt her heart sing and moved to kiss him and she felt all the barriers slip away.

"Marry me, Peter and give me sons that will grow up and love life and their families and their town like you love me."

He drew her into his arms, knowing what they had
would last forever. "That's a promise I'd love to keep."

Nefertiti, Dahia and Sheba celebrated their joy by
dancing late into the day. Decked in ethereal finery, each
wore the highest crown bestowed by their Heavenly
Father.

Dahia was dressed as any warrior priestess would be.
Metal from her neck to her feet, complete with a shiny
sword at her side. Sheba lounged on her cloud in shim-
mering silk, and Nefertiti looked regal in brilliant gold.

"Our work is done," Dahia said as Peter and Angel
jumped the broom New Years Eve with barely a minute
to spare.

"We almost didn't make it, but Angel is all of us and I
could never get anywhere on time. Ask Solomon,"
Sheba supplied.

"What will you do now, Sheba?" Dahia asked.

"Help lost souls who don't make it all the way here
after death."

"That is a good choice for you. I will join the fighting
Angel corps. They need leadership!"

Nefertiti and Sheba laughed.

Sheba turned to Nefertiti. "What will you do?"

"I'm glad you mentioned it," she said as she glided
toward them. "God used us to instill this legacy and He
is very proud. It seems there are Ongs in the tenth
dimension who can use our assistance saving their children from peril. God and I thought——"

Dahia and Sheba rose. "You mean work together
again? Are you wicked in the head? She wears metal
on her chest," Sheba said, moving away from Dahia.

"At least I don't shiver every time a strong Heavenly

wind blows. My metal protects me. I cannot do this with this queen who is no more help than a helpless rabbit. I won't," Dahia said.

"I won't," Sheba repeated.

"You will," Nefertiti said, and grabbed their hands.

The End

The Choice

Monica Jackson

Humph, that Angel Snowden nearly turned Mystic on its ear. But she had a lot of help from up above. She sure did. Naw, there's nothing strange about it all, least not here in Mystic. Just like it's not strange what happened to Evelyn Sweet that same year. Changed her sure enough, and those fast-talking sisters of hers too. They still talk about what happened, but only whisper it in the privacy of their home. Evelyn thought she was going plum crazy. Wasn't nothing crazy about Evelyn Sweet. No sir. It was just changes coming, changes in the making ...

Chapter One

Evelyn Sweet dropped her shopping bags on the couch and followed them. She eased low-heeled pumps off her feet and tried to rub the soreness away. The shopping mall had been a madhouse with the usual rush of people doing last-minute Christmas shopping. She'd always done her Christmas shopping early to avoid dealing with the crowds. But there had been a flurry of hints from her daughter and younger sisters about stuff they'd wanted and had to have. She was scared to see what her credit card statements would look like. A twinge of anxiety struck her about her bills.

She'd got the week of Christmas off work for the first time in her fifteen years of tenure as a registered nurse at the hospital. Instead of looking forward to the holidays, she was starting to dread the endless cooking and preparations. These sorts of thoughts nagging on the tired edges of her mind were unwelcome. Anxieties and a sense of dissatisfaction. Nope, thoughts of gratitude for her blessings, giving, and generosity were the sorts of things she tried to fill her mind with. She had health and the love of her family and friends. What blessings could be greater than those?

Evelyn moistened her lips. Suddenly, they felt like they'd been touched. Something like tender kisses. A masculine, musky scent wafted around her own longing. Evelyn frowned and stood. What was wrong with her lately? It was almost five o'clock. She had to get dinner started.

Cars always surrounded Evelyn's neat, but nonde-
script vinyl-sided white ranch around dinnertime in her
working and middle class neighborhood. Dinner was a
drop-in affair and well attended—her sisters and their
kids would be there. Her sisters might bring their men of
the moment. Friends from work might drop by, or folks
from church.

Evelyn cooked and catered and cleaned up after
them as well as she could. Folks seemed to think her
cooking was pretty good because her table was always
full of people and she loved it. Didn't she?

She put the bags in the closet and went into the
kitchen. Her kitchen was the heart of her home and she
loved it. It was straight from the fifties with big white old
fashioned appliances and white enameled metal cabinets with red trim and a big kitchen table to match. Her
one extravagance was the black granite counter tops she
had installed. She spent a lot of time in this kitchen and
it suited her.

Evelyn had decided to cook smothered pork chops
for tonight's dinner. She got the extra-large family-size
pack out and reached in the cabinet for the seasonings.
Suddenly Evelyn cocked her head and listened intently.
She heard singing. Smooth and soulful, like gospel
music. Did she leave a radio on somewhere?

"There you go cooking on the white folks' part of the
hog again."

Evelyn spun, her heart freezing. "Who's there?"

No answer.

She started to take a step forward and stopped, bit-
ing her lips nervously. There had to be an explanation.
Of course there was. She cocked her head and listened.
The homey and familiar hum of the refrigerator and the
tick of the wall clock were the only sounds she heard.
She was tired. That had to be it.

Evelyn bent over and put the big frying pan on the stove. Her eyes moistened. It was December 17. The anniversary of Sweet Mama's death was a week away. The grief had faded to a dull ache, but with her fatigue and the memory of her loss last Christmas . . . No wonder she heard her great aunt's voice, the woman who raised her and her sisters with a firm but loving hand.

The white folks' part of the hog. Sweet Mama liked the pork chops, the ham and the bacon, but she loved the parts of the pig reserved for the black folks way back when. Smoky ribs and crispy fried pigskin. Pig's feet and chitlins. That's good eating, child, she would say. We took the scraps and turned them into gourmet cuisine. That's how we black folks do it.

"Evelyn? You in the kitchen?"

"Yes, I'm back here, Deb."

Her youngest sister glided in sniffing. "You scared me for a moment. I didn't smell any food."

"I just haven't got it in the pan yet. I know you all would riot if I didn't cook."

Deb was beautiful, trim and small with smooth skin that looked like honey and long black relaxed hair hanging over her shoulders and down her back. Deb favored her other two younger sisters and her mother's sister, Aunt Jean. Not for the first time did Evelyn wonder why she'd gotten such a different set of numbers in the gene lottery, with her stocky body, dark skin and short, kinky hair.

Her mother and grandmother had drowned together in a flash flood so long ago that Evelyn's memories of being clasped to a full, soft chest by strong arms were all that remained of them besides a few photos. If it weren't for her looking so much like Sweet Mama and the old photos of her mother, she would have thought there had been some mistake.

Fair or dark, plain or pretty, the family legacy is

always the same, Sweet Mama would say. Evelyn had
frowned because that usually was a prelude to Sweet
Mama going on and on about the importance of choices
and dirty-doggish men. But everyone in Mystic Ridge
knew that Evelyn's choices had already been the wrong
ones.

"Pork chops? What are you cooking with them?"
Deb asked.

"I'm making smothered pork chops, rice and gravy,
sweet peas, yellow pound cake. Speaking of peas,
they're in the refrigerator. You can snap them for me and
put them on to boil with a pinch of sugar and lots of butter."

Deb heaved a sigh and went to the refrigerator.
"Sometimes I wonder why I show up early and don't have
the sense to wait for the food to be on the table like
everybody else."

Evelyn shrugged and unaccustomed resentment
touched her. She was forever cooking and tending to
other folks. What would it be like to come home to a
good meal for a change? She banished the thought.

"Let me tell you why I rushed over," Deb continued.
"I had to tell you the news. You aren't going to believe it.
David's back in town."

"David?" Evelyn put a questioning tone to the name,
but she knew who he was. Her heart thudded as she
remembered the handsome young man whom every single girl in the town wanted to call her own. They'd gone
to school together, first through twelfth grade. Not only
was he the best-looking, most athletic young man with
the highest test scores and grades, he was also one of
the nicest boys she'd ever met. David Douglas had been
born under a lucky star.

"I know you remember David. That man was so fine,
when he left, the echo of breaking hearts around this
town about broke the sound barrier."

"He went into the Foreign Service after college, right? What makes him decide to finally bring his family back to Mystic Ridge after all these years?"

"This is the good part, sis. He was in a car accident in Germany, serious injuries, and his second wife booked on him."

"That's the good part?"

"The man is unattached, broken-hearted and has been injured. He comes back to his hometown to heal and nurse his wounds. What could be better? He's ripe for the picking. The man is mine, do you hear me?"

Evelyn shot a sharp glance at her sister and shook her head. "The poor man," she murmured under her breath. "You were a kid when he left. What do you know about David?"

"I remember David quite well. And I'm not a kid anymore."

Evelyn started to open her mouth to reply when her daughter Ashley bounded in, all long legs and coltish energy. "Hi Mom."

Ashley glanced over at Deb. "What's going on, Aunt Deb?"

"We were talking about David," Deb replied.

"Who isn't? It's so romantic. Wounded hero returning home . . ."

"As far as I know Germany isn't a war zone anymore, and the Foreign Service hardly qualifies as military duty," Evelyn said dryly.

"Mom, you know what I mean."

Evelyn eyed her daughter, hardly believing that this tall beauty sprang from her loins. Ashley was home from the University of Maryland for Christmas break. She was staying in her own apartment and just dropping in occasionally. Evelyn barely got to see her. The apron strings were fraying. She'd be ready to graduate next year and she was already talking about heading off to the west coast for grad school.

Ashley was both the best and worst thing she'd ever done her entire life. She'd been a child having a child when she gave birth to her at fourteen. She could scarcely believe what was happening to her and to her body. When she brought forth this little wailing creature, she'd stared at it in disbelief.

"You've set a course for your life, child. You gave away your youth and you're a woman now," Sweet Mama had said.

And that was the way it had been. From that moment on, she'd been a mother to her child and her three younger sisters. She'd never looked back.

Her heart ached at the thought of her baby grown up and gone. Time had gone by so quickly. She was only thirty-five and she felt like a much older woman who'd never had the fiery juices of young womanhood fill her.

An hour and a half later, dinner was on the table. Folks were talking all at once and enjoying their food thoroughly. Evelyn hurried between the kitchen and the table, as was her habit, refilling glasses and serving platters, bringing out dessert.

Janet said, "I asked David to dinner over here tomorrow."

"Why?" The word from Deb was a sharp rap.

"I thought it would be a nice gesture."

"A nice gesture towards what?" Deb bit into a roll. "Don't get any ideas, now. That man has my name on him."

"I think it is a very good idea to be welcoming toward David," Beverly interrupted. "The man has been through so much."

"And Deb here is itching to put him through more drama," Janet said.

"You got that right," Deb replied.

Evelyn went in the kitchen and closed the door

behind her, shutting off the exchange. Her sisters kept a friendly rivalry going on between them over men. It had always been like that since they were teenagers, but they'd never seriously stepped on each other's toes. Beverly had been out of the loop with her marriage, then the bitter divorce such a short while later. Evelyn was happy to see her rejoin the banter. Apparently nobody ever considered that Evelyn could be interested in a man or that any man could be interested in her.

Although Deb's words had been joking, she'd obviously decided that David would be one of the very few men around Mystic Ridge worthy of her. Janet saw a catch too. Plenty of women would be after David Douglas—that was for sure. It should be interesting around Mystic Ridge with him back, and the Lord knew this town needed all the excitement it could get.

That night Evelyn woke suddenly to the whistling of the wind and cold so frigid her breath made white, ghostly puffs in the darkness of her bedroom.

She shivered and got out of the bed, drawing the blanket tightly around her. She slipped on her house shoes and made her way to the thermostat.

The heater kicked on immediately and she moved back to her bedroom to burrow under the warmth of the covers.

She stopped. Was that a voice she'd heard?

"Sweet Mama?" Her voice quavered and hung in the cold dark air.

Evelyn stifled the urge to turn on every light in the house and get back into bed. Remnants of a dream? A whisper from the grave? The hairs stood up on the back of Evelyn's neck. She sat up in the bed and reached out for the lamp. The yellow light from the lamp warmed her and she drew her knees up to her chest and wrapped her arms around them. The voice of Sweet Mama should be nothing to fear. If only she could hear her voice again, one more time. If only.

She picked up her watch by the bed stand. 12:03 and the date was December 18. Exactly one week before Sweet Mama died the year before on Christmas Eve. It had ruined Christmas for everybody, but Sweet Mama never put much stock in the holiday anyway although she claimed to love the time of the year. Fool commercialization, she'd murmur. Santa Claus and trinkets and spending too much money. Old gods own that time and don't you forget it.

The longest, darkest night of the year.

Evelyn's head snapped up. "Sweet Mama?" she whispered. There was a hint of pleading in her voice. She needed her now. Sweet Mama was the only one who'd cared for her in the way Evelyn gave and gave to others. Sweet Mama would cook the things she liked, rub her back and tell her to keep on putting one foot in front of the other when it seemed as if the world was against her. She missed her so much, and the year's passing had hardly dented the rock of her grief.

Evelyn cocked her head and listened hard. Was there the thrum of drumbeats, women's voices raised in joyous song, or was it the hum of the heater? Was she losing her mind?

She buried her face in her hands. Evelyn had thought this Christmas would be easier—a time of healing and renewal after the sad Christmas of last year. She'd wanted to make this Christmas special. But she was exhausted and broke and getting broker. Everything was falling on her as usual.

Her home was the hub of the family. She poured the money, time and energy to keep the traditions and family spirit alive, and her home was where they all gathered.

Four sisters, their men all gone or lost, and their children. They all lived in Mystic Ridge, tied there by reasons of circumstance and habit. A family of women was what they'd always been and family was all Evelyn had. All that was supposed to matter. Why the hole in her heart?

"Sweet Mama?" She needed her so much.

She turned off the light and lay back and closed her eyes. She felt sleep wash over her.

"Rest, child. You rest now. There's changes a comin' soon."

Chapter Two

Evelyn awoke with a start, feeling chilled to the bone. She gathered the bedcovers close to her and glanced over at the clock. It was six a.m., an hour after the time she normally woke. The morning dawn had yet to break the midnight gloom. It must be stormy. She tried to sit up, then groaned and fell back on the pillows. It felt as if someone had scraped the inside of her throat with sandpaper and replaced her bones with water.

Evelyn stumbled to the bathroom and stared with bleary eyes at her mirrored reflection. No doubt about it, she was sick as a dog on her first day of vacation from work. Figured. She brushed her teeth, swallowed two acetaminophen tablets and lay back down. Snuggling under the covers, she remembered the sound of Sweet Mama's voice. It had simply been a touch of the flu combined with missing Sweet Mama so. She didn't feel relieved at her conclusion, but rather, as if she'd lost something all over again. She closed her eyes and allowed herself to slip back into the soft cocoon of sleep.

When the ring of the doorbell cut into her sleep it seemed like mere minutes later. But when she rolled over and stared at the clock, it was almost noon.

"I saw your car in the driveway," Solomon said when Evelyn pulled open the door. "You doing all right?"

Solomon was one of the best things about Mystic Ridge. The mailman seemed ageless; he'd been there

for as long as she could remember, always a smile or
kind word for anyone who seemed to be in need.

"I could be better, but then again I could be worse,"
Evelyn replied.

He smiled at her. "Couldn't we all?"

She started to nod, then gasped. Beyond Solomon,
the landscape was white, glistening with snow and frost.
She couldn't remember the last time that snow covered
the ground in Mystic Ridge.

"It's something else, isn't it?" Solomon said. "The
town is frozen shut and stopped cold in its tracks.
Everything's closed."

"How is it at the hospital?"

"Half the nurses can't get in because of the roads. I
hear they're sending around trucks and snowplows to
bring them in."

"Oh my goodness. Maybe I should go in." Evelyn
started to back away from the door.

"Hold on. You're sick, it's your vacation and it's not
like you get off work more than once in a blue moon.
They'll be fine at the hospital."

Evelyn sagged against the doorframe. "You're right.
But Solomon, this bug couldn't have hit me at a worse
time."

"Go on and get out of this chill and I'll go get your
packages and bring them in. Pull that door shut now,
and settle yourself on the couch." Solomon hurried away
to his truck.

She went into the kitchen and put the teakettle on the
stove. It had started to whistle when Solomon came in
hidden behind a stack of packages.

"You can drop those under the tree. I'll go through
them later. Can you stop for a cup of tea?" Evelyn asked.
"I have some Christmas cookies too. They're from
Sweet Mama's recipes. I remember how you used to
love them."

"I can't resist that offer." Solomon carefully picked a ginger man from the plate she proffered and ate it in two bites. "You sure got Sweet Mama's touch in the kitchen." He looked around. "Yeah, Sweet Mama's spirit is here, as strong and proud as ever."

The hairs crept up on the back on Evelyn's neck. "I know what you mean," she whispered. "Sometimes it seems as if I can still hear her voice."

Solomon shot a glance at her. "Your family's roots are deep in Mystic Ridge's soil. Before Sweet Mama died she said it was about the time to set some wrongs right."

"What are you talking about?"

"Those old stories; your family curse."

"You're talking about the old family legend? That's ridiculous. The curse is just a myth to explain our run of bad luck with men. And how could you set some curse over a hundred and fifty years old right anyway?"

Solomon carefully chose a chocolate cookie and took a sip of tea before answering. "The only way to break any sort of darkness is with the power and light of love. Life is a circle, my dear. What goes around will always come around again. You can catch it if you're at the right time and place. A man cursed your ancestress in hate. Another man, the right one at the right time, can bless you with his love."

A bird trilled loudly and the church clock chimed. Solomon cocked his head. "Sounds like the time is close."

Evelyn shivered. "Solomon, quit it. You're scaring me. That old story doesn't make any sense. It's all confused and I don't believe it anyway."

A sad look covered Solomon's features. "It happened all right. Your ancestress, was a house slave. It was a coveted position and one she just gained. She was famous for her cooking and the cook's position was always fairly secure in the big house. She wouldn't have to worry about being sold or mistreated as long as she cared for others and dished up the food well.

"But she fell in love with a slave from a neighboring plantation. The personal servant of the owner's son, some say he was his brother. They had asked permission to marry and been refused. She became pregnant anyway. They made plans to run North. She was supposed to meet him by the old creek.

"She fretted and worried. She had a secure position and any child she had would be well cared for. If she ran up North she'd be risking it all. Was love worth it? She decided not. She sent her sister with a message that she couldn't meet him. Her sister told him that she didn't love him and offered herself in her sister's place. He spurned Clara's sister and she reported his intentions and whereabouts to his master.

"His master sent the dogs. It stormed that night and the creek was wild and swollen. He let the waters take him rather than return to his plantation as a slave. They say that the last words on his lips was a curse to the women of his lover's family... that they should be ever alone."

"And since then there have been no male children born that survive, no marriages that last, no man that stays or survives. We are a family of women," Evelyn finished.

"But the circle is closing. A change is coming soon." Solomon sat his teacup down and stood. "I got to get on my rounds. You take care of that flu, you hear?"

Evelyn nodded. She shivered again, but it wasn't from the cold.

෴

Evelyn went back to the bed after a generous dose

of nighttime cold medication. When the doorbell woke her again, she opened her eyes to the heavy headache of too much sleep. She looked at the clock and gasped. Five-thirty in the evening! She couldn't believe she slept that long.

The doorbell rang again. It wouldn't be her sisters. They all had keys and freely used them. She got up and pulled on her robe.

The bell rang. "Hold on, I'm coming," she yelled and immediately regretted the pain it caused to her sore throat.

She pulled open the door and further words dried on her tongue. The man standing on her doorstep was as handsome as a bronze Greek God or a gilded African prince. He smiled at her. His smile started at the corner of his mobile well-shaped lips and lit up his fire-touched tawny brown eyes. "Evelyn," he said. "It's good to see you after so many years."

Her eyes widened with alarm and she pulled her blue faded chenille bathrobe closer to her body. David Douglas was standing in front of her in the flesh and her hair was standing on end, she didn't have on a speck of makeup, and her sleep-swollen face probably looked as if she'd been through a prizefight.

"May I come in?" he asked.

"Uh, of course." She stepped back from the door. "Please sit down. Excuse me for a moment. I need to get dressed." She fled.

Back in her bedroom she pulled on a pair of jeans and a T-shirt and grabbed a brush and tried to scrape back her hair into a semblance of a ponytail.

She pulled open the bedroom door. What in heaven's name was David doing here? She took a deep breath and walked into the living room.

He was looking at her books. He withdrew a much-read volume from the bookshelves and turned to her. "I love this book. I must have read every single book from this writer at least three times." His thumb caressed the paperback cover lightly.

"Yes, Maya Angelou is one of my favorite authors too."

She hesitated. Asking someone what he was doing in her house could be awkward. "Won't you sit down?" she asked, gesturing toward the couch.

He sat and looked at her, obviously waiting for her to speak. Silence fell as Evelyn searched her mind frantically for the words to say.

"I expected your sisters to be here," David said. "Especially Janet, since she was so insistent that I come for dinner at your place tonight."

Dinner! That was it. She remembered the conversation from last night and her initial relief was followed immediately by alarm. She hadn't cooked a thing all day. She'd completely forgotten about dinner. Every piece of meat in the house was frozen. What was she going to do? She sneezed.

"God Bless You."

"Uh, thanks," she said, reaching for a Kleenex. "Excuse me," she said, and blew her nose.

"You've got a cold."

"Yes. I've been in bed all day. And I've got to confess, I completely forgot about dinner."

"I understand. But where are your sisters? After all, technically, they are the ones who invited me."

"I have no idea."

The phone rang and Evelyn reached for it.

"Girl, we slid down an embankment," Deb said as soon as the hello slipped out of Evelyn's mouth. "It's hell out here. The tow guys are going to have to winch out Janet's new car. She's been griping nonstop. She had the nerve to say it all my fault—"

"Are you two all right?" Evelyn interrupted.

"We're fine, but I don't see how we are going to make it over in time for dinner."

"David Douglas is here."

"Better you alone with him than that barracuda Janet. After you feed him be sure and invite him back."

"Deb . . . "

"I got to go. Here's our ride. See you." Then a click and the sound of a dial tone filled Evelyn's ear.

She slowly set the phone on the cradle. "My sister's car went off the road. They won't be able to make it for dinner."

"They're all right?"

"Deb says they're fine, although Janet's not happy about the damage to her new car."

"I'm sorry about that. And you're not feeling well. Maybe we should all get together another time?" he asked.

"Ummmmm, yes . . . another time."

He smiled at her and she swallowed hard. The man was so fine. He had the tall lean grace and chiseled good looks she remembered from high school, but his features were overlaid with a fine-polished patina of maturity, and his body radiated pure masculine sexuality.

David got up heavily and walked to the door. When she saw his limp, her heart went out to him. That touch of vulnerability made him even more appealing. "Are you okay?" she asked.

"I'm fine. The cold and damp have made me a little more stiff, but it'll pass."

He picked up his coat that he'd laid over a chair and pulled it on. "It's nice to see you again," he said. "You were one of my favorite people in high school."

She was? She wasn't in his crowd, but rather was simply one of a number of young women who had cast admiring glances his way.

"I hope you feel better," he was saying.

"I'll be fine. Uh, sorry about dinner. I hope you can come back soon."

"Sure. Give me a call." Then he was out the door. Evelyn leaned against the doorjamb, heedless of the frosty air and watched him make his way to his father's Buick on the curb.

The hole within her heart echoed with something like longing as she watched his lithe body move through the snow. What wouldn't she give for once in her life to have a man like that? Keep dreaming, sister. It wasn't about to happen. Not to a woman like her.

David's car motor revved. Evelyn started to move away from the door and drew it shut. But then his wheels spun in the ice with a sharp whine. He rocked his car forward and back again. Then Evelyn gave a little shriek as his car lurched forward suddenly and slipped past the curb into the gutter.

A moment passed and he slammed the car door behind him. He crunched through the snow back to her door. "Looks like I'm going to be here for a while," he said.

Evelyn nodded and stood aside to let him in.

Chapter Three

David paced as he talked on the phone. His strides were loose and easy instead of nervous or tight. Evelyn imagined she could see his high, rounded buttocks flex through his khakis. She bit her lower lip, filled with a mixture of worry, anticipation and excitement. David Douglas, the finest specimen of man she'd ever laid eyes on in her entire life was stranded in her house, probably for the night.

He laid the phone down and looked at her. "Seems like you're going to have to put up with me for the night," he said.

She was struck by a paroxysm of coughing and grabbed for a tissue.

David's brow creased as he looked down at her. "You're sick. Stretch out on the couch." She stared at him, confused.

"Now," he said reaching over her and picking up the afghan blanket draped over the back of the sofa. She lay down and he covered her with the blanket, tucking it in around her sides. He was close, too close. He smelled of sandalwood and spicy cloves. She closed her eyes for a moment and his hand grazed her hip.

"I make the best chicken soup in the state," David said.

Her eyes flew open. "What?"

"I make the best chicken soup in the state and I'm

going to go and make you some now."

"The chicken's frozen."

"You have a microwave, don't you?"

"Yes, but—" She started to struggle up.

"Please don't move. He gently pushed her back on the couch and handed her the television remote. "Here watch a little TV. I'll make you some tea and toast to hold you until the soup is done and I'll have some too."

"But—"

"No buts. I know my way around a kitchen. Let me take care of you. It's the least I can do for your having to put up with me all night when you're sick."

His words, "Let me take care of you" dried the protests on her tongue. Evelyn watched mutely as he disappeared into the kitchen. Nobody ever took care of her. It was her job to take care of everyone else.

Evelyn supposed she'd have him sleep in Ashley's old room tonight. She looked at her watch. It was barely six. The evening was young and she was going to spend it with the most eligible bachelor in town. She knew she looked a mess. She raised her head and it started pounding. She gave a little groan and let her head fall back on the pillow.

David walked in with a steaming cup of tea and a plate of hot buttered toast. "It's a good thing I got stranded here. You're far too sick to be alone tonight," he said. He put everything on the coffee table, and disappeared. A moment later he had two plump pillows from her bed. He raised her effortlessly with one hand and put the pillows behind her, plumping them and leaning her back against the fluffy softness. "You rest. I'm going into the kitchen and prepare to show off my stuff."

Evelyn smiled weakly at him and watched him walk away toward her kitchen. Lord, that man looked as good going as he did coming. She turned on the TV and sipped her tea. It was good. He'd sweetened it with honey and added a touch of lemon. The sound of canned laughter on the television soon became annoying and she clicked the TV off and snuggled back into the pillows. It felt both strange and good to hear someone rattling about her kitchen while she relaxed.

David Douglas still had the sweet charm she remembered from high school. He'd been unfailingly kind and usually cheerful. He was also still more than enough in the looks department to send any woman's pulse fluttering. She used to fantasize about him when she was a teenager along with half the female population of Mystic Ridge around her age, she was sure. Evelyn's eyes closed and she drifted away...

The smell of greenery and spring air sweet and fragrant with new and tender blooms assailed her nostrils. She was lying under a willow tree, in a soft bed of bruised young leaves and fresh cut hay, a long unbleached muslin dress pushed up around her smooth brown legs.

The leaves parted and there David stood, dressed only in trousers of the same sort of rough material. He went to her and she opened her arms as naturally as a plant turning her face to the sun. He eased his body over hers and his lips touched hers with a passion that was as familiar as it was blazing.

"Clara, my love," he whispered, his voice hoarse. She reached out and caressed his cheek.

"Daniel," she answered.

He kissed her again and their breathing became rushed, their bodies pressing against each others, seeking...

Their hands greedily reached for skin, pulling away clothing, skin against skin. He rained kisses on the curves of her breasts, lower and lower until he encircled her nipple with his tongue. The timeless moans of a woman wanting a man came from her throat. She wanted him, needed him, all of him.

*When he moved his hardness across her thighs, she
gasped with pleasure. This pleasure with this man felt so
right, so perfect, it was why she had been created.*

He poised himself above her, his weight on his arms.

*"Please, please," she begged, her hips churning.
Her feminine emptiness needed and wanted to be filled
with this man more than anything in the world.*

*Her legs grasped his slim hips and he started to
move against her.*

"Evelyn." Her eyes fluttered open and met
Daniel's—no, David's, warm brown eyes. "Evelyn, are
you all right? You were gasping..."

"I'm fine," she said, feeling heat under her skin. It
matched the warmth of her lingering arousal and the
moistness she felt between her thighs. "I was sleeping."

"I've got your soup." He set her food before her on a
wooden tray with a flourish. He handed a spoon and
napkin and settled back into the recliner with a glass of
ice tea and an expectant look.

She could hardly look at him without remembering
the vision of him unclothed in her dream, all lean rippling
muscles and smooth caramel skin. When had been the
last time she'd had a man? She couldn't readily remember, so obviously the experience hadn't been worth
remembering. She knew she'd remember a man like
David Douglas forever. What had she called him in her
dream? Daniel. And what had he called her?

"So how is the soup?"

"It's delicious," she said. It was. The soup was del-
icately spiced and rich with chunks of chicken, egg noo-
dles, carrots, onion and celery. He hadn't been lying
when he said he made good chicken soup.

"Aren't you eating?"

"I'm not hungry. I did my share of tasting in the
kitchen. Eating your own food is not nearly the fun of
cooking it."

"I know what you mean. Sometimes it seems as if I do most of my eating at the stove too."

"It's good to get a break from your own cooking once in a while." David looked at her closely. "You have a dreamy look yet around the eyes. Were your dreams good?"

She shot a glance at him, alarmed. How could he know?

"Or did you have nightmares?"

She dipped a corner of her toast into her soup and took a sip of the orange juice he'd put beside her plate before answering. "I dreamed of things that were out of my reach."

"Ahhh. I know. Sweet dreams that leave a taste of dissatisfaction with yourself or your life in your mouth."

"I can scarcely imagine you dissatisfied with either," Evelyn said.

David looked away. "A life lived without mistakes and regrets is a life not fully lived."

"Are regrets made lighter through sharing them?" she asked.

He met her eyes. "I don't know. Are they?"

"I've only made one mistake of any significance in my life and it was a doozy. But I can't bring myself to regret it."

"Your daughter."

"Yes, my daughter. What about you?"

"I have two children I hardly ever see. Those are my biggest regrets. Two women whose hearts I failed to hold. Mistakes. When I married, I always had this fantasy of happily-ever-after."

"Doesn't everyone?"

"I suppose." He sighed. "Did you ever marry?"

"No. I've never had the opportunity. I'm pretty busy, you know?"

"Do you have the inclination?"

"Sometimes the idea of the companionship is nice. But then I see some of my acquaintance's marriages and it seems as if I'm not doing too bad. We're a close family, my sisters and I."

"Yes, I remember. They are very different from you."

A wry smile crossed Evelyn's lips. "More attractive, more outgoing, you mean."

"Not necessarily. I find your company very easy and you know beauty is in the eye of the beholder."

Evelyn took another sip of soup, feeling flustered. "This soup is really good," she repeated.

"One thing about sharing regrets," David said.

"What is that?"

"It might not make the regrets lighter, but it does make the one you shared them with a friend." When he smiled at her, it felt as if the sun broke through the sky on a rainy day.

Evelyn inhaled and exhaled slowly. "I can't eat an more. My appetite . . ."

David stood to take her plate and touch her forehead. "You're burning up. You should be in bed."

She couldn't protest. He took her hand and pulled her up from the couch. She felt her hand trembling within his like a small, hot bird as he led her to her bedroom. He turned to her at the door and she thought her heart would stop when his head lowered toward hers. He dropped a friendly kiss on her forehead.

"The linen closet is outside the bathroom. There's bedding in there. You can sleep in Ashley's room," she managed to say.

"Take some aspirin," he said. He turned and left and she closed the door behind him feeling bemused. She felt as if she was in some sort of fairy tale, stranded alone with this fine man for the night. Just her luck she'd have a raging fever, cough and sniffles. She pulled off her clothes and had just dropped a flannel nightgown over her head when she heard a soft knock on the door.

"Your pillows," David said, holding them out. She took the pillows from him and held them to her chest. "Sweet dreams," he said. Suddenly, his head cocked to one side. "Do you hear that?"

She listened and her eyes widened. There was the faint sound of women singing.

"Have you left on a radio anywhere?" he asked.

"No. I haven't."

He shrugged. "Must have been the wind."

"No, I heard it too. Women singing."

It probably came from outside." He drew closer to her and she held her breath. "I had a really good time, probably a whole lot better than if things had turned out as planned."

Her heart pounded. "I don't feel as if I've been much of a hostess."

"You've been wonderful." A flash of that crooked smile and he was gone.

There was a sound like a slow, collective exhale after the door closed behind him. Evelyn looked around the room. "The last thing I need is to be haunted. Do you hear me, Sweet Mama?"

"You say something to me?" David called through the door?

"No. I didn't say anything. Good night." Evelyn crawled under the blankets. The smell of spring and freshly cut hay wafted across her face and she sat up in bed. It was the middle of winter in the biggest snowstorm in years. What was going on? She remembered David's cocked head and quizzical expression at the faint sound of women singing. If she was losing her mind, maybe she wasn't losing it alone.

She thought about what Solomon said about the circle of life going around. He had said another man, a man coming at just the right time would bless her with his love.

thus ending the family curse. Was David a part of that circle? Somehow it felt as if they belonged to each other, as unlikely as that seemed. But curses and old family legends were things dreams were made of. Dreams that a man like David really belonged to her were as elusive and unreal as magic.

Chapter Four

Evelyn opened her eyes to the aroma of coffee. Daniel was here, she thought, filled with a warm glow at the thought of his strong hands and loving heart. Daniel? David. David was here and she didn't know a thing about his strong hands on her body and she likely never would.

Evelyn stood and touched her head. She felt much better. At least the flu bug had been of short duration. Walking to the dresser mirror, she stared at herself and sighed. No, she had no hope of snaring a man like David. Her short black hair, barely long enough to scrape into a ponytail, stood straight up. Her relaxer sorely needed a touch up, because the naps on the back of her neck were threatening to take over.

Her body was sturdy and plump, not willowy with feminine curves like her sisters. Her skin was the color of Hershey's chocolate, her features distinctly African. Brothers who would turn all the way around when one of her sisters passed wouldn't give her a second glance on the street.

Evelyn Sweet was no one's flavor of choice. That had been just fine with her, seeing all the trifling men her sisters had racked up . . . until now. David Douglas pulled strings in her heart she didn't even know she had. There seemed to be some sort of indefinable connection between them. Like they knew each other—intimately. She sensed that he felt it too. She remembered her dream of Clara and Daniel. Evelyn and David? The circle turns.

She bit her lower lip and turned away from the mirror. She needed to stop thinking foolishness. She'd have to leave this room to face David sometime. It would be better to do it showered, groomed and dressed rather than sick and in disarray like she'd been yesterday.

Then she heard the shower come on and sank back on the bed. The thought of him in her shower, hot water sluicing over that perfect body . . . oh my. Then Evelyn shook her head to clear it. Her thoughts hadn't wandered so persistently in those directions since she'd been a teenager. Get a grip, girl.

David turned his face up to the showerhead. The warm water felt good. He'd had a good night's sleep, much better than he thought he'd have in a strange bed. But being here in Evelyn's house felt wholly comfortable to him. Her home was like her, warm, old-fashioned and comforting. He liked her immediately, more so than his usual somewhat guarded reactions to women. She was also quite unlike the type he usually dated. He couldn't imagine dating Evelyn, or any sort of casual relationship with her really. But he could imagine living with her . . . waking up next to her every morning of the rest of his life.

He turned off the shower with a quick motion. What was wrong with him? He barely knew the woman. At this stage of the game it was normal to think about what a woman looked like naked or their sweaty, heaving body underneath his own, but domestic bliss? Hardly.

He toweled himself off with a towel and wrapped it around his waist. He needed to shave badly. He remembered seeing a package of disposable razors in the linen closet outside the bathroom. He adjusted the towel and opened the door.

David looked up into the astonished faces of three women. Evelyn's sisters.

Evelyn heard the shower cut off. Keys jangled in the front door a few minutes later and Evelyn sat bolt upright in her bed. Oh Lord, her sisters. You know they'd find a way over at the crack of dawn to find out what the story was with David. She reached for her robe.

"Good morning," she called as she pulled open her bedroom door. Evelyn drew in a breath at the tableau that unfolded in front of her. David stood there, frozen like a bronzed god with only a towel draped around his middle. Her three sister's eyes bugged and their jaws dropped toward the carpet. For some reason the sight satisfied Evelyn. "I'm surprised you're here so early," she said calmly to her sisters.

Her words seemed to unfreeze David. "I'm going—going to get dressed now," he said and fled to the bathroom.

Evelyn smiled at her sisters and went into the kitchen. She poured herself a cup of coffee. It would probably take a minute or two for her sisters to pick their jaws up off the floor and make it into the kitchen. She started to get cups for them, but then settled back into her chair. They knew where the coffee cups were.

Sure enough, her sisters sailed in, wafting a residue of shock. "So what happened?" Janet demanded. "Why did that man spend the night?"

Beverly chuckled. "It's obvious what happened. It's about time you finally got some, Evelyn."

"I don't believe that for a moment David Douglas is that hard up," Deb snapped.

Evelyn sat her cup of coffee down so hard on the

table that it splashed and overflowed. She ignored the spill. "Excuse me, what do you mean, hard up? I see you need reminding that this is my house you're standing in."

Beverly pulled out a chair and sat. "I need a cup of coffee," she said.

"So do I," said Janet.

They both looked toward Evelyn. She didn't move.

Janet frowned, then got up and got herself a coffee mug out of the cabinet and poured herself a cup. "I don't know what's gotten into you," she muttered to Evelyn.

"How about David Douglas?" Beverly cracked.

"I wouldn't believe that until I saw it in action," Janet said.

"Where's my cup of coffee?" Beverly asked Janet.

"Get it yourself."

Deb was still glowering and pouting at Evelyn's retort.

Evelyn chuckled, stood and stretched. "I'm going to shower and dress," she announced. Her walk had a decided bounce to it as she walked out the door.

David entered the kitchen with some trepidation. Evelyn's three sisters sat around the table sipping coffee. From the way the conversation stopped when he walked into the room, he knew they'd been talking about him.

"Hello, everyone. I was wondering if any of you could give me a ride home."

"You're having car problems?" one of the sisters asked. Janet, he thought her name was. He always got them mixed up. They looked so similar and so different from Evelyn,

"My car slipped in the ice last night. It's stuck."

"Ahhh," said the smallest sister, the youngest one.

The syllable was laden with understanding. So that's why you spent the night with my ugly sister, she'd said without words.

David felt a surge of protectiveness toward Evelyn. "Yeah. I don't regret it though. If it wasn't for that I wouldn't have had the opportunity to... get to know Evelyn better." And with those words he strode from the kitchen.

He knocked on Evelyn's bedroom door.

"Come in," she said in her soft voice.

He closed the door behind him. Evelyn stood in front of her dresser mirror, makeup scattered in front of her.

"I'm going to ask one of your sisters for a ride home."

Her face closed like a shutter and she turned and faced the mirror. "Okay."

"How do you feel?" he asked.

"Much better."

"That's good," David said. "I wanted to let you know privately how much I enjoyed our conversation last night."

"It didn't seem like we talked much. I spent most of the evening asleep. But that chicken soup was wonderful. I should be thanking you."

"No thanks needed. Sleep and chicken soup are probably why you feel better today." He paused. "I wanted to also let you know that I'm not interested in your sisters."

Evelyn turned to the mirror and picked up her lipstick. "It would be none of my business if you were."

"I wish you could make it your business. I'd like to see you again."

She turned and faced him, a glint of anger in her eyes. "I don't need your pity, David Douglas."

"You don't have it. You do have my interest though."

She looked down in confusion and David caught her chin and pulled it out, forcing her eyes to meet his. The door flew open and her three sisters all fell into the room.

"That door latch must be broken," Janet said. "Sorry." Her sisters all backed out of the room and pulled the door shut again.

David and Evelyn looked at each other and simultaneously chuckled.

"Your sisters are a mess," he said.

"Don't you know it. A little shaking up is good for them."

"It's better for you. I sense you need a change in your life, Evelyn Sweet. I sense it with every bone in my body."

Her smile faded and David hated to see it go. Her smile lit up her face and the beauty of her soul radiated from her features. He didn't understand why she didn't consider herself attractive.

"It seems as if I've heard that I need a change from several different people," she said.

David caught her hand. "I think that your change is right here, Evelyn," he said.

Chapter Five

Evelyn looked out the window at the swirling snowflakes. It would be a white Christmas, the first one in Mystic Ridge in five years or more. The town was frozen, stopped cold, but the houses glowed with holiday lights and activities. Evelyn felt more alive than she had in years. There was a tingling quality there, a breathless anticipation. It had nothing to do with the Christmas season and everything to do with David Douglas.

The ring of the phone interrupted her thoughts.

"Hi Mom, I just wanted to tell you I'm not going to make it home until Christmas Eve," her daughter, Ashley, said.

Evelyn let her silence reply.

"Travis is having this great party and I've promised Melanie I'd go shopping with her," Ashley continued

"What about us?" Evelyn asked. What about me? She wanted scream the words. She missed Ashley so much sometimes. This growing up and growing apart hurt more than seemed fair.

"I'll be there for Christmas. Knowing you, I know you have all the Christmas arrangements under control and the sisters haven't lifted a finger to help."

"I miss you, Ashley."

"I miss you too, Mom. The best thing about Christmas for me wasn't the presents, but all the stuff we did together, especially the cooking."

"And the tasting," Evelyn added with a chuckle.

"It's just that now, well . . .my friends are important to me too. I just started dating Travis and he really wants me to be there for him."

"Do you want to ask him here for the holidays?"

"His family would freak if he didn't spend Christmas with them."

"Believe me, I understand. Speaking of—I think I'm going to ask David here for the Christmas Eve dinner."

"They put you up to that? Aunt Deb, I bet."

"No. I've been seeing him the last couple of days."

Silence. Then a shriek. "You're kidding, Mom!"

"Nooooo, I'm not kidding, although I can hardly believe it myself. It seems that he's taken an interest in me."

"You know, I'm not surprised. You know I love my aunts, but you're nicer than all of them put together."

A warm glow filled Evelyn at her daughter's words. "He might not be able to come, but I didn't want you to be surprised in case he shows up."

"You go, Mom. Don't let your sisters put a damper on this. I bet Aunt Deb is having a fit. It's about time you went for the gusto."

"David Douglas might be a little more gusto than I can handle."

"No woman would have any problem handling that. He might be old, but he's fine."

The beep of call waiting broke in. "Hold on, Mom," Ashley said. A second later, she was back. "I gotta go, it's Travis."

"Bye baby," Evelyn murmured before she hung up. Her daughter was right. It was about time she had a taste of the gusto.

~~◊)

Evelyn touched her hair nervously before she pulled

open the door.

David stood there, blindingly handsome in a suit and tie. "You look great," he said.

Evelyn smiled at him and picked up her coat. He took it from her and gently eased it over her shoulders.

"I had to make reservations," he said.

"At La Costa?" It was the only decent restaurant in town, but reservations had never been required before.

"Mystic Ridge is full of friends and family this holiday season and it seems as if a lot of people are eating out."

"I've eaten out more these last few days than I've done the past few years." Evelyn said, as they walked down the shoveled driveway to David's car."

"Good. Someone else needs to do the cooking for you once in a while. How are your sisters holding up under the strain?"

They'd discussed her sister's complaints about the lack of dinners at Evelyn's house the last few days.

"They're griping, but I notice that none of them look like they're going hungry."

The Maitre d' seated them in an intimate quiet spot. They ordered their food and Evelyn fingered her wine glass. David looked around. "It's good being home, but I could never live here again."

Evelyn's stomach fluttered and she lifted her wine glass to her lips. "Why not?" she asked.

"I've experienced all this town has to offer. There's too much out there. My heart has moved on."

"I don't think my heart could ever leave Mystic Ridge. It feels as if I'm a tree planted here. My roots are deep," Evelyn said.

"Nothing could persuade you to uproot yourself?" David touched her hand.

Her mouth dried. "I'm afraid I might wither," she whispered.

"Not if you're well cared for."

Evelyn looked away. She had to be reading in the undertones of this conversation. He couldn't possibly mean . . . It was far too soon.

"How is your father?" she asked.

"Dad is perfectly content. He's dating a widow from church and he's set in his routine. He's happy to see me, but it feels like I've unsettled his routine more than anything."

"So what are your Christmas plans?"

"Dad's going to celebrate Christmas with his lady friend, Gina Brown and her family. It's the third Christmas he's done so and I understand he's sort of expected. He's looking forward to it. I'm invited of course," David added.

"I'd love to have you join us for our Christmas Eve dinner. Christmas too, if you like," Evelyn murmured.

David's face lit up, and he intertwined his fingers with hers. "I'd like that," he said.

A rush of pure happiness filled Evelyn. Their eyes met and it felt as if the world stopped for a moment. It made no sense. They were so different and almost strangers, but being together felt so right.

"Our family has some Christmas traditions," she said. "On Christmas Eve the kids go over to Bev's and they tell stories and such. The adults go over to Sweet Mama's house and we have Christmas Eve dinner and exchange our gifts. Christmas Day the kids come to Sweet Mama's and open their presents. We generally eat all day and pass out in a stupor sometimes near evening."

David chuckled. "Sounds nice. Especially the eating part."

Despite the conversation, Evelyn's attention was focused on her hand in his. Electricity seemed to flow between their fingers.

"I'm looking forward to it," he said and paused.

"Evelyn— I wonder . . . Does it ever seem to you that we've met before?"

Evelyn withdrew her hand, shaken. "All the time."

"Are you thinking about high school?" he said. "I mean it's more than that. Sometimes it feels like we've been together before—like we've had a relationship before."

"Like a dream?" Evelyn whispered.

David frowned and looked away. "No. My dreams are disturbing lately. That's unusual. I've never remembered my dreams before."

"Tell me."

"I dreamed I was drowning in a rush of water. It was terrible. The water filling my lungs, the utter despair, then the blackness."

"My mother and grandmother drowned together."

"I'm sorry."

"We never found out what they were doing by the creek in the rain like that. A flash flood and they were washed away."

David's face was grave and his thumb rotated in the center of her palm.

"It was a long time ago," she continued. "I mentioned it because afterwards, for a long time I had dreams about drowning. I remember how awful it was."

"You understand. I've only had this dream once, but I remember it as if it actually happened."

"Sweet Mama told me that water in dreams means emotions. She said I was afraid of my emotions and grief overwhelming me."

David nodded. "That's a good explanation," he said and looked away. Evelyn looked at her plate and picked up her fork.

The subject of dreams was an uneasy one.

"The mailman, Solomon, told me something the other day. He was talking about our family legend," she said. The water is deep and you don't know where the currents lead, but jump on in.

"Family legend? That sounds interesting. Tell me about it."

Evelyn shifted with embarrassment. It wasn't easy to tell a man you're intensely attracted to about this particular sort of curse. "A slave from a neighboring plantation had fallen in love with our ancestress. They'd made plans to run north. At the last moment she changed her mind. He ended up drowning in Sorrow Creek and he cursed her with his dying breath." Evelyn paused and took a deep breath.

"What was the curse?" David asked.

"That there would be no men in our family."

"No men? How could that be?"

"We generally only have female children and our marriages don't last long. That is, if we're lucky enough to marry in the first place."

"That does seem like bad luck."

"I think it's just a made up story to account for our sorry track records with men."

"My family has nothing as romantic as a family legend and a curse."

"It would be our luck to have a curse that's the opposite of all things romantic. Solomon said that maybe our luck will change soon."

"Oh?"

"He said the time is coming where we can be decursed."

"How is that?"

"I'm not sure. Something with men."

"I'd sure hope so."

They both started laughing at the same time. Then the conversation turned to comfortable subjects—the past, mutual acquaintances, her job. Evelyn felt wholly relaxed in his presence. Meant to be.

Afterwards, when they stood at her front door, they turned toward each other. "Do you want to come in for coffee?" Evelyn asked.

"I better not." David's eyes were full of some unfathomable emotion. He bent his head toward her and pulled her close. When his lips touched hers, a spark of electricity traveled through her. His lips were mobile, firm, warm. His arms around her felt so right. *Too right.*

She trembled. She felt him tremble too and he drew away. They looked into each other's eyes and she could see the passion clouding his and she knew it clouded hers. This was unbelievable. *Too fast.*

The emotions between them were like a silent freight train rushing. He touched her cheek, turned wordlessly and walked to his car. They both knew if he came in what would happen. *Too soon.*

The phone was ringing as she entered the house, but she ignored it and let the answering machine pick it up. She dropped her shoes in the middle of the living room floor and headed for her bedroom. She uncharacteristically left her clothes on the bedroom floor. As she brushed her teeth, all she could think of were dreams and magic and David Douglas. Her feelings for him had turned into wildfire, quick and all-consuming.

No, it wasn't like her at all. She was a naturally cautious person, a person unused to and leery of change. She was letting this man sweep her away as if he were a river and she was helpless against the current. With him she wasn't afraid of drowning. She crawled in bed and closed her eyes, welcoming her dreams.

Chapter Six

*C*lara woke with a start. The morning sky was turning pink already and she could hear the song of birds. She'd overslept again. She'd have to hurry to get breakfast ready. Tillie would have started the preparations, but the family wouldn't be satisfied without her own soft, fluffy white biscuits.

She didn't want to rise from her coarse bedding and straw mattress. Lately she'd felt tired down to the bones. She touched the soft swell of her belly and her eyes widened. Suddenly she knew. A smile curved her lips. A wondrous thing. A perfect thing. She was going to have Daniel's baby. A part of her was a part of the man whom she loved more than life itself. With her position in this house, his child would be safe. They would never sell her child away from her. Ever.

"Evelyn!" Tillie's voice called...

"Evelyn, wake up, girl!" Deb was sitting on the bed, a cigarette dangling from her fingers.

Evelyn sat up in the bed, still disoriented from her dream. "Put that thing out. You know better than to smoke in my house."

"Well, excuse me," Deb said, but she went into the bathroom and dropped the cigarette in the toilet. "I had to have a cig because I waited forever for you to wake up. You were in here snoring like a wild boar—"

"A wild boar?"

"Okay, so you were just breathing heavy. I made a pot of coffee."

"Good. I need a cup." Evelyn pushed the covers away and got up and went into the bathroom. "Pour me one will you?" she called. "Lots of cream, no sugar."

"When did I start looking like your maid?" Deb answered.

It was too early in the morning for Deb's crap. Evelyn pushed the door open and came out of the bathroom with her jaw tight. But before she could say a word, Deb threw up her hands and said, "All right. I'm going to get you a cup," and switched out of the room muttering about grumpy sisters.

Twenty minutes later, Deb came back into Evelyn's bedroom proffering a mug of coffee. Evelyn took it, went into the living room and turned on the television to the morning news. Deb trailed her and sat on the chair adjacent nursing her own coffee.

"What happened with you and David last night?" Deb asked, too casually. "I heard you two were seen at La Costa.

"We had a nice meal," Evelyn answered, her attention pointedly on the television.

"What did he say about me?"

Evelyn looked at Deb. "Why do think he said something about you?"

"Well, that's obviously the reason he asked you out. He must be hesitant to ask me out directly—"

Evelyn snorted in a purposeful imitation of a wild boar. "I'm going to get dressed."

"So what did he say about me?"

Evelyn turned slowly to face her sister and put her hand on her hip. "He didn't say a thing about you. He had quite a bit to say to me though. He'll be over here Christmas Eve."

"He's coming to spend Christmas Eve! He must really want to see me. What shall I wear?"

Evelyn shook her head. "You just don't get it, do

you?"

"Get what?"

Evelyn raised her hand and went into her room, shutting the door behind her. Lord, give her strength. She thought. Deb worked her last nerve.

꿍

At precisely seven on Christmas Eve, Evelyn pulled the door open for David. He was loaded down with an armful of presents wrapped in bright paper. Deb, overdressed in a short, tight red velvet dress rushed to him, practically knocking Evelyn over.

"David, I've been looking to seeing you again," Deb gushed. "Please come in. I hope those all aren't for me?"

David looked bowled over by this torrent of words. "Uh, they're for everybody," he said.

Deb grabbed the presents from his arms and went to the tree with them, shaking each one carefully before she set them under the Christmas tree. Evelyn noticed her frowning as she stuck a small box way in the back.

She left him to the ministrations of her sisters while she went to the kitchen and poured him some hot buttered rum. He looked like he might need some fortification. Dinner was ready to go on the table. She stood inhaling the aroma-laden air. Duck with lemon sauce, wild rice dressing and Virginia ham, greens and cornbread dressing. Cakes, pies and her special homemade candy cane ice cream, and more. She'd been up all night and it smelled like it would be worth the effort.

Bev came in. "Time to put the food on the table?"

"Yes. Give me a hand."

"All right." Bev moved toward the table. "Deb's got that poor man cornered," she said. "But I think this is one trophy she's not going to be able to put on her mantle. I doubt if she'll take it well," Bev said.

"Me either."

Bev looked at her out of the corners of her eyes as she poured the gravy into the boat. "I hear that you and David might be an item. Deb says it's not possible."

"Last time I checked, I was just as much a woman as her," Evelyn said.

"I didn't mean it like that. It's just that you've never shown much of an interest in men before."

"Things change," Evelyn said as she picked up the platter of the family's traditional Christmas duck and wild rice dressing. She caught the speculative look Bev gave her as she sailed out of the door.

Let them worry and wonder, she thought. She hugged what she and David had shared together to herself like a delicious secret.

Deb sure was showing her tail, Evelyn thought as she savored her last bite of duck in the delicate lemon sauce. She slid a piece of rum cake on her dessert plate. Deb was laughing too loudly in David's face. How did she know that he hated that? There was nothing she could do to check Deb, so she just watched and inwardly shook her head. How did she know that Deb was making David feel uncomfortable? He was behaving with perfect courtesy, showing no evidence of discomfort whatsoever.

Why did she feel she knew this man so well, body and soul? Heaven knew they weren't a perfect match, she a small-town homebody with plain looks, he an exciting, handsome well-traveled man. Her gifts were a flair for cooking and the ability and love of giving. But with her family she had to admit the giving was wearing thin.

"We need some more whipped cream, Evelyn," Janet said.

"You know where the kitchen is," she answered pleasantly, right before she ate a forkful of rum cake. The cake was really good. She knew she'd outdone herself for the entire meal, but no one had expressed appreciation except David.

Maybe she'd done her sisters a disservice by trying so hard to fill Sweet Mama's shoes. They were dissatisfied women. It wasn't because they didn't have enough money or a good man. It was because they weren't grateful enough for what they did have. That was another thing that made her different. If nothing else, she'd always been grateful. Grateful for her health, for the people she had to love and loved her. Not that her life was perfect, but it was good. The Lord had blessed her. She smiled and glanced at David and he met her eyes and smiled back.

Suddenly it was just the two of them celebrating the advent of Christ into the world. Deb broke the spell by clearing her throat loudly. "The kids are expecting us back soon so we'd better go open our presents. I can't wait to see what David bought me."

Janet rolled her eyes and Evelyn stifled a giggle.

That girl has always been stubborn.

Evelyn's head snapped up. Sweet Mama was whispering in her ear. The hairs and the back of her neck rose and she could feel the goose bumps forming on her arms. Well, if she was losing her mind, she could at least lose it quietly until the holidays were over.

She followed her sisters in the living room where they sat around the Christmas tree like they'd done every Christmas Eve except the last one, the one when Sweet Mama died. Evelyn could scarcely believe that she hadn't thought of her all day until the ghostly whisper in her ear. How could she be losing her mind? She'd never felt more alive and sane in her life.

"Sweet Mama always said a prayer before we started opening our presents," Evelyn said.

Janet sighed and looked away. "It almost feels like she's here." She looked over at David. "Sweet Mama was our great aunt who raised us. She passed away a year ago on Christmas Eve. We missed Christmas last year."

"I know," David said. "I'm sorry."

"Sometimes it does feel as if Sweet Mama's still here in this house," Evelyn said.

"If Sweet Mama was going to haunt anybody, it would be you, Evelyn. You were always her favorite," Bev said. "You took after her while the rest of us took after mother."

Evelyn took a deep breath. "Maybe Sweet Mama hasn't moved on yet. It's as if she's waiting for something."

Bev shivered and looked around.

"Are we going to ever open the presents or do you all just want to talk about Sweet Mama and that depressing Christmas we had last year?" Deb complained.

"Isn't that just like you?" Janet said. "Always thinking of yourself and some presents when the woman who raised us—"

"I'm going to say the prayer in Sweet Mama's stead this year," Evelyn interrupted.

"Go ahead and say the prayer, Evelyn. Sweet Mama would have wanted that," Janet said.

Evelyn closed her eyes and reached out for the Spirit that had been her main comfort this past year.

"Heavenly Father We praise your Name every day and especially in this season. Thank you for the precious gift of your blood and the salvation Sweet Savior Lord Jesus has given us. Help us not to forget this true meaning of Christmas. Let us be willing and able to give with the power and spirit you pour out your blessings onto us. We thank you for the gift of life, of health and family. We thank You for the love we share . . . All this in the name of the Father, Son and Spirit, Almighty God.

She stopped. Sweet Mama's strength and love filled her like a wind and a blessing.

"The longest, darkest night of the year is upon us. The circle turns and the time for the choice comes once again. It's the time to set old wrongs right and the time to make the choice. Choose to walk the path of trust, faith, and love rather than fear. May the binding be broken and our blood set free once again."

She heard a gasp and her eyes flew open. All her sisters were staring at her in consternation and even David looked concerned. "What's wrong?" Evelyn asked.

"You were going to say a prayer and you started, but everything changed. Your voice changed," Bev said, looking worried.

"What are you talking about?" Evelyn asked.

"You sounded spooky, girl," Janet said.

Evelyn got to her feet. Fear replaced the warm loving feel of Sweet Mama's presence and memory of the words she spoke flooded her. They weren't her words. "I'm going to my room for a moment. Go ahead and open the presents. I'll be back."

She walked to her room and threw the door closed behind her. She heard Deb explain. "It's hard on her with the anniversary of Sweet's Mama's death."

Evelyn lay on the bed and closed her eyes. "Sweet Mama?" she whispered. There was no answer, but the wind blowing against the windows.

She felt someone enter the room and sit on the bed bedside her. Evelyn turned and opened her eyes and looked into David's concerned brown ones.

"I don't know what's happening to me," she said. "Sometimes I wonder if I'm losing my mind."

David gave a tiny shake of his head. "You're not los-

ing your mind. Your sisters say it's grief and stress, but—
maybe it's more than that."

"Do you feel something too? There's a strangeness."

David looked away, silent. He handed her a small
box. "For you," he said.

She sat up and ripped away the paper, feeling like a
child on Christmas morning. It was a black velvet box,
the type of box that holds promises. She held it in her fingers, hesitating.

"Go on, open it," David urged.

She lifted the lid and a pear shaped diamond
sparked on a delicate chain. Tears filled her eyes. It was
so beautiful.

"I—I can't. It's too much."

"It's not enough." He took the box from her hand and
gently put the chain around her neck.

The diamond fell to the cleft of her breast and
sparkled near her heart. A promise. David leaned forward and their lips met. Stars swirled around them.
Evelyn wrapped her arms around his neck and they cradled each other. This was where she was supposed to
be, with this man. She knew him. She wanted him more
than life itself.

"Why do we know each other?" she whispered.

"I don't know. I can't understand it, but I do know
you. I can't fight what I feel."

"It's crazy. We don't know the details of each other's
pasts or anything about each other really." Evelyn bit her
lip. "It's as if I see your soul."

"Like we've known each other in another life," he
said.

Evelyn's head snapped up.

David smiled down at her. "You know what? Let's
not fight this."

Evelyn smiled back at him. "Let's not."

There was a sharp rap at the door. "Are you two all

right in there?" Deb's voice called.

"We're just fine." David answered.

"We should go back out," Evelyn said. "They're probably worried."

When Evelyn came from the room with David following behind her, all eyes went to the glittering diamond at her breast. Janet gasped, Bev's eyebrows raised and Deb frowned.

"Isn't it beautiful?" Evelyn asked.

Apparently her sisters had been struck speechless because nobody answered.

The phone rang and Deb moved to answer it. She listened a moment and put the phone back in the cradle. "That was Ashley. She's wondering where we are. The kids are expecting us. We'd better hurry and open our presents."

"The presents will still be here tomorrow morning," Evelyn said. "Why don't we open ours with the kids?"

"But we've always opened our presents on Christmas Eve," Janet said.

"Maybe it's time for a change," Evelyn said.

"Whatever," Bev said, obviously impatient. "Let's get going then.

"I'm not going," Evelyn said. She felt in every cell of her body that her place was here with David this night.

The sister's stared at David. Speechless again, they got into their coats.

"Don't come by too early in the morning," Evelyn said. "I think I'm going to sleep in."

Deb looked like she itched to slap her. "Thanks for ruining Christmas," she said.

"Ruin Christmas? I didn't ruin Christmas Eve. Dinner was lovely," Evelyn answered. She felt serene. No negativity could touch her with David at her side.

"Dinner was great," Janet said.

"Sure was," Bev added. "See you tomorrow." She

reached out and grabbed Deb's arm, practically dragging her out the door.

"Merry Christmas," David and Evelyn called out to them in unison, standing together in the doorway. All the sisters stood stock-still, turned around and stared at them again. Janet and Bev finally waved back, with Bev keeping a firm hand on Deb's arm.

Chapter Seven

The sisters gone, David and Evelyn faced each other. It was as if a chasm was between them, wide open and yawning. A chasm full of uncertainty, doubts and possibilities. The possibility of bliss and the possibility of pain that always comes with intimacy. If they jumped there was no returning.

David stepped toward her and Evelyn raised her face to his. Their bodies came together and they soared through the air. They cleared the chasm. There was no stopping them and no going back.

She didn't know how they made it to her bedroom, but their clothes were falling away and her fingers were touching his body, his fingers learning hers. Blazing, urgent heat flared between them that Evelyn had never experienced before nor even knew existed. Time stopped and her world constricted to the aching need to have him inside her.

When he slid himself into her, she gasped with the wonder and rightness of it. Moving within her with a basic and elemental rhythm, he took her to a place where they were no longer flesh, but where their spirits mingled somewhere beyond ecstasy. The song of the stars and the dance of electrons. Magic. That's what it had to be.

ᴄ❧

Evelyn awoke with David spooned around her, his arm holding her to him, feeling his warm breath on the back of her neck. There had been no self-consciousness as they loved each other for hours with their bodies along with their souls.

It wasn't that she hated her body or had any huge hang-ups about it, but Evelyn knew she didn't quite fit into the norms of beauty. That's the reason she usually felt self-conscious when exposing her body to a man for the first time. But with David it was different. There was no feeling of inadequacy or, what was that term in the song? Unpretty. She knew her body was perfectly right to him. Ying and yang, male and female.

The truth slipped into her consciousness with a rightness that made her draw in a breath. The shape and size of the body was totally irrelevant. The outer changed, failed and eventually died. What was inside was what mattered. She was far more than the size of her hips or the shape of her breasts. Her stretchmarks and slight blemishes were simply a part of her, a natural byproduct of being a woman and human. She knew David didn't see her as any trophy whose cultural physical attractiveness would boost his own esteem. David saw her as the other half of his soul.

David's extreme good looks were a liability because of the way other women reacted, like Deb. David was who he was inside, a man, as perfect and imperfect as any. A man completely unique and forever hers.

He stirred behind her and she felt his lips at the back of her neck. "Merry Christmas."

"Merry Christmas."

He turned her toward him and nestled her into the curve of his hips. She felt his hardness and it aroused an answering moistness within her.

"We've gone so fast. I know we've had to skip some steps of relationship building, but everything with you has felt so right. Regrets?" David asked in a husky voice.

"How could I regret the most wonderful thing that has

ever happened to me?"

He drew her in his arms and they started the day with the sweetest celebration of all.

☙

Evelyn knew it was her family when the doorbell rang at ten that morning although they rang instead of using their key and walking in like they usually did. She'd been bustling around the kitchen in a last minute rush and David was helping her.

"I'll get the door," David said as Evelyn bent to pull a sheet of cookies from the oven.

She started to say no, thinking about her sisters' reaction when he answered the door, but then she decided to let him go ahead. They were going to have to get used to David being a part of her life. Then she wondered why was she so certain that was so?

She soon heard the shrieks of excitement of her nieces as they spied their presents under the tree. But she didn't hear the raised voices of her sisters like she usually did when they first came into the house. They were probably in shock to see David still there. Probably, shoot. The odds were one hundred per cent that they were tripping. He might be out there performing CPR. She'd better go rescue the man. Evelyn wiped her hands on her apron and started to hang it on the hook.

Baby, it's only begun. The circle turns and the choice comes.

Evelyn froze. "Sweet Mama?"

The circle turns and the choice comes.

Terror rushed in on her. This was not her imagination and she wasn't losing her mind. This was Sweet Mama. That was the only reason she was still standing in the state of Maryland, much less the room. Sweet Mama, dead or alive would never hurt her. There had never been anything but love between them and it had to have survived the grave.

"Evelyn?" Bev called as she walked into the kitchen. She stopped at the sight of her sister. "What's wrong with you? You look like you've seen a ghost."

"No. I've just heard one."

"What?"

Evelyn turned to her sister. "Sweet Mama is haunting me."

"Girl, that man has made you lose your marbles. Not to say I don't blame you. If he looked twice at me, I'd toss some marbles his way too—"

"Bev, I'm serious."

The expression on Bev's face changed to one of fear. "I know," she said.

"You know?" echoed Evelyn, hardly believing her ears.

Bev looked around the room and wrapped her arms around herself as if warding off a chill. "I've felt something every time I've walked into this house the past few weeks."

A mixture of fear and relief filled Evelyn. She was right about not being crazy. Someone else had felt it too.

"What's been happening?" Evelyn asked.

"I can't describe it easily. It's like walking into a dream. And there's cold spots in the house."

"Cold spots like what?"

"Like when you walk in a refrigerator. Also it feels as if someone is watching me whenever I'm alone in this house, even in the bathroom. You know that feeling?"

"You've discussed it with Janet and Deb?"

"No. We've never talked about it, but I think they know too."

"I hear Sweet Mama's voice," Evelyn said.

Bev drew in a breath. "What does she say?"

"It doesn't make a lot of sense. She talks about circles and choices."

"What are you going to do? Should we get an exor-
cist or something?"

"Do you really think Sweet Mama could be exorcised
from anywhere if she didn't want to go."

Bev shook her head. "Uh-uh. But it's Christmas.
Maybe we should take everything over to my place. You
can stay over there for a while. Solomon would know
what to do, but it's Christmas and we can't call him to
come over, " Bev continued.

"Yes, Solomon knows. He's the one who talked
about circles for the first time. He talked about the old
family legend."

"The curse," Bev whispered.

"Yes, the curse."

"Solomon will know what to do."

"I got the feeling that he thinks everything is as it
should be. There's something that he feels I'm supposed
to do," Evelyn said.

They stood together silently for a while, each with
their own thoughts.

"We've lived with Sweet Mama all out lives," Evelyn
said. "What's the big deal? Let's invite her out for
Christmas. Sweet Mama?" Evelyn called.

Bev looked as if she was going to have a stroke.

But there was no answer but silence.

"What are you doing? Why are you calling for Sweet
Mama?" Janet asked, coming into the kitchen.

Bev and Evelyn looked at each other. "She's here,"
Evelyn finally said.

"Please. Aren't you two going to come out and see
the kids unwrap their presents? And Evelyn, let me help
you get the food out on the table." Janet grabbed a pot.

"Wait," Evelyn said, but Janet was already gone.

"See, she couldn't wait to get out of this kitchen," Bev
said.

"I needed to put that in a bowl," Evelyn murmured and followed Janet out the door. Christmas was here and now and so was David. They could worry about ghosts later.

Chapter Eight

Evelyn sat alone in her house and stared out her window at the dark, icy landscape of Mystic Ridge. The Christmas lights and tinsel suddenly looked more garish than festive as soon as the day was over. Still, that view was far better than turning around and looking at her house. The house was a wreck with remnants of the Christmas celebration and dirty dishes scattered everywhere. But it was always like that after Christmas passed. Usually at this time she was busy washing up dishes and straightening up the messes.

This Christmas was totally different. Everything had changed. She was looking out of her window waiting for the man she loved to return to her. She was also waiting for something else. Sweet Mama. Ever since Bev and she discussed the reality of Sweet Mama's lingering spirit, there had been emptiness. No hairs rising along her arms, no cold areas in the room, no ghostly whispers. It felt as if Sweet Mama had gone at the moment of acknowledgement. That made Evelyn feel bereft instead of relieved. Sweet Mama's shadow was better than no Sweet Mama at all.

Tears burned her eyes. Emotions she hardly knew she had tumbled and churned within her. How could she be sad with so much new joy? She heard a car door slam and looked up. There he was, David. The sudden warmth of love flooded her with happiness.

He came in and hung his coat on the rack, then

turned to her. He kissed her forehead, then raised her chin and looked into her eyes. "Tired?" he asked.

"No. I was just thinking. Can we talk?"

David sat on the couch next to her. "Sure we can talk. I guess there's a lot to talk about."

He had no idea how much, Evelyn thought. "Let me go get us some coffee first. Do you want anything to eat?"

David groaned. "I feel like I've eaten enough the past two days to feed a third world country for a week."

Evelyn grinned, and went to put on the pot of coffee. She took the time to organize what she wanted to tell him.

Setting the cup of coffee on the coffee table in front of him, she nestled next to the arm of the sofa and pulled her legs up beneath her.

"Do you believe in ghosts?" she asked.

David's eyes shot up. "Not really, since I've never met one before." He reached for his cup. "I thought when you said you wanted to talk it would be about us."

"Why would I want to talk about us?"

"Why?" David looked nonplussed. "Why? Because we've known each other a whole week and we have this amazing connection. We've made love. Notice I said made love, not had sex. And we need to be together."

"I agree completely. So what is there to talk about?"

"You don't know a thing about me for one."

"I know who you are."

"Evelyn. Most women want to talk any relationship to death. What's up with you?"

"I'm not most women. If what you say about us is right, we have plenty of time to talk anyway, don't we? I want to tell you about being haunted by Sweet Mama."

David sat back with a strange look in his eye. "This is the first time in my life I've heard 'can we talk?' from a woman and not been embroiled in some emotional relationship dissection for at least three hours," he muttered.

"Give us time, hon. But pay attention. I want to tell you about Sweet Mama's ghost and what Solomon said."

"I'm all ears."

"I've been hearing Sweet Mama's voice the last week. At first I talked myself into thinking it was a dream or stress, but then I heard her this morning in the kitchen. She said something to me twice, David. It was no dream."

He studied her for a moment. "I suppose I can deal with it if you're somewhat eccentric." He started to reach for her, lust in his eye."

"C'mon, I'm serious. And you know I'm not crazy. Bev said she felt Sweet Mama's presence too and Janet about jumped out of her skin when I mentioned Sweet Mama's ghost."

"Ummm. I can't really buy the ghost thing, Evelyn. If there was such a thing as ghosts, we'd hardly be able to turn around without bumping into some dead person. Why would Sweet Mama want to hang around here instead of going on to her heavenly reward anyway?"

"I think there is something for me to do. It involves the family curse and it involves you."

"And what is that?"

"I don't know yet."

David had inched closer and closer until he was a mere inch from her. He dipped his head and kissed the hollow of her throat. He worked his way up her chin with tiny kisses.

"Were you listening to me?"

"Every word. I thought you were done."

He covered her lips with her own. When he raised her head, she looked into his brown eyes. "I guess I am done after all," Evelyn whispered, and reached for him again."

Much later, they lay together, legs and bedding tangled, satiated from their loving. "I've been married twice and it's never been like this," David said. He turned to his side and traced the line of Evelyn's breast.

"What was it like?"

"I married too young the first time."

"You two weren't right for each other?"

"More like I was too young to know how to build the relationship we needed. I was concentrating on my vision of what I wanted our family to be, working hard, trying to get ahead. Several years and two children later we looked at each other over the dining room table and realized we were two strangers who didn't like each other all that well."

"Ouch," Evelyn said.

"The divorce was amiable, but expensive."

"You married again."

"I lived with her for five years before we married. A German woman. Right before I had the car accident, it was pretty much over anyway. It had been a practical relationship that turned into a habit that had pretty much run its course."

"Have you ever been in love with a woman?"

"Before? It depends on how you define love. I've cared, I've committed, but I've never felt I belonged there."

A moment passed in silence. "Why did you never marry?" he asked.

"No one asked me to. My experience with men has been rather limited here in Mystic Ridge. I never thought I'd ever find . . . "

"Love. Until now," David whispered.

He'd said it. Evelyn turned to him, and touched his

cheek. "Until now," she echoed.

"What is happening to us? I've never been an impulsive sort of man, especially in relationships of this sort."

"It's meant to be, I think."

"I think so too. When we leave Mystic Ridge . . ."

"Leave Mystic Ridge? Why do we have to leave Mystic Ridge?" Evelyn asked.

"My new job starts in a few weeks. It's in San Francisco. You'll love it there. It's the most beautiful city in the world."

"I can't leave Mystic Ridge."

"Why can't you?"

Evelyn sat up against the headboard. "I just can't. This is the soil I was raised in, my roots. Why can't you stay? The cost of living is low and almost any business here would be happy to hire you."

"I can't stay here. I've made a commitment to the position in San Francisco, and furthermore, it's a job I really want in a place where I want to be."

"I thought you said there was an 'us'."

"There is. If there was any good reason why you couldn't leave Mystic Ridge, I'd have to reconsider my plans."

"I just gave you a very good reason that I can't leave. So are you are going to reconsider?"

David sighed. "We need to talk about it more. Is it that you're afraid of leaving without any formal commitment to me? If so we can—"

"That's not it. It feels as if we have a bond together deeper than any papers. You're right. We need to talk about it more when we're not so tired."

They straightened the covers and settled down in each other's arms. Evelyn wasn't worried; she knew deep in her bones that David's place was with her in Mystic Ridge.

ᕫᘓᎫ

Two weeks later, Evelyn opened the door for the realtor. "This area is in high demand and I can see you've kept things up," the plump red haired woman said as she moved through the door. "It'll probably go fast."

The realtor thrust a sheaf of papers into Evelyn's hands. "Here's a checklist and there's that other list of things that need to be done within the week."

Evelyn stared at the list of cosmetic things to do to the house. Her heart sank as the idea of leaving Mystic Ridge forever moved further toward a reality.

The realtor stood in the middle of the living room and turned three-hundred-and-sixty degrees. "Yes, it'll go fast," she repeated. "You must be the luckiest woman in the country, no, the world." The woman smiled at Evelyn. "What wouldn't I give to have a man like David Douglas come into town, sweep me off my feet and take me away to glamorous San Francisco. Why, it's like a fairy tale."

"I'm truly blessed," Evelyn agreed readily.

But later, after she closed the door behind the realtor, she felt a sense of dissatisfaction. She and David had discussed it and she had to agree, it made more sense for her to go to San Francisco with him. He had a job that he'd been wanting for years and she could work as an RN anywhere. She had no family ties that couldn't be maintained long distance. Her sisters were adults and her daughter was grown and living her own life.

But still it felt like leaving Mystic Ridge was akin to tearing out her heart. Evelyn sank on the sofa. She almost wished she had continued to hear the other-worldly whispers from Sweet Mama and to have strange dreams. She so needed someone to confide in, and failing that, to distract her. Her sisters had been stunned to hear the news, to make an understatement.

She had not spent much time with them the past couple of weeks because of David. That part felt healthy. With perspective she could see that her constant doing for them had actually done none of them much good, including herself.

She'd started to confide her reluctance to leave Mystic Ridge to Bev. Bev promptly responded that if Evelyn didn't go with that man, she was going to personally beat her ass and haul her off to the State Hospital afterwards because it would be clear that she'd lost her mind.

Evelyn smiled at the memory. But still, it was crazy, running off with a man she'd only known for a few weeks, soul mates or not. No, that wasn't true. Following David anywhere, any way and any time wouldn't be crazy. He was just as much a part of her as her heart.

Then why the anxiety? Was it simply because she'd grown up here and had never lived anywhere else? Her entire family had been raised on this soil for generations. She'd built a life and security for herself here in Mystic Ridge.

But she knew it was more than that, way more. It didn't have to do with David or Mystic Ridge or her past as much as it had to do with her own fear. She was afraid. So very afraid. She was not a person who took to change easily. And this was almost more than she could handle. She was leaving everything she'd known all her life and jumping into the unknown.

Don't worry so. You made the right choice, baby.

Chapter Nine

Clara and Daniel lay wrapped in each other's arms after their lovemaking. The drooping arms of the weeping willow shielded and shaded them. Daniel had covered the ground with soft pine needles, grasses, and crushed clover that gave off a sweet fragrance. It was their own place, their secret room where they escaped to whenever they could.

"I have something to tell you," Clara said.

Daniel propped himself on his elbow and tickled her nose with a soft brushy stalk of grass. "And what is that?"

"I'm going to have a baby."

He didn't fill the silence, but sat upright, looking off into the gently waving green willow walls instead of at her.

"I thought you'd be happy," she said. She didn't quite know what to make of his reaction. She knew with every particle of her body that he loved her, so she'd assumed he'd be thrilled to hear about the child.

He reached out and touched her hand. "It's not that I regret any child of ours. It's that... I vowed to myself that when I had a child, he would not be born into slavery."

Clara sat up beside them and wrapped her arms around her knees. "How would that be? Our stations are what they are. The only thing we can do is accept—"

"It is not the only thing we can do," he said, his dark

face was fierce and intense. Clara felt a fear that iced her soul. Black men who showed that sort of anger didn't live long. Black men with Daniel's intelligence and strength who didn't carefully tread the paths set out for them, lived even shorter lives—no matter how valuable they were.

"We can run, Clara. We can run. I know a way, a special way called the slave's railroad. We can go North. We can be free, Clara. We can live our own lives. Our own lives, can you imagine? And we can give our children lives of their own too."

Her fear intensified. "What if they catch you? They nearly always do. They kill you for sure, but only after they torture you for their sport and for an example to the other slaves."

"I don't believe my owner would do that. He is my brother."

"When have they ever cared about that? He would laugh as he burned you alive."

"I know this way will be safe. I know of people who will help us. How else could I ask you to join me in this risk?"

She saw by the tilt of his jaw that he had made up his mind and she wanted to scream and cry and rip out her hair. How could she ever live without her Daniel? How could she leave the safety and security she had as the cook for the family who owned her for the unknown North and the similarly unknown promise of freedom?

Evelyn woke like a crack across a mirror and sat straight up in the bed with a strangled groan in her throat.

"What's wrong?" David asked her, his voice blurry with sleep, but alarmed.

"I had a nightmare." She lay back down. "Sorry I woke you."

"Are you sure you're all right? It sounded pretty bad."

"I've had it before. Not the same dream, but the same people. You and me." She paused and picked at the bedding nervously.

"Go on," David said. "It might help to talk about it."

"It's back in slave times. We're lovers."

"I hope that wasn't part of the nightmare."

Evelyn smiled at him. "No. Your name is Daniel and mine is Clara. You want to run North and I'm terrified."

David became very still, too still.

"David?"

"Maybe we both learned about those people in school. We had a lot of classes together," he said.

"What are you talking about?"

"I've dreamed about Clara and Daniel too."

"Oh, my God."

"It's a coincidence. Like I said, we've probably both heard of them."

"How could it be a coincidence? It doesn't make sense. What do you think it means?"

"I don't know."

"We should talk to Solomon . . ."

"I don't want to talk about it any more." David's voice was sharp and strained, so uncharacteristic of him that Evelyn stared at him.

"I'm sorry, but let's just drop it." He turned on his side, his back facing her. "I'm going back to sleep."

Evelyn let herself into the dark house, loaded down with presents from her going away party at work.

"Surprise!" she heard voices scream and screamed right back at them in shock. Lights clicked on and her sisters and a few of her closest friends stood there dressed in nightgowns, pajamas and lingerie.

"What's going on?" Evelyn asked. She didn't know if

she really wanted to hear the answer.

"You didn't think we were going to let you get out of here without a bridal shower, did you?" Janet said.

"We forgive you for planning to elope and get married on some South Pacific cruise, but we deserve our bachelorette party," Bev added.

"So get on your pajamas and let's swing," said Toni, a good friend since high school.

"Uh, why pajamas?" Evelyn asked.

"Because it's a pajama party silly. Hurry up, now, before the strippers get here."

More than a few hours and several drinks later, she'd lost count, Evelyn waved goodbye to Toni, who'd kept changing her lingerie. Toni had progressed through flannel to Victoria's Secret and finally to Frederick's of Hollywood. Toni waved happily back to Evelyn from over the stripper's muscular shoulder as he carried her out the door.

Evelyn collapsed on the couch amidst her sisters. "Thank you all. I had a great time."

"So did we, sis," Bev said. "We're going to miss you."

"You guys are so great."

"Yep, sis, you're breaking up a great team."

Evelyn grabbed a throw pillow from behind her and buried her face in it, her shoulders heaving.

"What's wrong?" asked Deb.

"I can't stand it. I can't do it. I can't, I just can't. I'm not going to leave you guys," Evelyn said through her sobs.

Janet, Bev and Deb looked at each other over Evelyn's heaving shoulders. "I think it was that Long Island Ice Tea," Janet said. "All those liquors mixed up. Why did you give that to her, Deb?

"It was in the spirit of celebration," Deb answered.

"You know Evelyn didn't know how potent that stuff was. She can't hold her liquor."

"I can too," Evelyn's resentful, muffled voice came from the pillow.

"Stop sitting there yakking and help me get her to bed," Bev said. "You know Evelyn is going to be mad when she wakes up with a hangover in the morning."

"Lord, I don't think she's ever hardly drunk mixed drinks before, she usually sticks to wine."

"Stop talking about me like I ain't here," Evelyn bawled from the pillow.

"C'mon. Get up and help me with her," Bev said.

It was far too soon for her to feel the quickening movements of her babe within her. Clara laid her hands on the slight swell of her belly. She walked to the stool, sank down and buried her face in her hands.

The plans were in place and the time set for Daniel and her to go. The secret burned within her. She would not be able to tell her sisters good-bye or how to reach her. The slightest suspicion, and that slave would be tortured until they revealed what they knew. Even so, they would certainly whip her sisters.

She imagined she heard the whistle of the whip through the air and the screams of her sisters. The ripped flesh and dripping blood. That was nothing compared to what they would do to Daniel if they were caught. What they would do to her and her unborn baby.

Silas had run from the farm a few years ago. It was said that he had got the crazy notion to go up North, get a job and save enough money to buy his family. Silas had been the best blacksmith within three counties and maybe he could have done it. They caught him three

*days later. They tore out his entrails while he was still liv-
ing and let the dogs eat them while he dangled from the
cottonwood tree where they'd hung him. Silas' white
skull still hung in the cottonwood tree as a reminder.
They trained no other slaves in any craft or skill after that.*

*Her fear built within her until she could taste it, bitter
as bile in her mouth. She couldn't go with Daniel. She
wouldn't let him go either. They were valuable livestock.
If they did their work and caused no trouble, they and
their children would be safe. Freedom was nothing but a
dream. Getting up to breathe yet another day, that's
what mattered, wasn't it?*

*Mary walked into the kitchen: "What's wrong with
you?" she asked.*

*Clara straightened and dried her eyes. "You must do
something for me. Go to the Bushes. You can take
those eggs over there and say they are a gift from the
mistress. It's a matter of life and death, Mary. Tell Daniel
that—that I can't go with him tonight. I cannot. Tell him
to wait for the time until we can meet again."*

"Go with him?" Mary asked. "Go with him where?"

*Clara shook her head. Mary studied her sister's tear-
swollen face. "You were going to run," she breathed.*

"Just go, Mary, go now. Please."

*Mary started to speak, but at another pleading look
from Clara, she turned and hurried out of the room.*

David chewed his knuckle. He'd woken up from
another dream of the dogs and the rushing waters. . . A
dream sharper and more real than a memory. His
dreams had never disturbed him as they did now and
he'd never remembered them with such clarity. What
should he do about it? Therapy? He rebelled against
that thought because he was happier now than he'd once

dreamed possible.

His love for Evelyn fit him like a buttery leather glove, comfortable and natural. He didn't know what he would have done if she hadn't agreed to go to San Francisco with him. He tried to empathize with her at the loss she felt at giving up familiar Mystic Ridge, but it was hard. He got excited at the thought of what he could show her in the world beyond this town. What they would experience together. He couldn't have picked a better woman to have by his side and grow old with. Certainly they'd travel the world.

He rolled out of bed. It was one of the few nights in the past weeks he'd slept without Evelyn and already he didn't like it. Her sisters were giving Evelyn a wedding shower and they said they might be a little late. He had some things to finish up in preparation for their move.

He heard the doorbell ring and almost groaned. Not before he had a cup of coffee. These dreams were sapping his usual morning energy. He pulled on a pair of jeans and a t-shirt over his head and went to answer the door. He blinked twice when he saw Evelyn's sister Deb there. "May I come in?" she asked?

"Are you here for Dad? He's already left for work." David was unable to fathom what she would want with him.

Deb walked past him into the living room. "I'm not here to see your father. I'm here to see you."

Chapter Ten

Something must have crawled down her throat and died in her stomach last night, Evelyn decided. That was the only thing that could account for the misery she was presently experiencing. She groaned and rose up from the bed, squinting her eyes against the pain pounding in her head.

Stumbling to the bathroom she swallowed three extra strength acetaminophen. She started to close the medicine cabinet, reconsidered, and took three ibuprofen also. Lurching back to her bed, she closed her eyes. Sleep was unthinkable, but she could lie perfectly still for the twenty or so minutes for the drugs to kick in.

Exactly thirty minutes later, she opened her eyes. She threw back the covers, stood and stretched. Much better. She started to reach for the phone to call David.

The river will churn as the circle closes. Go to him now.

"Sweet Mama? Why are you here?"

For this. Go to him. Remember the choice you've made for trust and love. Remember that fear is the enemy.

❦

"What's up, Deb?" David asked.
"Please sit down. I want to talk to you."

"Sure. But let me get some coffee first. Want a cup?"

"That would be great," Deb said.

He went in the kitchen and poured two cups, wondering again what Deb had to talk to him about. Whatever it was, he hoped it was quick. He had a ton of stuff to do today. "Want cream or sugar?" he called.

"No. Black will be fine."

He handed her the cup and saucer and sat in an adjacent chair. "So what can I do for you?" he asked.

"It's about Evelyn."

"Oh."

"What happened last night terribly concerned me."

David put down the cup and listened.

Deb took a sip. He noticed she seemed a little nervous. "Evelyn was crying and carrying on so. She said that she really didn't want to leave Mystic Ridge. That she felt you were forcing her to leave everything she loved."

David picked up his cup again. "Hmmmm," he said.

"I'm worried sick about her, David. You know she was recently hearing voices. If she puts herself under the kind of stress that I think will happen if she leaves Mystic Ridge, well, I don't know what she'll do."

"Hmmmm"

"What do you think we should do?"

David drained his cup of coffee and stood to get another one. He poured himself a cup and added a dollop of cream. No need to offer Evelyn's sister a refill.

When he returned to the living room Deb was perched on the edge of the couch.

"What do you think we should do?" she repeated.

David shrugged.

Deb waited.

"Aren't you going to say something?" she finally asked.

"No."

"Aren't you concerned about Evelyn?"

"Very concerned."

"So why aren't you saying anything?"

"I was waiting for you to tell me something that made a lick of sense." He stood again. "Since you haven't done so, I have a lot to do today. I'll see you to the door."

Deb's face crumpled and she set her coffee cup carefully on the coffee table. "I just wanted you to see my sister for what she is."

"All you showed me was what you are." He walked to the door and pulled it open. Evelyn was standing there, and she stepped in past him and rushed straight to Deb.

The boy ran up to Daniel while he rubbed the horse down in the stable. "There's a woman here to see you waiting on the rock in the field. She says it's important."

He straightened and wiped his hands on his rough trousers. When he got out to where she sat at the edge of the field, he saw it was Clara's sister, Mary. Disappointment filled him. He had hoped it would be Clara.

"How can I help you, Mary?" he asked.

She looked around furtively and his heart sank. Clara couldn't have told her their plans.

"I have a message from Clara," she said.

He waited.

"She realizes she made a mistake. She no longer loves you Daniel. She is not going to run with you tonight."

A beat of time passed.

"You lie," he said.

"She will not be meeting you tonight, you will see."

Daniel could say nothing. He felt as if a giant had hit him in the stomach. Since Clara had told her sister of their plans . . . it might be true. He could not believe that Clara would put them in such danger by entrusting such a thing to this woman.

"But I will meet you in her stead," Mary said. She moved close to him. "I have wanted you for a long time. I'll go North with you since she no longer cares for you. You're too good for the likes of my sister."

His eyes narrowed. "No. I'm too good for the likes of you."

"What did you say?"

"You heard me. I would not have you."

She gasped in disbelief. "But I'm far more beautiful than Clara."

Pity filled him. "You've always believed that, but you're wrong. Clara's beauty outshines yours like the sun to a sputtering candle."

"You have no idea how much I've wanted you," she said, obviously not able to hear the meaning of his words. She reached out for him and he stepped away.

Mary stumbled.

"I do not want you, woman. Go," Daniel said.

Her face turned into a mask of fury.

"She told me herself that she hates you. That you were crazy thinking she would run North with you," Mary spat.

"I know Clara would never forsake me." With those words he turned and walked away.

⌒◞⌒

Deb gasped when she saw Evelyn bearing down on her. David wheeled in surprise, and rushed to follow. But all Evelyn did was to grasp Deb's hand tightly.

Then she held out her hand to David. "Quickly. Take

my hand. The circle closes."

He caught her hand and there was a cracking in the very air of the room, shattering like glass, breaking into a million pieces. He thought he heard Deb scream. Then suddenly he was thrust into some cold and wet darkness.

Daniel crouched under a tree to provide him some shelter against the pouring rain. He had waited hours for Clara. The sky was lightening to gray in the east. He was numb and cold inside and out. His Clara hadn't shown up, just as Mary said.

His tears mixed with the rain and he didn't wipe them away. He was man enough to cry. He stared toward the rushing, swollen waters of Sorrow Creek, trying to decide what to do. That was when he heard the baying of the hounds. He knew instantly they were after him. There was no way his owner would have set the hounds after him for one's night absence unless he had been tipped to the fact that Daniel had run away. Mary, he thought, with his teeth grinding. May that wench roast in hell.

The sound of the hounds came closer and he did all that he could do. He ran.

Chapter Eleven

aniel's breath ripped through his chest like sharp knives. His muscles were screaming with every step. He wouldn't be able to run for much longer and the dogs were gaining on him. Daniel looked toward the creek, now a raging torrent of muddy brown water after the hard rains. The snarl of a dog echoed behind him, and he knew he could hesitate no longer. He used his last burst of energy to sprint toward the flooded creek. Possibly it would carry him along to a place where the dogs would lose his scent on the other side.

He threw himself into the boiling rush of dark water and within a few seconds knew he was lost. The raging waters were too much for him. They wrestled and worried him, finally pulling him under. Daniel stopped struggling and let the new river take him home. His last thought was of Clara. Such a love as they had surely could never pass away...

Clara felt as if she was going to lose her mind. She'd been waiting all night for Mary to return. Clara had watched her sister Tillie sleep, wake and start a fire with her usual cheerful unconcern. Clara envied her.

She stood to leave for the neighboring farm where Daniel lived, no matter the trouble it would cost her.

Then her hand flew to her mouth as she saw Mary stumble into the cabin. Tillie gasped. Her sister was disheveled and wet, but it was more than that. It was the expression on her face. Anguish, regret, and fear mixed all together. Mary wasn't one given to strong emotion.

"What happened to you?" Tillie cried.

"Let me talk to Mary alone," Clara said. "Tillie please leave us."

"But it's raining outside!"

"Go stay in the barn awhile. I need you to leave us."

Something in Clara's voice made Tillie gather her skirts and hurry out the door.

Mary sank to floor in front of the fire and Clara waited until she heard Tillie's footsteps fade away.

"Tell me what happened."

Mary said nothing but continued to stare into the fire.

Clara walked around and crouched down. She looked into Mary's eyes and Mary looked away. "What did Daniel have to say?"

When Mary didn't answer, Clara pulled her hand back and slapped it with all the force she could muster across Mary's cheek. "Tell me what happened to him," she screamed, her fear turning to panic and her breath coming in deep, fast gasps. She could see it in Mary's eyes . . . She could see the worst.

"They set the dogs on him."

Clara doubled in pain, a moan like a wounded animal coming from her throat. A black mountain of despair crashed down on her and she didn't think she could survive the impact.

Tillie rushed in and ran to Clara. Mary turned her face away and stared back into the fire.

A crack like thunder and they were in a room dressed

in strange clothes and holding tight to each other's hands. Mary, Daniel and Clara stared at each other in fear and alarm.

Evelyn. She was Evelyn, not Clara. But she was and had always been Clara too. They were Deb, David and Evelyn in another world and another life. She saw similar knowledge cross their faces and Deb's mouth opened in a scream and David pulled back in horror. Evelyn held on to Deb's hands as tightly as she could despite the struggle. *The circle still closes.* She held on to Deb with every bit of strength she had as the world shattered around them.

Clara ran through the muddy field through the pouring rain lit with the brackish light of dawn. She ran toward her love, toward Daniel and the place she'd promised to meet him. She heard hounds baying in the far distance and stumbled and fell. She lay face down while her fingers dug in the mud in anguish and pain. She knew, felt it in her heart. He was gone. Gone.

It wasn't until the rain, had stopped, the sun had risen higher in the sky when a boy from the farm where Daniel had lived found her face down in the field. He touched her shoulder and she lifted her head a little. The boy screamed and jumped back. "I thought you was dead," he said.

"I only feel that way," Clara answered. Her voice coming raw and husky from her throat. She struggled to sit up and finally righted herself.

The little boy peered at her. "Aren't you the cook-lady from over yonder?" He pointed.

"That I am."

"I've seen you before. I'm the houseboy. I saw your sister yesterday in the stables. She was looking for your

man. The boy's face clouded. "I'm sorry," he whispered, and looked down.

"What happened to Daniel?" she whispered.

"The dogs chased him into the creek during the flood. They found his body a mile downstream.

So it was true. Daniel was dead. Clara closed her eyes in agony. She'd known it was so, but still she'd held on to that little flame of hope.

"You look so sad. So why did your sister tell them that Daniel was going to run? Everybody wants to know that."

Clara stared at the boy.

Clara stirred the stew with loving attention. She ladled three bowls. One for her, one for Tillie, and one for Mary. She gave Mary's bowl an extra stir to hide the extra seasoning.

They ate in silence, not an unaccustomed thing lately. Clara's new silence was attributed to her grief. She left her food untouched. They also mistook her lack of appetite. Clara grieved, but hatred burned within her also.

When her sisters finished eating, she took their bowls for cleaning in silence.

It wasn't until later that night when Mary's stomach cramps started. An hour later she was screaming and sweating in agony. By daybreak, she was dead.

Everyone immediately knew that Clara had poisoned her own sister. Not that the evil wench didn't deserve it, but still she was valuable property.

Clara would have to be punished. Shame to have to whip her in her delicate state, but it had to be done.

They strung her up on the cottonwood, and the overseer flexed the whip and then sent it whistling through the air to rip through the brown skin of Clara's back again and again.

Legend was made more than once that day, because it was said that Clara never screamed. Not once. But she did speak. She cursed her sister, her own lineage. She said since her sister let a man cause her to betray her blood, let her blood ever be without a man.

Everybody knew it would be so, because Clara died that night and a curse spoken before death always comes true.

As the years passed the story changed. For some reason a man often gets the credit for the glory—and the evil.

Chapter Twelve

velyn and Deb dropped each other's hands as if they were hot coals.

"You killed me," Deb whispered.

Evelyn felt drained and exhausted, but light in spirit. The circle had closed. The wrongs had finally been righted and the right choices made. She forgave and was forgiven.

"What the hell happened?" David sat heavily on the sofa, his eyes glazed. "Mass hallucination?"

"You know better, David." Daniel, my Daniel, her spirit sang. He was here with her finally, this time forever.

Deb sank to the floor, her shoulders heaving with silent sobs, and her face buried in her hands. Evelyn sat down beside her and stretched an arm across her shoulder.

"I never meant for . . ." Deb's voice trailed away. "I was mad and I just wasn't thinking. I was never thinking. That was my problem. I deserved to die. Forgive me, please forgive me."

"All is forgiven. Everything is all right now. Don't you understand? There's forgiveness instead of hate and vengeance, love instead of fear."

"Tell me what happened, Evelyn. I—I can't quite understand," David said, his face pained.

"The spirit never dies," she said. Evelyn stared at

her hand. The skin, meat, sinew and bone. The beauty of it. "The body might be long crumbled into dust, but the spirit remains and in some sense the deeds of that person," she continued. "What Clara did resonated through time, trapping our spirits into an unfulfilling circle of dreams denied, jealousy, fear, and bitterness. This was the only time that the circle could be broken."

"Why now?"

"We've never been together before. This time and place brought our three spirits together. We had to touch. And to break the curse, Clara had to set things right. I had to set things right. I had to make the choices of love instead of fear, compassion instead of anger, and forgiveness instead of vengeance. Even if the situations were only a milder, shadowy sense of the tragedies that happened before, the ultimate choices are the same."

"Why did we remember?" Deb asked.

"The veil that separates us from the other side and the memories of past lives that would overwhelm us, was ripped when we three connected at that particular time."

"I think that the memories were a gift also," David said.

"Why?" Evelyn asked.

"So we could remember the joy along with the pain." He gazed at Evelyn, his eyes full of love.

Then David looked at Deb. "So we could learn a lesson, change and grow."

Deb stood, and wiped the traces of tears from her cheeks. "Yes," she whispered, her voice husky with her own pain. "I'm sorry for coming over here and saying the things I did David. It won't happen again. Evelyn—"

Evelyn met Deb's gaze. "It was jealousy. Not new jealousy over David, old jealousy. I've always envied your peace, your contentment, and how you always have people around who care about you. I'm sorry."

"I love you, Deb."

"I love you too, Evelyn." Then Deb turned and walked out the door back into her new life.

Evelyn pulled a sweater over her shoulders before she walked out on their large deck overlooking the San Francisco Bay. The Golden Gate Bridge glittered in the background while glorious sunset colors played across the sky and burnished the mountaintops gold. This view from Marin County had to be one of the most breathtaking in the world, and it took her breath away every time she came out here.

She sat in the chair and took a sip of her lemonade. Now was the time to tell her husband. She scarcely finished her thought when he came out, carrying steaming brown paper bags that smelled heavenly.

"I made sure to order no MSG," David said, as he set the bags on the deck table and started to pull the cartons from the bags.

"Can we talk?" Evelyn asked.

David froze.

Evelyn chuckled. "I should have reworded the request. I remember how you once said those three words coming from a woman can strike terror within the breast of any man."

"And you said that you weren't just any women. You were completely right."

She touched his hand and he sat down next to her. "What is it, Evelyn?"

"I'm going to have a baby."

Silence. Then David whooped so loud that Evelyn was sure that the folks in Oakland heard him.

"Sounds like you're happy about it," she said with a grin.

"Happy? I'm two powers squared past happy. Our child. Evelyn, we are finally going to have our child."

Evelyn nodded, happiness overflowing in her own heart. The circles of life turned and everything was as it should be. Such are the blessings that exist in the world.

The End

Home for the Holidays

By Leslie Esdaile

Mystic is sure gonna miss Evelyn Sweet and David, too. But they'll be back. Folks can't stay away from Mystic once they've found it—always figure out a reason to return. Just like that young couple Colette and Franklin, even though their visit started out as an unhappy occasion. But by the time the spirits hit that family, none of 'em were the same, and a good thing too. What a ruckus went on up in old Nana Johnson's house. Folks in Mystic are still laughing about it and shaking their heads. And I'd bet money Nana Johnson had a hand in it. Yessir...

Chapter One

Colette Johnson-Morris sighed as she watched her husband drift off into the routine slumber that always seemed to follow their lackluster lovemaking these days. With twenty minutes to spare before the alarm clock sounded, she reached over to the nightstand and turned off the offending technology, and tried to stave off her physical frustration that was now merging with resilient anger.

She resented the way his long, thick-built chocolate frame seemed to rest, satiated, without a care in the world, and it annoyed her that his easy smile and deep brown eyes could always coax her into this position – agreeing to be unfulfilled. She wondered if he'd rest so peacefully if he had to lie in the wet-spot and hover on the verge of an orgasm that never ignited? It was so easy for men.

But how could one year of marriage have changed so much between them? she worried, as she shuffled to the bathroom. It wasn't always like this. Maybe this was just a six-month-long phase? There was a time when his voice over the telephone would make her mound swell and dampen... or the way he towered over her to pull her into his arms would simply make her melt. There was a time when his back, that now always seemed to face her, was an edifice of muscular ridges to be honored with a touch... revered for the sheer pleasure of indulgence alone. And there was a time when his fingers trembled as they brushed her skin. There was also a time when they talked about his business, and her community work — which led to dreaming, which led to lovemaking, and hoping they were pregnant.

But that was almost six months ago... After waiting until she was almost forty to marry... after getting her education and shoring up her career, and foregoing babies... after choosing so wisely and so precisely on a mate... All of that gave way to constant arguments about bills, responsibilities, personal space... No one could have prepared her for this—not even Nana. Even that sage, with her parables dropped between the creation of biscuits and gravy, was gone.

During the weeks that had followed Nana's funeral, she'd told herself not to be sad, carefully reminding herself that her grandmother had led a full life, had died calmly of natural causes in her sleep, and had lived to the ripe old age of eighty-seven. Colette repeated this mantra as she flushed the toilet, washed her hands, and turned on the shower without turning on the light—peering briefly in the mirror, then deciding that it was too early to look at her own reflection in stark florescent.

The warm, steady pelt of water soothed the tight muscles in her neck, and she stretched and rolled her head from side to side, trying to stave off the heated sensations that had collected between her legs. What had happened to her grandmother was normal, to be expected. But the new distance between her and Franklin was not. It was an ache that lingered, like incomplete lovemaking.

As she turned herself to face the shower jet, its rhythmic pulse sent another wave of memory through her body. It had been so long since he'd touched her the way the water now caressed her skin, making her nipples rise and sting for attention. She brought her hands to her breasts and cupped them, kneading each hard, tiny pebble between her forefingers and thumbs. There was only one bathroom in the house down in Mystic Ridge, Maryland, and the house would be filled with her sister, her brother, his wife, her cousin, Wilton, and his pregnant wife, plus her cousin, Bey, and his trifling self... and, of course, Franklin... for a whole week. Feeling like this. Needing a release. With no private space to find it. She closed her eyes.

Her fingers worked against the angry flesh, gently rubbing the smooth surface of each globe in her hand, then reveling in the change of texture at each tip. As a shudder added a new source of moist warmth between her legs, she allowed the water to replace Franklin's kisses along her neck, slowly sliding her hands down to her lower belly and stopping to caress where they'd both hoped a baby would reside. She wasn't ready. Her hands returned a slow trail up her body. That's what he couldn't seem to remember. It took time to make love to a woman.

Foreplay started in the morning with a pleasant kiss, and a caring gesture, like bringing a cup of coffee up to bed to wake one's lover, followed by light conversation, and a deep kiss goodbye as they each went off to work. The dull ache within her had now turned into a throb, but she kept her hands moving in a slow circle around her breasts as she reminded her skin how lovemaking was supposed to be done.

She reached out and turned up the hot water, and reduced the coolness, then returned her hands to her belly. That was how it was supposed to be—anticipation created throughout the day. A telephone call to the job, just to say, "I love you." A little note slipped into a brown-bag lunch, with an appointment for a home-bath-date hastily scribbled. Her inner thighs burned with repressed

need as she parted them to allow the water entrance followed by her palms. She forced herself to be patient to
make the desire grow, and abandoned her skin to lather
her hands with soap.

Massaging the tender surface of the areas she'd
already given attention, she dropped her head into the
spray to drown out the sound of street traffic. Yes, that
was how it was supposed to be... patient. After a kiss
hello, and solid conversation about one's day. Making
dinner together, with jazz on in the background, and
removing the dishes while talking, waiting, and wondering when the right opportunity would present itself for
touch.

Her fingers slid to the outer delicate folds that had
now become so swollen that they opened on their own
for affection. Then, she mentally whispered, they would
curl up on the sofa by candle light with glasses of wine,
and relax, holding each other, making plans for the
future, dreaming. Her fingers kept time with the water,
occasionally grazing the tiny bud of skin that now peeked
through the pouting flower as they moved back and forth.

Another shudder made her wince with pleasure
when she withdrew from the attention-starved nub, and
gave affection to the aching areas around it. Time, it took
time, to sit on the sofa and dream... and to let one's hand
slide down an arm, then a hip, and to land well-placed
kisses down a neck. It took time to gather a lover up into
one's arms, and to whisper your deepest dreams. It took
time to touch all the places they wanted you to touch,
and to avoid all the places they desperately needed you
to touch. It took time to slowly remove layers of clothes,
one by one, and to land kisses behind every shred of
cloth on each section of exposed skin. And, Lord, it took
time to have your mouth revere their body in ways your
hands could not. Only after that would they be ready.

Her fingers found a deep well and entered, then

retreated to pay staccato homage to the ignored and angry bud, while her other hand found its way back up to her breasts, which were now throbbing and jealous. The final shudder that wracked her forced her to lean against the cool tile for a moment, and she stifled the moan that tried to pry its way up from her abdomen. Why couldn't Franklin understand that?

Tears blurred her vision as she hastily soaped and rinsed, then stepped out of the shower. This time when she looked in the mirror, she lingered. The unfocused image of herself became a space in time when one broke beans on the porch, or helped peel apples for the end-less array of pies needed at the church, or one simply stirred the iced-tea as the wise woman chef responded with a textured phrase from a hymn.

She had planned to use her time at Mystic Ridge to gain much-needed knowledge, but time had run out. She was going to ask Nana how to rekindle a dying flame, how to stay married to the same man for fifty years, and how to make her body respond to him the way it once had—all the while knowing that she could ask these questions with a single sigh, and that question would be addressed in an answer without direct words from a sage that had become an accomplished telepath within her eighty-seven years of reading between the lines.

Instead, she'd only be going home to a horde of greedy cousins, siblings, and irritating spouses of sib-lings—there only with the intent to scavenge what they could from the dead, and to put the family's only true homestead on the market. The family peacekeeper was gone, and the one who had the wisdom, fortitude, and magic to bring all of these disparate tribes together, in peace, had gone Home herself.

It was almost too painful to fathom, as she brought a cold splash of water to her face and shook off the feeling of dread. Nana would have been the only person alive that could have repaired what was going so wrong with her and Franklin. There was no sense dwelling on it. She released another sigh and began brushing her teeth.

He'd become accustomed to awaking to an empty space on her side of the bed, just as he was getting used to the way she responded to him by rote—without true passion, or tenderness, anymore. This was not the way he'd envisioned spending the rest of his life, or their first Christmas together. Why couldn't they wait until January to go through Nana Johnson's things, and to put the house on the market? They already had everything.

Franklin pulled himself upright, and threw his legs over the side of the bed, and tried to shake the morning chill that crept up his shins and into his mind. What if Colette was really like them, the rest of her bourgeois family—down deep, and her independent, down-to-earth vibe was really just a lure to get him hooked? The only reason he'd agreed to this mess during his busy season was because of his love for Nana Johnson!

He could hear Colette washing up, and hesitated, remembering that there was a time when he would have slipped into the shower with her... just like there was a time when she couldn't get enough of him. Now, there were boundaries. Now, there were limitations. And, now, he was quite sure that, his wife had touched herself again this morning to complete her pleasure, instead of him... Just the way he had to, since the word "No" flowed from her lips more often than a "Yes."

Franklin listened and waited until the water in the sink stopped. Again, after they'd made love, she'd gotten up and had taken an unusually long time in the bathroom—alone. He'd heard the sound of the lock click, then the shower go on, then the rush of water stop after a while. It was a new sound that was becoming oddly familiar, one that he just couldn't get used to.

But, in truth, this morning was a pattern, like a timing belt that had gone wrong in an engine. The reality felt like cinder blocks had landed on his shoulders as he stood slowly and approached the door. He closed his eyes and thought of her lean cinnamon skin and petite breasts, with their darker brown nipples that no longer became erect for his touch... her short, thick auburn curls that called to his fingers, and her deep brown eyes that always looked sad these days. He wanted to hold her again, and to ask her what was wrong, beyond losing Nana – but the door was locked.

After waiting until he was damn near forty to marry, he'd imagined it to be different than his home-boys had warned. But it wasn't.

Chapter Two

She watched him from the corner of her eye as their massive black four-by-four pulled onto Route 13 in Delaware. No matter what he said, and what they'd agreed upon, this was his car. Why that was so important to her now, she hadn't a clue. She only wished that she didn't have to leave Philadelphia to travel back home for this reason.

Oddly, her mind drifted in and out of the little vignettes of their morning conversation, and now the vehicle reminded her too much of Franklin. Black, dependable, silent... with a soft interior and strong motor, crooning jazz, and warm.

The previous forty-five minutes of interminable silence was wearing on her, but she decided not to let it show. Even his selection of jazz CDs was getting on her nerves, and his quiet civility made her want to scream. He had everything he wanted, it seemed – even down to their choice of what to listen to on the drive down to Nana's.

"Well, looks like the weather will hold till we get down there," she offered as a mild transition to a deeper conversation.

"Yup. If it's this clear on the way home, then it's all good."

She just looked at him briefly then focused her attention on the clear blue sky.

"Glad we got an early start before the traffic picked up."

"Uhm, hum."

"I think we'll get to the house first, and that way, we can settle in, choose the room we want, and get situated before the drama kings and queens arrive."

She did notice that a slight smile had formed at the corner of his mouth. She liked his mouth.

"Like I said, it's all good, baby."

"Is that all you can say?"

For the first time since they'd entered the car, he looked over at her for moment then returned his attention to the road. He knew that a conflict was probable this morning, and had been trying his best to avoid one. It was all in the way she got dressed, literally snatching on her clothes, and in the way she gave him one-word responses over breakfast, and snapped off orders and details about how much and what to pack. He could feel it, sense it was on its way — just like birds take cover for a pending rain storm long before people even notice the winds have picked up.

"Tell me, during what part of this conversation was I supposed to say something more?"

"Don't patronize me," she whispered.

Okay, it was on.

He'd put forth the question without looking at her, and her answer came with a soft click of annoyance as she sucked her teeth and huddled herself more closely against the passenger's door. He knew the sound. It was the response that black women offer when truly disgusted.

More silence. Five more miles of silence. Maybe she'd let it go.

"It's just that, you never have anything to say anymore."

He knew the drill. She wasn't going to let it go. That

left two options. Either get it all out and try to resolve it
before they got to the house, or he could leave it be, and
drive in peace. But then he'd have to try to resolve whatever it was after they got there, and after everybody else
got there. Fighting in Mom Johnson's house, with her
family reinforcements present, was out of the question.

"What do you mean I don't have anything to say any
more? We talk."

He watched her from the corner of his eye. After a
moment of apparent contemplation, she seemed to relax
and turn her body more in his direction. Oh, yeah, this
was going to be a long one.

"No, Franklin, we don't."

"I don't get it. It's not like I don't say good morning...
or like I don't—"

"—You don't say good morning like you used to."

His mind searched for any shred of logic that could
be salvaged. "What's that supposed to mean?"

"See, now you're getting defensive, which is why we
can never talk about what we need to talk about."

He let out his breath slowly, and tried to remain calm.

"Look, I know you miss your grandmother. So do I.
She was a lovely woman. I also know how much you
don't want to be going down to the house, right before
Christmas to pack up her things, but they overruled your
vote, and mine, so we have to go. I can't imagine having to deal with this, especially after losing your Mom and
Dad five years ago to cancer and a heart attack. And,
maybe I didn't want to talk about it, because I knew you
had to be hurt to the bone. Truthfully, I haven't quite
known what to say to you about any of it."

"That's not the issue, and that's not what I'm talking
about and you know it. We've been over that already."

When she let out a long sigh, he extended his arm
across her shoulders and held the steering wheel with
one hand. "Listen, I know it's still bothering you, no mat-

ter what you say. That's why I'm here. I gotchure back.
Okay? Me and you. We'll deal with your people the
same way we've gotta deal with mine, with a long-han-
dled spoon, as my grandmother would say. Then, we'll
come home and make Christmas for just the two of us."

He noticed that her eyes were glistening when she
leaned against his shoulder.

"But I've dealt with losing Mom and Dad, you know.
Mom was the hard one, because we didn't expect the
cancer, and it came on her and took her so fast... Dad's
heart attack was almost a blessing for him. He loved her
so much."

"Yeah," he offered quietly, "but, sometimes, one thing
has a way of triggering a memory about something else.
You know?"

"Maybe," she nearly whispered, "but Nana was
eighty-seven, and wasn't even sick. So, when she
passed in her sleep, we all knew it was time."

"True, but, it still don't take away all the hurt."

"I know," she said in a soft voice, "but it still doesn't
answer why we've been having problems for the last six
months. Nana wasn't sick when this marriage started
unraveling."

He had no answer to that, nor had he expected such
an honest statement of fact.

"I don't know, baby. Maybe relationships just have
an ebb and flow? For a while, we was flowin' pretty
good; then we had a little ebb... and that low tide ran
right into this situation making everything feel dried out.
Now, it's hard to tell what has you down."

"It's not just me, Franklin. We're both going through
something."

Again, he had no answer. She was digging deep this
morning. He allowed the road to consume him as he
pondered what she'd just said.

They rode for miles in companionable silence, her

head resting on his shoulder. He was glad that she did-n't appear hostile and withdrawn, but he hated the sad-ness that enveloped her. When he pulled off the main highway onto the narrow two-lane divide, he looked at the barren trees and bleak ice-covered hills that had once been lush and green and full of life. The truth was everything had its own season... but that didn't make winter any easier to endure.

The single lane road that they turned onto was icy, but it was passable. The branches of the trees hung heavy within a clear crystalline casing, laden from their burden, and seeming to bow as their four-by-four passed them. Deep, frozen tire ruts within stiff mud made Franklin withdraw his arm from her shoulder and hold the steering wheel with both hands. The change in sensa-tion allowed a renewed chill to seep into her bones.

Small farmhouses dotted the landscape, each sitting back from the main road like silent observers protected from encroachment by wide front yards and fields. It was so peaceful, motionless, where the absolute quiet almost forbade one to speak.

Nana's house soon came into plain view. Colette's stomach lurched. It was just as she'd last seen it only a few weeks ago. But it was so still. It was also covered with a delicate coating of ice that created a spectacular prism of light which appeared to bounce from the sur-faces. Almost as if the entire house had been wrapped and sealed in cellophane, and put away for something special, she thought, wondering how beautiful it would be in Mystic Ridge if it ever snowed.

Yes... for the moment, home was still there. The large bay window stood watch over the wooden porch that rimmed the property, with yellow shutters winking a

welcome to all visitors. Wide wooden steps formed an
apron against the long dirt path, framed by two fenced-in
vegetable gardens that now lay fallow under winter.
Everything was the same—except the fact that Nana
wasn't on the porch to look down the lane and wave.
Now, a sparkling icy blanket of silence replaced her smile
and made the house vacant.

"You think I should pull up in front of the shed, or the
barn?"

Colette shrugged and sighed. The front path to the
house had been salted, as well as the driveways leading
to both structures—no doubt, courtesy of the members of
the church, and Miss Julia's son, Juney's, home training.
"Closer would be better, I suppose."

Without a response, Franklin pulled the vehicle to a
stop in front of the large outdoor tool shed, pushed the
back-hatch button, and hopped out. Colette kept her
gaze on the house, then exited the vehicle with another
sigh, and headed up the path after she'd grabbed her
garment bag. It took a moment to find the keys in the
bottom of her large satchel purse, and he took her luggage so she could dig for them.

"Looks like everything is in order," Franklin murmured, as they entered the large sun-lit foyer and closed
the door behind them.

Colette nodded, and allowed her gaze to scan the
spacious rooms that faced her. Everything was in order.
Too much order. The brightly colored hook rug under
their feet seemed newly vacuumed, and each of her
grandmother's hand-made, needlepoint pillows in the living room was in its place, resting in the corners of the two
overstuffed armchairs by the fireplace. Clean, crisp
doilies frocked the plump, floral sofa, and the floors and
wooden mantle glistened with a coat of fresh furniture
polish. Stained glass sun-catchers merrily spilled colored prisms along the adjacent walls, and her line of

vision scanned for the merest hint of unwanted intrusion. Relief swept through her when she spied the row of sil-ver-framed pictures on the mantle. Those were the true house treasures, each one bearing an irreplaceable moment in time captured on yellowing celluloid.

"I think everything is okay, Colette."

He watched her shoulders drop an inch before she spoke.

"So pretty... and such a shame that it's going out of the family. I hate the fact that people were in here from the church after we left, to clean it."

"I just think folks was trying to help, and to do a little something nice, is all—like the way they did the drive-ways for us. I don't think nobody meant no harm, honey. They all loved Ester, and this was all they could do to show their respects. C'mon. Tell me which room you want us to be in, and I'll put the bags up there."

"I want to check the dining room and kitchen, first."

He didn't argue with her—that she appreciated. He also didn't follow her. That, too, she appreciated.

Without looking back, she crossed the living room and went into the dining area. Her eyes settled on the large oak ellipse of a table and matching spoke chairs that were handmade by her grandfather's patient craft. She touched one of the needlepoint seat cushions, and smiled, remembering the fuss Nana always made when they'd accidentally spill something on them as children.

Each dish, and rows of crystal stemware, were still arranged museum-style behind the beveled glass of her grandfather's family-famous breakfront, with large serv-ing platters displayed prominently in plate-holders across the top. Her fingers slid across the ivory crocheted table-cloth that her mother had given Nana as an anniversary present. It had taken her mother so long to finish it, so many years ago, and the Tiffany lamp still added a splash of color to the pale yellows and blues in the room... it was a gift from her brother, one that Nana cherished. "She loved that, Wilton," Colette whispered, "Glad she and Pop got to enjoy it." She ignored the ostentatious chandelier that Bey had competitively added to the room the following year.

Moving into the kitchen, and flicking the overhead light on, Colette stood in the middle of what had once seemed like Grand Central Station. She remembered teaming with her sister to replace the old linoleum table with a genuine butcher block one and low oak stools that now took center stage. Her cousins had replaced the cutlery that was now motionless. But nobody, not even her father, could get Nana to part with her cast-iron skillets. The best they'd been able to do was to buy her a suitable rack upon which to retrieve and store her magic pots.

How many meals, she wondered, had been prepared at that six-foot wooden room divider? Biscuits, and breads, and green beans, and stews, and chickens had even been beheaded there. Iced-tea, and fresh lemonade had been squeezed, as local and family gossip got poured into pitchers along with the seeds and sugar.

This was the real family room, not the living room. Colette allowed her gaze to travel to the refrigerator, and she suddenly stopped. A note with an elderly scrawl made her do a double take and catch her breath. That wasn't there before, when they'd come down for the funeral. But she relaxed as she approached it. The note was simplistic, and the message clear.

We washed up the linens for you, baby. Refrigerator is cleaned out, save some fresh eggs and milk for breakfast. You know our Ester, jams and mason vegetables been put up since early Fall, and God bless her, her pantry was full when she passed. You young folk don't need to go to the market for nothing much—you family, love you like my own. Come see me when you get set-tled in. I got mail from the house, as Mr. Whitfield brings it to me now like Ester told him to. —Love, Miss Julie

Colette stood there for a moment, and fought back the tears. Exiting the kitchen quietly, she clicked off the light and joined Franklin at the bottom of the staircase.

Accepting his gentle lead, she headed up the steps, glad that they had been the first to arrive. As they reached the top of the landing, she hesitated not know-ing which direction to turn.

To her left was her grandparents' bedroom. She def-initely didn't want to sleep in there, even with Franklin beside her, and despite the fact that it was one of the closest rooms to the bathroom.

"Let me walk the halls a bit by myself, okay?"

Franklin set the bags down and waited. At the moment, she appreciated his silent acquiescence. She knew he understood her need to drink in the pure quiet, with only the large grandfather clock in the hall ticking. This space had never been so still, not even during the funeral. And there would never be another opportunity like this again.

Colette walked down the hallway alone, leaving Franklin where he stood. She poked her head into what had been her grandparents' room, first. The neat four-posted bed sat high off the floor and donned a pristine set of lemon-yellow linen beneath the same clean, white quilt with doves and white roses on it that had been in her Nana's wedding trousseau.

Mending that quilt had been an ongoing labor of love for her grandmother for years. Now, looking at it with new eyes, she finally understood why. That's where they'd probably talked. That's where they'd shared secrets. That's where they'd made enough love to pro-duce three wonderful children. That's the place in the house where her grandmother and grandfather had probably formed their life's dreams... where intimacy and warmth privately resided... and that's why her grand- mother could never part with her new-bride's quilt, no matter how tattered and frayed it became. It was a shrine of memories, lovingly repaired every season by a woman who remembered.

The vanity had also withstood the test of time, and still held her grandmother's silver comb and brush set— another wedding present from a lifetime of love.

"She used to brush our hair with that when we were little," Colette whispered to herself, her eyes filling with unshed tears. Then she turned away.

It was clear that whoever had come in to clean had been honest and diligent to a flaw. What had been wrong with her for begrudging those loving hands a last connection to Nana? She'd been living in the city too long, and infested with its twisted values. Ester Johnson was a community treasure, to be shared by all, and missed by all. Colette drew another slow breath and relaxed.

The entire house almost looked as if Nana Johnson had carefully cleaned everything herself. Someone had even taken down and washed the yellow and white dot- ted Swiss curtains at the windows, and dusted the end tables, and dutifully returned the family Bible to its famil- iar perch on the night-stand by the bed on a doily. Her brother and his wife were older, had been married the longest, and deserved to be here, she thought, mentally arranging things as she walked.

She made her way down the hall and peered into her uncles' rooms. The same neat, tidy appearance of order faced her, and the twin beds made her smile. She and her sister used to share that room during their summers in the country, happily bouncing from bed to bed until Nana hollered at them to stop. Yes, it wouldn't be hard to convince her sister to take this room at all. She now wondered why they'd all chosen to stay at a motel in the center of town for those three days of the funeral, instead of coming home?

As she approached her father's room, she drew another steadying breath. He was gone too, just like her mother, but the neat little room was cozy, and had a queen-sized bed and a broad window with a cushioned window-seat and large armchair. It was perfect for Wilton and Deidre. She did need her rest, being eight months pregnant, and everything. The large feather bed would make her comfortable... plus, it was directly across the hall from the bathroom—which would be a definite asset. It was probably good that her father was the eldest son, and therefore had been given the best room in the house, second to Nana and Pop's. At least, there was an extra couple-comfortable room, so no unnecessary squabbles would occur on that issue, anyway.

Colette slipped into the last room, and just as she'd expected, the bathroom was spotless. The white claw-footed tub and porcelain sink sparkled with an old-fashioned brand of elbow grease. The sight almost made her weep with gratitude, and it took the last edge off her misgivings about other people intruding.

She touched the edges of the silver frames that graced the hall as she made her way back to Franklin's side, adjusting pictures ever so slightly, and relaxing, finding the old rhythms of Southern easy speech and a slower gait, simply remembering as her fingers grazed them.

"Everything all right?" he murmured when she reached him.

"Yeah," she whispered, going ahead of him toward the other end of the second floor. "There's nothing to do to get ready for the others. Every room has been done. I need to go by Miss Julie's house and thank her personally when I get Nana's mail."

"You know where you want us to be?" he asked in a quiet tone before picking up the bags, still reverent of her mood.

"I'm gonna put Wilton and Diedre in Daddy's old room, Brother and Nancy in Nana's—that's only right, he's the oldest. Nicole can go in the room we used to share as kids, since she'll be the only one sleeping alone up here, and knowing my sister, she'll be trying to jump into bed with us if something goes bump in the night."

Franklin chuckled, and for the first time that day, she joined him.

"Now, you know, that'll put Beynard next to us, if we take the extension and he and his lady take Pop Johnson's little reading room."

"Yeah, I know," she sighed. "But I like Nana's sewing room. Pop built it for her with his own hands... and they put a big daybed in there, with windows all around... a comfy chair... and he even put his tiny room beside it so they could talk without him getting in her way." A small chuckle at the thought surprised her, and she smiled as she remembered how her grandmother and grandfather lovingly and constantly fussed at each other in an age-old repartee. "He even made her a full length floor-mirror, so she could let her clients see her handiwork and do gown fittings. He really, really loved her."

"A lotta love went into all of this house," Franklin said in earnest from his vantage point behind her close to the room, all the while appreciating the craftsmanship that had gone into the exposed beams and hand-hung windowpanes. "Always admired your grandpop. Was a true artisan. Don't teach cabinet-making and carpentry to them young boys, like they used to. Everything was done by hand, no fancy machines."

"He built the extension for her because she always wanted the boys' rooms to be intact for when they came

home with their wives and kids... guess he got tired of sitting on her pins in the living room furniture," she chuckled again sadly. "She never got used to any of her children being gone. Guess I'll know what that feels like one
day." Before Franklin could comment, she turned away
from him and paced toward the room. "It gets all the
light, and at night, the stars and trees look so beautiful.
And she made every curtain, and pillow, and bedspread
in here herself, too. This room has both of them in it...
laughing and talking, with a door in-between, and one to
enter from the hall, if they needed individual space. I
love this new little nook they created."

"You don't have to sell me," he whispered, catching
up to her and landing a kiss against her neck as they
moved deeper into the room. "It's just that Bey keeps
strange hours, and might keep you up with his hootin'
and loud talkin'."

She turned and considered the comment, then
walked over to the small room that hosted a pull-out sofa,
desk, bookshelves, and wooden chair, and looked in. "If
trifling-ass Bey brings that same floozie to this house
again, and screws her under Nana's roof while we're trying to deal with serious business, like he did during the
funeral, I'll kick his natural behind. I'm not havin' it! I will
not keep quiet this time! Why, I'll unlock that damned
door and turn on the light, and—"

"—Slow down, slow down, baby," Franklin urged with
a smile. "Now, the man is grown, and has a right to have
his lady friend join him, and it ain't our business what
they—"

"—Oh, so, now, you're taking his side!"

Franklin set his load of bags down very carefully and
walked over to the adjoining room door, closed it, and
threw the latch. "Why don't you just put Sissey in there?"

"Because, Sissey shouldn't have to be put out of
what's familiar to her just because Bey's a pig!"

"Well, everybody mourns a little different, honey. Bey just got tore up the day before the funeral, and grieved in some flesh... you can't hold a man hostage for—"

"—What!"

"All I'm saying is..." Franklin stifled a smile, let the comment trail off, and began arranging the bags neatly at the foot of the daybed.

"Oh, and I suppose you have the same intentions while we're here? Well, forget it. This is Nana's house!"

"Now, don't jump to conclusions, and go killin' the messenger. I just think once everyone is here, and we get to workin', we should all let bygones be bygones. I brought my tools, and I'll fix anything that's out of order... noticed the mailbox was leaning a bit. I'll get on that this afternoon. Will walk the perimeter and see if there's anything that could hurt the selling price, and fix it, okay? That's my contribution, and all I'ma say—for now."

Franklin gave her an impish grin, then walked toward the door. The man truly got on her nerves!

Chapter Three

He hadn't been able to pry Colette out of the house all morning, not even to stop in on Miss Julia to pay her respects. She seemed determined to set out towels on the foot of each bed, and to thaw out meats and greens for dinner, and determined most of all to be the first presence in the house everyone else encountered when they arrived. It was some sort of weird female squatter's rights ritual, if not a territorial marking ceremony—the way she took absolute physical possession of the kitchen. But, the house was still going on the market within the week. It had been decided. So her attempt was futile, and sure to only get the feathers flying around there. Besides, what was the point? Pure crazy. At least that's what it seemed like to his way of looking at it; however, even that rational argument didn't change things. The woman would not be moved.

His retreat had been to go outside and work on straightening the leaning mailbox post. It was a safer distance than standing idly by, chatting with a half-angry, half-crying woman. And there was definitely no reasoning with her.

"How do? Looks like you workin' mighty hard on that post."

Solomon Whitfield's voice startled him, and Franklin pulled his head up quickly, then relaxed and smiled as he squinted in the afternoon sun to make out the local postman's face.

"Yo! Mr. Whitfield, how you be?"

"Jus' fine, son. Jus' fine. No aches, pains, no complains. But was, and still am, sorry to hear about Miz Ester. Beautiful lady. Everybody's gonna miss her."

Franklin pulled off his baseball cap and wiped his brow with the forearm portion of his down jacket. Even though it was cold outside, the exertion of digging up the post from the frozen earth was beginning to take its toll. He leaned back on the fence and nodded in agreement with Mr. Whitfield. He liked talking to a fellow Southerner. It relaxed his tongue, and his mind, as he could easily slip into the comfortable dialect without feeling any sense of being on-guard the way he normally did around Colette's family.

"You ain't said a mumblin' word, brother." He allowed each syllable to escape in a slow, patient drawl. "I'm just fixin' a few things, and trying to stay outta harm's way until the rest of the family gets down here."

Whitfield adjusted the mailbag on his shoulder, and shook his head in a gesture of understanding; then he cast his line of vision down the road in the direction of Miss Julia's house.

"Yeah, I imagine Colette took it the worse, which means, you gonna have to weather the worse, sorry to say."

A companionable silence enveloped them, and Franklin let his breath out slowly.

"Her brother, Girard, should be here soon, which'll be good," Franklin offered after a moment. "He's the executor, and the family attorney. Good people, fair people, so... I know he'll handle things the way Mom Johnson wanted. That oughta take some'a the load off of Colette."

"Hmmm... maybe," Whitfield mumbled, rubbing his chin and squinting at the late afternoon sky. "You know,

Ester never wanted this house to be sold to no developers. Wanted it kept in the family."

Again, all Franklin could do for a moment was shake his head in agreement. "Yup, but that ain't my call, man. I'm just the hired help," he added with a sad chuckle. "Right shame, too. This place is like something people dream of... but all of 'em couldn't make it a week in here together, so I guess Girard is gonna do the only rational thing. Sell it, split the proceeds, and move on."

The statement seemed to take the conversation out of Solomon Whitfield for a moment. He just leaned against the fence with Franklin and looked down the road in the same direction. After a while, he pushed himself away from the leaning white pickets and adjusted his mailbag again.

"You know, this house has been in the Johnson family since just after slavery. One of the last Negro strongholds in this tiny town of nobodies. History. Why, the folks that held onto this house saw two World Wars, The Great Depression, Jim Crow... buried kin in the family plot out back, and raised generations here."

"Sir," Franklin offered quietly, "you preaching to the choir. My Colette has been like a Wild West pioneer about the decision, since she heard it... wouldn't be surprised if she stood on the porch with a rifle and dared the revenuers to come on her land."

"Don't laugh," Whitfield chuckled, "I saw old man Johnson chase off a sheriff from the next town over, one time, just like that—rifle in hand, back in the Klan riding days.

"Yeah, well, it might come to that in here this week."

"That bad, really?"

"Really," Franklin sighed, straightening himself away from the fence, and to get closer to Whitfield's good ear. "Got bad about six months ago. We'd come down for a visit, and Mom Johnson was moving slower than normal.

Was showing Colette who was to get what in the house, and singing hymns more than usual. Told Colette that even though Brother Girard had the solid mind, Colette had the fairer heart. Scared my poor wife to death. She said it was a sign. When we got home, Colette cried and cried like a baby, and there was no talkin' to her, neither. I couldn't do nothin' about the way she felt, and all she kept telling me was, time was short. So I started working crazy hours, trying to make my auto-body business rake in enough to possibly buy the house—if said dark hour ever came. But then we started fighting about money and bills... 'cause I stopped taking her out and stuff... was trying to hold onto every penny, though I never told her why. I mean, we argued about who was to do what in the house—stupid stuff... I was so tired, and takin' on too many body-jobs to help out and make things easier, like I used to... and I sorta lost interest in the day to day things, if'n you know what I mean."

Franklin cast his gaze to the ground, and for the first time, his admission felt like a heavy burden had been lifted from his shoulders. Whitfield's reassuring slap across his back made him feel better.

"You tell your wife any of this?"

"You crazy?" Franklin muttered, shaking his head no. "Look, I waited till I was damned near forty to marry her... watched her lose both her Mom and her Dad, then her Grandpop, before I could get myself together to give her a date to go along with the ring. Engaged the woman for five and a half years... Hell, her brother had to be the one to walk her down the dag-gone aisle... all the while, I was claiming that I wouldn't be ready to make things official until I got my business together. Stupid! Short-sighted."

"Don't be too hard on yourself, son—"

"—No. Truth is naked truth. 'Cause, then, when I finally did marry her, all I can do is put her in a row house. Sure, I make a decent livin' now, but it still ain't enough to cover what we dreamed about. What I promised her our life would be. You understand?"

"Dreams gotsta be pursued together. It ain't all on the one. I know if Ester Johnson was here right now, she'd tell you that much."

"Yeah, but I'm still the man of the house. The weight's on me."

Whitfield placed his hand on Franklin's shoulder and looked him straight in the eyes. "If I know our Colette, and I been knowin' her ever since she was in her mother's belly, she wouldn't hold you responsible for tryin' as hard as you did—no matter what the outcome. In fact, she'd love you even more because you even cared to try."

Franklin pulled away and sought the fence to lean on again. "Tryin' don't cut it, no offense, Mr. Whitfield. I didn't produce. She got men in her family that can put their money where their mouth is, and that's what they'll be doin' when they come down here today. I can't say diddly on the subject of what happens. All I can do is hold her hand as they run her out of town on a rail and let her take a few boxes."

"Her grandpop didn't have nothin' when he and Miz Ester started, and—"

"—Not to cut you off, or to get philosophical, but she's used to men in her family that have achieved something of note. Grandpop Johnson started out as a furniture-maker, and built his business to the point where he made this house into a national treasure... you should see the work that man put into his home. Like something I always dreamed of doing for my family one day—never could stand the city life," he added on an exhale. "Always wanted to go back south, home."

"You can't compare yourself to a man that had no other options. In Pops Johnson's day, a black man had to work for hisself, or die tryin', and that seems to be

whatchure doin' in Philadelphia. Right? A woman can't
ask for more than that. Can't get blood from no turnip. I
seen ya, and Ester done tol' me plenty times, you work
hard, boy. She was proudest of you... said you reminded
her so much of her husband, Ezekiel."

"No excuses, Mr. Whitfield. The fact is, the next generation did okay for themselve. Got a solid education
and good jobs. Me, I went into the service, then went to
vo-tech school. Stupid. Colette's brother's a lawyer, a
big time lawyer."

"He ain't do that by hisself. Ester scrubbed floors to
send her son, his Dad, to Morehouse College. And, her
brother, Girard, missed Vietnam by the skin of his chin-
ny-chin-chin—Ester's prayers being heard On High, no
doubt. And he only went to law school 'cause his grandmother encouraged him to fight for Civil Rights—now,
what he did with that degree ain't have nothin' to do with
what Ester originally intended. That much, I do know."

Franklin ignored Solomon Whitfield's argument,
and pressed on. "Even her Dad was an engineer, at
Boeing, back in the day—"

"—All 'cause he was in the right place at the right
time after a lawsuit, which is why Ester was so high on
law for Girard. Law got his daddy into Boeing. Civil
Rights."

Not to be dissuaded, Franklin continued without
missing a beat as he ticked off the lineage on his fingers.
"Her cousin, Wilton, has some muck-t-muck post down at
Hampton University—"

"— Cause he married the right girl at the right time,
whose family was in the Virginia upper crust Negro soci-
ety."

"—Even triflin' Bey is a dentist."

"Now, you got me there. That's still one of the eighth
wonders of the world!" Solomon Whitfield slapped his
knee and laughed at his own joke, and poked Franklin in

the chest when he couldn't even get him to chuckle. "Aw, c'mon, son. Life's too short to be woulda, coulda, shoulda-ing. You never know what's gonna happen. Ester was the one who always said, it's a long road that has no turn."

Still caught up in his own litany, Franklin let out a breath and watched it turn to steam. "Why Colette picked me, out of all her choices, only God knows. Shoot. The woman can't even quit her job and do her grants to start that community center she dreamed about. She needs to get out of that dead-end city job at DHS, people with problems too serious to solve day in, day out. And too much bureaucracy to help 'em. All the girl really ever wanted to do was work with kids, under her own terms, and teach 'em basic stuff like Ester Johnson taught them."

Franklin held up his hand to stop Mr. Whitfield from defending him further. "What's worse is, truth be told, Mr. Whitfield—since we speakin' man to man. I couldn't even do the easiest thing, and the simplest thing, she wanted... then, I'd have to tell her that I couldn't even save her grandma's house. Nah... no use in tellin' her about failing one more stupid dream."

The postman looked at him hard now, and set down his bag. "What's the simplest thing?"

"I don't even need to be bothering you with this nonsense. You a working man, got letters to deliver, and it's ass-biting cold out here." Franklin turned his back to Solomon Whitfield and lunged at the stubborn post that refused to budge.

"You know, stress'll make a lot of things stop workin' the way dey normally would. Now, I maybe an ole country boy... but, I hear tell your people is from North Carolina good stock. Blessin's will come to you soon, son, in God's time. But, in the meantime, y'all needta get Miss Julia to give you somea her medicinals, and have a

talk with your wife about how you been feelin'. All dat
stress ain't good to keep bottled up. Gotta release it, and
let go and let God. Young folk can die of heart attacks
too, ya know. Dreams is good medicine—goes along
with prayers, but you gotta share 'em for it to work."

Although Franklin kept working at the post without
turning around, half talking to himself as he did so, he
grunted out a question-part-statement to Solomon
Whitfield that was so quiet, he was sure the old man did-
n't hear it.

"When Wilton's very pregnant wife gets down here,
all Hell is gonna break lose on-top of everything else, and
if," he added with a pant of exertion as he took a second
lunge at the post, "Miss Julie got some magic in her
kitchen, I'd be much obliged."

He heard the postman's bag lift, and when he finally
looked up, Solomon Whitfield was on his way down the
road heading for Miss Julia's house.

The sound of a large sedan pulling into the driveway
brought her to the kitchen window. Her brother Girard's
gleaming black Mercedes seemed so out of place
against the simple country backdrop of the front yard.
She watched and nearly held her breath as her brother
rounded the exterior of the vehicle and opened the door
for her sister-in-law. Her jaw went slack as a sleek black
mink-covered arm appeared first, and the always-elegant
Nancy descended from her chariot.

"Well, it's on, now, Nana," she whispered into the
open space. "The carpet-baggers are here to break your
home up and box it away into a million pieces."

Colette wiped the flour from her hands onto her
grandmother's apron. She'd be sure to lean in without
bodily touching Nancy when she greeted her. The

crunch of icy driveway brought her to the window again, only to see that a steel gray Volvo had pulled in next to the Mercedes. "All right. Wilton and Deidre got here," she sighed. Now all she had to do was wait for Bey to bring his red BMW careening into the yard. If she knew Nicole, she'd probably paid for a cab all the way from the airport.

As expected, Nancy had laced her arm around Franklin's waist, and it took both her brother and Franklin to haul in the assorted heavy Louis Vitton luggage while duly escorting Nancy up the steps. God forbid the queen shoul take a skid on the ice. Colette steadied her nerves and stood at the front screen door with a pasted-on smile, braving the cold and bracing for impact.

Chapter Four

Standing in the middle of the kitchen high-traffic zone, Colette wondered almost aloud, why it seemed that when Nana was alive, the same number of bodies in the same space would flow in a more orchestrated fashion. This was sheer chaos!

Somehow, her grandmother could seem to talk, and dispatch duties effectively and in accordance to skill levels, all the while never missing a beat. Now, however, the once-calm terrain seemed to be manned by an uninitiated and confused air-traffic controller—her.

Nancy, her sister-in-law, was swinging her immaculate jet-black bob hair-cut at every opportunity, and trying desperately not to chip a French-manicured fingernail, or to splash food on her Nile-blue silk dress. God forbid that any organic particle might get trapped in the setting of the four-karat rock her brother had given the woman, and Heaven forbid that she take off her Rolex watch to avoid getting it wet while making dinner. How in the Hell was she going to call herself helping in the kitchen with that get-up on? Colette had to admit that the woman looked good, athletically trim, no hint of gray, full-face make-up—beat down, always, upon flawless cappuccino skin. She had to admit it, even if begrudgingly so, that she didn't know a woman alive who exuded Nancy's level of elegance. But the heifer was in the way, nonetheless, and was always trying to Grand Stand.

Without thinking about it twice, Colette had simply reached in the drawer and handed Nancy a full apron, and a designated spot to be on the other side of the butcher's block, yet in the middle of the kitchen, which ended the circling and directing from Nancy—for the moment.

Colette knew she was getting tired, just by the way she was starting to answer people. She was almost ready to give her tall, stylish sister, Nicole, a shower cap to cover her short, curly blonde-brown ringlets—if she didn't stop playing with her hair and twisting it while preparing food! At least Nicole didn't require full hazmat covering, since her tie-dyed, New York chic outfit could get splashed, and no one would know the difference.

Even though Beynard's friend, Sandra, annoyed her with her constant coos and overtly sexual commentary thrown in Bey's direction, at least the young woman held to a basic standard of food prep cleanliness. In fact, Sandra was growing on her, even though she was only twenty-five and had everything hanging out in the dead of winter, she was much less of a pain than Wilton's wife, Deidre—who got in the way, whined, and complained at every turn. If Deidre would just sit her big, water-buffalo butt down!

Between Sandra's squeaky, cutesie voice emanating from her tiny coffee-colored, half-naked frame, Deidra's constant deer-in-the-headlights look of sheer confusion coming from her wide brown eyes, and her sister's know-it-all news-anchor voice competing with Nancy's too-bored-to-be-bothered-and-where's-the-maid approach to cooking a basic family dinner, Colette thought she'd pass out.

Finally, when a mid-air collision occurred between her sister, Nicole, and Bey's friend, Sandra, Colette held her hands out and stopped all motion.

"STOP! Freeze. Nobody move."

The bewildered members of the near pile-up laughed and screeched to a halt.

"Y'all, this don't make no sense," Colette chuckled. "Okay, Diedre, get your big self into that chair that your husband brought in, out of the way in the corner, and sit down like Wilton told you to. You can fold the napkins for dinner on what's left of your lap."

"Yes, Ma'am," Deidre giggled, and scurried into the corner and flopped down with a grunt that made everyone laugh even harder.

"Sissey, get on that high stool by the sink – no, not in front of the sink—you ain't at work at the news desk, and there's no cameras here. Sit to the side of it, so everybody can get to the water. Thank you, and make the iced tea. Everything you need is right there. And, Sandra, I know this is your first time at this, but it's all about chore-ographed rhythm. Stay to your side of the butcher block next to Nancy—our resident expert, follow her lead, she's slicing what you peel, try not to cut her, and stay up on a stool while you're peeling those yams, and you won't cut your dang self."

Sandra laughed, and joined in with the rest of the giggles. "Bey!" she exclaimed, when Nicole slapped his wrist as he leaned over her to get to the sink, "Go get water for your scotch from up in the bathroom. Stop running in and out of here for stuff. That's how I almost wiped-out Nicole, trying to rinse off this knife and not bump into you!"

"That's right, Bey," Nancy chimed in. "It's bad enough that Wilton is sashaying in here every five minutes to check on his wife, and Girard and Franklin are hovering in the doorway like two yard dogs waiting for a scrap to fall... why don't you fellas just go somewhere?"

"You tell 'em, Nance," Colette added, popping the back of Franklin's knuckles with a wooden spoon as he tried to open her vat of greens for a peek. "Stop sweatin' the pots!"

"Dag, y'all are some mean women," Bey laughed amiably, then smoothed his fingers through his short, silky, salt and pepper hair. "I'm just adding to my cups. Why y'all so mean to old Bey—they treat me bad, Frank."

"Totally vicious," Franklin belly-laughed as he rubbed his knuckles and tried to avoid another whack from Colette's spoon. "Mom Johnson would let us come in and get a taste, but yall are just plain evil."

Nancy put one hand on her hip and brandished a flat skillet filled with warm butter in it with the other. "Mom Johnson ain't here to save your sorry butts. Now move it, and make yourselves useful by setting the table, at least."

"Dag, a man can't even get a little taste of hooch before dinner. What's the world coming to?" Bey added in an overly dramatic tone. He flashed Sandra a wide, perfect smile, and she giggled at the attention. "What we having for dinner, anyway... somethin' sure smells good."

"Colette was nice enough to get things started this morning when she got here. She made three apple pies, plus we got baked chicken, fried yams, greens, biscuits, potato salad, and iced tea. Satisfied? Now scram!" Deidre ordered with a laugh.

"Gentlemen, I say we retreat, now, while we have a fighting chance," Girard chimed in with a wide smile. "We're outnumbered and out-gunned, and they have sophisticated culinary weapons."

"But, I think it's too hot in here for Deidre," Wilton protested.

A collective groan echoed out from the group. It was enough of an indictment to make the other three men bodily carry Wilton away from his wife, and into the dining room.

"We got one wounded," Franklin laughed as they hoisted a wiggling, chubby Wilton up by his arms.

"I say we shoot him, and put him out of his misery," Bey laughed as they all struggled to get through the door arch at the same time.

"No, can't shoot him," Girard bellowed in a faux-military voice. "We're Marines, and we never leave our wounded behind."

As soon as the men had gotten to the other side of the doorway, all the women doubled-over and laughed. Nancy was the first one to salute Colette. The fact that her sister-in-law did so made Colette further disarm.

"Well defended, Captain Cole!" Nancy quipped with a grin, accidentally getting yam sugar on her forehead in the process. "Every station present and accounted for. I'd say we couldn't have done this better."

Each woman stood up a bit straighter, and then made a grimace to denote her intention to bravely protect her position in the kitchen, which brought another round of uproarious laughter.

"Lord have Mercy!" Deidre sighed, "I never thought we'd get rid of them!"

"Girl!" her sister, Nicole, huffed, "I don't see how you all stand it? That's why I'm still single."

"It's just like when we were kids, remember," Colette laughed, setting biscuits on a cookie sheet from her post. "Grandma had to have her hands full with that bunch under foot all the time."

"Oh, like the time when we were out back, hanging sheets for Nana, and crazy Bey and Girard were chasing poor Wilton with a dead field mouse. He came tearing around the corner, got tangled in the wet sheets, took out the entire clothes line, and we had to scrub all that yard-dirt outta Nana's linens—by hand. She was so mad at us, and all of us got a whippin' for messing up her laundry." Nicole, leaned back and roared with laughter at the memory.

"No!" Nancy, exclaimed. "Girard never told me that."

"Oh, girl," Colette added in, wiping her eyes with mirth, "my brother, your husband, was a terror. I'm sure there's plenty he didn't tell. Don't let that sedate façade of Mr. Attorney fool you. He tortured me and Nicole, all the time. Bey was his running buddy, and they would gang up on poor chubby little Wilton... me and Sissey used to feel sorry for that chile."

"Bey and Girard?" Nancy said in shock, but accepted the statement as both Nicole and Colette nodded in unison.

Deidre shook her head. "Now see, why'd they abuse my poor Wilton like that?"

"Cause he was a cry-baby butterball," Nicole chuckled, "and used to tell on everybody."

"You wasn't much better," Colette chuckled, finishing her placement of homemade buttermilk biscuits on the sheet before casting them into the oven.

"I was not that bad!"

"Yes you were," Colette countered, "Y'all, that's how she became a journalist. We used to call Sissey, Eye Witness News."

Even Nicole had to laugh, and she bent her head in mock shame.

"I heard about the time you dimed on Bey," Nancy giggled, making a face at Nicole and sticking her tongue out at her, as she moved a filled pan of yams over to the stove to begin frying them.

"Aw, sookie sookie, now. But, you're gonna have to be more specific, Nance – 'cause Sissey was always tellin' on Bey." Colette put both hands on her hips and sauntered over to Nicole, who had covered her head in anticipation of a tickle as her sister then began to try to pinch her. "Got Brother incriminated as well. Poor Girard."

"The *Playboy* incident," Nancy said with a wink. "I heard that was one that almost made Mom Johnson lose her religion."

"What?" Deidre exclaimed, looking from one woman to the next while they all slapped each other five and screamed and laughed.

"Y'all telling lies in Mom's kitchen ain't Christian," a male voice boomed from the other room.

"Mind your bizness," Colette yelled back, "if y'all wanna eat sometime tonight."

"C'mon, yall, tell me," Deidre insisted in a conspiratorial whisper. "What'd Bey do?"

"Well," Colette began with dramatic emphasis. "Our poor cousin, Bey, was feelin' Spring mighty hard, you might say."

Nancy shook her head and laughed, bending over the butcher block.

"Had this little church girl in his mind, and she had his nose wide open. Back in the day, Bey couldn't get none, even though he thought he was the lover, with his skinny yellow self. But, Brother—Girard, being older, had gotten ahold of some *Playboy* magazines. Big-mouthed Sissey, our one and only Nicole, told Bey that Girard had a bunch of nasty pictures."

"Uh, ahhh! I did not tell Bey about the magazine, like that. He found it himself! Sort of...." Nicole protested, trying to defend her honor.

"That's not the way I heard it," Colette countered.

"Wait," Nancy added in, pointing her finger at Colette, "Girard never told me it was his magazine... or, that there was more than one. He blamed the whole thing on Bey."

"Why am I not surprised?" Deidre chimed in.

"Gurl, lemme tell ya," Colette giggled, "Girard was fine, I mean tall, dark, handsome, and an athlete. He loved the ladies, and the ladies loved him—and he'd get so close to a kill, then either the girl would get scared, or

Nana would bust him before he could go all the way. My poor brother would come upstairs all mean and crabby, hollering at me and Sissey. Then, I would say, betchu didn't get none, did ya? And he'd chase me and pluck me in my head until I cried... or, till I said, I'ma tell Nana."

"How you know all this?" Deidre asked wide-eyed, and hanging on every word.

"'Cause Girard would pay me to keep my mouth shut, and to be his alibi."

"Let the child tell the story," Nancy insisted, becoming engrossed and laughing all the while.

"Like I said," Colette continued, "Girard was always able to talk his way out of a jam. Probably how he ended up as a lawyer. But Nana didn't play no hanky-panky in her house. So, when Girard and us would come down here for the summer, all Girard could do was smooth-talk Mr. Gibson into letting him buy a magazine on the sly. He'd always beg me for my hush money to get it, and I'd say okay—only if he showed me what he bought, and if he gave me fifty cents interest on the dollar. Nobody was gettin' any tail in those days. So the boy was desperate, and I stayed paid all summer... and Girard stayed in the barn, up in the loft, with his secret magazine stash—until Sissey told on him and Bey."

"That's not how it went," Nicole jumped in. "See, Bey took my babysitting money, and tried to go buy a magazine, but Mr. Gibson wouldn't sell it to him... told him to go borrow one of his cousin's. Old man Gibson's daughter overheard it, 'cause she worked at the store in the summers, and she was my best friend, so she told me. So, I told Colette that the same amount of money I was missing was the price of one of those nasty books. Colette put it together, and we went up into Girard's hayloft stash, and saw there wasn't no new issue up there. So I confronted Bey, and told him that I knew there wasn't no new magazine in Girard's stash, so he'd better

give me back my money. Then, Bey tricked me, and told
me to show him that there wasn't no new magazine—for
evidence, and if there wasn't, he'd give me the money he
supposedly found."

By this time, every woman in the kitchen was doubled over with laughter. Female hands waved in the air,
and whimpers and hoots implored the central storytellers
to stop. Poor Deidre squeezed her legs together tightly
and begged the team of Colette and Nicole to wait for her
to recover, lest she pee her pants.

"Oh, no, we can't stop now. Y'all wanted to know,"
Colette panted through the giggles. "Nicole's got it right.
My bad."

Sandra was laid out across the butcher block. "Stop,
please, I can't take it. I can only imagine Bey's face
when he hit the mother-load of Girard's collection."

"See, Girard is such a liar," Nancy screeched, wiping
her eyes, "He said there was only one magazine."

"One?" Colette nearly yelled.

"Gurl, pulleeease," Nicole went on. "Bey almost
wept when he saw all them big tittied women in stacks up
in that loft. The boy pulled out a knot of ones, shoved
them into my hands, and told me to git. I ran so fast with
my loot, that I bumped into Nana on the way to find
Colette, and all those bills fell on the floor."

"Oh, my God!" Deidre hollered.

"Nana hauled me into the kitchen, and threatened to
take my life if I've been stealing. So I told her that I did-
n't steal, Bey gave it to me. She asked me where Bey
was, and I said in the barn cleaning up. Now, since Bey's
narrow, yellow ass wouldn't hit a lick at a snake of
chores, Nana knew something was fishy. I wasn't as fast
at tellin' tales as Colette," Nicole said with a wink, "so
Nana took off with a broom in hand towards the barn,
talking about no child of hers was gonna do drugs on her
property, 'cause that's the only place Bey coulda got ten

dollars—was from selling that whacky weed mess."

"No, lie," Colette reinforced with a hoot. "Nana tore outta this house like a rampaging bull. Poor Bey was up in the loft, surrounded by paper women, his pants down to his knees—"

"Girl, stop it!" Nancy shrieked.

"He started givin' up the tapes as Nana climbed the ladder. The boy was talkin' fast, pullin' up his pants, tellin' her that he found Girard's books and they wasn't his, and Ester was praying out loud to Jesus, calling for Girard, and yellin' to me and Colette to fetch Grandpop and a switch—all at the same time. Nana was talkin' 'bout necket white women desecratin' the sanctity of her home... in between screamin', 'Jesus, Father, help me,' then she'd go back to a burst of, ' I'll kill you dead, boy! Bringing necketness into my house!' Poor Girard was on his way home with a girl, headed for the barn, when Bey flew out, Nana on his tail, and me and Colette was runnin' as fast as our legs could carry us—trying to wave him down and tell him to go the other way. But honey-chile, honey-chile—Nana was steam-rolling in his direction, speaking in tongues, and then, like in slow motion, Girard turned to run, bumped into his date, knocked the poor girl down, was trying to get up and pull her up.... But it was too late. Nana was on him—beatin' his natural ass in the front yard with a broom, in front of his date, while she had Bey by the shirt-tail... callin' them dogs. Grandpop couldn't get to the boys fast enough. He had to literally pick Nana up by her waist and carry her into the house. That's the story, and the only reason Girard and Bey lived. Grandpop saved them!"

Deidre hauled herself out of the chair and waddled quickly to the door, tears from laughter streaming down her face. "Wilton, help me get to the bathroom! Fast!"

Nicole was standing in the middle of the room now, stomping her feet, and Colette was leaning against the sink. Sandra had completely covered her face with her hands, and a collective scream brought the men running into the kitchen.

Franklin was the first to burst through the door. "Everybody all right?" His gaze searched the laughing faces of the women, and Bey and Girard tumbled in behind him.

Female hands waved and shooed them back.

"Go 'head on," Sandra gasped. "You all don't even need to be in here."

Franklin, Bey, and Girard looked at each other and folded their arms over their chests.

"I think our reputations are under attack, Counselor," Bey said with a chuckle.

"That could be liable. Slander," Girard retorted, then went over to hug his giggling wife. "What lies did you tell them about me?"

"I didn't say a word," Nancy gasped, still unable to recover. "Your sisters told it all."

"Well, since y'all are in here tellin' lies on us," Franklin chuckled, "can anybody tell us when we're gonna eat?"

The pitiful looks on the three male faces at the door brought another round of screams and giggles from the group of kitchen conferencers. But it was Franklin's pained expression of acute hunger that made Colette cross the room to kiss him.

"I haven't thought about, or laughed about that mess for years," Colette giggled, still unable to fully catch her breath. "Dinner's in twenty minutes."

Chapter Five

L aughter rang throughout the house during dinner, until the call for dessert made everyone stand up to make room in their stomachs in order to merely breathe. The entire female part of the family contingent had deftly moved in unison from the dining room into the kitchen, continuing the reverie while they handed dessert plates through the door to men, then received them back — returned with only crumbs. During the process, they had not broken their rhythm while cheerfully cleaning up dinner dishes and putting away the remaining food. The men had brought in a few plates, promising that they would help, but then, one by one, defected into the living room with pie slices to go. By the time the kitchen lights had been turned out, each man had staked out a corner of the room with a drink in hand.

Girard had claimed one of the armchairs by the fire, which in turn meant, the other one, adjacent to it, was for Nancy. Wilton had made a comfortable space for himself and Deidre in the center of the sofa, which also meant that no one else, but Nicole, could fit on it. Bey had pulled two dining room chairs together for himself and Sandra, and Franklin had sprawled mid-floor in front of the fire on the rug.

Colette smiled as she looked at the lounging males. Tradition in this house had not been interrupted, not even by the final passing of Nana, and she wondered how many dinners, holidays, and family gatherings had borne witness to the same, oddly comforting routine?

Her brother was still handsome and athletic looking, with the firelight casting shimmers of gold against the silver gray at his temples and bringing out the reds in his rich, dark chocolate skin. He looked positively regal, and was clearly in charge, as he sat in the high-back chair nursing his brandy. Bey, on the other hand, looked like a graying teenager, and the flickering light brought out the bronze in his complexion that was always cheery, but becoming a little gaunt, she'd noticed. Wilton looked like he hadn't aged a day... still brown, and pudgy with a tender, baby-face. But somehow, her Franklin looked like a lean, sated panther, sensually laid out in the evening light after a healthy kill. He seemed so content that she was almost waiting for him to lick his paws and purr. It was the first time anything in her close to recognizable as being a sexual urge had stirred toward him in a long while.

"Whew, man! You ladies sure out-did yourselves tonight," Girard exclaimed as he rubbed his belly and took a sip of brandy. "Thanks, Bey, too, for providing adequate libations to top off the evening."

"Here, here," Franklin added, raising his glass of cognac in Bey's direction from his outstretched position. "Brother Bey brought a little somethin' to take the chill off after dinner. We thank you, good brother. Ladies, my highest compliments to the chefs."

Bey beamed and nodded. "For real, you all done Mom Johnson proud, and I couldn't come down here without taking care of my boys. And I brought you ladies your favorite wines, too. Our turn to serve you."

"Oh no, not that easy," Nicole laughed. "Breakfast is on you, gentlemen. We left plenty of eggs, bacon, and left-over biscuits in there. I'll take my coffee black and strong, just like I like my men. Thank you."

"No problem," Wilton answered through a sip of his beer.

"Aw, man, don't be givin' in so easy," Bey fussed as he stood and went into the dining room, bringing back stem glasses and an assortment of Merlot, Chardonnay, champagne, and a cold bottle of sparkling cider for Deidre.

"Too late now," Nancy announced, "We have witnesses, and Wilton agreed to it for you, boys. We, the ladies, are sleeping in."

"My wife, the court stenographer," Girard sighed, taking a healthy sip from his goblet.

"That's cool, brothers," Franklin said cheerfully, obviously trying to diffuse a possible gender battle. "Breakfast is the easiest meal of the day."

"Bey... you sweetheart," Deidre crooned, accepting the sparkling cider.

"Yeah, man, thanks," Wilton chuckled, "she's had her eye on my beer all night.

Deidre slapped Wilton's arm and snuggled into him, while Bey poured champagne for Sandra, Merlot for Nancy and Nicole, and knelt to pour a glass of Chardonnay for Colette, then returned to his chair and snuggled up against his date.

The warmth of the fire enveloped the group, interweaving itself between the easy tempo of conversation and soft jazz that Franklin had provided. Colette found herself lying on the floor cuddled into the crook of Franklin's shoulder, the wine taking effect and making her yawn and giggle at the fragments of passing sentences. But every now and then she noticed her sister's far-away look, and how a hint of sadness flickered within her hazel eyes. Her sister's line of vision kept traveling past the group to the photos on the mantle, and Colette said a quiet prayer that one day her sister would have a permanent somebody to lean against by the fire.

"Been a long day of on the road," Girard said in a sensible tone that began dispelling the mood. "We've got a lot of packing and decisions to make in the morning, and maybe it's best that we all make it an early night."

"I hear you, my brother," Wilton yawned, helping Deidre up. "Thanks for putting us close to the bathroom. C'mon, baby, let's get you upstairs to bed."

Nicole stood with them and walked over to the mantle. Her fingers lovingly touched the edges of the picture frames as she considered the photos. "We had some good times in this house," she whispered.

Colette felt a lump beginning to form in her throat. "Tomorrow, baby. We'll figure it all out tomorrow."

Girard nodded, stood, and pushed the remaining embers back deep within the fireplace so that the smoldering timber could burn out on its own. Once he had completed the task to his liking, he held out his hand to Nancy. Being the champion of grace, she made her rounds, kissing everyone good night, then floated out of the room ahead of the rest. The momentary gesture of refinement made Colette smile. Nancy had her ways, but admittedly, she was the perfect match for Girard.

"Well, y'all gonna lie there on the floor all night, or what?" Bey chuckled, helping Franklin to his feet.

"You putting me and Cole out?" Franklin asked with a sly wink before he reached back to pull Colette up.

"Well, now, you gettin' into my bizness," Bey slurred while threading his arm around Sandra's waist, and trying without success to kiss her neck. When she squirmed away from him, he laughed and tried to pull her closer, then gave chase as she fled up the steps laughing.

Franklin chuckled and pecked Colette on the mouth with a kiss before she could say anything, then gave her a wink as he led her out of the room toward the stairs behind Bey. Turning off the lights as they passed each room, Franklin stopped at the base of the staircase and held Colette close.

"Don't begrudge him a little fun for the last time here," Franklin whispered close to her face.

His breath was filled with the sweetness of pie and a hint of cognac, and the warmth of his gentle hug magnetically forced her body to seal the small gap between them. Darkness covered the two as they stood at the bottom of the steps, with only the low red glow from the fireplace making shadows dance against the wall. His kiss began as a soft brush against her lips, then deepened until she could taste the remnants of dessert laced with drink. Yet, it was not forceful. Then, he pulled away, landing tiny kisses upon her eyelids, then down the bridge of her nose, finding her mouth again, and abandoning it for her neck, and the edge of her sweater-covered shoulder.

"This is the best time I can remember in this house," she whispered. "The first time that we all just got along, and nothing came up between any of us."

"I heard you girls laughing in the kitchen, and me and the fellas had a blast trying to figure out which one of us was in the dog house."

"Hmmm…" she murmured through a giggle, as his hands found the center of her lower back. "I'll never tell."

"You sure?" he whispered against her cheek, then grazed her earlobe with a nip.

"I'm sure," she whispered low within her throat, "that you're starting something we can't finish in this house tonight."

He let his breath out slow and warm against her ear.

"I promise to be really, really quiet," he murmured against her neck, "and, to go so slow that neither one of us will care where we are."

The comment combined with the moist heat from his mouth was sending shivers of anticipation through her.

"I'm not making any promises," she whispered, moving away to lead him up the steps, "at least not while everybody is still awake."

She saw him smile from the corner of her eye, and gave him her back to consider as she walked up the steps slowly—very slowly. When she felt his palm graze her backside, lingering for a moment before taking hold of the banister, she swallowed hard. It was going to be difficult to remain respectful in Nana's house, for sure.

"Don't turn on the light," he urged when they entered the room. Gathering her in his arms, he held her in the dark until their eyes focused. "See, isn't this better... and, isn't this why you wanted to be in here? Look out the window."

Moonlight cast a bluish light in the room, and the stars added magnificent splendor. Her body melted against his, and again his mouth captured hers, although, this time, not as tentatively. His hands slipped under her bulky knit sweater and tee-shirt, then began to unhook her bra. As his hands glided around her torso in an upward motion, her skin ignited, setting off a molten flow of desire between her legs.

But a loud creak, then a woman's laughter, made her flinch and giggle, momentarily breaking her trance.

"Oh, Lord. We can't do this. Not with Bey and Sandra at it in the next room."

Franklin chuckled, and released her. "Well let's get in bed. We can't stand in the middle of the floor all night," he quipped in an amiable tone, and stripped before her and tossed his clothes on the floor by the daybed. "Come on, get in, and go to sleep."

"Didn't you bring any pajamas... or, some sweats?" she countered, totally shocked, as she tore off her clothes and found her nightgown in the dark.

"Yeah... I did, but..."

"But, nothing, boy," she laughed in a whisper, "at least put on some pants."

"Yeah, okay," he mumbled, fishing for a pair of sweat pants in his duffel bag at the bedside without getting up. Finding them, he pulled the sweats under the covers to her satisfaction, and motioned for her to join him.

His hot length of skin sent another wave of desire through her, and she chuckled and nipped his chest to chastise him for not having put on the pants he'd found.

"You are really making this hard, for me," she fussed, pushing him away.

"No, correction," he whispered, strategically placing her hand against him, "you are really making this hard for me."

Another deep moan and a loud female gasp from the room next door, followed by the unmistakable rhythmic squeak of springs, made them put their foreheads together and laugh under the covers.

"Oh, my God," Colette whispered, "I can't listen to this."

"From the sound of things, it won't be long now," Franklin chuckled. "I give the brother ten more strokes."

"Shut up, boy... you're terrible!"

Laughter consumed them both, as they burrowed deeper under the covers.

"How're we gonna look Bey and Sandra in the face in the morning?"

Franklin rolled over on his back and pulled the covers down. "After a cold shower and a cup of coffee, I'll be as mean as a hound dog, and it won't matter."

Her laughter joined his as he began counting down and she pinched at his side.

"Ten, nine, eight," he counted, while pushing her hand away, "it's like jazz, all in the syncopation... five,"

"Boy, shut up, before they hear you!" she whispered

through her teeth.

"No they won't," he argued, sitting up, "I could be a marching band, and Bey won't know it until... ... wait a minute, wait a minute... one... done, baby. How much you wanna bet."

"Oh, God, Franklin... there are no words." Colette covered her face with her hands and laughed hard.

"None whatsoever. That's what I've been trying to tell you," he growled, slipping down beside her. "Now, it's our turn."

"Can't we just talk tonight?" she groaned, giving into the hug, but chasing his fingers away from her breast.

"Okay, how about a compromise. You talk, I'll listen, and try to convince you with my mouth not to talk."

"That's not playing fair."

"Uhmmm hmmm," he whispered, from trailing her shoulder down under the covers.

"Just think," she said in a shaky voice, "if it could be like this all the time... if we didn't have to sell this piece of history away, and all of us could come here for the holidays... just like it used to be. Tonight was wonderful."

Her comment made him stop his progressive journey towards her breast, and he brought his mouth up to briefly meet hers. For the first time tonight, and since he'd unloaded his burden on Solomon Whitfield earlier in the day, he remembered his failings.

"Yeah, tonight was the way it was supposed to be," he whispered, then reached down and put on his sweatpants.

"What's the matter?"

"Nothing," he said gently, coaxing her head back against his chest as he reclined. "You were right... this ain't the place."

Chapter Six

The house was so still in the early morning hours. The sense of peace that engulfed him was both a comfort and a plaguing reminder of what had not happened with Colette. Silence gave him time to calibrate his sense of internal balance, but it also gave him time to think. Too much time, in fact.

He loved his wife. That had never been the question. But, how long would it be before she became disillusioned and dissatisfied with his inability to provide for her in the manner that they'd both always dreamed? His business allowing her to raise a family and work in the community... And, worse yet, what if a baby was never created between them... a child, children, to share in a loving home? In truth, he knew that was all she ever wanted. Not money, not elaborate things... but, a family. That was what he loved so dearly about her. The thought he couldn't reconcile was, how long would it be before her disappointment turned into disgust, and she no longer loved him?

Franklin made his way down to the kitchen in the dim morning light, bent on at least keeping the promise to corral the guys to fix a hearty breakfast. He knew that today was actually D-Day, when all laughter would turn to serious business, and he'd have to quietly witness Colette's childhood being dismantled. In his mind, a good meal together might begin the conversation on a brighter note, giving her another pleasant memory in this house before it became somebody else's.

Entering what had been Mom Johnson's sanctuary, he stood at the threshold and stared out toward the well-equipped terrain. Although he was no stranger to flipping pancakes and scrambling a few eggs for a bunch of hungry mouths—his siblings had been excellent boot-camp preparation for that—it was still somewhat intimidating to try his hand at it in this space. After all, this was the nerve center of the Johnson family home.

A large Mason jar on the counter caught his eye, and he moved toward it with pleased expectation. Colette had remembered. Maybe his fears of her beginning to not care about him the way she'd used to had been just that, a fear, not a reality? As he scooped up the wide-mouthed glass container and inspected it, he was right. Sure enough, his baby had set out some of Mom Johnson's peach preserves. It amazed him how such a little thing could bring so much comfort to his embattled spirit.

The thought of that warm, sweet confection poured over buttermilk biscuits inspired him to hunt in the refrigerator for the eggs, and in the freezer for the possibility of sausage. Then a bright idea flashed into his mind. Fish. Fried, country fish, with bacon, eggs, sausage, and fried smokehouse ham slices. It would be perfect for a peace-summit at the dining room table. He was now on a mission.

To his delight, the freezer in the shed-kitchen offered a selection of frozen meats, and there, in ziplock baggies, cleaned and scaled, were several local river caught catfish carcasses that had been preserved for a coming meal. He greedily snatched out two heavy-laden bags, and lifted a ham down from the shed hook, before dashing with his loot toward the sink. Now, the question was, how would he defrost the rock-solid quarry? Mom Johnson didn't own a microwave, as the appliance had seemed to go against her religion.

"Well, guess this will have to be done the old-fashioned way," Franklin mumbled to himself as he worked. Pulling out a bowl, he filled it with hot water, and dropped the bags of fish into it.

"Thought I heard somebody moving around down here," Girard yawned, peering at him through sleepy eyes from the doorway.

"Yeah, man," Franklin returned with a smile, "You know if we don't pull our act together this morning, we'll never hear the end of it."

Girard just nodded, and went over to the coffee maker. "I can't get the mental gears rolling until I've had at least the first cup. How long you been up, anyway?"

Franklin glimpsed at Colette's brother from the corner of his eye as he worked on slicing down the ham. "'Bout an hour."

Girard took his time measuring scoops of dark coffee grounds, and adding water, but somehow, both men knew that Franklin's comment wasn't lost in the mundane chore.

"She's taking this hard, isn't she?" Girard finally murmured, as the smell of coffee began to permeate the kitchen and seemed to wake him up.

"Yup." Franklin's response, though terse, was not intended to offend. There just wasn't a whole lot more than that to be said on the subject.

"You all okay?"

"Can't complain." Again, Franklin knew that the short question was loaded, and he felt like a game of Russian roulette had begun.

"I know my sister."

Franklin declined comment and moved over to the drain-board to begin breaking eggs in a large metal bowl.

"I also know," Girard continued, after an assessment of Franklin's non-response, "that she loves you, man.

Never forget that."

Although Franklin never turned around, he appreciated the statement. "I love her too... more than I can tell
her sometimes."

Girard sat down heavily on a stool and brought his
mug of coffee to his lips. He took a deep slurp, closed
his eyes, and sucked in the aroma that wafted in the
steam above it through his nose.

"Then, why you up so early, and all by yourself?"
Girard murmured through another sip, this time bringing
the cup away from his face and setting it down on the
counter.

For a moment, the two men made eye contact, and
Franklin looked away in the direction of the kitchen window without responding.

"That's the kind of situation that you all haven't been
married long enough to be going through," Girard said in
a low, confidential tone. "That's for me and Nancy, not
you."

Franklin stared at the man.

"Look," Girard said hastily, his line of vision traveling
out of the door before he leaned in toward Franklin
across the butcher block, "I know having to cope with
Deidre being here is probably causing a lot of unspoken
drama between you— but, you've got time." Girard sat
back and picked up his mug again, this time focusing on
the dark liquid before he sipped it. "I used to tell myself
that it didn't matter... and used to tell her that she was
my baby... and, I made it my business to spoil her at
every turn... just like Wilton waits on his wife now, hand
and foot. But, it never fails. Every time one of Nancy's
girlfriends got pregnant, and had a baby shower, or their
kid got a first tooth, my poor wife would go into this deep
funk. And, no matter what I said, what I bought her, or
how I tried to make up the difference, it never made a difference. Got so that time just wore on us, and now, we

live in the same house, but we go our separate ways."

Not knowing how to respond to the confession, Franklin watched the pain etch its way across Girard's normally confident eyes. The hurt that emanated back from them tore at his gizzards. At a loss, and wanting to stop his brother-in-law's suffering, he reached for solutions, none of which felt good as they came to his lips.

"Did you ever think about adopting?" Franklin proposed quietly, and not addressing the part of Girard's statement about going separate ways.

Girard's breath pushed out in a heavy, troubled gush. "She wouldn't hear of it, initially. She wanted to be pregnant herself, to experience a life we created together inside of her. Then, all these legal custody battles started coming into the public eye... and time had begun to harden her outlook on such compromises. Franklin, twenty years ago when we married, they didn't have all these fertility treatments, and new technology. In the last ten years, alone, the industry has taken enormous strides, but, alas, my Nancy is beyond the window of time. Her clock ran out. She'll be fifty in March — and she never forgave me... then, she stopped sleeping with me and wrapped herself up in good deeds done through women's organizations and the sorority. And, I became very discrete."

"Damn," Franklin whispered, not knowing whether or not to walk around the counter and give his brother-in-law a hug, or to head for the hills.

"Yeah," Girard whispered back, "you know how hard it is to love your wife more than anything in the world, but to always feel a wall between you? Or, to watch our good brother, Wilton, pull his wife up to him and rub her belly and kiss it, watching his child move within her... or, to hear your boy, Bey, rocking his girlfriend and her calling his name back, the way your own wife used to? That's why I'm up this morning. I thought I would come into this kitchen and ask Mom what to do."

Franklin looked down at the counter as the last part of what Girard had said trailed off with a raspy tone. Dear God in Heaven, no man should have to suffer like that. Every envious thought he'd ever had about Girard went by the by, and he rounded the counter between them to place a hand on his shoulder.

"Yeah, I do know how it feels, man. You ain't alone, but we're all family and gotta help each other through this kinda stuff."

"When I saw you up... I figured something was wrong with you and Colette. I was up all night, couldn't sleep. From the way you two were acting towards each other last night, before we all went upstairs, your room shouldn't have been that quiet. That's how I knew. Once you've lived it, you know it when you see it."

"You know, counselor," Franklin said in an empathetic and paced manner, avoiding the reference to his problems with Colette, "it may be too late to have the children, but, it might not be too late to bring back the love between you?"

"Hopeful thought." Girard iterated in a monotone voice. "I was going to take Nancy down to the Islands for Christmas, since she can't bear to really deal with that holiday—it's really for kids—and all the hoopla around children... thought I'd get her to relax with me down on the beach. That's why I wanted to dispense with this house, and close this door, too, as quickly as possible. No fuss, no muss."

"Then, that's what you should do, man." Franklin tried his best to sound upbeat, but it was obviously having no effect on Girard.

"It's not that simple, although, it could be. Me and Nancy have all the furniture and things we need, and money is not a problem. Bey don't want nothin' but cash—as he's a glass and chrome kinda guy," Girard said with a sad chuckle. "Wilton and Deidre might want a few sentimental items, but, by and large, with a baby on the way, they need to begin a trust fund. Her parents already set them up well, in a very nicely established house on campus when they arranged for Wilton's appointment to the administration. Heavy furniture would just clutter their environment and would not be appreciated."

Girard ticked off his mental laundry list, and Franklin remained quiet, fully understanding that the man had been wrestling with how to dispense of things for a long time. Suddenly, the burden of the responsibility of it all seemed to momentarily eclipse his own problems with Colette. Solomon Whitfield's comments came back to him. Odd, Franklin mused to himself, as Girard droned on, nothing had been as it had originally seemed to be on the surface. What he had, and didn't have, materially, was quickly becoming irrelevant.

"Nicole... well..." Girard went on, "I thought the photos would help her deal, and being single, she could probably use the cash to help her rainy day fund. She's a minimalist and Swedish-modern type, and always traveling, so, what's she going to do with a big floral sofa, huh? Then, I thought about you guys... an infusion could probably help your business, and maybe some of the more substantial pieces of furniture would help give Colette some peace about this. That's why I was pressing for the sale. It would make everybody happy, give us a knot to evenly divide without argument, and, nobody is prepared to live here, pay the taxes and upkeep on it from afar—plus, the likelihood of family gatherings here, after another year or so, will render the point moot. So, I said to myself, Girard, ole boy, you've gotta sell it. I don't know..."

"It's cool, brother. Whatever you decide, it's cool. Nobody's really financially hurting, and—"

"—But, then, I saw Colette and Nicole's faces," Girard protested. "It's not cool. And, it's not going to go as swiftly and cut-and-dried as I'd hoped. My sisters are still not resolved about the sale, and I don't think I can take having them resent me for the rest of our lives. Not for something like this. Not the same way Nancy has kept the frozen undercurrent between us fed... I can't take it from Nance and them too. Can you understand that?"

"They'll get over it," Franklin offered quietly. "Time is all they need."

"No, Frank, you don't understand. Last night, I could see the change-over beginning to happen to Nancy."

"What do you mean?" Franklin held Girard's gaze.

"She was fine, more relaxed than I've seen her in a long time, until she heard Bey and Sandra. Then, the fortress wall went up. She was already on the verge of a bitch-session when Wil was all hugged-up with sweet D. But, the wine, and the good food sort of pre-empted that battle. I even got to kiss her goodnight," he murmured in a far-away tone. "Then, Bey started, and she began cutting up Wilton, and Deidre. It was the same old litany about how D was a black American princess without a clue, and how Wil was a weak sonofabitch, who couldn't have achieved anything without his wife's family —so why should they take anything out of the house... yada, yada, yada. Then, she started ragging and going off about how she just wanted to get the hell out of this house. Then she turned on Colette and Nicole, saying they had everything in the world already, and had been spoiled rotten, so why did they need to be worrying about some old stuff that didn't even have real antique value. It was ugly. The only one she didn't have anything to say about was you. I won't tell you what she said about that little girl Bey brought in here. Poor child doesn't stand a chance, now that Nancy has grown fangs again."

"That's deep, brother... I don't know what to tell you."

"Trust me," Girard sighed, then walked over to get a pan for the sliced ham, "when Nancy comes down this morning, she'll be finding fault with everyone and everything."

Franklin shook his head, and let out his breath slowly. "And, that's only going to make Bey snap, and start cussin' and fussin' and drinkin'... and Deidre will be in tears, and Wilton will call his Momma and get her in the middle of it. Man, oh, man."

"And, my sister, Colette, will insist on going through this house with a fine-toothed comb to be sure that nothing of sentimental value is left in it before the realtors come... and, we'll have to get a restraining order on Nicole to keep her from squaring off with Nancy, the dining room."

"And, my wife, your sister, will be done until the end of time. You know Colette. When she's through with you, she's done—and, that's gonna make it real hard for all of us to ever get together under anybody's roof again. We gotta solve this, man. And, you've gotta talk to your wife before she comes down here loaded for bear. I know it'll be hard, and I understand, now, why she is the way she is, but everybody's nerves are on edge. It's going to take time for them to even accept that this stuff in this house has to go up the highway."

"Can I be honest with you," Girard murmured in a low tone, looking up at Franklin like a bewildered child.

The gaze stunned Franklin, and it made him stop all movement.

"I don't know what to do, really. Frank, Nana never had a will. There is no will. She made me the executor, but didn't write anything down. About six months ago, she started talking about missing Grandpop, then called me into her bedroom and had me sit on the side of the bed. Me and Colette knew then that it wouldn't be long.

We never said anything to Nicole. We didn't want her to be afraid, like we were, especially since she was alone. Colette had you. I was the eldest, and a man. That's the way it is."

Franklin's mind tore at the facts and recompiled a million pieces of fragmented conversations with Colette in one instant. His wife knew... she had been afraid... terrified of losing the last parent, and not having given any of them a child as a gift, a remembrance that the line would go on... afraid that there would be no mother, or grandmother, to seek womanly advice from while pregnant... no one to share the secrets of mothering a child in the expert way her own mother and grandmother raised multiple generations... and no grandma days for her child down at the house in Maryland... no summers of fun and pure innocent glee... no repeat of what had made her who she was to pass on to her own. Time had run out, in Colette's mind, and he now understood that, the grieving had really started way back then. If Girard's voice hadn't been so compelling, he would have bound up the stairs and swept Colette in his arms, just to let her know that he'd be there for her, even when the elders could not.

"Man," Franklin whispered, swallowing hard, "you'll do the right thing—by them, and Mom Johnson."

"But, all she'd say was, follow your heart, son. Be fair, and be honest, and keep the family together—and don't let 'em fight like dogs over these scraps of me and your grandfather. I'm countin' on..."

Girard's voice broke, and two large tears filled his eyes and spilled down against his robust, dark face. All authority had gone out of him, and only the man-child remained. Franklin's full embrace seemed to make his shoulders shake, but no sound ever came from Girard as he struggled against the deep well of emotions and gripped onto his dignity in silence.

"The old lady is gone, man," Girard finally whispered, then pulled away from Franklin, rubbed his face hard and stood, his authority having returned instantly. "I'm sorry... it just messes me up, sometimes. They broke the mold... they just broke the freakin' mold. Both Mom, and now, Nana."

"I know, brother," Franklin whispered. "Let's make breakfast."

Chapter Seven

"You don't need to talk to my lady like that, Nancy," Bey warned as he reached for his second helping from the platter of eggs.

"It's just that, this is family business we're conducting here, and I should think that all non-family members would understand the need to remove themselves from the conversation upon their own volition."

"Thanks for setting out the peaches for me, honey," Franklin interjected, trying to stave off a battle between Bey, Sandra, and Nancy.

"I didn't put out any peaches," Colette quipped, her ire growing as she watched Nancy's pseudo control of the discussion.

Franklin glanced at her nervously. It was in the way his wife snatched up the orange juice container, and set it down just a little too hard before she spoke. He could tell she was near the edge.

"There weren't any peach preserves left, just strawberry. I checked yesterday when I went in the pantry to get the ingredients to make the pies."

Colette's precise diction concerned him.

"And, good pies they were indeed," Girard mumbled through a mouthful of fish, aiding Franklin's attempt to restore civility.

Oh, yeah, Franklin thought, Girard felt it too.

"Well, somebody around here knows peach is my favorite, and I thank you."

The combatants glanced around the room at each other, then dismissed Franklin's comment.

"Well, I would have brought you some up from Virginia, had I known," Deidre added in tentatively, joining the peace-keeping forces. "And, thanks, Colette, for leaving that delicate old christening gown out on the window seat for me and Wilton this morning. It's beautiful. Where did you find it... was it yours, or Nicole's, when you were a baby?"

Confusion captured Colette for a moment, but before she could answer that she didn't leave it, and hadn't seen it, Nancy was on Deidre like a summer wasp.

"First of all, I thought we had all agreed not to start moving things until Girard had gone through the paperwork and final wishes. So, why anyone is leaving things for people, is beyond me."

Colette opened and closed her mouth, stopping her first reaction to curse Nancy out. "I didn't leave the christening gown. I didn't even know Nana had put one up for any of us to use when we had children."

"Well, since that doesn't look like an eventuality for either you or me, Colette, then I guess it doesn't really matter—but, there is the principle of the situation."

Fury tore through Colette, as well as gashed at a very tender, and very secret wound within her. Her gaze narrowed on Nancy. That bitch...

"Gooood Morning," Nicole crooned as she slipped into the dining room. "You brothers sure have been burning, and something smells so good!"

Nicole swept past the group, clutching a small photo, and went to wrap her arms around her brother who was seated at the head of the table.

"I love you, Girard," she said with a peck on his cheek, hugging him from behind and closing her eyes. "How did you know this was my favorite picture in the whole house?" She turned the photo over for him to inspect, her eyes glistened with tears of appreciation and joy. "Oh, look at us," she nearly whispered, stooping down beside him. "Nana in the middle on the front steps, you behind her whittling, Colette sitting next to her holding the hair grease—with a fresh done head of plaits, and me in-between Nana's knees, my face all scrinched up, getting mine done. If that doesn't say it all... One day, I'm going to gather up all of these pictures, and do a documentary with interviews of the people who lived in this little town for generations. Oh, Girard... I just love you so much for this."

Bewildered, Girard held the photo in his hands, and looked down at it. "This was on the mantle when we all went upstairs. I didn't leave it."

"Oh, pullease, Girard," Nancy hissed. "You have always spoiled that girl, and it's time to stop. You are going against your own word that nothing in here would be moved, or decided, without group consent. Now, everybody is going for self, collecting stash, and—"

"—What's it to you, Nancy?" Colette fired. "Truth be told, you ain't family!" On that note, she stood, and grabbed her plate and pushed back her chair. "If my brother, Girard, wants to give my sister, Nicole, a picture from our grandmother, it is none of your business. And, if my cousin, Wilton, wants to give his wife, Deidre, a christening gown he found on my grandmother's window seat, it's none of your business. And, if my other cousin, Beynard, wants to share the proceeds of my grandmother's house with his girlfriend, Sandra, it's none of, your, business!"

"It is my business!" Nancy shrieked, standing to follow Colette into the kitchen, "because, my husband, Girard, is the executor of all of your so-called business!"

"No, the hell it isn't!" Nicole screamed behind her, fleeing Girard's side, and following the procession of angry kitchen-bound marchers.

"And, what would you know about the disposition of property, and wills, and legal matters?" Nancy countered, spinning on Nicole, who slid to a halt before her. "You have never been married, never buried anyone without dissolving into a useless heap at the funeral, and definitely have never coordinated anything of magnitude on your own in your life."

"C'mon, y'all, don't fight like this," Deidre begged, searching the faces of the men who seemed to have decided telepathically to steer clear of the fray.

"You're no better," Nancy yelled in Deidre's direction. "Your parents are still here handling everything for you, including your husband!"

"What!" Deidre seethed through her teeth as she wobbled to get up.

"That's enough," Girard warned under his breath in his wife's direction.

"Don't you dare take their side against me—at least not in public!" Nancy's eyes had narrowed to slits as she'd spoken. But, the fact that Girard never lost eye contact with her and had stood up was not lost on the group.

"That's right, you'd better put your woman in check, Brother," Wilton volleyed back in an unsure tone, then seemed to withdraw when both Nancy and Girard turned quickly to glare him down.

"Now, you have gone too far!" Colette yelled as she paced from the kitchen entrance back into the dining room, marching up to Nancy with her sister, Nicole, on her heels. "My brother may not put you in check, but I will. Don't you ever yell at D when she's pregnant, heifer!"

Franklin could tell that Bey and Sandra's smug glances across the table had ignited the situation beyond the point of no return, and had made retreat now impossible for either contestant. Weighing his options, Franklin stood up.

"What did you call me?" Nancy's expression was incredulous, and her voice came out like a low, quiet growl of a guard dog.

"You heard her," Nicole warned in a slow rumble of her own, and angling for the battle that had been long overdue.

Then, there was a moment of silence, just like the seconds before a tornado impact.

"That's enough, y'all. Let it rest," Franklin interceded. "Nobody meant any harm with the small things that got moved. And, there was no need to call Nancy out of her name, Cole. Everybody chill."

What he was not prepared for was the glare of pure rage that filled Colette's eyes as she stared in his direction. If looks could kill, he would have been laid out cold.

"You're standing here, callin' yourself my husband, and takin' this heifer's side? Are you crazy, Franklin Morris?" Colette's voice was barely audible, but the message was clear. It was on.

"Oh damn..." Sandra and Bey whispered, lowering their eyes and seeming to brace for an unwanted ricochet turn of events.

"Look, Big Sis, Franklin didn't mean no harm," Nicole tried to sooth, coming between Franklin and Colette.

"Get from between me and my husband," Colette whispered through her teeth, "now."

Although Nicole moved away, it was Nancy who stood her ground with haunting satisfaction. She crossed her arms over the chest, creating a slight ripple in her peach silk robe.

"Isn't pleasant to have your husband side with someone else, is it?" Nancy spat out in a venomous tone, "You'll get used to it. Even in public." It was a double-edged, Wilkinson's stainless steel blade that Nancy unsheathed, and it cut down both Colette and her brother in one fell swoop.

"Listen Cole, this is not the place—"

"—No, it isn't," Colette said to him calmly. Too calmly. "Just like it wasn't last night."

When Franklin stepped away from her, she'd been prepared to win the verbal confrontation with him, but nothing could have prepared her for the sheer hurt that etched its way across his face. In the second that followed her lethal interjection, she wished that she could have taken it back. She was hurt, too, and angry, and enraged that he would side with Nancy—but totally unprepared for his reaction to being gored in public. They'd never fought that way—ever. What was worse, was her brother's look of pain as he hung his head and moved away from the table.

It had been a total verbal massacre, and everyone instinctively seemed to know that the battle was over. One by one they each filed out of the room, leaving dishes and food on the table, and heading for a private healing corner of the house. It was time to get dressed and go visit Miss Julia—alone.

Chapter Eight

Ice crunched beneath Colette's feet as she trudged to Miss Julia's house. Somehow, the brisk pace and stinging cold helped to diffuse her anger. After about a hundred yards, her stride began to slow, just as her patterns of speech had effortlessly transitioned back to her mother-tongue once she felt at home. She took in the serene landscape with newfound reverence. Why did any of them have to leave from place?

It was so still and pretty out here, she thought, passing the old Tilman farm and stopping briefly at their gate. Two fat lazy cows roamed in the enclosure and her mind grazed with them, remembering where she'd received her first awkward kiss from Junior Tilman on the front porch after a summer dance. She wondered what had happened to all those kids? Did each child in the town eventually pull away from it to seek their fortunes in the bright lights of the big city? Did they still come home for the holidays, married, with children, returning to the loving arms of parents and grandparents who had held onto this little piece of Heaven for them all?

Colette dragged herself away from the momentary replay of her childhood, and began walking again. Small crystalline flakes had begun to fall, lightly dusting all that was beneath them, and clinging ever so gently to her lashes. Even with the frozen dirt under her feet, the ground felt softer than city streets.

People had it all wrong, she mused, thinking of how

different a snowfall impacted her urban place in the world. True, cities had their conveniences, like buses and trains and easy access to airports and cabs, but there was a softness, if not a tenderness here, that couldn't be denied.

In the city, it seemed, things were physically easier. Flat pavements, street lights to organize crossings, corner stores that stayed open all night, transportation, and a million options of different things to eat, and do. One didn't have to thaw out, or catch, food. You could pick up the telephone and order any type of cuisine, at nearly any hour, from any nationality.

But, here, one had to work at the basics. There were no right-around-the-corner stores. Sometimes, the power went out, and it could be days before the problem was resolved—which meant firewood was essential, and even that had to be chopped and brought in. One had to be physically fit to deal with the long, unpaved stretches between homesteads, she noted as she trudged along. You had to be self-contained on a snowy day, finding ways to amuse yourself in the home with books, and mending, and music. If you had a television, you'd better have cable out here, she chuckled to herself, because the nearest, and poorly stocked, video rental store was in the center of town, along with the gas station, the bed and breakfast, a tiny one-star motel for the en-route-to-somewhere-else-truckers, the diner, the supermarket, the bar and pool hall, the hardware store, general store, tobacco shop, and a plethora of little one-product shops, down the street from the school.... and, of course, the church. There was no mall.

However, it was still, oddly, easier. For all of the inconveniences, there were also no sirens, and loud voices, and constant on-guard fears to keep one stiff and mean. People sort of meandered about, and that was okay, because nobody rushed to get to, or to do, any-

thing. The pace, Colette told herself, that was it, the
pace was different. Here, the physical amenities
required near athletic stamina, but your soul was always
at rest. There, in the city, you had every material and
physical want at your disposal, but your soul could die of
starvation in the midst of frenetic, joy-less activity.

She stopped briefly to catch her breath as she made
it up Miss Julia's path. The frigid weather and long hike
had almost stripped the air from her lungs by the time
she'd reached her destination but, yet, it felt good.

"My, my, my," Miss Julia exclaimed as she opened
the front door, "Now ain't you a sight for sore eyes!
Come in here, baby," she laughed, scooping Colette into
her wide arms and half smothering her with ample
breasts. "Dis here is my Christmas present."

Colette laughed and gave the elderly woman a deep
hug before wriggling away so that she could breathe.
"I've been so remiss. You're the first person I shoulda
come to see... but, there was a lot going on the first day.
How've you been?"

Miss Julia sucked her dental plate and flipped her
wrist to dismiss the concept.

"Honey chile, you all have plenty to contend with. I
knew you'd get to me when the time was right. Now, let's
get you some hot tea, and a little somethin' on your stomach, then we can catch up. C'mon into the kitchen. I'm
workin' on some pies."

Colette giggled as she followed Miss Julia into the
kitchen, knowing that one had to eat as a visitor's right-
of-passage, or major offense would be taken. Down
here, food symbolized love, friendship, caring, and could
even stand witness as an apology between neighbors.
You had to sit down and take your time, and highly compliment all of the superb chefs that labored on the way-
farer's behalf in their alchemy chambers with love.

Entering the small warm room, her eye spotted a

basket on the linoleum table filled with a little wiggling thing that gurgled. Anticipation swept through her, and she took off her coat quickly and rushed to the basket, while silently hoping that Miss Julia wasn't in the process of preparing a chicken for dinner.

"A baby!" Colette exclaimed as she moved closer to the basket. "Oh, whose, Miss Julia? Juney had another baby?"

Miss Julia chuckled and came up behind Colette to peer into the basket with her.

"No, this ain't Juney. Dat boy don't need to make no more younguns. Him and Cherl already got six, and about to drive me outta my natchel mind with 'em all running around here."

Colette giggled and leaned into the basket as the baby curled a fat fist around her pinky finger and hung on.

"She likes you," Miss Julia cooed. "Ain't she just a precious angel."

"Oh, yes..." Colette whispered, looking down into the round, wide eyes and chubby little face that greeted her with a smile. "Just look at this child..."

The elderly woman let her breath out slowly, and moved to the stove, then brought Colette a hot biscuit with jam and tea. "Beautiful little thang almost didn't make it here, and didn't half stand a chance," she sighed, turning Colette's attention away from the baby's face for a moment to stare at her.

"Triflin' mother," Miss Julia explained with defeat, going back to her post at the sink. "You know, Juney lives here with me, since Paul passed. Him and Cherl didn't have nowhere to go, and he used to look in on your Grandmaw, and old man Tilman. My other younguns been tryin' to coax dem two to follow behind them to Washington, but, Juney stays here to look out for me and Miss Pat, Cherl's Momma. Her Momma's my other best

friend, next to Ester, who's gone now. She got three
daughters of her own, all livin' in the city with their kids
living with her. Ester woulda took the baby, when
Reverend came to us with her. But, then, Ester closed
her eyes."

"But, where's the baby's parents?" Colette asked,
unable to follow the long weaving trend of the explanation. In reflex while still standing, she bit into the biscuit
and sipped the tea—her finger still locked in the baby's
grip.

"Drugs. Died on that crack. Don't know how, but the
Lord spared the chile any defect. The girl passed right
before her Momma. Some say, seeing the daughter die,
killed the mother. They don't know who or where the
father is... and, I suspec' he ain't worth findin'—so,
Reverend brought her to Ester, then to me after Ester
passed. If it hadn't been for the fact that Juney looked in
on Ester every day, and Solomon Whitfield told that he
hadn't seen Ester that morning when he delivered the
mail, that po' chile mighta cried herself to death and coulda starved in the house all by her lonesome."

Colette sat down slowly, and could only stare at the
elderly woman who was now lacing pie-crust with apples.
"But, Miss Julia," she whispered, ignoring her tea and
biscuit. "You've got so many children of your own, and
they have children... and all of the town is mostly grand-
mothers and seniors, all of whom have a lot of grandchildren to watch. Didn't the girl have any sisters or
brothers who'd take the baby?"

"Not a one left livin'," Miss Julia said with a huff. "The
city kilt 'em all, that's why her Momma took to her bed
and called upon Jesus to bring her home."

Miss Julia stopped her pie-making and looked at
Colette. "You know, me with my arth-a-ri-tis, and Pat,
with her bad hip... and, all our chillen barely makin'
due... we couldn't put this baby on a generation down.

So, me, I said, da Lord don't put no more on ya, den ye kin bear. And, I figured, I'm not long for Glory, myself, so, I best not be turning away no lamb of da flock. You know what I mean?" Before Colette could speak, she went on. "When ole Rev brought this bundle to me, I said, Now Julia Davis, dis here might jus' be your last blessin' from above. You never know what's in a chile of God. Amen. So, I signed them papers to keep her. And, that's all there is to tell about it."

The firm dignity and sureness with which Miss Julia had spoken made Colette sit up straighter in her chair. She searched the lined dark face to understand where the well of strength came from, fully knowing that this was how black people had made it from slavery to freedom. Unconditional love, extended families, people going above and beyond and making a way out of no way. And, with that glimpse into the strength of age and wisdom before her, came her shame. How meaningless had all of her family squabbles been in the face of such adversity, and unwavering faith?

"Let me bring you some things from the house, at least," Colette murmured, not knowing what else to say.

"Chile!" Miss Julia scoffed with a wave of her broad hand. "We don't need a thing."

"But—"

"—But nothin', baby," Miss Julia soothed in her timeless, buttermilk smooth voice. "Your grandmother gave us everything we'll ever need. Like dis here apron, dat I'll cherish till I see her again. And," she said, holding up her hand to stop the protest, "she gave us blankets, and children's clothes for all my grands, not to mention, all her front yard hens. Ester would bring a little gift for each of us at the church every Sunday, that's how we knew she was markin' time. Even gave Juney some tools, so he could keep fixin' people's houses, and work on cars in town. But, most of all, she gave us all of her love while she was here. That's tucked away safe in my heart. She was my best-ever friend. Don't need no mo' den dat."

Colette watched tears well up, and then fade away from the old woman's eyes that shined with unashamed emotion.

"I miss her, too," Colette whispered.

"We all do, baby, but that's jus' how life goes. It was her season, and she lived a good, clean Christian life— so, the Father called her home." Julia Davis crossed the small kitchen and placed a warm thick palm against Colette's cheek. "Now, you lissen here," she whispered. "Ester ain't gone, she right there with you like an angel on your shoulder. I talk to her all da time."

"You do?" Colette murmured, covering the gnarled hand with her own.

"Oh, yes, siree!" Miss Julia chuckled, removing her hand from Colette's cheek to dab the corners of her eyes. "In fact, I fussed hard at Ester the other day when this here chile was ballin'. I said, Ester Johnson, you the one named after the good woman in the Bible, the one who supposed to be watchin' babies past your season. You the one who done raised fine, educated children, with good children of they own—so, you the expert, not me," she laughed again. "So, why I gots to be the one here with this squawlin' little thing? You were the calm one, the smart one. Me, I was the wild one. So, what I'm supposed to do?"

Colette laughed, trying to conjure up the image of a wild Miss Julia in her mind, to no avail. The image was too incongruent.

"Well," Colette chuckled, "you still are a looker, Miss Julia, and have enough energy to get Mr. Tilman to help you out, I'm sure."

Miss Julia laughed harder and placed a kiss on Colette's forehead. "Mayhaps I do, chile," she giggled. "But, these days, the only thing that I can do to warm him

up and git his motor runnin', is to bring him a hot pie.
Now, a few years ago, mighta been able to intres' him wit
somethin' else."

The shock that swept through Colette had obviously
registered plainly on her face, because Miss Julia's
response to it was to laugh even harder.

"Now, jus' 'cause we seniors don't mean that all the
life done gone outta our bones. A man is still a man," she
chuckled, moving back toward the stove. "Speakin' of
which, how's that Franklin of yours?"

Before Colette could formulate an answer, Miss Julia
began again. "Now, that's a man," she pronounced. "A
good one. Hard-workin', kind, responsible, good-lookin',
too. Ester tol' me all about him. Wish my own dang kids
had followed suit. Been tellin' Juney to get over there
and talk to your Franklin, while y'all here, so maybe he
could learn himself a thing or two 'bout auto-mechanics,
and could learn how to open his own real business,
instead of piece-mealin' his way through life. Ac'hally,
Franklin could teach a lotta dese fellas dats left 'round
here how to do. You know?"

Colette just nodded, but didn't speak. Too many
thoughts jumped through her mind to sort them out
before Miss Julia started up again.

"Now, you look at this here town," the older woman
warned. "See, all the young has gone out of it, and the
ones dats left, ain't worth a damn, pardon my French,
Jesus. All us grandmaws and grandpaws is raising
babies they made out in the city then bring home, or pro-
vidin' room and board for everybody. The men my
Juney's age, don't know what ta do wit deyselves, and
the women dats left, humpf," she added in disgust.
"Can't tell which is mother or chile."

"There's a few jobs and stores left, Miss Julia. And,
I know Doc Miller still needs help."

"Yeah, I suppose, but ain't nobody to pass on know-

how to. Like, what's gonna happen when old Carter can't
fix cars no mo', or Doc Miller finally retires, like he shoulda ten years ago, or Doc Pearson gives up on doin' people's dentures? An', whose gonna take over Gibson's
General Store, huh, tell me? It's enough we's raising all
the babies, we can't run all the businesses too, and keep
house, and everything, honey. Ain't no replacements.
Sooner or later, everybody gonna haft to travel for miles
to Virginia or Washington to get anythin' done, and at our
age, that's more than a notion."

   "Maybe..." Colette's voice trailed off. What could she
say?

   "We's tired," Julia Davis exclaimed with righteous
determination. "Broke down, like old Georgia cotton
mules. But, we gotta press on, 'cause all dese little
chillen don't have nothin' to do, nothin' to expand dey
minds, and there ain't much recreation we can provide.
Only a few teachers left, and dey don't even teach Negro
history good any more. If we don't watch ourselfs, 'fore
long, this will be a ghost town, and we'll all be turnin' in
our graves watchin' properties get sold, and all the history lost, like what almost happened when Angela
Snowden came."

   "This town used to be so lively, and has so much
potential... that would be a crime," Colette whispered in
agreement.

   "Uhmmm hmmm," Miss Julia confirmed. "Is hal-
lowed ground, too. Did you know that the Indians had it
first, but no tribe claimed it, so they never warred over it.
In fact, they say, no blood ever spilt here in no war. It
was the pass-thru, fer white, black, and red alike, they
believed, from this world to the spirit world. It sat on the
border of three tribes, don't remember which, but it was
considered the safe haven, and it turned out to be so for
colored folk."

   "Didn't the church take it over first?" Colette said in a

distant voice, trying to scavenge the remote facts in her mind.

"Yep, da white Methodists bought these twelve square miles, and it was abolistionist territory, before AME took it over. They willed each parcel to the colored and Indian families that escaped up here, and anointed every property with oil in a big call-on-Jesus ceremony. Made even the Klan scairt to come on people's land, so, anyone who built here felt protected. Strange, but, no matter what was going on, things would happen all around this town, but never to the town. Was only like fifty original families, Johnsons and Davises among 'em. Colors sorta all blended together, 'cause we was all so close-knit. Den, people had children, who married children. Humph," she exclaimed, "probably everybody here's related, in one way or another... so, how'd I know if this pretty little baby girl wasn't one of mine no-way?"

As she stood, Colette gazed at the caramel face and wide brown eyes again, leaning into the basket to kiss the baby's warm cheek. The wafting scent of fresh, new life filled her nostrils, and her arms ached to scoop up the bundle and press the child to her breasts.

"May I," she whispered, looking toward Miss Julia for permission.

"You sure can," Miss Julia graciously offered, "but, be careful, she'll grow on you."

Reaching down ever so tentatively, Colette slid her hands under the child's body, supporting the wobbly head with her palm. She cradled the infant against her, nuzzled her face against the tender flesh, and breathed in the child's scent with a sigh. "Oh, you are such a beautiful gift to the world, and so lucky to have a Mom-mom Julia to raise you up," she cooed, "God bless you, little one." Tears blurred her vision, and Colette carefully returned the infant in the basket, knowing that a stronger dose of holding her would make it impossible to part with her.

"Look like you a natchel," Miss Julia beamed.
"Holdin' a baby like dat, when you jus' married, they say,
brings on good luck. I'ma say me a prayer, or two, on it.
Just keep da faith, chile."

Somehow, the old woman's words brought a sense
of immediate comfort that she could have only received
from her own Nana's mouth. Colette knew that what
Mrs. Julia Davis had said was not only a blessing, but a
promise, that had been given to her in that simple statement. It was a commitment to contact God directly on
her behalf, and to pray that a child would come into her
and Franklin's lives... a perfect baby, at the right time...
and knowing that she'd receive said blessing, she could
go back to the house filled with spirit and patience. An
elder woman-shaman-survivor had filled her body with
food, her mind with history, and her soul with hope, and
only an elder from back home could perform such
kitchen magic... this was what she'd needed from Nana.
Colette considered the sense of community and lineage
that went back countless generations. They were indeed
all one family, one tribe, and one enduring testimony of
survival.

"Well, Miss Julia," she said quietly, "I need to get
back and start the process that I came down here for."

"But, you hardly touched your tea, and just took one
pitiful bite of that biscuit."

She looked at the old woman's crestfallen face, and
crossed the room to hug her.

"I'll be back," Colette promised, "and, I won't be
empty-handed. I'll have some of Ester's strawberry preserves for you. There's plenty to share. Franklin ate up
the one jar of peaches he found."

"Now, for that, and the company, I'd be much
obliged," Miss Julia murmured, squeezing Colette to her
harder. "Nobody made preserves as well as our Ester.

But, I'm surprised Franklin found peaches," she said with a puzzled look. "We only put up strawberry this year." She dismissed the thought with a smile. "No matter."

"And, my manners are really long gone," Colette added with shame, "I didn't even thank you for filling up the freezer, and cleaning the house so nice. You didn't have to go to the trouble... making all those beds... We really appreciated it, honestly."

Miss Julia laughed, and kissed her. But her expression contained a hint of curiosity.

"Baby, now you know, I can't take the credit for all-a that. Me and Pat sent Juney to go fetch the laundry, and we had him carry everything back to the house. We told him to deliver my note when he did—put it on the fridge to letcha know the laundry was done. He just put away the linens in the closet like we asked him to, knowing y'all was comin,' and had him put a few little odds and ends in the ice box for ya, that we pulled together—but, we didn't go to no lengths. Was anything missing? Why, I'll tan that boy's—"

"—Oh, no!" Colette assured her, becoming alarmed that such a concept would ever enter Miss Julia's mind. "I guess we have Juney to thank, then, for not only salting the driveway, but for cleaning up the entire house. I just assumed it was you?"

"Do, say..." Miss Julia began slowly, her gaze becoming distant. "Naw, my Juney wouldn't clean no house, not even for a million dollars. And, as to my cleanin,' and such—there was a day when it wouldn'ta been a passin' thought to do for a neighbor... Then came my Arthur, which don't allow me to bend and git 'round like I used to, and dear Pat, her hip is so bad, she kin barely make it up da steps. But, lest I forget, lemme give you back the key. Like I said, as to food, we put a few eggs and stuff in there, like I said in that little note— all so's you'd know what was in there. We didn't have to add no meats or can nothin', 'cause you know your grandmother, she had everything put up and ready for the holidays—just like she always did, God bless her soul. You know how she'd put up November greens and freeze 'em... No baby, since Ester was doin' good on her feet, we just didn't think that far."

The two women stared at each other without breaking their embrace.

"The house was spotless," Colette whispered.

"Well," Miss Julia shrugged. "Is it any wonder? That was our Ester."

Chapter Nine

As she made her way up the path towards Nana Johnson's house, Colette paused for a moment. Something was wrong. Where was Girard's black Mercedes, and Beynard's red BMW?

She quickly bounded up the steps, inserted the key in the door, and breezed into the house. Wilton greeted her with an expression on his face that told her not to speak until they could get close enough to one another to whisper. From his reclining position on the sofa, he reinforced the telepathic message by looking up from his laptop computer, briefly casting his line of vision toward the kitchen, and putting his finger to his lips to ensure her silence.

"What happened?" she murmured, as he made room for her to sit next to him. "Where is everybody?"

"Brother is in the kitchen, cleaning up from breakfast. Franklin's out back—and has been out there, chopping wood, for the last hour and a half. Bey, Sandra, and Nicole took Bey's car and went into town to the diner, since everybody refused to eat another meal together. Deidre is finally taking a nap, and I'm going to take her into town to eat when she wakes up soon."

"And, Nancy?" Colette whispered hard. "Where's she?"

"Oh, gurl," Wilton said with a deep rush of air, "She left him."

"What?" Incredulous, Colette leaned into Wilton and

held his arm.

"After you went down to Miss Julia's, Colette, all hell broke loose." Wilton glanced toward the kitchen door, and began again, only when he was convinced that he could speak confidentially. "It's so complicated, I'm not even sure I can pull it all together in the right order. But, here's the best to my knowledge. Nancy and Girard went into their room, and stared hollering and screaming at each other."

"Wait," Colette demanded under her breath, trying to gather her thoughts and picture the scenario. "My brother was hollering?"

"You gonna let me tell you what happened, or keep interrupting until Brother comes in here?" Wilton fussed through his teeth.

"Okay, okay, I'm sorry, but, I just can't imagine..."

"Yeah, neither could we," Wilton admitted. "We all know that things get strained between them two, every now and then, but they were really going at it... bringing up things that shouldn't be said... and, talking divorce."

"What!"

"I said," Wilton reminded her, "let me finish." Once he seemed appeased that she wouldn't interject, Wilton continued. "I didn't think it was my place to go in there, unless it got physical." Wilton ignored the shocked expression on Colette's face, knowing that she now understood just how heated the argument had become between her brother and sister-in-law. "But Bey and Sandra ran down the hall."

"Oh, my God..." Colette couldn't contain herself, the comment had come out from sheer reflex as her hand covered her mouth. "Where was Franklin?"

"Outside, I told you. Now be quiet, I've gotta get through this fast." Receiving Colette's nod, he picked up where he'd left off. "I heard Bey, which I knew was going to boil the pot over. That's when D and I went across the hall into the room. We thought they'd be squared off, but instead, we saw Bey sitting on the edge of the bed, wailing... somebody had left Nana's silver heart locket—with a picture of the four of us when we were boys, on his bed... musta been while we were down at breakfast, and they also left Grandpop's gold pocket-watch on the chair in Bey's room. Sandra was on her knees in front of Bey, trying to get him not to cry, and he was blubbering—I'm telling you, baby-wailing, telling Girard how much the tiny locket-photo meant, how good Nana and Pop had been to raise him, since his own mother was so trifling and his own father had left... all how they was the only family he had, and we were his brothers, not his cousins, in his mind. That's when Nancy went off, stormed out of the room and challenged Nicole."

"Oh, damn...."

This time, Wilton kept pace despite her interjection. "That's what I said. Nicole was packing to leave on the next thing smokin' when Nancy burst in her room, and accused her of giving Bey valuables without telling anybody. Nicole—and you know littl' sis—flipped, claiming she didn't give anybody doodley-squat. Nancy called her a bold-faced liar, and that's when Nicole cussed Nancy out so bad that, even me and Girard had to stop it. That's when Nancy started screaming about how he didn't need to protect her from his bitch sister, then slapped Girard's face, and everything went still."

"Oh. My. God." There were no further words that she could employ as she stared at Wilton.

"I thought Girard was going to deck her, and me and Bey jumped up and grabbed his arms outta instinct. I mean, it was the look in his eye... I've never seen Girard's face look like that. Then he left the room, and came down to the kitchen. Nancy grabbed her suitcase and headed for Miss Ruth's bed and breakfast in town. Me, Bey, and Deidre ran behind Girard, but he told us to

get away from him, it was over. Nicole went out back to
get Franklin to talk to Girard, but he said, it was married
folks' business, and this was a long time comin' – and he
kept choppin' wood. Baby-doll, this is the worst it's ever
gotten in this family."

"And, you're in here doing University work, instead of
talking to Girard?" Colette stood up with disgust.

"I'm working on my novel, if you must know," Wilton
hedged defensively. "It's the only thing that gives me any
peace any more."

She stared at her cousin. "Your novel? Since
when—"

"—Since my wife's family took over my life!" he suddenly yelled, breaking the whispered exchange. "Every
man has to have something to claim as his own—to be
proud of accomplishing on his own. Yes, even quiet,
book worm, fat Wilton, okay!"

Again, all she could do was stare at her cousin as he
now stood and glared at her. "Wilton," she began quietly, "I never—"

"—Never thought it mattered, huh, Colette? Never
thought I had any dreams or aspirations, or even a god-
damned backbone! Never thought me and Deidre
haven't gone through our problems, or ever thought
about what's it's like to have your whole career decided
for you, and to not be able to touch your wife for a year
because she might lose the baby you've had to go to a
fertility specialist to make? I'm going to the diner after I
get D up, and we may even stay in the hotel in town. I
hate this house, and don't want a thing from it—not the
money, not the furniture, and not the memories, nothing.
Bey, and Nicole said the same thing, as did, ironically
enough, Nancy. Funny how things work out," he raged
through his teeth, then spun on his heels and stormed up
the steps.

She stood in the middle of the living room floor for a

moment, trying to process everything that had been said, and had occurred, and every emotion that the series of outbursts had invoked. What was happening to her family? Girard's slamming of pots and pans drew her into the kitchen.

Entering the room quietly, she slipped in and found a perch on one of the tall stools. From her seat, she watched him move around without speaking, fully knowing that he was aware of, but ignoring her presence.

"Rough morning," she murmured, in a feeble attempt to coax him into a conversation.

"So, you've heard," he grumbled back, working without making eye contact.

"You need to go get her," she whispered. "She's hurting bad, I'm sure."

"And I'm not!" he yelled in a sudden outburst. "I'm not?"

"You both are, and have been," she said calmly, keeping her voice even. Standing, she walked over to the wounded bear that was her brother, and risked getting bitten. But, for some reason, she was not afraid. Years of watching Nana heal hurts ebbed into her cellular memory, and she reached for her brother despite his protests, wrapping his rigid form in her arms. "Go to her, Girard, and tell her how much you need her to be in your life."

His body grew stiffer, yet his voice gave way to a gravelly tone when he attempted to argue. That's when she knew for sure, there was hope.

"There's too much water under the bridge, Colette." His voice quavered and he took deep breaths in between each word. "It's not all her fault, either."

"I know," she whispered against his shoulder, "and it's not all yours, either."

Her comment drew his arms around her, and he released deep breaths of attempted emotional control against her hair.

"I wasted so much time, Cole... I started off doing what I loved. I should have kept working on civil rights claims with the NAACP. But, it didn't pay well. Ambition took hold of me, and I told her we should wait until I got a better job. And, she listened to me. Then, high-stakes corporate law got good to me... it possessed me, and the adrenaline rush, and feeling of power when I won a big case. I was moving up, made partner, then senior part-ner, and she was always there—the perfect executive's wife, assisting my career rise, and every year that went by, I kept saying, not yet, when the time's right... until we ran out of time, and she started hating me. She had a right to, because I cheated her out of creating life itself... I got the things I wanted, but never stopped long enough to realize, all she ever wanted was children. All the mate-rial possessions and fat bank accounts were what I needed to make me feel whole. I was so afraid of not making the grade, not living up to her and her family's expectations, and being thought of as some country bumpkin..."

Colette rubbed her brother's back and swayed against him in the timeless rocking rhythm that soothes the soul of even the most savage beast. She closed her eyes and said a mental prayer, and in that moment, she saw her own Franklin's struggle. The image was so clear, so recognizable that, it brought tears to her eyes. "Go to her, Girard. Go bring your wife home for the hol-idays."

"I can't," he whispered. "She won't have me, and I don't blame her. I can't remember the last time I even touched my wife... got so that I started working late, but she knew what that meant... even though I only go out like that now, maybe once every coupla months... still. There's so much water under the bridge. I can't even admit it to you, let alone myself."

Colette held her brother back and looked at him tenderly. "Do, or did, you love any of them?" she asked in a quiet, but firm tone.

"No," he confessed, then dropped his gaze. "All I want for Christmas is my wife back."

"Then," she murmured, tracing his tears away from his face with her forefinger. "I suggest you go downtown and pick up your present."

"Now, Girard Johnson, boy, come on over here and give Miss Ruth a hug!"

Girard leaned across the front counter of the bed and breakfast inn, forced a smile and complied, trying his best to camouflage his distress and nervousness about having to inquire about his wife's whereabouts.

"Oh, my goodness, it's so good to see you," the elderly lady exclaimed, rounding the desk, and bringing him a key. "Now, lookie here," she whispered, "it ain't my bizness, but I'm an old wida woman, and kin see what don' hafta be said. You go on upstairs and tend to ya wife. She came in here all upset and cryin', and I know she love you, 'cause she wouldn'ta been a-weepin' her eyes out, tryin'ta act all reserved, and what not, if she didn't... and, I know Ester Johnson's boy ain't do nuthin' too despicable to no woman. So. There's hope. Mr. Whitfield even brought her your letters. So. I know you wanta re-open a conversation with her, and she don't look like da type to be runnin' on 'er husband. So. Like I said. Dere's hope."

The intimacy of the town wore on his nerves, but in that moment, all he could do was accept the key with grace, kiss the old lady's forehead, and quicken his pace up the steps to find his wife.

Nancy let out her breath in exasperation as she

heard the key in the door. The old woman who ran the place had practically talked her ear off with non-requested Biblical marital advice, given that it was slow season—and all Mystic Ridge visitors were staying with family members, and not another guest was around to distract her. She wiped her face with the backs of her hands, and then quickly folded the letters in her lap.

When Girard's form entered the room, a wave of relief washed over her. New tears filled her eyes, and this time she allowed them to drop without censure.

"I read your letters," she whispered to him as he closed the door and faced her.

"I didn't write any letters," he managed, not moving from where he stood.

"Yes, you did," she murmured, standing up, and grasping the envelopes, as well as a small purple ribbon. She extended the evidence in her hands for him to inspect, but stayed close to him. "You wrote your Nana all the time ... and told her how much you loved me... and asked her advice ... and told her how sorry you were that no grandchildren were on the way."

As she kept her gaze fixed upon him, he reached out and touched the moisture on her cheeks and trailed his fingers in them. "I felt so guilty, baby... I wanted Nana to tell me something, anything at all, that I could fix this ... that I could give you something, anything to make up for it ... I even prayed to God, but He didn't hear me ... and, I asked Nana to help Him hear me ..."

She brought her fingers to his lips and stopped the flow of words, then replaced her fingers with her mouth for the first time in many, many years.

Chapter Ten

Colette kept stirring the large pot of homemade soup that had absorbed her thoughts as she listened to the sound of the back door banging open. She didn't flinch, or look up from the steaming vessel as a cold blast of air whipped about her.

"Mighty chilly out there," she remarked casually, stirring the rich mixture of ham chunks, lima-beans, and vegetables. "Want a warm up?"

"I'll be just fine," Franklin grunted, hauling an armload of wood through the door into the living room.

The heavy thud of timber hitting the fireplace traveled into the kitchen, and she smiled. "Was that you, or the wood? Even a workhorse's gotta eat, or fall down dead."

"I told you, I'm fine," he bellowed, then paced across the floor and out to the back yard.

"That you are," she yelled behind him in a good-natured tone.

When he came in again, his pace had slowed a bit, but she could tell that he was still very annoyed.

"Two bowls are in the dining room, with some hot tea and biscuits. Care to join me, or, are you going to go to the diner like everybody else did, and leave me here all by myself?"

Although he didn't answer, this time, he closed the back door, and kicked the snow off his boots and grabbed a mop. She watched him from the corner of her eye as he cleaned up the chunks of packed snow that had fallen on the floor, returned the mop to the shed kitchen, and took off his coat, cap, and gloves, carefully placing them on the radiator to dry. Still, without a word, he went to the sink, washed his hands, and then went into the dining room. She smiled from the doorway between the rooms as he stood at the table for a moment, looked confused, then relaxed—seeming quietly pleased that she had put a bowl at the head of it where Girard normally sat.

Colette slid into the seat adjacent to him and bowed her head, and said the short meal-time prayer that had been ingrained in her since childhood. When she looked up, he dropped his gaze down to his bowl and began to heartily devour its contents.

"Need to talk to you, Franklin," she said in a slow easy manner.

"Can't a man eat in peace, Colette?" he grumbled through a slurp, then broke off a piece of biscuit and sopped at the thick concoction in his bowl.

"Been owing you an apology," she said plainly, glimpsing him from the corner of her eye.

His grunt was all the affirmation she required, and his moodiness made her smile widen—despite her attempts to hide it.

"You know, sometimes a woman can be wrong," she said casually, and his scoff made her chuckle.

"She can be wrong for a long, long time, did you know that?"

"We can just let sleepin' dogs lie," him mumbled. "It's squashed."

"Naw," she countered, chuckling when he cast a glare in her direction, "a dog that sleeps too long can get up mighty evil in the morning."

"Now, what's that supposed to mean?" he huffed, then washed down his mouthful of biscuit with a swig of tea.

"Means that, a woman can be wrong for like... I don't know, six months, or more, and not even know it."

He stared at her for a moment, then went back to his soup.

"Then, if she's not careful, six months can go to a year, which can go into many years... and, then, the dog either gotta runaway to get fed, or gotta be put outta its misery, once it's gone mad and turned."

"Colette, I'm not getting into your brother's business. Girard's a grown man, and—"

"—And, I'm not talking about Girard and Nancy."

"So, what, then? Me and you?"

"Anybody else in this house?"

"I can't rightly say. Been outside minding my own beeswax."

She laughed, and began eating her soup.

"Yeah, guess a person could, and should, mind their own business, but, in this town, that's hard to do."

He glimpsed up at her, then stood, taking his empty bowl into the kitchen. She could hear him dishing himself another bowl, and she waited for him to come back and sit down before she continued.

"Seems like nothing got moved, or done, but a lotta arguing and fussing this past few days, and its almost Christmas Eve."

"I knew this was how it was gonna go down," he muttered, "and why I said it coulda waited until after the holidays."

"That's one of the reasons I owe you an apology," she said amiably, finishing her own soup in the long stretches between their comments.

After he turned his bowl up to his mouth, polishing off what remained in it, she took his dishes along with hers into the kitchen—not surprised that he followed her.

"You didn't have to dress me down in front of your

family, though," he countered in a low voice, with his comment aimed at her turned back.

"No, I didn't," she said quietly, rinsing the bowls and spoons and tea-cups.

"It was a pure lack of respect," he argued on, his voice issuing from low in his throat with hurt.

"It was, and very inconsiderate."

She turned around and looked at him, and his gaze slid to the floor.

"I may not have degrees and money, and all, but I'm still a man, and have my pride, Colette."

He was on the other side of the butcher block, and she knew that closing the space between them was imperative now. Slowly making her way to him, she touched his jaw-line and brushed his mouth with a kiss when she reached him, then pulled back so that she could look him directly in the eyes.

"I'm sorry," she whispered. "For real, for real... and not just for today. But, for the pressure."

Franklin shrugged and then nodded.

"I saw first hand what it can do. I saw it in Girard, in Bey... in Wilton... my Lord."

Again he nodded, but this time his stance relaxed enough to accept an embrace from her.

"Where's everybody?" he whispered, while enfolding her in his arms as he'd asked the question.

"Girard went to go bring his wife home," she murmured against his cheek. "Wilton went to feed his wife and join Bey, Sandra, and Nicole at the diner."

"If it keeps snowing like this, they'll all have to wind up staying in town at Miss Ruth's," he whispered slowly, closing his eyes as her lips caressed his neck.

"Yeah, and they'll all come home here, tomorrow morning, after Juney plows the road... to pick up their clothes, and get on the road," she said in an even lower tone aimed at his ear, and designed to send a warm rush of breath into it.

"Uh, you think so?" he barely whispered back, pulling her against him harder.

"I hope so," she murmured as her mouth found his and captured it.

"Then, let's go upstairs."

The long walk through the house, up the steps, and down the hall to their room had been cloaked with silent understanding. Small twinges of anticipation made flip-flops inside her lower belly that gradually singed her inner thighs as her husband held the door open for her—then locked it behind them. No words we're exchanged as he held her gaze and gently unbuttoned her sweater, peeling layers of winter clothing off, and trailing kisses against her flushed skin as each garment was removed. She returned the favor, and was rewarded with his deep gasp each time her mouth found a new section of his skin to adore.

Desire returned, unfamiliar, yet recognizable, and he seemed to revere it with trembling hands that played in the key that also understood that it took time to love a woman ... a chord of love sublime that insisted on taking its sweet ole' time to arch her back and make her knuckles turn white as she grasped the corners of the sheets ... baby, please ... and she seemed to remember the song better now upon each slow, burning thrust ... it was the memory-laden instinct of how to follow his lead, and lead him to follow her anywhere—because she fully loved him back enough to make him call her name, and to bring tears to the man's eyes that she cherished, oh, so much ... not yet ... just as her body remembered how minutes could feel like hours, and hours like minutes, until time stood still, and the metronome in their bodies and breathing synchronized, and repeated the stanza of short breaths that led to deep, resounding moans of syncopated rhythms that oozed into shudders, and off-key sharps and flats which snuck up on you as they slid up and down the scale of a backbone, and ended on a pant then a sigh. Oh yes, she remembered the music that they'd once listened to together ... it was called real jazz.

Dawn washed across them, and she turned over lazily to break their fitted-spoons position to find his mouth for a kiss. "Baby," she whispered. "You hungry?"

"Hmmm... " he grumbled low in his throat. "Starved."

"Wanna raid the refrigerator?" she chuckled, snuggling against him.

"Yeah, but my legs feel like Jello," he murmured, then kissed her deeply. "What time is it?"

"C'mon, man," she giggled, reaching over to the nightstand to turn and see the clock. Then she stopped and drew herself up into a ball at the headboard, gathering her knees under her arms and began to rock.

Franklin immediately sat up and reached out for her, looking alarmed. "What's the matter?"

"The quilt," she whispered.

Shaking his head, he glanced at it, rubbed his face, and returned his gaze to hers. "What, baby? What is it?"

"Nana's wedding quilt. This wasn't on the bed when we came up here! It always stays in her room."

Franklin jumped out of his side of the bed, and quickly drew on his sweat pants and a tee-shirt, and found his sneakers. Colette found her nightgown, robe, and slippers, and they both headed for the door, paused briefly to inspect the lock, then raced down to the kitchen.

"You thinkin' what I'm thinkin'?" he exclaimed, as they flipped on the lights on their way through the house.

Both stopped and looked at each other as they entered the room of destination, then stared wide-eyed at the new, unopened jar of peach preserves that sat on the counter.

"I'm calling Girard," she whispered, but did not move. "We can't sell the house."

"No lie," Franklin affirmed, "call every dag-gone body."

He stood beside her as she dialed the numbers, and woke up the clan one by one, navigating calls past sleepy and curious front desk clerks, all of whom wanted to chat and felt they had a right to—because they knew the family well. She kept her information exchange brief; get home quick, Nana's leaving signs. Then they sat and waited in the parlor, neither one saying a word.

The sound of Juney's plow truck coming down the road was a welcomed noise that made them hurry in unison to the front porch. When the motor idled, Colette turned the door lock and opened it, not allowing Franklin to get far from her side.

Impervious to the cold, they watched him come up the steps to the door, holding a basket very carefully, along with a pink bag over his shoulder. Colette squeezed Franklin's hand, and squinted as a caravan of headlights began to make their way down the road in the distance.

"Look, I know this is a terrible inconvenience, but I didn't know where else to go," Juney said quietly, refusing to come into the house as he thrust the basket forward to Franklin, and handed the pink bag to Colette when she opened the screen door. "Mom, don't look too good. I think her sugar's up ... so, I need to take her down to see Doc Pearson, and Cherl's got the kids over at her mother's across town. Too cold, Mom said, to take her all around in a truck in the snow ... and Mom said if Jesus call her, that Girard is a lawyer, might know some people who would want a little lamb like this." Apology etched across Juney's ashen face. "Me and Cherl can't barely manage wit the ones we got, so—"

"—Oh, Lord above..." Colette whispered, dropping the diaper bag, and hushing Juney with a kiss. "You tell your Momma that this chile will be looked after by Johnsons, and she don't have to worry about nothin' but getting herself better."

Juney extended his hand to Franklin, and gave Colette a hug before he backed out of the doorway. "Y'all always been good people, 'Lette. You and Frankie both. Much obliged. I gotta get Mom to the doctor's."

She watched him leave, and waved at Miss Julia, who she knew could see her from the truck, then closed the door, gathering up the little bundle within the basket, and pressing her cheek to the sleepy face as it yawned.

"Colette... a baby?"

"Oh, Franklin," she whispered, "look at her..."

He peered inside the blanket and immediately the child reached for his finger, and wrapped its fist around the thick, rough appendage and tried to suckle it.

"Look at this pretty little girl," he whispered in awe. "So delicate... who could leave a child like this?"

Tears filled her eyes, and she kissed her husband's brow. "This house has been giving everybody what they needed, not what they wanted—and she's been keeping it in order, cleaned, just like she used to prepare for all of us coming home for the holidays. Miss Julia said neither she, nor Juney, nor Miss Pat did it. Don't you see the blessings?"

Franklin didn't comment, but cast her an uneasy glance as his line of vision traveled over his shoulder.

"There's nothing to be afraid of, honey," she soothed with confidence. "Nana gave you another taste of her sweetness to remember—in those mysteriously appearing jars of peaches—even though Miss Julia said she'd only canned berries this year. Then she gave Nicole her pictures, and me a taste of history in Miss Julia's kitchen to share with my sister. My cousin, Wilton, and his wife,

Deidre, got a christening gown—to let them know that there was no need to worry, and their baby would be born and live. She gave my cousin, Bey, a reminder—her silver heart and Grand Daddy's gold watch, to be sure he knew that he was loved by both her and Pop, and that he was a sibling, not just a cousin. She gave us her quilt, the one that was her wedding quilt... for good luck in making our own babies. But, this child is for Brother and Nancy. This little thing was here when she passed on, probably the last living soul to see Nana alive ... here, in this house, just like this little girl was already family. It's a good sign. Trust me."

He stared at her and his eyes misted, then cleared as he looked from her to the baby and back. "That's the only right thing to do, honey. We've got time to wait for our blessings. They don't."

They both chuckled as the baby began to wiggle and kick, making little grunting sounds of hunger on its way to a full-blown wail.

"Go sit on the couch out of the draft, and see if Miss Julia packed some formula. I'll crack the door open, 'cause everybody just pulled up."

Girard was the first one through the door, followed by Bey, then Wilton, with the women all following in a terrified-looking huddle of humanity behind them.

"Nancy, Girard," Colette whispered, "look what Nana gave you for Christmas," she beamed as they approached her on the sofa.

"What?" Nancy whispered back, tears rising and streaming down her face when Colette handed the child out to her to hold.

Girard laced his arm around Nancy's waist, and all the family members fought to get a good look at the wriggling bundle of life.

Nicole whispered, "Nana's in this house, isn't she?"

Franklin nodded, and his admission of belief sent a

collective gasp through the women in the room.

"All the gifts... everything being just what was the true sentimental thing for each person," Deidre whispered, covering her mouth.

"Whose baby is it?" Sandra whispered, "Somebody just left it, like that—out in the snow?"

"Appears old Miss Davis took a turn this mornin'," Franklin said in a low, serious voice. "Sent Juney by here with this baby for the family to watch, and said to give these papers to Girard." He handed Girard a manila envelope, and proceeded to hug him as he accepted it. "Me and Colette couldn't think of a better father and mother in the family... so..." he shrugged, "Merry Christmas, Daddy."

Girard went over to the armchair, sat down, and covered his face with his hands and wept quietly. Nancy drew to his side, and knelt before him, placing the baby on his lap.

"Tell them all what we talked about in bed last night," Nancy murmured, kissing her husband's hands until he removed them from his eyes.

"We thought," Girard said in an unsteady voice, "that the house should stay in the family... and, Nicole should have all the pictures—like Mom Johnson would have wanted. And, Bey should have a lot of Pop's things, because Pop was like a father to him. And, Wilton and Deidre should have the baby things, all those handmade toys, and crib, and bassinet... but, the house, should be filled with love, and someone sentimental... with a good woman and a good man that knows how to fix things, and care for more than things—that's Colette and Franklin. Y'all take it. Case closed," he quietly added, allowing the baby to suckle his finger tip. "'Cause, if it wasn't for my sister..." his voice trailed off, "Wouldn't be no glue left to hold this family tight."

"Girard," Franklin protested. "We got a house up in

Philly, and I've got an auto-body business to run."

"Ain't no argument to it," Nicole fussed with a smile. "Nana left the signs. Like Girard said, case closed."

"And," Bey protested, "you got a barn out back, that would make an excellent recreation center, if fixed up. Lord knows, we did some recreatin' out there in our day," he laughed, pulling Sandra to him.

"And, there's the big, ole shed," Wilton added, that could use some equipment to teach vo-tech skills to these young boys in town."

"Who might get a scholarship from a historically black college or a university, if there was an after-school program that could help both the girls and the boys get prepared," Deidre added with a wide grin. "I think my people can see to that."

"And," Nicole chuckled, "there might be a news correspondent that might be able to get the program some national recognition and media attention, which could help ensure solid grants to run the place."

"And," Nancy nodded, taking the baby from Girard to walk around the room, bouncing the infant on her shoulder, "I'm sure that an influential attorney could do the 501c3 paperwork to establish the non-profit... and a well-orchestrated letter-writing campaign from several well-respected black women's organizations, could ensure foundation support in this historic black enclave... which would definitely call for documentary attention," she said, smiling in Nicole's direction.

"No doubt," Girard murmured from his chair, "that well-placed political connections could even coax private contributions for a school bus, and to hire a local driver, like Juney, and to get in solid speakers. But, I'm sure that a good attorney could also negotiate a stellar sales price on a thriving Philadelphia-based auto-body business, enough to install state-of-the-art new equipment in a vocational training center... and that same attorney could reasonably manage row house rental property."

"Yes," Bey chimed in, "might even find that a dental facility might open in town, to assist with internships and teaching office management and dental technician skills, if he retained the proper office manager to support his efforts. You never know." Bey's smiled and looked and Sandra who looked away and giggled.

Suggestions rang out amid Colette and Franklin's feeble protests, until a small wail brought the group to harmonious laughter that trailed them all as they went into the kitchen.

Colette stood at the sink, her eyes shining with tears of gratitude and joy. Franklin absorbed her against his body like hot butter on warm baked bread. Nancy nursed the baby with such tenderness that the group fell silent for a moment while Girard stroked the dark, tight ringlets of infant hair in pure awe. Wilton touched his wife's stomach and nuzzled against her.

"Marry me," Bey said quietly against Sandra's cheek. When she filled his arms, Nicole squealed, and another round of commotion broke out as everyone tried to talk at once.

"I say we all stay here for Christmas," Nicole whimpered, crying as she danced between each couple. "We been blessed... don't you feel the energy in this house? I've gotta get this on tape."

They all agreed, while laughing and bumping into each other, hugging and kissing, and talking a mile a minute. But then, Franklin held up his hand, and the group settled into silent expectation.

"I say before we do anything, we say a prayer of thanks." He looked around the room at all the faces that had become riveted on him.

"I stand down, Franklin Morris," Girard whispered. "It's all yours, brother."

Franklin cleared his throat and bowed his head, holding Colette against him. "May God bless Mom and Pop Johnson for their wisdom, courage, and the spirit of love that they shared... and we thank you Heavenly Father above, for all the true gifts of immeasurable value that you have bestowed upon this family. And, we thank you for allowing us to finally give back the gift of collective effort and harmony and love to those already gone home to Glory. And, I thank you, for giving me back my wife— along with a way to fulfill all of our hopes and dreams... Merry Christmas."

"Merry Christmas," Colette whispered, an instant before she met her husband's lips with her own, sealing their hearts and their future.

Miracle at Midnight

By Gwynne Forster

*T*hat Nana Johnson was something else, gave that family of hers a good shaking up, she sure did. Now every time you look around Colette and Franklin have a house full of family, the very same folks who didn't want no parts of it. Funny how things work out, ain't it? They say the old ancestors are still walking the roads here in Mystic, checking on things, watching over folks—like angels, you know. I'd bet money that's what happened with Page and Nelson. Who would have thought those two unlikely folks would have found their way to each other—without some help? Can't say if it was pure coincidence, or something … more. You judge for yourself…

Chapter One

Nelson Pettiford flipped off the television newscast and blew out a tired breath. Two solid years of electioneering for the presidency, and not one candidate had produced an original idea he thought. As a political cartoonist, he made his living by exposing politicians to ridicule, but lately the actors on Capitol Hill rarely inspired him. he supplemented his income with his other love—writing novels, which garnered him best sellers. Overall he had a good life, although a lonely one. He got up from his favorite living-room chair and ambled across the hall to his studio, selected some pens and set down to draw. An hour later, he stood back and surveyed Quigley the cat, his alter ego. A smile flashed over his face as he appraised his work. The big, haughty tomcat gave Odessa-Cat, his onetime girlfriend, the lowdown on the ways in which human beings made life miserable for each other. To Quigley's way of thinking, people could chose incompetent leaders without spending a penny. Yet, every two years, they threw away millions, like bettors at slot machines. He signed the political cartoon as he always did with his pen name, Slim Wisdom, put it in an envelope, drove to the post office and mailed it to the distributor of his syndicated column.

As he left the post office, he stopped and held the

door for the woman behind him.

"Thanks," she said, then gazed up at him, grinned and winked. "Wow! How's the weather up there?"

Nelson stared down at the woman until he could see her wince. Why did people feel they had a right to say whatever they thought at the expense of others? When he was in the third grade, he was suspended from school for giving a boy who'd taunted him about his height a reality check. And a harsh one at that. That transgression earned him a lecture from his father on the importance of controlling his temper, and he hadn't forgotten it.

He'd suffered through every insulting name and numerous taunts. Slim, bean pole, skinny, stick. You must be a basketball player. What's the weather forecast? He'd endured the pain of being a spectacle until he'd become inured to it. Men didn't like looking up at other men, so they resorted to ridicule, and women judged him as a man who ought to appreciate any attention they paid him. He'd locked them out, all of them. He walked alone.

On the way home, he took a detour and drove past Lake Linganore as the last rays of the setting sun painted the sky in brilliant hues of red, orange and blue. He'd planned to go straight back home, but he seemed propelled—almost against his will, as if pulled in that direction—to drive past the lake. He drove slowly so as to prolong one of the pleasures of a lonely man, a view of nature at it most majestic.

Page Sutherland pressed the accelerator to the floor, then pumped the gas a few times. Nothing. Four o'clock on a chilly October afternoon on a strange road, an isolated road, and her car wouldn't move. She'd had a tune-up the previous week and filled the tank with gas less than fifty miles back and, apart from driving a car, that was all she knew to do to one. Strange. The car had just stopped without a warning. Not a change in the engine or locked brakes. Nothing. The thought of getting out of the car in that out-of-the-way-spot sent cold prickles from her neck to the base of her spine. Even if she were willing to risk walking, she had no idea how far it was to Mystic Ridge. She'd been huddled in the car for all of forty-five minutes when she saw the headlights of the approaching car.

The sight of a Chevy parked on the other side of the highway got Nelson's attention, and he stopped and crossed the two-lane roadway to where a lone woman huddled in the front seat. As he approached, she rolled up the window.

"Are you all right?" he asked her. "Can I help you in some way?"

Something, maybe it was fear or, it could have been caution, mirrored in her eyes. The eyes of a woman in jeopardy, or who believed she was. He stared down at her long-lashed dreamy eyes, framed in a flawless brown face, and inexplicably connected with her from his scalp to the pit of his gut.

"Well?"

She shook her head. "Uh... No. I...I'm fine," he thought she said, though he couldn't be sure because she didn't roll down the window.

"You're sure you're all right?"

She nodded so vigorously that he didn't believe her, but what could he do? In the circumstances, any intelligent woman would be wary. He turned away and walked back to his car, but he didn't like leaving her there. He didn't like it one bit.

Maybe she should have trusted him, but how could she go off with a stranger on that deserted road in the encroaching darkness. His was the only car she'd seen in the last hour or so. And who was he? She didn't think she'd ever seen such a tall man. Dark, elegant and handsome, too. As uneasy as she was out there alone, he could have been an illusion, an image she conjured up. Still... Something moved in the thicket beside the highway, or so she thought. She checked the windows and the locks on the doors. Another movement, this time closer to her. Her breathing accelerated and she rubbed her moist hands. The night sounds began in earnest, as crickets chirped out an anthem and frogs began to croak in a seesaw rhythm. A far-away boom with the sound of roaring thunder split the silence, and she wrapped her arms around her body.

In a brief flash of lightning, she caught a glimpse of the most exquisite looking rust-colored tom cat sitting regally on the road. In a blink, the cat was gone. Page burrowed deeper in the seat, a sensation of the surreal filling her. Yet, she felt perfectly safe, even as she wondered what she'd gotten herself into.

Six hours earlier—it felt like six years—she'd set out from Washington, D.C. looking for a life of her own, away from her mother's career, popularity and maddening social life. A journalist, she'd accepted a position as reporter for a weekly paper in Mystic Ridge and a chance to be her own person. If she made friends and succeeded as a journalist, it would at least be the result of her own efforts and abilities and not because she was Millie Shipley's daughter. And she'd be away from her glamorous mother's notoriety and have a life of her own. She and her mother loved each other, but they were as different as two women could be. She'd left Washington glowing with expectation as to what might happen in her new life, but so far she was batting zero.

Thunder crashed and bellowed closer this time, and she lay down in the seat, frightened by the sound of dogs barking nearby. *Probably after that poor cat.*

The headlights of a motor vehicle lit up her car, and she sat up with such suddenness that her head hit the steering wheel. Fear shot through her as a pickup truck parked across the highway and the driver's door opened, but her heartbeat slowed to normal when she recognized the tall man. He'd come back, and somehow she knew he wouldn't harm her. If he'd wanted to, he could have done that two hours earlier. She opened the window a crack.

"It's too dangerous for you to spend the night out here," he said. "If you're afraid of me, you can stay in your car, and I'll tow you to Mystic Ridge. If you won't do that, I'll just sit across there in my truck to make sure nobody bothers you, but I can't leave you alone out here."

Lightning streaked through the sky and shivers raced through her. It was silly, she knew, but lightning always made her uneasy. Maybe...

She rolled down the window. "I...uh..." If she didn't go with him, she could become someone else's victim. "If you'll tow my car, I'll... I'll ride with you. I'm headed for Mystic Ridge."

"Well, go sit in the truck before it begins to rain."

She liked his voice. Strong and authoritative. A voice that commanded respect. She did as he suggested, and she'd never been more grateful than when he got in the truck, made a U-turn and got out without touching her. He succeeded in hooking her car to the truck as drops of rain began to fall.

"Where're you staying in Mystic?"

"I was going to the Ridgewood Inn, but it's already nine-thirty, and it's probably full."

"Mystic Ridge is a small place and it isn't a tourist

attraction. So your room will be there for you."

He stopped in front of the Ridgewood Inn. "I'll help you with your things."

She noticed that the receptionist stared from her to the tall man, and Page hastened to waylay any suggestion that she might be checking in with him.

"I reserved a single room and bath for today, but I had engine trouble. I hope you still have the room."

The woman nodded, though she stared at the man who'd proved to be Page's salvation.

"You're all right now," he said to her. "I'll leave your car out front."

She turned to thank him, but he strode out of the door, and when she followed him, he stopped, turned and said, "I'm glad you're safe. Goodbye."

The sharp finality of his tone stunned her, leaving her with no choice but to walk back into the hotel.

"What is that man's name?" she asked the receptionist. "Do you know who he is?"

"Me?" the woman asked, pointing to her chest. "'Deed I don't know a thing about that man. People say he's strange, but don't ask me."

Frowning, Page went to her room, ordered a chicken breast sandwich, ate it, showered and went to bed. And when she closed her eyes, she saw again the face of the tall man who rescued her.

A week later, having found a suitable house and settled into her new job at *The Mystic Ridge Observer*, Page focused on finding a niche for herself in the place she hoped would become her home. Already, she had a sense of freedom and of opportunity to find out who she was and what she could do away from the glare, commotion and excitement that continually surrounded her mother.

But first, she had to find the man and thank him. She described the man to the handyman who worked around the neighboring houses. "Do you know who he is?"

"Well, I've seen him, Ma'am, but people say he does-n't talk to anybody. I'm not even sure he can talk, and they say he's weird, too. Stays in a big house with a high fence and they say he's got ten or fifteen bad dogs in there. Must be hiding from the law is all I can say."

She didn't know about the dogs, but the rest of it was off the mark. She questioned Phyllis, the copy editor at *The Observer*, as the local folk called it.

"What you want to know about him for? He's some kind of hermit. Walks around looking straight ahead and ignoring everybody like they say witches do. People here have gotten used to him, but nobody knows where he came from. You'd think the wind would blow him over, he's so tall." She chuckled at her own joke.

Page had had enough of the speculations. Living in a small town had some disadvantages, and ruinous gos-sip topped the list. "Where does he live?"

"Last house on Fritchie Road going toward Frederick. It's practically on the spot where Barbara Fritchie is supposed to have stonewalled old Stonewall Jackson himself when he marched through these parts during the Civil War. Why do you want to know anyway?"

"I'm a reporter, and all this stuff I hear about him has peaked my curiosity."

"Oh yeah? Well, you might as well forget about an interview. That man don't talk to nobody."

"Did I hear you asking about that string bean out on Fritchie Road?" James Rodgers, editor of *The Observer*, asked, as he knocked and walked into the office Page shared with Phyllis. "You know him?" Page explained how they met. "Doesn't sound like the same guy, but if it is and you get to meet him, I want a story." She promised to do her best. Her curiosity at fever pitch, she made up her mind to visit him the following day. When she awoke that morning, Saturday, Nelson Pettiford was her first thought. Around noon, she dressed to go to his house, but decided she'd better call her mother first.

It seemed as if a hundred people talking at once stood directly behind her mother when she answered the phone. "Oh, darling, I'm just having a few people over for lunch. I owe everybody, and in this town, that's not good. As a member of the House of Representatives, I can be powerful and make a difference or I can be as useful as a wet match. Darling how are you?"

"Me?" asked Page, winded by the speed at which her mother's words flew out. "I'm fine. I called to see how you are."

"Never better, darling. You know me. I'd planned to call and remind you of the Urban League gala. I can't go to that place alone, and I hate being obligated to these excuses for men. Look, I have to go. Senator Lucus just arrived."

Same old. Same old. "Love you." She hung up. It wasn't ever going to change.

Chapter Two

Nelson dashed out of the house and down to the gate when he recognized Mr. Whitfield's buzz. The man had a special way of pushing the buzzer. One, three, two, one buzzes, so he always knew when his mail had arrived.

"Morning, Mr. Whitfield. You're late today. I was afraid something had happened to you."

Whitfield removed his government regulation blue postman's hat and scratched his head. "I had to get signatures on a lot of packages, and you can't just hand Miss Laura a letter, she has to talk for half an hour. I don't mind, though, 'cause I'm the only person she gets to talk with. Here's your mail."

"Thanks." Miss Laura wasn't alone. Whitfield was often the only person to whom he spoke for days, so he understood the woman's reluctance to let the man continue his rounds. "See you tomorrow," he said and turned back to the house, but before he reached halfway the buzzer sounded again.

Now, who could that be? He wasn't expecting his brother, Logan, and his only other visitor was the man who took care of his house. The buzzing persisted. Instead of speaking over the intercom, he walked out to the gate and stopped dead in his tracts. It couldn't be.

She'd stayed in his head, lived in his dreams and frol-
icked in and out of his thoughts since that night when
she'd taken over his life. He walked closer. Her radiant
smile changed to a grin. Excitement raced through him.

"Hi. It's me, the woman you rescued on Old Mills
Road the other night. I had to find you and thank you. It
wasn't easy either."

He walked all the way to the gate, looked into her
long-lashed, brownish gray eyes and felt her sink into
him and burrow her way into his soul. He shook his head
to clear it, to retrieve himself, but she was in him, he
knew it.

She sniffed. "What do I smell that's so tantalizing?"

"Forgive me," he managed. "I must seem rude. I'm
roasting chestnuts that I gathered from my tree this
morning. They're wonderful. Would you..." He hesitated.
If she said no or acted as if she was turned off by him, he
didn't think he could bear it.

"Would I what? Like some chestnuts? I warn you, I
love them."

He unlocked the gate and opened it, scared that
she'd hear his heart pounding. "Would you like to come
in? I've got a fire around back where I'm roasting the
nuts, and it's warm there."

"Thanks. My name is Page Sutherland. You didn't tell
me yours, and nobody seems to know it." Something
akin to empathy surfaced in her eyes, and she stopped
herself as she nearly grasped his arm.

He took the hand she extended. Soft and feminine.
"I'm Nelson Pettiford."

Recognition of the name seemed to flicker in her
eyes, but to his relief, all she said was, "Thank you for
being so kind to me the other night. It's something I'll
never forget."

He shrugged. "I'm glad I came back for you."

She walked beside him, obviously at ease, and he

recognized in himself an expansive feeling, a sensation of belonging with someone. A feeling as alien to him as any he could imagine. He breathed deeply, and allowed himself to enjoy it, if only for a little while.

"Have a seat," he said, pointing to one of the lounge chairs that he kept there. He hooded his eyes and watched her. More than once, he'd seen people run from him, but she didn't hesitate to take a seat and, in almost slow motion, crossed the shapeliest pair of legs he'd seen in years.

"What a soothing environment! And the music. I love Mozart's chamber music."

He stopped turning the nuts and looked steadily at her. "I could listen to it twenty-four hours a day and never get tired of it. I like other music, but I need this. I don't know how I could get along without it for long."

She leaned back and closed her eyes. "It's wonderful. I like jazz when I'm doing chores around the house, and I love opera, but this makes me feel alive."

The tongs fell from his hand down to the hot coals, but he paid no attention. Had fate, or an angel sent her to him? Or was this another of the strange happenings in his life since some force beyond himself had pulled him onto Old Mills Road where she sat stranded. He didn't believe in coincidences anymore than he believed in predestination, but from the minute he'd first looked into her eyes, he'd lost himself. Over a week later, nothing had changed that. She smiled, and he knew he'd been staring at her.

"What is it?" she asked.

He raked the tongs away from the coals with a stick. "I don't remember having been so comfortable with anyone as I am with you, except maybe my brother. It's been... I don't know ... maybe never. Don't tell me you like walking in the woods."

A smile drifted over her face, mesmerizing him. "All

right. I won't. But I will say that, during summer camp, I
spent many hours in the woods. As a child, I couldn't wait
for spring, so I could do my studying in a tree in our garden. I'm a card-carrying nature lover."

He peeled the roasted chestnuts, gave her some in
a small bowl and watched her eyes blaze with delight as
she anticipated eating them. "Are you warm enough? I
could get you a sweater or a blanket."

"I'm fine. The fire is wonderful, and I enjoy looking at
the flames. They're like puppets dancing to an imaginary
tune. Central heating has its drawbacks."

"I have central heating, but I also have fireplaces in
most rooms. They make it so much more....well, like
home."

He glanced down at her feet. When had he seen
anybody tap their toes to Mozart's music? What an inviting woman! He realized he could care a lot for her and
checked himself. He didn't know her, and he didn't plan
to lose his heart to any woman only to regret it.

Page leaned back, savored the delicious nuts and
considered Nelson Pettiford. Thoughtful. Kind. It hadn't
occurred to her that he'd peel those hot chestnuts so she
could eat them while they were warm. She wanted to ask
him why the townspeople had such peculiar opinions of
him when nothing they'd told her about him bore any
semblance of the truth, but she sensed he'd shut her out
if she put him on the defensive. Weird? Definitely not. His
handsome brown face boasted the dreamiest eyes she
remembered looking at. And she liked his mouth, too.
Firm lips. Not too thin and not too... She sat forward.
What was she doing lolling there fantasizing about a
strange man?

"It's been a wonderful few minutes, Nelson, but I'd
better go." When he looked at his watch, and a half smile
formed around his lips, she looked at her own watch.

"Good Lord, I've been here almost three hours." She

frowned, confused. "But how could that be? I didn't intend to ... You've wasted a whole afternoon with me. I—"

"This afternoon was not wasted. It was ... something very special."

She stood, and he got up immediately and walked down to the gate with her. If she'd had the nerve to do what she wanted, she would have kissed his cheek in gratitude for the most pleasant afternoon she could remember. Instead, she thanked him again, shook hands with him and left.

He watched her car until it turned the corner. *Yes, I felt it too, Page, that sensation of being lost in time, transported somehow.* He shook his head, dispelling the weird notion, and returned to the grill. He stood there gazing at it for long minutes. Its flames still crackled, Mozart's music continued to fill the air with romance and the aroma of the chestnuts still clung to his nostrils, but he doused the fire, stopped the music and went inside. The awful emptiness. He pushed it back, sat down at his drawing table and got to work. Damned if he'd let it beat him.

"Did you get anything good on Pettiford?" James Rodgers asked Page the following Monday morning.

She couldn't lie, but she wouldn't betray Nelson either. "You said he wouldn't see me, didn't you? Don't tell me you came in here to gloat."

"Truth is I didn't hold out much hope for it, but since you're new in town and didn't know anything about him...." He let the thought hang, shrugged and went back to his office.

"I'm not gloating either," Phyllis sang out.

Page locked her computer, dusted her key board and

considered ignoring Phyllis, but she wanted to prove she could make friends on her own, so she said to her office mate, "I'll give you a little of my late father's philosophy: don't expect too much of your friends, and you'll always have them. The boss didn't expect anything, and he's not disappointed."

"Yeah," Phyllis drawled, "but if you'd gotten that interview, he'd be dancing on the ceiling."

"Can't you just see those bowed legs tripping over each other while he does a two-step on the ceiling? I'm going to the City Council meeting. See you tomorrow."

"Right."

Page grabbed her briefcase and camera, dashed out of the building and stopped as she opened the door of her car. "Hmmm." Something could be going on there. Phyllis never made jokes about James and didn't comment if anybody else did. Boredom quickly overtook her during the Council meeting and her mind drifted back to the previous Saturday afternoon and the idyllic moments with Nelson. She'd thought only of him since she'd left his house, flustered by her easy acceptance of him. She'd actually closed her eyes, relaxed and daydreamed while he sat less than four feet from her. She didn't care what the gossips said; she trusted him because her instincts said she should and, so far, he'd proved worthy of it.

Why couldn't she see him again? He didn't suggest it, and she knew he wouldn't. She wanted to spend time with him, to know him. She suspected he was the same Nelson Pettiford who'd written three national best selling novels, but if he wanted her to know that, he'd tell her. And the longer he kept it to himself, the more attractive he'd be. If there was anything she could do without, it was another seeker of notoriety. Life with her headline-grabbing mother, as much as she loved her, had erased her tolerance for people who needed the spotlight. She fished in her pocketbook for a quarter, went to the phone and called him. She reached his answering machine.

"Mr. Pettiford," she said, speaking to the answering machine, "this is Page Sutherland. I'm sorry you're not at home. I hate talking to these infernal things. I'll—"

"Hello, Page. I can't imagine a more pleasant surprise or a more welcome one. But how'd you get my number?"

"Bribery. The boss' sister works for the phone company, and I promised her dinner if she'd give me your number.I hope you don't mind. I...I spent such a wonderful afternoon with you that I... Well, I don't know anyone else whose company suited me like... Oh, for goodness sake, Nelson, can't we see each other again?"

"Do you... Yes. Yes, I want to see you. I've hardly thought of anything else since you left here. What's your phone number, and what time do you get home?"

Her heart started a shaky waltz in her chest, and she took a deep breath and leaned against the side of the building. "711-1177. I'll be there about four-thirty," she managed to say. What was it about the man's voice? It seemed to soothe her, to wrap her in a dreamy kind of peace.

"If you're free for dinner this evening, we can talk about it when I call you. Around six?"

"If you're just being a gentleman, I want to know it right now, and I'll excuse you."

"Ha ha." His laughter had the ring of honest relief. "I'm thirty-six, Page, so unless someone needs my help, I'm not likely to agree to do something I don't want to do. I'd like to see you, and I've already begun to anticipate the pleasure of being with you again."

Oh, dear. This one didn't let any weeds grow under his feet. "Till then."

"Right. Call you at six."

She hung up and made herself walk the half block to

her car. Where had she gotten the nerve to call a strange man and tell him she wanted to see him again? His immediate response was more than she'd hoped for, but she definitely wasn't going to make a habit of seeking him out.

What should she wear to dinner with him? If she were in Washington, she'd go for broke, but women in Mystic Ridge didn't seem to dress up except on special occasions. She'd wait till he called and take her cue from him.

Nelson propped his elbows on his drawing table, leaned forward and rested his face in his hands. If this was a joke, he couldn't find the humor in it. The phone rang and his head snapped up. He stared at the phone and let it ring. Was she calling to say she'd acted on impulse?

"I thought you said you'd be home this evening, and—"

He grabbed the phone, flipped off the answering machine and interrupted his brother. "Good grief! I did, didn't I? But—"

"Look, man, if you gotta go somewhere, I can take a rain check. No problem."

He'd forgotten that his brother planned to spend the night with him, as he did once every two or three weeks. "It's okay. I...uh...I forgot about it. But come on over. You have a key, so let yourself in. I'll...uh...I ought to be back around ten."

He heard the silence on the other end of the wire and waited, knowing that Logan would place his shots accurately.

"Who's the girl?" Logan's deep baritone always seemed to come from the pit of his belly. Although two inches shorter than he, Logan had always seemed bigger for he wore the aura of strength that a boy finds in an older brother. His good looks made him a favorite with women, but he was a man who did his own choosing.

"Not anyone I care to talk about. I just met her, Nelson said."

"I see. When and where?"

Nelson allowed himself a hearty laugh. "The eighteen months difference in our ages hardly entitles you to the status of father, buddy, but I'll humor you." He gave his older brother a watered down account of his acquaintance with Page.

"Hmmm. I think you've hooked yourself into something."

"Wrong. She got to me."

"Well, hallelujah! Hope it works out. I'll be over tomorrow night instead. The full evening's yours, Brother. I wouldn't take a gal I liked home at ten o'clock, not even in a small town."

Nelson exhaled sharply. "Neither would I if I hadn't wanted to accommodate you. I'll see you tomorrow evening. Thanks."

Butterflies still flitted around in his belly, when he let himself remember that she'd wanted to see him badly enough to call him up and tell him so. But would she prove to be like the others? Satisfying their curiosity. Lord, he hoped and prayed she'd be different, that she'd be... He told himself to back up; she was new in town and probably wanted nothing more than friendship.

He telephoned Page precisely at six o'clock, and when she answered, her voice rested softly on his ears. "Hello."

"This is Nelson. Can you be ready at seven? I thought we'd go over to Frederick."

"Great. I don't know the customs around here. What are you wearing?"

He wondered at the question, then remembered that she came from Washington where the socially conscious were always on the ready. "A business suit. That all right?"

"Sure. People here go to dinner in jeans, and I guess I'm not used to that."

She hadn't struck him as being pretentious. Quite the contrary, but you never could tell, and he wasn't going to second guess her. "Till seven," he said, though what he wanted right then was more of her voice caressing his ears.

"B... Bye."

He had the feeling she'd wanted to say something else but dismissed it. After quickly showering and dressing, he remembered that he didn't know where she lived and called her.

"What is your address, Page?"

Her laughter rumbled to him through the wires. "I hadn't thought of that. I'm at 91-A Cochrane Drive."

He hung up and braced his hands against the wall. Watch it buddy. That's pure quicksand. You'd better remember who your are.

Chapter Three

*B*usiness suit, huh? She dressed in a simple sleeveless, red silk sheath that reached her knee, added pearls, pearl earrings, a pair of plain two-inch patent leather shoes and a splash of Dior's Opium. Her heart skipped a few beats when she opened her door and looked up at him. Gray suit, yellow tie and those dreamy eyes that promised paradise. He gazed down at her, liking what he saw and made no effort to hide it. After he helped her with her coat, she handed him her keys, and both his eyebrows shot up.

"What's this for?"

Had she somehow made a mistake? She'd soon know. "After you lock my door, keep them in your pocket until we get back."

He trained his gaze on her, and she battled the effect of his penetrating stare. "You aren't bringing a pocketbook? Your confidence honors me."

He took Route 144 and made it to Frederick at seven thirty-five. He doesn't play games, she reflected when he made none of the childish moves of some men she'd dated who used phony excuses to touch her. After the waiter seated them, she looked around at the other diners and was glad she'd dressed.

"It's lovely here," she told him. She hadn't expected such elegant fare or such a posh restaurant in that relatively small town.

He leaned forward, "So are you. I'm glad you're pleased."

Nelson leaned back in his chair, tapped his long fingers on the white linen tablecloth and cut to the chase. "I haven't gotten over your telephone call. What did it mean?"

Though surprised, his blunt honesty pleased her. She made herself look directly at him and hold his gaze while those eyes played havoc with her senses.

"It meant that I realized you weren't going to call me. I didn't know if you wanted to see me again, but I thought you might, and I...well, I...wanted to be with you again. Those few minutes by the fire in your back garden were so peaceful and...and...wonderful."

If only he wouldn't look at her like that. Brown eyes ablaze with... Lord, she didn't know what. But it certainly wasn't disinterest she saw in them.

"Do you want us to see each other on a regular basis?"

Doggoned if she'd do his work for him. "If I say no, that ends it. If I say yes, I'm at a disadvantage. What do you want?"

She watched, mesmerized, as a smile played around his lips, lit up his cheek bones and then claimed his entire face. Then, to her amazement, laughter poured out of him. The first time she'd seen him laugh, really laugh.

After a minute or so, he controlled it. "I wouldn't take good money for that remark. You're a woman and a half. I want as much of your company as I can get."

She wanted to hug him. "Better not be too hasty. I've got a supply of Chuck Berry and Mahalia Jackson records right beside my Mozart and Louis Armstrong collections."

White teeth glistened against his bronze skin. "I can handle Berry and Jackson if you can stomach my Bruce Springsteen CDs."

In their delight in each other's company, they barely ate the food. He reached across the table, but before his fingers touched her hand, he stopped himself and withdrew it, and she could see him pulling back.

"You're not comfortable with our becoming...uh...better friends. Why?"

He dragged his left hand across his face, over his eyes. Then his gaze bored into her. "Comfortable? You sailed into my life like a comet streaking across a black sky. And we...uh—"

"Clicked," she supplied, since he wouldn't let himself say it.

"Yes. We clicked, and... Well, I'm trying to believe it's... that you're real."

She reached across the table and grasped his right hand. "I'm real, Nelson. If you've been alone, so have I, but I'm putting a period to that right now. What about you?"

His long, tapered fingers stroked his chin giving the impression that he mused over her words. "You don't pull your punches, do you?"

She lifted her left shoulder in a quick shrug. "I'm tired of pretending not to be interested in a man so he can fool himself into believing he's chasing me. I'm grown, and I plan to act like it."

He sipped his coffee, savoring it to the last drop. "Why would you ever have done that?"

"In these matters, besides being a southern belle, my mother belongs to a different era, though I suspect she must have been one of the first modern women to keep her maiden name after marriage. She's brilliant, but she hardly ever touches earth. Anyway, I absorbed some of her attitudes." The thought that she was out of Millie's mad-cap environment warmed her and she couldn't help smiling. "I think you're interesting so why can't I let you know it?"

"Keep talking. You'll never get rid of me."

She released his right hand. "Really? Any more tips?"

"Tips?" He winked at her. "I've got a bag full. Be sweet to me, and I'll write 'em down for you."

"Good heavens! It's almost eleven," she said after glancing at the watch that lay among the hairs at his wrist. I had no idea it was so late. Hadn't we better go?"

He grinned at her. "Chicken. Scared of what you might do if I give you my bag of tips?" He stood and extended his hand to her.

"Don't bet on it," she said. "I'd check them out one after the other, so hand them over soon as you get the nerve."

He paid the bill and wrapped his fingers around hers as they left the restaurant. "What makes you think I don't have the nerve? I chart my own course, and no challenge or temptation has yet made me waver from it."

"First time for everything."

"Yeah? Mind if I call you tomorrow around six?"

She squeezed his fingers. "I'll mind if you don't."

On the drive back to Mystic Ridge, he didn't talk though he glanced at her from time to time, smiled and rubbed the back of her left hand. Sweet contentment flowed out of him and enveloped her. She turned up the palm of her left hand to receive his caress.

He slowed down as they entered Mystic Ridge and paused at the red light. "I've sworn off women, Page. I've been a curio to a lot of them, a challenge. To be as tall as I am doesn't mean that I'm different from other men. I'm constructed just as they are, and I'm not immune to pain. If your goal is to conquer, forget it. I've walked over so many proverbial hot coals that my feet no longer burn. I like you a lot. I mean a lot. But I don't have to do anything about it."

She laced her fingers through his, squeezed his hand and, stunned by the fiery ripples that flashed through her, withdrew from him. "You're a sensitive man, so you recognize the difference between your past relationships and the way ours is developing. If we're going anywhere, you'll have to trust me."

The light changed, and he eased the Mercury Sable forward. "You play it close to the chest, and I don't blame you." He remained quiet for a few minutes, and she realized he was testing a thought. "My brother's spending tomorrow evening with me, and I'd like you to join us for dinner. How about it?"

"I'd like that. Is he like you?"

His short laugh surprised her. "I never thought so. Logan says whatever he thinks. And some of what he thinks can make you mad as the devil."

She blinked rapidly, wondering what would come next. "Don't you like him?"

"Logan? I love my brother. He's my closest friend. He's just a pain in the butt sometime. You'll see." He grinned as though enjoying a private joke.

Relief coursed through her. "With that recommendation, I can hardly wait."

Nelson parked in front of her house, took her hand and walked with her to the door. Would he hold her and kiss her, banish the awful feeling that he could slip away from her like a ship easing out to the ocean. He opened her door, handed her the key and stood there looking down at her, his eyes unfathomable. She gazed up at him knowing that her eyes mirrored her expectation, her need for some semblance of intimacy with him. A kiss. A caress.

"See you tomorrow around seven," he said.

She didn't trust her voice, and her words came out in a whisper. "Okay. I'll be here."

For the longest time, he stared down at her, heat blazing in his eyes. Heat for her.

She wanted to touch him, to feel his hands on her, but she'd taken the first step, she'd called him, and she wouldn't go further. She smiled to make it easier for him, and blatant desire simmered in his eyes and proclaimed its wildness in his stance. He stepped closer, but he only stroked her cheek with gentle fingers, turned and, without a word, left her standing there.

She closed the door, walked into the darkness of her home and of her life and sat on the edge of her living room sofa. Empty. She'd needed him to hold her if only for a second. He liked her, just as he'd said, and he wanted her, but... Either he meant to take his time, or he needed some kind of assurance. She couldn't give him that. She sat up straight. What was that he'd said about his height? Oh, yes, he seemed to consider it a problem. Well, she didn't; when she looked at him, she saw a great looking man who made her think things she wouldn't mention to her mother.

Something about him drew her the way a flame lures a moth. His vulnerability? She didn't think so. His quiet calm and the peace she felt in his presence? She didn't know, but with him she felt serene, untroubled. For so long, her mother's headline grabbing antics and the media glare that went with them had kept her life in chaos, though Millie Shipley regarded it as necessary fuel for her political career.

"Dress casual," Nelson said when he called her the next day.

When he arrived, he looked at her long, narrow black leather skirt and jacket, red sweater blouse and low heeled black leather boots. "Well, I guess you could call that casual, but the effect certainly isn't. We're going to my place. Logan's cooking dinner." At her raised eyebrow, he added, "All right with you?"

She trusted him, didn't she? "Can he cook?"

He rolled his tongue around his right cheek and

inclined his head slightly. "Oh, yes. That he can. I'd planned for us to go to Frederick for dinner and then stop by The Watering Hole to hear some good jazz."

What changed your mind?"

"Logan. He's a good cook, so don't worry."

She slid into the front seat of his car, and he closed the door. "It doesn't occur to me to worry when I'm with you," she said.

He paused in the act of turning the key in the ignition. "Nobody's perfect, Page. I don't have a halo; I'm a man."

"Thank God for that," she murmured under her breath.

"What? Did you say what I think you said?"

She wasn't getting into that one. "How old is Logan?"

He didn't answer until he reached his house, drove through the gate and into his garage. "He's thirty-eight. He lost his family in an accident. You didn't answer my question."

His intense stare scattered her nerves, raising her temperature, and she resisted the urge to peel off her leather jacket. Annoyed at her reaction to him, she said, "You know the answer, and stop pushing me."

He cut the ignition. "What's the matter? Did I do something to upset you?"

"Yes, you did. What was wrong with kissing me good night last night? The occasion didn't call for a fifty minute clinch, so you didn't risk losing your soul. But you—"

With his hand gripping her shoulder, he turned her fully to face him. "But I...what?"

She lowered her eyelids and tried to move from his grasp, but he held her. "Open your eyes and look at me. There's something going on here, and it's nothing to play with. Are you ready for...I mean... Look! Once we get started, we're going to invest a lot of ourselves in this, and not all of it will be sweetness and bliss. You know that."

"No, I don't."

His big hand dragged her into his arms, and she stared into the dark and fierce wantonness that his eyes had become. Hunger radiated from him. Desire so fierce that she smelled it. Tasted it. Without warning, his mouth was on her hard and hot and demanding, and she opened to him as the unfamiliar softening of her heart battled the fire that raged in her loins. Closer, tighter he held her. His tongue danced wildly in her mouth until reason deserted her, and she moaned her need for relief. She sucked his tongue deeper into her mouth and tightened her grip on him, and he thrust his hand into her blouse and stroked her already beaded aureole. Her nerves rioted as he claimed her with his tongue and his stroking fingers, exhilarating her and drowning her in a pool of sensuality. And still he kneaded and stroked her while his velvet tongue plunged in and out of her. She thought she'd die if she didn't have him.

But he broke the embrace, reduced the tension and folded her gently in his arms. She couldn't speak, and when his hands cupped her face with exquisite tenderness, tears pooled in her eyes.

"I want you, and you want me, Sweetheart," he whispered, "but I feel in my gut that we need to go slow. The chemistry between us is mind boggling, but I need more. Don't you?"

She buried her face in the curve of his shoulder. "There is more, at least for me," she whispered.

He stroked her cheek. "And for me. But I can't gamble with my feelings anymore. The price of losing is too high."

Her heart constricted as tendrils of fear streaked through her. "Are you saying you won't give us a chance? This is it?"

His long fingers caressed her back in soothing strokes. "Far from it. I want us to get to know each other.

I want to know if the way I feel about you makes any sense, and I think we should make a serious attempt to explore this friendship."

She moved away from him and told herself to keep a lid on it. "I've got girlfriends already, Nelson. And one more thing. I don't think I said I want to have an affair with you."

His long-lashed gaze swept over her face. Then, to her astonishment, the sound of mirth erupted from his throat, captivating her, and she thought she could listen to him laugh forever.

He rubbed the tip of her nose with his thumb. "Honey, you're a piece of work. Tell you what, soon as I'm convinced your intentions toward me are honorable, we'll get down to business."

For long minutes, she looked at him, at the twinkling devilment in his eyes, looked until a grin spread over his face. She didn't know how it happened, but they were tight in each other's arms, hugging and laughing.

"As I said before, I'm not much on mysticism, but I don't believe we met by accident. Fate had a hand in this thing or something, so let's be patient and see what's in it for us. You seeing anybody? I mean, are you committed in any way?"

She shook her head. "I don't have any ties."

"All right. Neither do I." He straightened up and reached for the door handle. "I don't know what Logan thinks we're doing out here, and I'd as soon not give him a reason to be clever. Let's go in." He locked the car and the garage door, took her hand and started for the house.

Chapter Four

S o you're Page," Logan said, the three of them standing in the doorway of the kitchen. "I can't say Nelson talked about you a lot, because he didn't, which is why I'm cooking dinner tonight. I wanted to meet you. Getting anything personal out of him is like pulling hens' teeth, and they don't have any." He grasped both of her hands. "I'm glad you agreed to come."

All she could say was, "It's a pleasure to meet you, Logan." Tall and well proportioned with a strong masculine persona and skin the color of pecan shells, he was so much like Nelson that he almost unnerved her, but she didn't flinch. He'd trained his eagle-like eyes on her, the golden rim around his brown irises accentuating the intensity of his stare. So unlike the mesmerizing sensuality of Nelson's brown eyes.

"Cut it out, Logan. You'll make her nervous. You can't decide everything about her just by looking." Nelson's arm snaked around her waist in what she recognized as a protective gesture, but she'd already decided to pull Logan down a peg if he needled her.

Logan winked at her. "I hope you like Maryland crab cakes. I got the crab meat at the Inner Harbor this afternoon." With his thumb, he motioned them out of the kitchen. "Why waste your time in here with me when you could be enjoying each other's company?"

Nelson looked at his brother, and she couldn't miss the understanding that passed between them. Two individuals attuned to each other's feelings and emotions. Nelson's expression bore nothing short of relief and, with her hand in his, he took her to the living room.

"Did I pass muster?" she asked him, though she knew the answer.

It pleased him that she cared whether his brother liked her. "What do you think?" he teased.

"I think you'd rather not say, but if I go back in there and ask him, he'll tell me."

"That, he will. Want to go cycling after church Sunday?" *Now, where had that come from?*

She nodded. "What time?"

None of the coyness he so often got from women. She grew on him with each passing second. They agreed on the time he'd pick her up and, in spite of his lectures to himself to move with care, he stepped close to her, caressed her cheek with the palm of his hand and gave her a little more of himself.

"Dinner's ready," Logan said, announcing his presence. Page shook herself back to reality and stepped away from Nelson as Logan trained his gaze on her. "Is he scared you'll disappear?"

That was a devious way of getting a confession; she had to watch it with Logan Pettiford. "Do I look that frivolous? What woman would want to escape this man?" She pointed to Nelson. *Let them digest that.*

Later, as she sipped espresso coffee, she couldn't remember having had a better meal. "You're some cook."

"Glad you enjoyed it. Tell me, what's a sophisticated woman like you doing out here in the boondocks? Running away from anything?"

Nelson's antennae shot up. He'd wondered about that, but had decided it might be too soon to question her, since he had a string of things he wasn't ready to share with her.

"I'm not running," he heard her say. "I'm looking—for

myself, for my independence and..." something else, she thought suddenly. "I want to stretch myself to my limits."

"And you think you'll find all of that here?"

Nelson intervened. He wouldn't let Logan, an accomplished attorney, interrogate her. "Ease up, Logan. Aren't her reasons for being here the same as mine?"

"All right, man, but you know me." He winked at Page. "Stick with him. No matter how it looks, he's worth it."

Nelson stood. "It's time I took you home." He pointed to Logan. "When that philosopher's got his belly full and a snifter of good cognac in his hands, he's ready to roll." Logan walked with them to the door and, to Nelson's amazement, embraced Page.

"That's a first," Nelson told her, standing with her at her front door. "Logan is not a demonstrative man. I'll be out of town tomorrow, but I'll be at your place Sunday at one. Okay?" Unwilling either to draw them into heated passion or to leave without kissing her, he looked down at her willing lips, brushed them with his own and turned away.

"Now, who's chicken?" she called after him.

"Me. I freely admit it. See you Sunday." Her laughter wrapped around him, warming his heart as he headed home.

How could she know what it meant to him to have a woman who attracted him as she did behave as if his height was not unusual? A woman who didn't comment on the obvious and who seemed to accept what she saw of him. A woman who, with her intelligence, had to know about Nelson Pettiford, the writer; and with what she'd seen of his lifestyle, she had to know he was that man. Either she liked him for himself or she was someone special in her own right and unfazed by celebrity. Whichever, he liked the result. If their relationship continued to progress, he'd know it all, but he believed in biding his time.

He'd meant to go straight to bed, get up early and sketch some cartoons, but his entire system seemed charged, an engine revved and ready to go. He knew he wouldn't sleep, so he went into his den and started work on a cartoon. He sketched several but couldn't bring Quigley to life. Finally, with Odessa-Cat frolicking beside him, the big tom prowled along Old Mills Road complaining about human beings.

"Only an idiot would think of putting street lights on this road. What do people think moonlight's for?" Quigley said to Odessa-Cat.

"Don't ask me," Odessa-Cat said. "I long since forgot what moonlight-light's for."

Quigley slanted his gray eyes in her direction, "You had your day, girl, and I sure enjoyed you."

Suddenly, Quigley stopped walking. "I always get an eerie feeling out here on Old Mills Road, but I still can't seem to stay away from here. Let's go back."

Odessa-Cat rubbed herself against Quigley, but the wily tomcat merely stretched lazily and licked his chops. "Ain't no point in sidling up to me, girl. Come on."

Nelson stared at his creation, nonplussed as to where the idea had come from. Musing over it, he realized that he often got an eerie feeling on that very same road, but he loved to drive along it at sunset, when the multi-hued rays of the dying sun enthralled him and made him feel alive. Funny, that it was there he had met Page. Hmmm.

Page kicked off her shoes, put on her stack of Louis Armstrong CDs and danced herself into exhaustion. What was the matter with her? In all her twenty-nine years, never before had a man kicked her libido into perpetual over-drive. She ought to be suspicious of the whole thing, but he was so sweet, and being with him exhilarated her. She thought back to earlier that evening with him and his brother. Logan liked her and encouraged her relationship with Nelson. They saw something admirable in her, wanted her friendship and they weren't trying through her to get anything from Millie Shipley, weren't courting her mother for favors.

She went to the phone and called her mother's private number. She didn't telephone her mother often, because just talking with Millie wore her out.

"Darling," Millie began as soon as she said hello, "I was going to call you, but this town is one living cyclone. Congressman Boney is going to get a piece of my mind. You just wait. Oh, yes. We're going to the White House Tuesday after next for the reception preceding the Kennedy Center Honors. So get a new formal. Not pink. That's what I'm wearing. Mary Jasper is on the honors list. What for, I don't know, but they always have to have at least one African American out of the five. When are you coming home? Call me to make sure I'm here.You know—"

Page took a deep breath and broke into Millie's torrent of words. "Mama, I'm not going to that reception. So get somebody else to go with you. I'll let you know when I can get over to Washington. The job is—"

"All right, Honey. My other line is flashing. Mother loves you. Bye."

Page fell back on the bed. "How'd I ever stand the stress of living in the house with her?" she said aloud. "Much as I love her, I sure am glad I left there."

Sunday afternoon, she dressed warmly in down pants and jacket, got her head gear and waited for Nelson's one-one-three-one ring. She opened the door and laughed when she saw that he'd chosen down pants and jacket the same shade of blue as her own. His quick kiss didn't satisfy her, but she knew that was all she'd get right then. He took her bike from her and stored it with his own on the rack over his bumper.

"Where're we going?"

"Stone Mountain Park, about forty minutes from here. The trails are fantastic. I've always biked over there by myself, but it's so peaceful, so quiet and so...so beautiful that... Well, at least today I'll be able to enjoy it with someone...with you."

He'd been lonely, she surmised, maybe even lonelier than she, who had hungered for meaningful friendships to replace the superficial relationships she experienced in the rarefied atmosphere of her famous mother's orbit.

"I'm...I'm glad my car stalled out on Old Mills Road and that you happened along."

He didn't look at her, but she knew from the way his jaw worked that he was dealing with an emotion she'd stirred in him. He reached over and laid his right hand on her left one.

"I told you once, that I didn't believe in things I couldn't understand. Like Fate. But I'm not so sure now. The evening we met, I turned into that road by mistake because my thoughts weren't on my driving. I was sure I'd already passed Old Mills Road. Fate? I just don't know."

In the park, they cycled for almost an hour, not speaking, enjoying the beauty of autumn's last gasp. Then, he guided them back to the car. "I brought some snacks if you'd like something." They sat on an old stone bench beneath the trees that seemed to reach the sky, while the evening sun hovered closer and closer to its place of rest. "You can have ham, smoked salmon and chicken sandwiches, and I've got a thermos of coffee and some ginger ale, since you don't drink colas."

She looked up at him, saw the concern for her com-

fort reflected in his face and in his whole demeanor and
asked herself how she'd gotten so lucky. She told him
she'd start with the chicken sandwich and coffee. He
poured a cup of coffee for her and added milk. So he'd
noticed that she didn't add sugar. Taking it from him, she
smiled as best she could, because if she cried...

"Want some grapes?" he asked after she'd eaten
three sandwiches.

She nodded, and he picked one from the cluster and
held it to her mouth. Her lips accepted it and the next and
the next until she made herself look into eyes that shim-
mered with a sweet something that wrung a gasp from
her throat. In spite of her vow of prudence, she reached
for him; she couldn't help it, and in a split second, he had
her in his arms. Holding her. Stroking her. Wanting to feel
his mouth on her, she kissed his cheek and, when he
looked at her, she claimed him. He slipped his tongue
between her parted lips, but only for a second and then
hugged her to him. Every molecule of her body warmed
to his cherishing, his gentle loving.

Her heart told her that he'd seeped deep into her,
that because of him, she knew what she'd missed and
what she needed and that if they walked away from each
other, she'd never be the same. Now's the time to tell him
who you are, her conscience advised, but she couldn't
risk dragging her mother's fame into their relationship.
She'd better tell him about her work, though, because
she didn't want him to suspect her of using him.

With her hand still in his, she shifted her body to face
him. "Before we go any further, I'd better tell you something."

She sensed his tension in the hand she held, and his
defensiveness mirrored itself in his eyes like a swords-
man en garde.

"What is it?"

"I'm a journalist, and I work for *The Mystic Ridge*

Observer."

He stared at her and eased his fingers out of her hand. "Are you kidding me?"

She shook her head. "That's what I do, but I will never write one word about you. Never! When I asked my boss where you lived and told him why I wanted to find you, he gave me your address and asked me to interview you. But after those precious hours I spent with you that afternoon, no one could have paid me to invade your privacy. When I got to work that next Monday morning, I told him you refused to see me."

The fingers of his right hand moved back and forth across his chin, and while she waited for his response, tiny needles pierced every nerve in her body.

"I see."

"D...don't you believe me?"

"I do believe you. It's been almost two months, so you've had opportunities to write about me. But I read that paper, and I haven't seen your bye. How's that?"

"My column's in the features section under the name, Twice Shy."

"I know the people in Mystic Ridge are curious about me, and I know they've imagined all kinds of things about me. I'm also certain you've heard a lot of it. Rodgers has too, and when he discovers we're friends—and small towns being what they are, he certainly will—he'll pressure you. Then what?"

"It won't be the first time I've changed jobs."

He nodded. "That's the only paper in Mystic Ridge. You'd have to leave here."

"I'm not going to write a story on you. Period."

His gaze lingered on her. And then, as though having arrived at an important conclusion, he leaned back against the bench. "I'll be in Washington Tuesday night and Wednesday morning. Can we be together Wednesday evening?"

Her heartbeat returned to normal and she let herself smile. "I'm already looking forward to it."

After emptying their refuse in the wire basket that rested beside an elm, he walked back and took her hand. "It gets dark earlier and earlier these days. I think we ought to head back to Mystic."

He drove slowly over the two-lane highway that wound its way between trees that seemed to touch the sky, the last of their leaves fluttering gracefully to the earth. The only words that came to her mind were those that said peace, contentment, paradise.

"Do you think we can do this again before it gets too cold?" he asked.

She nodded. "I love the outdoors and especially the water. Next time, let's ride around the lake. We can go anytime; just whistle."

"Yeah? If I did that, you'd think I'd lost my mind."

He braked quickly, and his right arm shot out as though to protect her. A smile had taken possession of his face, and she glanced at the highway in front of them expecting to see a deer or a bear. But strolling casually across the paved road were a goose and her five little goslings.

"Nature's wonderful," he said, when the birds disappeared into the underbrush.

What a sweet man, she thought, folded her arms and settled back into the comfort of the aura that his presence wrapped around her. James Rodgers could beg all he pleased; he'd never get a story about Nelson Pettiford out of her.

Chapter Five

Nelson flexed his shoulders to get used to the cut of the tux he hadn't worn in nearly a year, stepped out of the Willard Hotel and into a Capital Cab.

"The White House, please."

"You got a pass, buddy? I ain't gittin' in that long line for nothin'."

He showed the driver the pass and, fifteen minutes later, stepped out of the taxi and into the White House. He'd had his jacket tailored with an extra inside pocket so he'd have places to keep his little note pads as well as his miniature recorder. His status as best-selling author thrice over got him more invitations than he bothered to accept, but he wasn't so blasé or jaded as to turn down a White House reception for the Kennedy Center Honorees. The President surprised him with the comment that he'd read and liked his last book; he thought the First Lady warmer and more feminine than her press and pictures suggested.

He ordered a wine glass of ginger ale with ice and mingled. He'd thought Art Buchwald taller, and Brokaw didn't look nearly his age.

Congresswoman Dr. Millie Shipley held court with three first-year congressmen and one old pro whose demeanor suggested an interest in more than her words.

Her eyes reminded him of someone; he couldn't figure out who, but he didn't give much thought to it. He spied two senators in heated discussion and inched close enough to discern that Senator Painter wanted the health care bill floored and Ballard swore it wouldn't happen. Power. Power. The entertainment at the Kennedy Center proved uninspired; he thought the honorees deserved better. The applause had hardly ceased before he was back in the Willard Hotel.

He ate a light supper in his room and listened to his recorded notes. He sketched Quigley snarling at a tom-cat that had invaded his territory.

"There's room enough here for both of us," the intruder said.

"But my space is germ free, Brother Tom," Quigley said, "and the way you chase these little hot trollops, you're full of disease. Stay out. I don't have any health insurance."

Brother Tom stuck his tail between his legs, his face, a caricature of Congressman Ballard, glum and arrogant. "Ain't no way you can stay healthy, Quigley, if my little hot trollops are full of disease. No amount of insurance will save you, so forget that."

"That's how you feel about all the poor cats in this country," Quigley said, raising his head and prancing off. "Later for you, Brother Tom."

Satisfied with the piece, he reached for the phone and dialed Page's number. "This is Nelson, I hope you hadn't gone to bed."

"No. I was editing my story."

He marveled that they had so much in common, but he couldn't tell her about that. Not yet. "Remember our date tomorrow? If you like, we could drive over to Baltimore. The choice is between an African American Arts Show, The Soloisti di Zagreb with a program of Mozart chamber music and the Preservation Hall Jazz

Band. If we leave early, we can take in the art show and one of the other two. What's your pleasure?"

"Whatever you can get tickets for. Just tell me what to wear and what time to be ready."

She never pretended, never fuzzed an issue. "I'll call you as soon as I have something definite."

"You can call me before then."

He rolled over in the bed and lay flat on his back. "Is that so? You aren't playing with me, are you?"

The silence lasted a little longer than he'd anticipated. "Uh...no. Well, not really. I mean, I may be teasing, but I mean it."

"What kind of double talk is that?" He fell over on his belly, ready to test her mettle. "I mean business."

Her giggle reached him through the wires, soothing him and exciting him as well. She said, "Me too."

A grin crawled over his face, and he waited, certain that she'd back down. "No kidding. You write a great score, Baby," he said when she didn't, "but I want to hear you sing the tune."

He could imagine that her eyes widened as they did when she got a surprise.

"Soprano or mezzo? I've got a wide range, and I'm no stranger to the scales."

"How often do you practice?" he asked, warming up to the game.

She cleared her throat. "That's the problem. I don't remember when I last practiced. I must be kind of rusty."

How much truth was in that jostling? He propped himself up on his elbows, more serious now. "A serious musician rehearses regularly."

"Is that what we're talking about? Music? I must have gotten lost somewhere."

"Be careful, Page," he growled. "I can be in Mystic Ridge in an hour and a half."

"But I wouldn't want you to get jacked up for speeding or maybe get in an accident."

"Why don't you just say `uncle'? You're chicken and you're backing down."

"Am not. If you want to come all the way here just to kiss me good night, I wouldn't think of objecting."

He held the phone away and stared at it. Whether she knew it or not, she was definitely kidding.

"You still there?" she asked.

"Yeah, but you give me one reason, and I'll be out of here in fifteen minutes."

"What's here for you will wait till tomorrow, and you can get a good night's sleep and drive refreshed in the morning."

"What's there for me, Page?" Maybe he ought to stop before he said more than he intended, but right then all he could think of was the heat of her body when he touched her and the hunger that racked his loins. Hunger for her alone.

"You told me to be careful; I'm giving you the same advice," she said. "You're not ready to know where I stand, but if you urge me the tiniest bit, I'll tell you. Can I have a kiss?"

"Can you have... open your mouth. Baby."

Arousal slammed into him, and his breath came in short gasps. What the hell had he done to himself? Get it together, man.

"Good night." He whispered it lest she detect his total disarray.

"Good night, Love." She hung up, and he lay there. Unstrung.

Nelson hadn't reached the point of commitment, and he'd intimated that he wanted to be prudent and let them care for and understand each other before they became intimate. She knew he didn't intend to have a casual affair, and if he decided he wasn't in it for the long haul, she doubted he'd let her get any closer to him. That suited her perfectly, and it told her more about him than he could explain with words. But tonight, he'd come close to breaching the bounds he set for himself, and it behooved her not to play with him. If she caused him to violate his own standards, he might hold it against her.

The next morning, she dressed in a burnt-orange colored woolen suit, a beige blouse and brown shoes and accessories. She wasn't overdressed, but she figured she could go wherever he took her that evening.

"Hey, Girl, you really hung it on this morning," Phyllis said. "Who is he?"

Page let her have a slow burn. "I dress to please myself, and my mood this morning said burnt orange. Since this is the only thing I own this color, this is what I'm wearing."

"Well, go out and buy a slew of stuff that color."

"Yeah, it suits you." She turned around to see James Rodgers, her boss standing in the doorway.

How does he know what color I'm wearing? she wanted to ask him. He'd glued his gaze on Phyllis, his copy editor. The phone rang and she reached for it, but Phyllis grabbed it first.

"*Observer.* How may I help you?" She listened for a second. "Uh ... she's right here."

Page took the phone, covered the mouthpiece with her hand and said, "Let that be the last time you answer my phone when I'm sitting here, unless I ask you to do it."

"Well kiss my grits."

Page turned her back to them. "Hello."

"Hi. This is Nelson."

"I know. What did you find out?"

"That's not the greeting I expected. You got company?"

"Yes. Sorry. I'll make up for it."

"I'll pick you up at four-thirty. Office or home?"

"I'll be at the office," she told him.

"I'll call you around one. Okay?"

"Right. Kiss me, and make it good."

"You'll be sorry for that one. Talk with you later."

She hung up, turned and it didn't surprise her that she had the attention of both James and Phyllis. A couple of sharp comments came to mind, but she swallowed them.

"Can I do something for either one of you?" she asked, instead.

Phyllis shrugged. "You been here a couple of months, and you're already whispering to some guy on the phone. Way to go, Girl."

Page chose not to comment, finished retyping her column and took it across the hall to the features editor.

"Is it good?" he asked her.

"Flawless," she said and headed for the elevator. She wanted to talk with Nelson, and she didn't want to wait another hour and a half. She called him from a phone booth in the building's lobby. After the fifth ring, she heard his voice on the answering machine. Deep and soothing.

"This is Page, I—"

"What a surprise! I'm glad you called. Our earlier conversation left me dissatisfied and wanting more. Much more."

"I suspect those busybodies will be watching to see whether anyone meets me this evening. I'll be proud to have you come to my office for me. It's your call."

"In that case, I'll be at your office at four-thirty."

"I'm in room four-sixteen. Turn left at the top of the stairs."

"Are you sure, Babe?"

"I've never been more positive of anything. See you at four-thirty."

She saw no reason why they shouldn't see each other when and wherever they wished. They were both single. The good citizens of Mystic Ridge may have peculiar notions about him, but she knew how wrong they were, and if being seen with him would change their minds, she was more than happy to walk hand-in-hand with him.

"But you'll have to wait for your kiss; I don't think I should do that in my office."

His laughter caressed her ears, and she suspected not for the first time that, if he let her, she could love him. Yes, if he'll let you, her mind challenged.

Nelson hung up, braced his elbows on his drafting board and gave in to his emotions as tremor after tremor slashed through his body. A companion, a woman who enjoyed his company, who wanted her colleagues to know that he was important to her and who asked nothing of him other than his friendship. A woman, who in two months hadn't alluded to his status as a celebrity author and who had never mentioned his height of nearly seven feet. Had he finally found a woman to love, to care for and who would cherish him above all others? He went to the refrigerator and got a glass of orange juice in the hope that the potassium would slow his heartbeat. After a few minutes, he sat down to put the finishing touches on the cartoon he'd begun the night before in the hotel. He gave Quigley an added bit of tabby hair in the forehead and signed it Slim Wisdom as he always did.

Nelson prepared himself for the astonishment that

Page's colleagues would exhibit when they saw him, and he appreciated Page's efforts to forestall that, though he didn't need their approval nor their good manners.

The door stood ajar, and when he entered, the sweet woman rounded her desk immediately, took his hand and reached up to him with her face upturned. Thinking she wanted to tell him something, he leaned down and, to his amazement, she kissed his cheek.

"Phyllis, this is Nelson."

"Hi. Well, hi. I have to say I never expected to meet you."

"Hello, Phyllis," he said, with amusement. "I'm glad to know you." Just for the hell of it, he winked at her. "Was it you who answered the phone when I called this morning?"

Phyllis swallowed hard. "That was you?"

He looked down at Page. "Was it?"

He felt her fingers tug at his hand. "You know it was, and stop pulling her leg."

He helped Page into her coat and, for reasons he didn't guess at, put his arm around her. As if to reward him for the audacious act, she let a brilliant smile light up her face and warmth suffused him.

"We'd better be going. Nice meeting you, Phyllis."

"Sure thing, Nelson," Phyllis said, and he could see that she was practically in a stupor.

"See you in the morning," Page called to her colleague over her shoulder.

"Why'd you kiss me on the cheek in your office?" he asked as they sped toward Baltimore.

"Just spreading the word that you are not available. By noon tomorrow, this town will know that you and I are seeing each other, and you'll have to step around the women."

He slowed down to seventy. "You couldn't be serious. They've left me alone for eighteen months."

Her laughter was gentle, yet invigorating like a rustling spring breeze. "You ever heard of royal tasters? They tasted the food before the sovereign ate it to make sure it wasn't poisoned. You could say these women will regard me as a tester, if not taster."

Lord, it felt good to laugh, and he let himself enjoy it. "You're pure joy. I'm already forgetting what my life was like before you walked into it."

From the moment they stepped into the art gallery, she appeared captivated by the paintings, most of which were abstracts, and he had to bide his time until they reached the drawings.

She commented on his preference for them. "You seem more interested in the drawings than in the paintings. I like the drawings, but I'm not sure I understand what the artist is saying. I love paintings."

"I love both," he said. Better not get into a discussion of their relative merits; he might give himself away. That thought brought to mind another issue that he'd better do something about. He hadn't told her he was Nelson Pettiford the author, though he suspected that with her sophistication, she knew. But if she didn't, he'd rather she didn't learn it through the media.

A group of Romare Bearden drawings caught his eye. So many black artists painted with great power and, yet, with so much less recognition than they deserved. He stood before the man's work, admiring the craftsmanship and inventiveness until her fingers slipped through his, warm and tender.

"You really like these, don't you? I've never paid much attention to them. Maybe you'll explain them to me sometime so I'll know what to look for."

He heard her words, but had no idea what she'd said. His mind, his whole being had focussed on her smile, on the evidence that she knew she had the right to take his hand and hold it.

"What's the matter?"

He'd been staring at her. But how could he not? A woman who seemed to fit him perfectly. At times, he'd swear he was deep in a dream.

"I know you're real," he said, "but sometimes I don't see how you could be."

"You mean because we like the same things?"

He shook his head. "That too. But everything about you appeals to me. At my age, I never expected to meet a woman who would touch me as you have and who would...well..." He couldn't finish because he wasn't that sure, didn't know what he was to her.

"And who would enjoy being with you and...and—"

"And what, Page?" The urgency in his voice shocked him as his words flew out to her on wings of prayer.

She didn't hesitate, nor did she take her eyes from his gaze. "And who thinks you're the most wonderful man she's ever met."

As though of their own accord, both of his hands grasped her shoulders, and he stared down at her knowing his eyes mirrored what was in his heart. "There's so much you don't know. I haven't felt alone since I've known you. Don't encourage me unless you're serious, unless you mean what you say. You're a lovely woman, and you don't have to take second best. Unless you care for me, I need to put on the brakes right this minute."

She looked up at him, her face open and vulnerable. "You don't care more for me than I care for you. If you put on the brakes, as you termed it, I'll have to do the same. I understand what you're telling me, but the citizens of Mystic Ridge are foolish." Suddenly, she grinned. "Imagine, I can go out and buy a slew of spiked-heel shoes and even if that puts me over six feet, it won't matter."

"You say all that in here in the presence of all these people when I can't..." His pounding heart sent his blood speeding through his body as the force and meaning of her words planted themselves in his brain. This wasn't the time to explore with her what he felt and needed, not there in that crowded gallery. He glanced at his watch.

"We'd better get something to eat. The concert begins at eight."

While they walked to his car, he took her hand in his and tucked them both in his coat pocket. Gusts of wind pelted his face as they strode along, and he wanted to shield her from the stinging air. But with her face up and head back, she seemed to glory in it. In the car at last, he locked the doors and reached across her to buckle her seat belt. He knew she could do it, but it pleased him to buckle it for her.

She leaned back against the headrest and treated him to a smile that shot pinions of desire straight through him.

"You can kiss me now." She wet her lips, parted them and raised her long-lashed gaze in an electrifying invitation. He'd have taken her to his body even if there had been a trap door beneath his feet. At the touch of his tongue against her lips, she pulled him into her and loved him as if she'd been starved for his touch, his taste, as if she couldn't get enough of him. Her fingers caressed his nape, and he tightened his hold on her. Moans erupted from her throat, exciting and thrilling him, and in his deceptive mind he had her beneath his naked body thrashing and undulating against him. He had to brake it or he'd lose control, had to stop the sweet and awful fire she'd built in his loins. But she let herself go, sucking on his tongue as if it were the essence of her life. *Stop it, man.* But it felt so good and for so long, all of his life, he'd needed the loving she gave him.

He had to ... With all the control he could muster, he pushed himself away.

She stared up at him, as if trying to see through a

fog. "What ... what is it?"

He let his hand brush her cheek in the only intimacy he dared permit himself. "Honey, you had me close to the point of explosion. I'm...I'm anything but hungry for food right now, but we ..." He cleared his throat. *Get it together, man.* "We have to eat." She continued to gaze at him, the picture of innocence. He shook his head in bemusement. "Baby, you're lethal." He turned the key in the ignition and prayed he could keep his mind on his driving.

Chapter Six

At the Crystal Cove Restaurant, they took their seats in a booth facing the Baltimore Bay. Reflections of lights from The Inner Harbor danced across Nelson's face. His precious face, Page thought, and acknowledged to herself that he was the man she wanted. Their explosive passion minutes earlier had taken her appetite, at least for food, so she ordered a poached filet of sole, the least filling entree on the menu.

"I think I'll have the same," Nelson said, and she didn't miss his lack of enthusiasm for it.

They finished the meal, and he moved around and sat beside her in the booth. "Maybe I should have told you this earlier, but I didn't. Anyhow, I suspect you may already know that I'm the same Nelson Pettiford who wrote three novels that made the *New York Times* list. I didn't mention it, because I wanted you to like me for myself."

She didn't need his confession, but it pleased her that he trusted her enough to tell her. "You're right; I knew it, and I liked the fact that you didn't try to impress me. Nothing would have sent me running from you faster. I've had my fill of that. That night on Old Mills Road, you told me that if I wouldn't let you take me into town, you'd park on the other side of the road from me and stay there all night to make certain no one bothered me. I wouldn't have been more impressed with you if you had won a Nobel prize."

He stared at her so long that tension gathered in her, and a restlessness suffused her. As though realizing that he unsettled her, he squeezed her fingers in reassurance, but that exacerbated the damage, and desire shot through her like a twister. His right arm brought her to him, and he patted her shoulder. But she wasn't fooled; he needed to touch her, and a pat was all he risked right then.

Three hours later they walked out of the concert hall and into the biting, early-December wind. "It'll probably be too cold to bike," he said, his voice tinged with regret, " but we could drive over to the Monocacy River, fish and cook the catch on the river bank. We could build a nice fire. Want to?"

She did, though she'd never had a fishing pole in her hands. For the remainder of that week and on the weekend, they explored Mystic Ridge and its environs, fishing in Monocacy River, walking in Stone Mountain Park and cycling through nearby woods and alongside Lake Linganore. For the first time, she had a companion, and she told him in many little ways that he had a special place in her life.

The following Monday morning, Page met Mr. Whitfield as he strode up with the mail. He tipped his hat and took the mail from his sack.

"Young lady, you've set this town on its head. At every stop I make, people are asking me about Pettiford. They're not sure they've read him right because if they had, a sane woman like you wouldn't be walking around holding hands with him. Unless there's something special about you, too." He chuckled. "You watch out when the sistahs realize they passed on the real thing."

She felt good. For two cents, she'd spread her wings and fly. "Serves them right. Every one of them," she said. "They isolated him, treated him as if he weren't human. But he is, and he's wonderful."

"I won't ask how you happened to figure that out, but I tip my hat to you. He's a fine man. Solid as they come."

No sooner had she walked into her office and sat at her desk than her boss appeared at the door. "I'd say you're a fast worker. "

She remembered Mr. Whitfield's words, and a cold dampness settled around her neck and on her forehead. Here it comes, she thought, and braced herself for the worst.

"I want a story on Pettiford for the next issue. It'll go right on the front page under your real name. A sell out. Can you get me a picture of him, preferably with you or somebody standing right beside him?"

Anger furled up in her, and she told herself not to lose her temper. "So you noticed we're friends, and you want me to do a story on him to appease the curiosity of people who've shunned him for the eighteen months he's been here? If you wanted a story on him, why didn't you call him, invite him to lunch and interview him? Sorry!"

Incredulity masked his face. "You're saying you won't do it?"

She unlocked her computer. "You got it. We're friends, James, and I don't intend for him to think I've developed a friendship with him in order to get a story."

He walked to her desk, and she could see that he

didn't believe she'd said it. "You're a reporter, and I'm only telling you to do your job. He was here, and he knows you work for a newspaper."

From his stance, she didn't expect to win, but she made one last appeal. "I care for him, James, and he's given me his trust. I won't betray him, not for this job or anything else. If you wish, I'll give you my resignation."

He stared at her. "You don't know a thing about that guy, and yet you'd ditch your job for him?"

She released a long, tired breath. "You're the one who doesn't know anything about him. You and these people who call him weird, crazy, dangerous, an outlaw and a lot of other things that would hurt him if he knew. If you want me to leave, just say so."

His shoulders sagged. "I won't ask you to leave, but you've just ruined your chance to report hard news, and I'm dropping your column. Go down to the senior center and find out if anything's going on there that would interest anybody."

"But—"

"You asked for it. Take it or leave it." With that he turned on his heels and stomped away.

"I'm sorry," Phyllis said. "I wish I hadn't mentioned it to him. But he was so happy when he figured he'd finally get that story. Maybe if I talk to him—"

"It's all right, Phyllis. I'm a good reporter, and I know it. When I get tired of visiting with the seniors, I'll move on." She consoled herself with the thought that it ought to be more fun working in Frederick.

"I didn't see your byline in the paper this week," Nelson said to her several evenings later as they sat in her kitchen making pecan pralines. "What happened? You missed your deadline?"

"Naaah," she said, as if the matter were of no importance. "I'm checking out the seniors at the center on Boyers Mill Road. Fascinating." She hadn't meant to sound sarcastic, but nearly a week of boredom had that effect.

"You mean... Wait a minute. Back up. You've been demoted. That's what this is about, isn't it?"

"It's nothing," she hedged, "I got a new assignment is all."

He stopped placing pecans in the middle of the candies and got up from the table."Did he ask you to write a story about me?" When she didn't answer and wouldn't look at him, he persisted. "Did he? I'll hound you till you tell me the whole story."

She let the air out of her lungs. "Okay, so he asked me. I told him I wouldn't do it." She related the remainder of it while he paced from one end of the kitchen to the other and back.

"He can't do this to you. I'll give you the interview. Carte blanche. Ask me anything."

She had expected he'd react this way. "Please stop pacing and sit down before this stuff gets hard. I am not, repeat not, going to write a story on you for this newspaper or any other. Period. I told you that, and I'm good as my word. Besides, I refuse to satisfy the curiosity of the gossip mongers in this town. And that's final."

"Well—"

She wasn't sure she was ready for what the expression on his face implied. "Well what?"

"Is it just a matter of keeping your word, or do you care this much for me?"

She stiffened. Until he told her how he felt about her, she'd let him figure it out from her behavior. Besides, she wasn't jumping over that bridge before she got to it.

"I care about you," she said, fumbling her way. "You're old enough to figure out things yourself."

The smile nearly made it to his eyes. Eyes that made her think and feel things she couldn't share with a living soul. He needed to know where he stood; she knew that, but he'd have to give a little.

He lifted his right shoulder in a light shrug. "I know you light up like a furnace when I touch you and that you care about me. Yes." He trained his mesmeric gaze on her for a long minute. "But you've given me something I never had, and—"

She scrambled from the table, stood and faced him. "You wanted to take it slow. Well so do I. That doesn't mean you aren't important to me because you are—"

Warm and eager, his mouth covered her own, and his hands held her to him, his caress gentle. The touch of his fingers stroking her hair, her cheeks and her shoulder in feather-soft touches bound her to him with the strength of ancient chains. His lips adored her eyes, the tip of her nose and her chin, swathing her in the bittersweet agony of love. Tremors rippled through her, as he cherished her, and she locked her arms around his waist. Not the mind-blowing passion into which he'd always drawn her, but a sweet and exquisite caring. He folded her to him and tucked her head to his breast, and her tears of happiness soaked his shirt.

"I think I'd better go now."

Torn between her head and her emotions, she hugged him. "You make me so happy."

She could see that he forced the smile. "I'm happy too, but it's best I leave. Make no mistake, Page, one of these nights I won't leave you unless you tell me to go. Is that clear?"

She nodded. He kissed her quickly and left, but if he had wanted to stay... She let the thought hang. Your days are numbered, girl, she said to herself as she closed the door behind him.

Nelson walked into his house and sat down to gather his thoughts. Maybe he shouldn't have left Page, but she had become a part of him, had buried herself into his every sinew, every molecule of his body from his feet to his scalp. Yet, they didn't know each other. Hell, he didn't even know her birthday, the names of her parents or where she was born. As much as they talked, and they talked all the time, they hadn't talked enough about themselves. He intended to correct that, because he was leaning toward the point of no return. His gaze landed on *The Washington Post*. He scrutinized an item in the lower left-hand corner, turned to page nineteen and read the remainder. With the paper in hand, he went to his drafting board. Millie Shipley was visiting local African American beauty parlors in support of small businesses, and she'd already had her hair done at three of them that day. When asked whether she planned to charge the government for her hairdos, she had replied, "It's part of the job, at least for today." Partly amused and partly vexed, he began his cartoon.

"Where you going tonight, Quigley?" Odessa-Cat asked.

"Staying home, Odessa-Cat. At thirty dollars for a hair trim, I can't afford to leave this alley. Where you going?"

"I found an expense account voucher for the House of Representatives that somebody lost, so I guess that ought to take care of things. I'm gonna have a night on the town."

"You're not scared you'll get into trouble with Taxpayer advocate Millie-Cat? You know how she rages about every little thing."

"No problem," Odessa-Cat said. "Millie-Cat's getting

her hair done at every beauty parlor in Washington and charging it to the government. She can't raise the devil about me this time."

Quigley licked his fur. "She should be glad she's not representing me. I'd picket her on Capitol Hill."

He sketched Millie-Cat's face to resemble Millie Shipley and signed it Slim Wisdom.

The phone rang, and he hoped he'd hear Page's voice. "How's it going, Brother? You sound disappointed. How're things with you and Page?"

He settled back for a long talk with Logan. "Page is fine. How's it going with you?" He didn't want to talk about her, not even with his brother, so he changed the subject. "A while back, I set up a foundation to help children, and I've decided to help the kids who suffer because they're different, as I have. Living in this conservative town has made me more aware than ever of what it means to stand out."

They discussed Nelson's plans for his foundation a bit more, then turned the talk to the case Logan was trying in civil court, but Nelson's heart wasn't in the conversation and their talk soon ended. He wanted to speak with Page, to tell her everything about himself, though he didn't consider that prudent at the time. He'd never doubted himself before, but he'd never loved a woman either.

In the library several days later, he noticed a group of children who were returning some books and checking out others. Two boys and a girl were severely deformed and one boy spoke with difficulty. All were well behaved for their age, around five or six.

"Who are those children?" Nelson asked a boy who was shelving books.

"They're from the group home."

A little girl with sad eyes covered the left side of her face with her hand when she caught him looking at her, and his heart turned over when he saw the mark she tried to hide. She signed for her book and walked past him with her head turned away from him. The next day, he went to the group home where he learned that all the children there had been abandoned, and he vowed to help as much as he could.

"What are you telling me?" he asked Page several evenings later when they spoke by phone.

"The Ridgeway Senior Center is not the dullest place in Mystic Ridge. A Mrs. Cook claimed that she always missed money out of her pocket book when she came back from lunch. It seems they are encouraged to leave their belongings in their little lockers. I then discovered that over half the seniors I spoke with there last Tuesday complained about the same thing," Page said with a ring of excitement in her voice. "They're afraid to tell the management, because the center is their whole life. It's that or stay home alone. If that weren't enough, I find that some of the workers borrow money from the seniors and don't repay it. We're speaking fifty, a hundred and more at a time. James Rodgers thought he was punishing me, but he may have done me a favor."

"If I were you, I'd keep it under my hat till I was ready to hand it in."

She told him she planned doing volunteer work at the senior center. He thought for a minute. "Unless you must be at that center, I've got a suggestion."

He told her that a year earlier he'd established a foundation to help children who weren't physically handicapped but who, like him, had traits that made them different.

"I need to publicize it, but I haven't been able to do that here and remain anonymous. Whether it's counselling they need, surgery, whatever. I know what it's like, and I want to help."

Her voice floated to him like music. "That's wonderful. I'll get a notice in the paper. Since it's charity, it won't cost anything."

"Great," he said. "How about a movie tomorrow night? Robert di Niro. There's a Danny Glover, too, but I've seen it."

He imagined that she grinned because he knew she loved di Nero. "Say no more. What time?"i

"Five thirty. Let's eat dinner after the movie."

She told him goodbye.

"Hey," he yelled. "What about my kiss?"

"Well, you didn't ask."

"I didn't ask? Since when did I have to ask?"

"I like to know you want it."

"You like to..." He got up and walked as far as the phone line would permit. "Page, are you trying to send me to an insane asylum? Well, Lady, let me tell you I want that and more." He lowered his voice and spoke in soft tones. "I want you, Page, in every way that a man can want a woman. I thought you knew that, but if you don't, I plan to remind you often. Very often. Got that?"

She laughed, and he wished he'd been looking at her so he could figure out what that laugh meant. "You make it sound like a punishment," she said. "I thought I was getting something super special, but——"

"I realize you like to challenge me sometime, but could we just skip that right now? I want a kiss, and if you can't manage it over the phone the way you usually do, I'm coming over there."

"I'll meet you at my front door, but you can't stay."

"I'll be right there."

He pressed the brakes just as his car was about to swing into Old Mills Road. He didn't remember driving past the turn to Page's street. Something about that old road pulled him and, as he thought back, he realized he'd been drawn to the area—almost unwillingly—since his arrival in Mystic Ridge. Furthermore, something there connected him to Page. He was sure of it.

Chapter Seven

ifteen minutes later, her doorbell rang. Quickly,
she washed the taste of mint out of her mouth,
dabbed some Dior perfume behind her ears
and beside her nose and rushed to the door. She slipped
the chain and the lock, and he turned the doorknob,
stepped inside and she was in his arms. His grip,
stronger than she'd known it to be, locked her to him and
fear battled with excitement as his tongue slipped
between her lips and dueled with her own. She tried to
control him, to suck him into her and still the dancing
torch, but he wouldn't give a quarter, stroking and promising what he had in store for them. Her heart hammered
out an erratic rhythm and shivers betrayed her body as
he loved her with the sweet and wild torture of his
tongue. Giddy with the aphrodisiac in front of her and all
around her, she grasped his hips and rocked against
him.

He moved her from him at once and spoke, tremors
lacing his words. "I want to make love with you; I need it
as I need air. But I want us to go away for a weekend,
somewhere where we'll be on equal terms, and I want us
to talk. Not about what we think and feel, but about who
we are, what makes us happy and what hurts us. And
when we leave there, I want us both to know what we

need and expect from each other. I've been let down, and I know what pain is. I want to avoid both. Are you with me in this?"

She shuffled through the pages of her mind to try to figure out what he was talking about. Wasn't she in his arms and wasn't he taking her to her bed? Oh Lord, if she couldn't...if...

With a smile that told her he knew he'd practically hypnotized her, she asked, "When?"

"Does weekend after next suit you? You'll have handed in your report on the senior citizens. What do you say?"

She couldn't imagine anything more exciting than a weekend idyll with him, but she said, "I'll let you know in a couple of days."

His cool and solemn stare unnerved her for it was not in his character, at least as she knew him. "All right. I expect you'll call me and let me know."

"Oh, Nelson! Honey, I don't doubt what I feel for you, but when I take that step, the rest will be out of my hands."

"Do you trust me?"

Warm coils of comfort flowed from him, and she gazed into his eyes until tension danced between them like an unharnessed electric current, wild and dangerous.

"You don't have to ask that," she whispered, "because you know I'd trust you with my life."

He bent to her, claimed her mouth and unleashed the force of his passion until she was drunk on him as on a gallon of spirits.

When she could get her breath, she whispered, "Leave, if you're going."

He hugged her and, like a woodland sprite, slipped out of the door and left her there. Alone.

She'd have to work like the devil to finish that story,

but she'd do it if she had to stay up nights for the next two weeks. Becoming lovers was not the only kind of intimate knowledge, and he was right in insisting that they experience every level of intimacy before committing to each other. He wanted her, but he didn't let his libido rule him. She liked that. With a light and happy heart, she went to bed.

Several mornings later, as she walked into her office, James stopped her. "Finding anything interesting at the senior center? I'd like to have an article for next week's issue."

She treated him to a withering look. "You serious?"

He had the grace to appear embarrassed. "Well... Uh... Yeah. I figured you could find something by now. You know, like how they spend the day."

"I'll do my best, Boss."

"Now, Page, don't take it personal. I needed some information about the seniors, and—"

"I know. I know. It's never personal." She looked him in the eye. "Now, would you please let me work."

He held up both hands, palms out. "All right. All right. I just didn't want us to have any hard feelings over this." He couldn't match the hard stare she threw his way. Instead, he lowered his gaze and walked out.

Page sucked her teeth and looked at Phyllis. "A man breaks an egg and thinks he's done a great thing when he cleans it up. It never occurs to him that there's no longer an egg."

Phyllis bowed her head as though embarrassed.

"Sorry," Page said. "I forget sometimes that you two are sweet on each other and I open my big mouth. Oooops! I wasn't supposed to know that, was I?"

"It's all right. When I saw how you were with Nelson Pettiford, both of you so proud of each other and all, I was sorry I told James we had to keep it quiet. Now, he doesn't even take me out."

Page supposed her shock was obvious from her widened eyes. "You can't be serious. Girl, I wouldn't put up with that. Pick the most public place you can think of and tell him you want to go there with him. If he refuses, tell him you'll go with somebody else. He's single. Put his feet to the fire."

Phyllis stared at her. "Is that how you got Nelson to come here and get you?"

"No indeed. He asked if he should pick me up here or at home, and I said here and gave him this room number."

"Gee! He's not...I mean, people think he's...that there's something wrong with him, but there isn't, is there? And when you see him close up, he's real handsome. I never saw such gorgeous eyes on a man."

Page turned to face her. "He's been mistreated here. Because of his height, he's considered weird, and heaven knows what else. You know what the gossip is. But I paid no attention to that talk. He's a wonderful man."

Phyllis looked down at her hands. "I know I sound disloyal to James, but I don't blame you for not doing that story on Nelson. I could see he cares for you. That wouldn't be right."

"And I care just as deeply for him," Page said. "I don't want anybody to think I don't." She uncovered her computer, signaling the end of the conversation. Over the next two hours, she outlined her story of the plight of the seniors. Then she took her notebook and headed for the center to check some facts. At the corner, she bought a copy of *The Maryland Journal* and put it in her briefcase to read when she got home.

"See this?" Mrs. Cook asked her when she entered the Center, "I cashed my social security check right next door on my way in here this morning. That's nine hundred and seventeen dollars. I ain't spent a single dime, and now I got eight hundred and seventeen dollars."

Page consoled the woman as best she could, recorded the names of the workers who were in the center at lunch time. After she turned in her report, she'd pass that information to the Sheriff. She did the work she'd gone there to do and went home.

She changed to her favorite at-home costume—a floor-length T-shirt—got a glass of ginger ale, kicked off her shoes and remembered to call her mother. Her calendar showed that Millie was in Alexandria, Virginia, preparing for a Town Hall meeting. She phoned Millie's cell number.

"Darling, I'm so glad you called. You won't believe how distraught I am. Of all the nerve! If I ever get my hands on that person who calls him or herself Slim Wisdom, you'll have to bail me out of jail."

Page took a deep breath and prepared for the worst. Her mother did everything possible to garner publicity, any publicity, and tried to die if she got bad notices. "What's it about? I haven't had a chance to read the paper."

"Well, don't. It's disgusting, and just as I'm about to start my campaign for reelection. All I did was publicize the plight of hairdressers in Washington, and just look at this. It's so unfair."

She had planned to tell Millie about her story on the senior center, but as usual, Millie didn't have time to listen to any voice but her own. They spoke a few minutes longer.

"Well, I'm on in a few minutes, so I have to catch my breath. Are you doing all right in that little old town? For the life of me, I don't know why you'd prefer that to the Capitol where everything important goes on," She paused for a few minutes, and Page knew the next words would come from her mother and not the public person Millie had created. "Be careful, Child. You're a very tender person, and mother worries about you."

"I will, Mama."

The orchestrated Millie reemerged at once. "My goodness, darling, I've only got two minutes. They gave me a dressing room two city blocks from the podium. I've got to run. Bye."

Page blew out the breath she'd been holding. Millie hadn't even bothered to find out why she'd called. One's own mother shouldn't be a source of stress, she told herself, as she opened her brief case to get the paper. She stared at Slim Wisdom's political cartoon strip, Quigley, and steamed in furor. Why did every news jock consider her mother fair game? The phone rang, and she directed her ire to the caller.

"Hello!"

"Wow! Who watered the gas in your engine?"

"Nelson? Oh. Hello. I was just looking at Quigley. Do you ever read that stuff? Why's he always picking on women? That tomcat is the reason why I can't stand any kind of feline."

She wondered at the lengthy silence. At last he said, "Yeah. I see it all the time. What strip are you talking about? There's nothing in today's strip that's anti-female. At least, it didn't seem that way to me."

She threw up her hands. "What did I expect? Men in congress do that sort of thing all the time, but if a woman does it, she's scandalized Capitol Hill."

To his credit, she thought, he refused to be drawn into an argument about it. "Page, I called to ask what you decided about our weekend?"

She thought for a minute. Oh, yes. Their weekend together. "Of course, I'll go. Why did you think I wouldn't?"

The silence was deafening. "I should have asked you that when we were together. If you're sure—"

She caught herself, because she knew she'd sounded flippant. But doggonit, her mind had been surfing elsewhere. "I'm sure, and I'm looking forward to it. Just let me in on the kind of weather I should expect."

"Warm weather and casual wear, but bring a couple of very dressy things."

"All right. How many days? I don't think I should ask for more than three or four."

"Four, if your boss will let you off, and bring your passport."

"He'll let me off, but you're kidding. Good Lord, Honey, you're risking the white slavery law. You're not only taking me across state lines for the purpose of... uh... you know, but you're taking me out of the country."

"You got it, Babe. If I'm gonna get thrown in the slammer, I intend to earn the right."

She fell back on the bed and crossed her knees. "I see you like to earn what you get. Works for me. I like to do the same, so if you're going to be so sweet, I'll have to cook you a gourmet dinner."

"Are you telling me you can cook?"

"You bet I can; otherwise I'd have starved. My mother can burn water and frequently did that. How about Friday night at seven?"

"I'll be there. Can I get my kiss?"

She blew him a kiss through the wire. "Good night, Love."

"Till tomorrow, Sweetheart."

Nelson hung up and stared at the receiver. Why would Page get so riled about that strip? Nobody could accuse him of denigrating women. And he didn't comment on them half as often as on men. Besides, he'd been gentle with the criticism. How would she have reacted if he'd ridiculed that woman the way he did Senator Thurman two days earlier? He flexed his shoul-

ders in a slight shrug, called his travel agent and confirmed their reservations. He intended to make it work; it
had to work. She was everything to him.

He walked into Page's house well aware that he had-
n't previously been any farther into it than the foyer. She
held his hand as he looked around her living room, hoping to broaden his knowledge of her through her tastes in
furnishings. An enormous bowl of yellow and burnt-
orange chrysanthemums graced the large glass-top coffee table. A brown sofa, over-sized beige and burnt-
orange chairs upholstered in velvet rested among
Oriental carpets of complementary colors, and two enormous desert cacti dominated the room. He pointed to a
painting of a group of jazz musicians.

"Who did that?"

"Doris Price. My mother has several of her things.
The one below it is a reproduction."

"I like them. What gallery is she in?"

She told him and added, "It's amazing. We really do
have similar tastes in art, except for drawings, and you
promised to teach me what to look for in those."

He cleared his throat. *Best to get off that topic, especially in view of her reaction to Quigley.* "It'll be my pleasure. He sniffed the odor that wafted his way. "I smell
something that's making me hungry."

"Like a drink?"

"Scotch on the rocks. A light one, please." She got a
glass of wine and joined him. "Welcome to my home,
Nelson."

He lifted his glass. "Here's to what nature had in
mind when she made woman. Thanks for inviting me."

She seemed embarrassed and proved it when she
said, "I...uh...better check the kitchen before I pull one of

my mother's tricks and burn the dinner."

He watched her lithe body with its rounded, mobile hips glide seductively away from him and downed his drink. Spending an evening with her in her apartment wasn't such a good idea.

An hour later with six courses of the best food he'd had in ages snug in his belly, he gazed around her dining room while she made coffee. White pillar candles of varying heights sat on the sideboard in a silver tray, the mirror above them giving their flickering lights added glow. And for the table she'd lighted more pillar candles and placed there a bowl of pink, white and purple dahlias. Feminine. Seductive. Like that lavender caftan that swished around her hips when she walked and outlined her high, generous breasts.

"You're quite a cook," he told her, walking with her to the living room where she'd placed a tray containing coffee and mints. "I take it, you cook as a hobby."

"If you want the truth, I hate daily cooking. It's boring. I get a bang out of preparing interesting meals for guests, especially guests who, like you, enjoy eating."

"The meal was wonderful. Tell me about some of your other talents."

"I don't have any. I sing with a choral group, and...oh yes, I'm a fair quilt maker. I enjoy that."

"How do you find time to make quilts?"

"I haven't recently. Want to see the one I'm working on?"

She got up, hesitant he thought. "It's...it's in here." He followed her to her bedroom and realized why she's seemed reluctant to lead him there. The flames of more pillar candles glowed on the dresser, a delicate perfume teased his nostrils and his eyes beheld what was possibly the most feminine setting he'd ever witnessed. White walls, white furniture and deep pile white wool floor covering relieved only by the pink silk cover on her bed. The epitome of femininity.

She opened a closet door and took out the unfin-ished quilt. "I have a lot more to do on this."

He saw it and he heard her, but neither her words nor her handiwork registered. Her voice, sweet and soft, promised him heaven, and he stared at her as he willed himself not to get out of line, to remember the stakes. But he was full of her. Though she was halfway across the room from him, he smelled her, tasted her. As she folded the quilt, she glanced up at him with a smile on her lips, and desire slammed into him with the force of a sledge-hammer. He whirled around and went back to the living room.

Inhale, count ten; exhale count ten, inhale—

"What happened? Didn't you like my quilt? I mean, do you think quilting is old fashioned or...or something?"

"It's...it's fantastic," he said, gulping coffee, "I would-n't have associated you with quilting. It must require a lot of concentration."

She walked right up to him, leaned over and placed a hand on his shoulder. "What's the matter? Anybody would think I aimed a gun at you. Why'd you—"

"Back off, Baby. Will you? The quilt's beautiful. The dinner was wonderful. I love your home. You're lovely, Page. I've got to get the hell out of here."

"But—"

He stood and headed for the foyer where she'd hung his coat. "Listen to me, Page and don't be hurt. Every vein, artery, muscle and sinew in my body is on fire for you, and the longer I stay in here, the worse it gets. What would surely follow isn't what I'd want for you or for myself. I'll call you when I get home." He opened the door, but she stopped him.

"Don't I get a kiss goodnight?"

He stared at her. "You're kidding. That would be the same as sticking a lighted match to a stick of dynamite.

I'll call you."

Outside he leaned against his car and gave thanks. He'd been a hair's breadth from putting her in that bed and losing himself in her. And what a disaster it would have been, because he wouldn't have had an ounce of control. Never before had desire sneaked up on him, infusing him with such a powerful urge. Tremors raced through him when he recalled how close he'd come to destroying what he planned for them.

At home, he took a cold shower, put on a pair of pajama bottoms and a robe, went in his den and telephoned Page. He didn't dare phone her from his bedroom.

"I'm sorry I had to leave abruptly, but it was best. The evening was...well, it was magical."

"Are you sure there's nothing wrong between us?"

He hadn't expected such a question, and for a few minutes, he pondered what he might say that would make her understand. "I'm surprised I got out of there without making a dunce of myself. Honey, you pack a wallop and me..." he grinned as he said it. "Me, I'm just a man."

As he'd hoped, her laughter floated to him through the wires. "You're full of beans. If that's really the reason why you cut out of here, I'm going to start wearing denim."

"And what do you think that will hide? I'm talking about that whole scene you spun out there. If you're all right, I'll say good night. I don't dare ask for a kiss."

She blew one to him. "Good night, Love."

"'Nite, Sweetheart."

He hung up and wiped the perspiration from his forehead. Thank God, she wasn't angry or pouting. Knowing that he wouldn't sleep immediately, he went to his den, tried some sketches, didn't like them and called it a night.

The next morning, he stood beside his kitchen window sipping coffee and mentally planning his day. He'd been so wrapped up in Page, so comfortable in their relationship that he'd almost forgotten how much he disliked going to the post office, to local stores and other public places where people gathered. Whenever he did, someone dampened his spirits with an incautious word or act, and he hated being treated as a curio.

On his way to the post office, he stopped at the library to return a book, but as he headed for the librarian's desk, two young women who seemed to have been shelving books pointed to him and giggled. He broke stride and walked toward them, but they scampered away. And a good thing, too, because he didn't know what he would have said to them. He thought he'd become inured to the cruelty, but could a man ever harden himself to ridicule? He turned and continued to the front desk.

The librarian beamed at him as he approached, a smile blanketing her face, and he turned around expecting to see someone in line behind him.

"Mr. Pettiford, I've been hoping you'd come in. We'd love to have you read for us and do a signing at the book store next door. Your books are very popular. We have a new readers' club that would be delighted to sponsor the event. If you don't want to read, you could talk about writing. We'd just love to have you."

Standing in that same spot, that woman had seen him at least twice a week for nearly two years and, until now, she'd managed never to look him straight in the face. And from her beet-red face and neck, he supposed his facial expression showed his astonishment and his indictment of her. He'd had the impression that the woman had never heard of Nelson Pettiford, author.

"Thank you," he managed with as much graciousness as he could muster. "I'll check my calendar and call you."

If her smiles weren't enough to floor him, she extended her hand. "This is wonderful. We'll look forward to the event."

Outside the library, he sat in his car wondering at the first impersonal gesture toward him as a man of worth that he'd experienced in Mystic Ridge. According to Whitfield, the mailman, everybody in town knew everything about everybody else, though that admittedly didn't include himself. He'd been seen holding hands with Page Sutherland, and it was as if some inexplicable transformation had happened to the townspeople of Mystic. Things had been decidedly different since the night he'd found her on the road. It was if she was the source of change. He shook off the strange notion and went home.

Seated at his desk, he shuffled through applications to his foundation. Two dozen young people had responded to the notice Page inserted in *The Mystic Ridge Observer*. He telephoned six applicants for additional information, but couldn't decide which had the most urgent need. He decided to work on his cartoon strip and then visit some of them.

An hour later, he looked over his effort, a piece in which Quigley expressed his opinion of members of congress.

"I'm more moral than you," Brother Tom said to Odessa-Cat. "I have family values."

"You sound like one of those TV know-it-alls, Brother Tom," Quigley said. "You're so boring. Always repeating yourself."

Odessa-Cat scratched her ear and turned to Quigley for sympathy. "How can he say that, the lazy tomcat, when he's the reason I've been fixed so I can't have any more fun?"

"Not true. Boys will be boys. I believe in family, the flag and God," Brother Tom replied. "If you liberal cats didn't prowl around in this alley all night, you'd still be intact."

"Oh, Quigley," Odessa-Cat moaned, "He's so cruel? Don't you remember all the...er...re great times we had before—"

Brother Tom stuck his tail up, ready to prance off. "Please don't remind me of my wicked days, Odessa-Cat. I've been reborn. If only you liberals would see the light and stop worrying about these other broken-down cats. Let them stop having kittens, get a job and go to work. Then, maybe Providence will take care of them."

"Oh dear me, you must be running for president of Cat Alley," Odessa-Cat said. "I don't think I want to be reborn."

Nelson drew the cartoon in final form and put it in a mailer. After reviewing the six applications once more, he decided to make his first visit the Mystic Ridge Group Home. The manager of the group home stared in aston-ishment when she learned that he was the foundation's benefactor, and he imagined how busy her tongue would be when he left there.

"I'd like to meet Ann. Of all the letters I received, hers, which you enclosed with your own, touched me most deeply. She wrote only four lines, but her misery jumped out to me." He smiled to put the woman at ease. "May I depend on your keeping my role in this confiden-tial?" If not..." He let her imagine the consequence.

"Of course, Mr. Pettiford. You're a generous man, and we in Mystic Ridge don't deserve your kindness."

He lifted his left shoulder in a dismissive shrug. "I hope I can save Ann the humiliation she hinted at in her note. I could hardly believe a six-year old could express pain so graphically."

"I'll get her. Please have a seat."

His heart nearly burst with pain, as the little brown-skinned girl with sad eyes who entered the reception room clung to the manager's hand.

*Miracle at Midnight***361**

"Hello, Ann. My name is Nelson. I read your note, and I can help you."

"With this?" She pointed to the patch of thick black hair that covered her brown cheek. "The children here laugh at me, and they won't play with me."

He took her hand and leaned toward her. "People laugh and make fun of me too, Ann, because I'm so tall. It hurts when they do that, so I know how you feel."

She gazed at him "You're tall? How tall?"

Did he risk standing? He decided to chance it, got up and raised to his full height.

The little girl stared up at him obviously in awe. "Gee whiz," she said. "Gee."

He sat down. "Well, I can't do anything about how tall I am, but I can get a doctor to remove this growth from your face, and that side will be just as pretty as the other one."

"You can do that?" Her eyes widened. Lovely eyes, and she would be a beautiful child when that growth was removed.

"I can do that if you want me to."

She jumped up and down, slapping her hands together, and ran over to the manager. "Can he, Miss Dodd? He said he'll fix my face. Please, Miss Dodd."

Miss Dodd fixed stern eyes on him. "It's burden enough to be left here for whoever'll take you, but to be laboring under something like this..." She took a deep breath. "You're a God-send. How soon can you arrange it?"

"I'll call the surgeon today. Let's hope she has that pretty face by the end of the year."

He looked into the little girl's smiling face and laughing eyes, transformed from the sad child of minutes earlier. He hadn't felt so good in—he didn't know when.

"I'll be with you through every step of this, Ann. In a day or two, you'll know when the doctor can see you."

She reached to him with outstretched arms, and he leaned forward to receive her hug. A desperate hug that communicated her hope and her fear that nothing would change. The first hug he'd ever received from a child, and he had to control the urge to hold her close.

"Two weeks," the surgeon told him the next morning. "Why's it so urgent?"

"For a child, an hour is like a year. I've raised her hopes, and I don't want her to feel that I've let her down. Is there a chance that she'll develop keloids?" he added in a moment of apprehension.

"I'm not known for botched jobs, so don't worry about it."

Nelson thanked him and phoned Miss Dodd with the news. Feeling good about the world and everything in it, he checked over the tickets and reservations for himself and Page the coming weekend. He promised himself nothing would go wrong; he wouldn't permit it.

He walked out on his porch, looked up at the sky and let the wall take his weight at the sight of clouds that literally smiled at him. He went inside, but the vision lingered in his mind's eye and he went back to the porch. And still they smiled at him. The trees bent his way as if paying homage to him, and birds chirped and sang. Page, they seemed to say. Yes. He'd swear that every bird sang "Page. Page." The townspeople may not have warmed up to him, but at every turn, Mystic Ridge welcomed him. Its sky, birds, trees and its Old Mills Road reached out to him.

Chapter Eight

*P*age zipped up her bags, placed them in the foyer and threw her raincoat across them. Standing before a floor length mirror, she checked her avocado-green linen suit, inspected her three-inch heeled shoes and took a last glance around her apartment. She'd watered the cacti, closed all the windows... Lord, she hated waiting, but he wasn't late. Her nerves had gotten so far out of control that she'd dressed early to give herself something to do.

The doorbell chimed, and with her heart pounding like a run-a-way train, she rushed to open the door.

Nelson stared down at her, and then a grin crawled over his face until it lit his eyes, and she knew everything would be all right. Lord, she loved his eyes. His lips brushed over hers fleetingly, but possessively, as if making a claim.

His smile turned to a grimace. "This all you're bringing?"

She glanced at the two twenty-two inch bags and wrinkled her nose. "Well, you said I should bring two real dressy things. To me, that means evening wear, which takes up space."

"No problem. Ready to go?"

She nodded, and he set the bags outside the door, locked it and looked steadily at her. "Any second thoughts? If so, now's the time to tell me."

"None whatever. You haven't told me where we're going."

With his grin in place, stars danced in his eyes. "That's right. I haven't. You'll know when we get there."

"You're splurging," she said as they waited in the first-class lounge at Baltimore International Airport.

"Why shouldn't I give you the best I can afford?" You'd do that for me." When she didn't respond, he urged her. "Wouldn't you?"

The man had a way of getting next to her when she least expected it. She winked at him, audaciously, in an effort to cover her flusteration. "I want the best for you, and I wouldn't offer you less than what was within my means." She patted the arm of the butter soft leather chair. So they were traveling first class. She should have known he'd do that.

From the plane, they took a chauffeured stretched-out Town Car, and after a lunch of sandwiches and a glass of wine, she laid her head on Nelson's shoulder and went to sleep.

"Wake up, Honey."

"We're there?"

"Well, partly."

She stepped out of the limousine and into sweltering heat, removed the linen jacket and looked around to get her bearings. Her gaze fell on the mammoth cruise ship that loomed before them, and shifted to the eager expression on Nelson's face and his concern that his choice pleased her.

She reached up and hugged him. "Did I tell you you're wonderful?

"Are you sure it's all right?" he asked.

She couldn't figure out why he was anxious; her

delight must surely shine on her face. "I've never been on a cruise or even on a big boat. This is...just wonderful."

He watched her as she twirled around in her state-room. "You like it?"

Hope shone in his magnificent eyes, and she stopped dancing around and walked over to him. "It's beautiful, and I know the furnishings and accessories are not an accident. You had them decorate it similar to my bedroom." She waved her hand around to encompass the entire room with its white rattan furniture, white shag rug and pink spread and draperies. "I love it. Uh... where did the porter put your things?"

He looked down at his feet. "Next door."

"Well, I hope there's a connecting door between us."

His steady gaze with its age-old man to woman message nearly unglued her. "There is."

She'd worry about her sudden attack of brazenness later. "Okay. Scat. I want to put on something comfortable and then see what this boat looks like. Twenty minutes?"

"No kiss?"

She kissed the side of his mouth. "Out, bright spot."

"Right. I'll be on deck."

She looked out of the window at the deck, the small craft nearby, the ocean and the sea gulls. "Nelson, this is a dream world. It's...it's a fairy tale."

"I'm happy you're pleased. After half an hour of safety training we can explore this thing. We sail at five."

Three hours later, the Princess eased away from shore bellowing her intentions as she pulled out. Page leaned against the railing in front of their state rooms with Nelson's strong right arm for her anchor. She looked up at him, then back at the receding shore.

"You're taking me on a cruise to give us a chance to know each other better. Where on earth will you take me on our honeymoon?"

She looked at him just in time to see his bottom lip drop and his eyes widen. But his shock apparently lasted only for a second. The fingers of his left hand tipped her chin upward as though to make certain that she not only heard his words but saw him say them.

"Marrying you is something I am neither willing to joke about nor to discuss lightly. My sense of humor does not cover that topic."

"Sorry." That sounded lame even to her, and maybe that was because his words sent a flush of delight throughout her body.

He moved away from the railing. "It's getting chilly. Shall we go in the lounge? What's your pleasure?" he asked, after they'd read the list of activities scheduled for the night.

"To sit here and talk with you." A smile played around his cheek bones, and she could see that her answer pleased him.

He ordered drinks. "I chose the second seating for dinner since I've noticed that you don't eat early."

"Fine." She reached over, took his left hand and examined it. Long tapered fingers with beautifully manicured nails and the smooth skin of a man who didn't use his hands for rough work.

"I like your hands," she said, unaware that she'd rimmed her lips with the tip of her tongue. "And I like their touch. Strong, but gentle."

At his silence, she glanced up to see eyes filled with passion and heat. Yes, and longing. Words she would have said hung in her throat as their gazes clung and she couldn't make herself look away."

"I like everything about you, Page. Everything. You take my breath away."

"Nelson, I—"

He waved his free hand. "Don't. I know it isn't the same with you, but if you'll let me, I aim to teach you."

She stared at him, bemused. How could a man be so blind? Or wasn't he able to accept that a woman he cared for could feel as deeply for him? While he's teaching me, I'll bring him up to date on a few things.

She stroked the back of his hand. "If it's not the same with me, why did I come on this trip with you, not even knowing or caring where you were taking me? You're a clever man. Figure that out."

His watch told him it was dinner time, but as they huddled close, holding hands in a quiet dream-like mood, he hated to interrupt the tender moment.

"Looks like it's time for dinner. Ready?" He took her hand and followed a crowd to the dining room.

They were seated at a table for eight with two couples and two single women. "How tall are you?" one of the men asked Nelson as soon as they'd introduced themselves.

Before he could react, he heard Page's voice slice through the air in a dagger-sharp reprimand. "Nelson's height will not be the subject of discussion at this table."

Stunned speechless, as their table mates also appeared to be, he stared at her with what he considered a silent caution. But she didn't back down.

"That's right. We'll enjoy our dinner if we don't get personal."

"Look, Nelson, I apologize. No offense meant," the man said, extending his hand.

"And none taken," Nelson replied, joining the man in a high-five.

He felt protective toward Page, had from the beginning, but it hadn't occurred to him that she might feel that way about him. He needed to sort that one out.

The waiters told jokes, sang, line danced and entertained the guests throughout the meal. His spirits high, he fed Page spoonfuls of caviar in between sips of champagne.

"You two must be newlyweds," one of the women ventured.

"Not yet," Page said. "On this trip, I'm just teaching him how to pronounce my first name. He insists on saying it with a French accent."

"But I thought you said your name is Page," the woman said with a note of uncertainty.

"It is," Page assured her. "Think what a problem we'd have if my name was Mary or April."

"All right. I get the message," the woman said, a sheepish grin on her face. "Nothing personal."

This was a side of Page to which he hadn't been exposed, this desire for privacy and the guts to insist upon it. He wondered at the reason for it. If he'd had any doubts that the cruise would give them a chance to know and understand each other, she had just dispelled them.

"Want to try the slots?" he asked Page as they left the dinning room, though he almost prayed she'd say no. He hated gambling, but they were supposed to be learning each other, so...

Her eyes widened and she stared up at him. "You mean the slot machines? Not me."

"Just checking. I don't gamble, But I wouldn't stand in your way if you wanted to."

"I don't gamble either, so..." She stopped walking. "Nelson, this is getting eerie. We have so much in common that it's beginning to scare me. And I'm starting to wonder why I chose *The Mystic Ridge Observer* when I also had job offers from *The Boston Globe*, *The New Orleans Tribune* and *The Baltimore Afro-American*. It's as if I was lured to Mystic Ridge."

He shrugged. "Maybe there's a reason why the place is called Mystic Ridge." He looked steadily at her, his mind racing. "I was watching TV one night, saw a short travel movie on Mystic Ridge, and I was ready to start packing. The place lured me the way a flame draws a moth. It didn't occur to me not to go there. Talking about weird! Let's sit over here in the lounge. It's cool on deck, and I'm not sure I want to join that frenzy going on upstairs."

They sipped the espresso coffee that he ordered and held hands as all kinds of people filed past them, but his mind was on Page's behavior at dinner.

"Why did you dress that man down when he asked about my height? Does my height bother you?"

Her stare was that of a person who'd been shot and couldn't believe it. "You didn't ask me that question. I don't wish that anything about you was different."

"Then why did you pounce on him so fast?"

"I'm sensitive to your feelings, and I'm tired of people who hurt others without thinking or caring."

"You didn't consider that I'd put him in his place?"

"If two men at that table had squared off, we wouldn't have had a pleasant meal. Right?"

"True." He rubbed his chin for a minute, deep in thought. "Are both your parents living? Tell me how you grew up."

She waited so long to answer that he wondered if she heard him.

At last, she said, "My mother's living, but not my father. I barely remember him, but I grew up in comfortable circumstances because my mother's a doctor. She's also something of a gad-about, attracts people the way sugar attracts ants. Since I'm an only child, I was always caught up in it, pulled from place to place—medical conferences, sorority meetings, speaking classes, trade shows. You name it. Loving though she is, life with her is one long stress scene. But what a woman she is!"

"She left you alone most of the time?"

"I wished she had. She dragged me every where she went; from the time I was nine, all I wanted was peace, a little calm and some privacy."

"But you love her."

"Of course, I do, and she loves me, but we aren't cut from the same cloth."

"I see." And indeed he did. "Where'd you grow up?"

"We lived in and around Alexandria. I moved to Mystic Ridge from Washington, D. C."

He settled back on the sofa with her left hand tucked snugly in his right one. "It's strange how different our lives have been and yet how similar in some important respects. My parents lived until I was grown, saw Logan and me through college and successful in what we'd chosen to do.

"They were older when we were born; we lost them a little over four years ago. Now, there's just Logan and me." His voice softened and suddenly seemed far away. "As you've no doubt guessed, they were both tall. Dad excelled at track and field, and he made a living as a lawyer just as Logan does. Mom taught music in the Baltimore public schools.

"Both you and I moved to Mystic Ridge seeking relief from notoriety, looking for peace and a private life," he went on. "After *Walking Tall*, my second book, came out, I was besieged wherever I went, and it wasn't all friendly. Taunts, jibes. That wasn't new to me, but that adults could be so... I'd as soon not go there."

She sat up abruptly. "So Rusty Orleans in your third book is actually you?"

He eased her back and into his arms. "Good Lord, no." She expelled a long breath in obvious relief. "He's a side of me, but the basic character is pure fiction."

"Boy, am I glad to know that. Now I understand why you established that foundation to help children whose handicaps subject them to ridicule. Did you get any responses?"

"A bag full. I've already chosen a six-year-old girl who has a growth on over a quarter of her face. When it's off, she'll be beautiful. I can't get her out of my mind's eye. Something about her—maybe it was the sadness when I first looked at her and the way she smiled at me when she left me—I don't know, but she haunts me."

"Will you let me meet her?"

He hugged her closer for she'd just said what he wanted to hear. "Sure, I will. Maybe we'd better turn in. Can I get you something first?"

She shook her head. "Nope. I'm feeling pretty good, Mr. Pettiford."

At her door, he asked her, "What time do you want to get up tomorrow morning?"

She looked him in the eye, letting him know with her cool regard that tonight wasn't their night. He didn't mind that because he knew the day's events had brought them closer. Much closer. And they still had a way to go.

"I want to see the sunrise."

"With or without coffee?" he asked, reminding her that he was right next door.

"Gosh, I hadn't thought of that."

He smiled to let her know that it was all right. "Knock, if you decide you want some, and if you don't feel like knocking, just open the door and come on in."

"You don't think I could forget that, do you? You'd better come inside and kiss me."

He looked down at the soft beige twin globes beneath the rim of the pink sheath that shielded the rest of her treasure from his eyes, brought his gaze up slowly to her glistening mouth and let his eyes feast on her luscious lips. He told himself not to look into her eyes and sink into the quicksand of desire. But he ignored caution, looked into those long-lashed grayish-brown pools of blatant need, and then her lips parted. He groaned, wrapped her to him and took the nectar from her mouth.

When she undulated against him, whatever she'd intended for the evening already forgotten, he broke the kiss. "Honey, do you want me to leave or stay?"

"Huh?" She hid her face in his shoulder. "I forgot where I was," she shuddered

That didn't surprise him. Gazing down at the bundle of feminine sweetness in his arms, he knew that she could bring him to his knees. "Go to bed, Sweetheart. We have to get up at five to catch the sunrise. I'll phone you."

She kissed him under his chin. "See you in the morning."

Chapter Nine

*P*age fought the noise droning in her ear for as long as she could, sat up, looked around and recognized the noise as the telephone's ring.

"Yes?"

"Morning, Sweetheart. I ordered breakfast, and the waiter will serve it on the deck beside our doors, so slip on something. Fifteen minutes?"

"Okay."

Fifteen minutes later, dressed in a yellow T-shirt and white cotton pants, she stepped out on deck where he sat in a deck chair with his hands locked behind his head and his feet stretched out before him.

"You're a cruel man; it's barely light."

"Come sit down. Here comes our breakfast table. "Still think I woke you up too early?" he asked as the first ray of red streaked across the horizon.

"This is unbelievable," she said, as pigments of red, gray, orange and blue flashed over nature's palette. "Look. Oh, Nelson, just look at that," she said as the red globe slipped up from the Atlantic Ocean, a woman easing away from her lover's bed. "I wouldn't have missed it for anything."

She thought her heart would burst with joy, and she wanted him to feel the same way. "Are you...happy?" she asked him.

He reached over and squeezed her hand. "More than I've ever been or thought I could be."

"You're not an Aquarian, are you?"

A grin claimed his face. "Unless somebody changed the astrological charts, I am. February sixteenth."

"Then this isn't so strange after all. I'm a Libra, and I love Aquarians."

His laugh warmed her like steam from sidewalk grates on a freezing day. Suddenly, he sobered. "So you love Aquarians. What about this one?"

She got up, dusted crumbs from her pants and looked past him. "Why do you think I'd make an exception of you? Thanks for the breakfast. I'll be back out here after I shower and dress."

"And I'll be waiting for you."

"I never thought you could find so many things to do on a ship," she told him later that afternoon as they lounged alone on the ship's lee. "Imagine swimming, fencing and line dancing in the space of a few hours. I needed that movie in order to sit down and get some rest."

"If you're tired——"

She turned on her side and faced him. "I'm not so tired I want to leave you."

"What's your idea of the best way to spend Sunday?" he asked.

So he's still not satisfied that he knows and understands me. "Stick my arm out the front door, get the Sunday papers, crawl back in bed with a mug of hot coffee and read till I fall asleep again. Of course, I have to make the coffee first."

"And then what?"

"In Washington, I'd go to a museum, or write letters, watch the political pundits on TV, go to dinner or something special with a friend. In Mystic Ridge, I do the paper and coffee thing, take a walk, write letters, watch TV, do my laundry. How do you spend Sunday?"

"When I have my choice, I get up early, read the papers and eat breakfast. Then I go to church. I come back and call Logan or he calls me, and after that, I may work, garden, go for a drive, go over to Frederick and check out the antique shops, eat dinner and back home."

"You grew up in Baltimore?"

He nodded. "On the corner from Druid Hill Park. As a child, I spent a lot of time in that park."

She reached for his hand. "Alone?"

He sat up. "Yeah. Want some frozen yogurt?"

He didn't have to tell her that those had been painful days of rejection by children his age such that, even now, it hurt to speak of them. "I'd love some," she said and wished with all her heart that she could take all his pain away.

They walked back to their state rooms holding hands and eating double cones of frozen vanilla yogurt.

"The captain's giving a party tonight. Want to go?"

"You bet I do. I brought these evening dresses, and I'm going to wear them even if I have to put them on for breakfast."

He raised an eyebrow. "And you'd do that, too. Get some rest, why don't you? I'll knock at seven thirty."

She waited for the kiss that would send her spinning, but he let a grin play around his lips. "Oh, no you don't. I'm drunk enough just looking at you." He kissed her cheek. "Later."

He looked around the tables at the captain's dinner

for first-class passengers and counted his blessings. On this night, he was just like other men of his status, enjoying the company of a beautiful woman whom he loved, who cared for him and wanted everyone to know it. On this night, he was not wishing for what he deemed impossible nor trying to pretend that he didn't need it.

"Dance with me?" he asked her, as the orchestra whipped into an old Duke Ellington ballad about what it meant to be blue.

She stepped easily into his embrace, with the confidence of a woman who knew what she wanted and took it. Her supple body moved against him, her steps matching his as if they had danced together all their lives. He stepped back from her so that he could focus on the music, on anything except the way she moved against him, but she closed those few inches and let him feel her breasts, her hips and her lover's promise. He held her away from him and gazed into her eyes trying to clarify her message, to know for certain what she intended to communicate. For a second, she let him see her need, then her long lashes closed that window and she moved back to him. But not before he saw the tips of her hardened breasts beneath the silk that barely covered them. He stopped dancing.

"Do you...want to... Can we leave here?"

"I want to go wherever you want to take me."

"And if I want to take you to my room?"

She took his hand turned toward the exit, and with his heart rioting in his chest, he followed her.

She didn't stop at his door, but led him to her own. His gaze seared her with the fiery storm of desire in his eyes, and as her trembling fingers slid the plastic card through the lock, she said a few words of prayer. Lord, please let him know and feel that I love him. She flipped on the light and waited for him to close the door behind him, but as though being sure of his ground, he left that task to her. She closed and locked it.

"Want some champagne?" she asked him, pointing to the bottle of Moet and Chandon that rested in a bucket of ice on her dresser.

He shook his head. "I'm not leaving unless you ask me to." Wasn't it typical of him to eschew small talk and get down to cases. However brazen she acted sometime, she wasn't really aggressive with men and she hoped he'd figure that out. How did you deal with a man who'd known little else but loneliness? She made herself say, "I haven't planned to ask you to leave. Don't...don't let me just stand here. Hold me."

He stepped closer. "There's no turning back for me after this. You understand? I'm deeply in love with you and when we make love, I'll only sink deeper. Do you love me?"

"Oh, yes. I love you. I've never loved anybody else."

She sensed the air bursting out of him, air that she knew had sought expulsion probably for decades. A smile enveloped his face, and his eyes shone as though sheltering millions of stars. His arms opened and she flew into them and gloried in his masculine strength as he crushed her to his body. His lips found hers, and she opened to him as he poured into her the fever that raged in him. She parted her lips and feasted on his tongue, welcoming him into her body. His fingers gripped her hips and when she undulated against him, he raised her to his level, pushed aside the shoulder strap of her gown and sucked her hard nipple into his mouth. The hot molten lava of desire shot through her, and she moaned her need aloud not caring that he knew how she longed to have him inside of her. She held his head to her breast as he teased and suckled, making her will his own, until in disregard for all but the feel of his mouth on her, she lowered her other shoulder strap and pushed her evening gown down to her waist.

As he moved from one breast to the other, she threw her head back and moaned, "Put me to bed; I can't stand this."

A gasp escaped her when he slid her down, and her belly skimmed over his powerful erection. His deft fingers unzipped her dress and tossed it onto the chaise lounge. Then he lifted her and carried her to her bed. He pulled back the cover, lay her in bed and his eyes feasted on the treasure that awaited him, hidden only by her slim bikini panties. Staring down into her eyes, he threw off his clothes and knelt beside the bed. His lips seared her belly and her inner thighs as he peeled the little G-string from her body. Frissons of heat singed her nerves as she felt his gaze on her naked body.

He joined her in bed, leaned over her and streamed kisses over her face, neck, ears and shoulders. "You're so sweet, so... Oh, God, I love you!"

Then he had her nipple in his mouth tugging and suckling until her hips swayed of their own volition as her need for him threatened to explode

"Honey, please, I..."

"I've waited all my life for this; let me enjoy loving you. I need to love you this way." His lips trailed down to her belly where he sipped, kissed and nipped until she thought her whole body had burst into flames. But he continued his onslaught, kissing his way as he went until he reached the ultimate, hooked her legs over his shoulders and loved her until she screamed for more. He took a minute to protect her.

"All right, baby," he said, rising above her. "Tell me if I hurt you."

She shifted her body upward to meet him and took him in her hands as she stared into his face and brought him to her lover's gate. He touched her and her body became a raging storm. The clutching began when, at last, he sank into her and she couldn't hold back the tears. Tears of joy that at last he was hers. She smiled to let him know her joy and, gazing into her face, he began the powerful strokes that sent jolts of electricity whistling through her veins to settle in her love nest as he rocked her. Almost immediately, the squeezing and pumping began, and he drove relentlessly while she thrashed beneath him, wanton and beyond control.

"Love me," he whispered. "I need you to love me."

"I do. I do. I love you so much."

His lips touched her in a possessive kiss as he increased his pace and power until she buckled under him in a shattering eruption. Then he wrapped her in his arms and cried aloud as he gave her the essence of himself.

His body shook with the power of his release, and he had to control what he felt for her lest he hold her too tight. With his elbows and forearms supporting his weight, he let himself relax, opened his eyes and gazed down at her in wonder. Awed that he held in his arms the perfect complement to himself.

"How do you feel?" he asked, his voice little more than a whisper.

Her smile was all the answer he needed, but her words soothed him. "Wonderful. I didn't know I could feel like this. Is... Is everything all right with you?"

"As never before in my life. I'm...to think that I might never have met you."

Her fingers stroked the side of his face, caressed his chin and then brushed over the tight curls on his head, loving him, cherishing him, and he'd have sworn that she could hear his heart thundering its mad rhythm. He stifled a groan. No matter how their song played out, he would love her forever.

Her grin told him to expect irreverence and she made good the promise. "If my car hadn't acted up, we wouldn't be here right now."

"At Gayne's Garage, where you took it, I was told there wasn't one thing wrong with your car. That entire event smacks of the supernatural. I tell you, it's creepy."

"Say what you please, my car is entitled to your gratitude."

Encouraging her frivolity, he said. "Convince me."

"Well, people get a physical examination every year, and—"

"Okay, I'll take it for another tune-up. That ought to square things."

She feigned surprise. "I hadn't even thought of that; I was thinking more of an oil change, but if you want to go that far..." She let the thought dangle when he spread kisses over her face and neck, brushed the tips of his fingers over her breasts and then sucked an aureola into his mouth. When she wrapped her legs around him, he shifted his hips and took her with him to the stars.

Nelson walked into his house that Monday evening, dropped his bags in his bedroom and looked around him. Nobody could tell him that he wasn't a brand new man starting a brand new life. He telephoned Logan.

"I thought you'd decided not to come back."

"I was only gone four days."

"How's Page? Did you take her with you?"

He didn't lie to his brother, the person who'd always been there for him. "We were together, and she... she's just fine."

"Great. Way to go, brother. Stay on top of it."

"If I don't, you can bet it won't be my fault."

"I thought as much. Why don't you come over next

weekend?"

"I may camp out at your place a few nights. I told you about Ann, the girl my foundation is helping, didn't I? Well her surgery is scheduled for next weekend, and I think I ought to see her through it. I'll let you know more later this week."

He hung up and called the surgeon. "Is the operation still on?" he asked after they greeted each other.

"Yes I was at the group home yesterday morning as promised, and I examined her. I don't expect any problems. Bring her in Thursday afternoon. I'll operate at seven thirty Friday morning. If all goes well, she should be out of there Tuesday or Wednesday, but I want her where I can watch her to see that she heals properly. If you don't know of a place, I can recommend one."

"Go ahead and make the necessary arrangements. I'll have her at the hospital Thursday."

After telephoning Miss Dodd and getting her cooperation, he sketched a few cartoon strips. In spite of what he planned to draw, his pen insisted on depicting Quigley strutting down Old Mills Road toward the lake. Finally, he let the big Tom have his way.

"I'm getting too old for this night prowling," Quigley said. "I need a cozy little nook with a cozy little cat."

Nelson stared down at what he'd drawn and gasped when he saw that the little cat had Page's face. He tore it up, phoned a Chinese take-out for his supper and thought over the weekend while he waited for the delivery. After their first night together, he and Page hadn't wanted to be away from each other and had spent the remaining two nights in each other's arms. And that last evening at the gala, she had been so breathtakingly beautiful that he'd seen the envy of other men. For once, he had the prize.

He'd had the company of any number of beautiful women, but he had been with them as ships passing through the night. And they, dangling themselves before him as precious jewels, had proved to be mere plastic at the core. He'd known no pleasure in being with them. He hadn't loved any of them nor had they loved him. Liaisons of convenience, all of them. But with Page, his soul had soared. He put on his coat and went down to the gate to get his supper from the delivery man. After eating, he phoned Page, talked with her for a few minutes and went to bed.

After lunch the next day, he went to visit Ann, to reassure her and tell her what to expect. She walked into the reception room, looked around and when she saw him, her face bloomed into a smile and she raced to him with open arms. He stooped down and lifted her into his arms. To his amazement, she kissed his cheek. Deeply moved, he kissed the ugly birth mark on her face and hugged her. When he sat down, she sat as close to him as she could while he outlined her treatment program.

"You're going to be there?" she asked him, her voice filled with hope.

"I'll be there, and I'll take care of you. You must be patient while your face heals and do exactly what Dr. Mack tells you to do."

"I will. Dr. Mack brought me some lollipops. He has a little girl, too."

"I'll come for you day after tomorrow."

The fierceness of her hug communicated to him more aptly than any words what his gesture meant to her. After apprising Miss Dodd of the arrangement and getting her agreement, he left, whistling as he strode with quickened steps to his car oblivious to the cold and biting wind. First Page and now this wonderful little girl lit up his life. He'd do his best for her.

Chapter Ten

Sitting at her desk across the small room from Phyllis, Page dialed the third number she had for her mother but got no answer. Fearing a tragedy, she called Millie's secretary.

"Dr. Shipley is in Mexico City, Ms. Sutherland, which is why you couldn't reach her by cell phone. She'll be back tomorrow."

Relieved, Page hung up. What business did a congresswoman from Virginia, United States of America, have in Mexico City, Mexico? She knew her mother loved to travel, but justifying some of her trips required a magician's skill. She hadn't spoken with her mother since she'd gotten back from that unbelievable idyll with Nelson. Thinking of him and their days and nights together, she hugged herself, remembered where she was and looked into the knowing eyes of Phyllis Watson.

"That had to be some weekend. You were a can of mush all day yesterday, and you're still pie-eyed. He must be some hot stuff."

Sobering at once, Page raised an eyebrow. "Since I didn't hear you say that, I don't have to tell you whose business you're meddling in, do I?"

"Sorry, Girl. I didn't say a thing. But I've been trying

to take a leaf out of your book. James took me to dinner at the Wild Duck right here in Mystic Ridge, and on a Sunday night, too. Can you beat that? I had it out with him, and he's been acting different."

"A man will give you what you let him know you deserve."

"I'm crazy about him, Page."

"If he floats your boat, go for it."

Phyllis stopped typing. "Do you love Nelson?"

"Would I love the most perfect, most precious human male the Lord ever made?"

Phyllis' lower lip dropped and her wide eyes stared as if seeing a supernatural being. "You get outta here, Girl."

Page couldn't help laughing—at the astonished woman before her and because the whole world was new and wonderful. Her feet barely touched the floor on her way to her boss' office.

"Here's your story on the seniors, James."

He glanced at what she'd placed on his desk and, displaying little interest in it, motioned for her to sit down. "Still don't intend to get me a story on Pettiford?"

She'd thought that issue closed and said as much. "You've already penalized me for that. Anyway, before you decide to get tough with me, read my story. I think you'll change your attitude toward both me and the seniors."

His eyebrows shot up. He picked up her story, looked at the heading and began to read. Half an hour later, he walked into her office. "All right. I'm taking you off features and putting you on news, and you get a couple-a-hundred bucks more in your check every month. You done good."

"You going to leave me alone about a story on Nelson?"

His gaze drifted toward Phyllis then back to Page.

"I'm not a louse, kid. I know how you feel about him. I'll get it myself."

"Can I thank you for that?" she asked Phyllis after James went back to his office.

"Maybe. I don't know. I did ask him how he'd feel if I did an expose on him? That could have had an effect."

Page walked over to Phyllis and hugged her. "Thanks, friend. I couldn't have done it, not even if he'd fired me."

Nelson put Ann's small suitcase in the trunk beside his bags and prepared to drive to Baltimore. "You're welcome to come with us, Miss Dodd," he told the manager, who stood by anxiously as he buckled the little girl in the back seat.

"Can't I sit up there with you?" she asked him.

Fortunately Miss Dodd explained that state law required children under twelve to sit in the back seat, for he wasn't sure he could have denied her request. He talked with her on the way and learned that she had rarely been in a car, that she loved music and reading was her favorite entertainment. How like himself as a child, he thought, living inside herself, shunning rejection. If only he could help all children who were burdened with being different. He checked her into the hospital and sat with her in her room until she slept because she'd begged him not to leave her.

He'd also chosen two other children, but he already knew that neither of them would touch him as Ann had. He stood by her bed at seven the next morning when attendants placed her on a gurney and anesthetized her and realized that he couldn't have been more anxious for her if she'd been his daughter. He got breakfast at the cafeteria, went to the gift shop and bought toys, a radio with a cassette player/recorder and several books of fairy tales. That done, he went to the waiting room, took out his sketch pad and made himself work.

Three hours later, Dr. Mack's voice came to him, a shadow emerging from the darkness as he sat staring at his empty sketch pad. "It's about as perfect a job as perfect can get. When the sedation wears off, she'll be in pain, but I've left a prescription to take care of that." Mack patted him on the shoulder. "Man, you're something special. That little girl is going to be a beauty."

Nelson said a word of thanks and used his cell phone to call Page.

"She's going to be just fine," he told her. "Waiting for the doctor to come out nearly drove me nuts. I'm going up to see her now."

She told him of James' reaction to her report on the senior center. "I'm senior staff reporter now. No more features. He's going to try and get an interview with you himself."

That wouldn't be unreasonable. "Perhaps in connection with my lecture at the Mystic Ridge Library, though I don't know when that will be. I'll call you tonight. Love you."

"I love you, too, Hon. Bye."

For the next four days, he sat with Ann during her waking hours, sketching while she read the books he brought her, and it pleased him that she always wanted to discuss with him what she read. He discovered that she delighted in Mozart's chamber music and in boisterous pieces such as Tchaikovsky's Romeo and Juliet, and that she loved the music of Louis Armstrong and Pete Fountain. His taste as well. Nursery rhymes held no interest for her. He didn't know much about children, but it hadn't occurred to him that a child would dislike the simple tunes that were written for children.

He marveled that she didn't complain of pain,

showed no restlessness or impatience and raised no objection when he told her she had to recuperate at Dr. Mack's sanatorium.

"I like Dr. Mack," she said. "He fixed my face."

If Page were with him to share his happiness about Ann's successful surgery, he'd be complete. He phoned her. "I miss you. I haven't seen you in a week. Can't you come over this weekend. You can stay with Logan and me, but if you'd rather stay in a—"

"I'd rather stay with you and Logan."

When he could stop laughing, he said, "I hadn't envisaged your staying at a hotel by yourself, Sweetheart."

He imagined that she raised her eyebrows when she replied, "Neither did I, Love. One week couldn't make me that crazy."

"Glad to hear it. I want you to meet Ann. With her calm acceptance of what is happening to her, her faith in those responsible for her care and her almost unbeliev-able equanimity, she is a revelation. I've learned much from her."

"I want to see her too; I can tell she's become very important to you."

"You think so?"

"I know it, and it's good. See you Friday night."

"Hey, woman! Where's my kiss?" She blew him one through the wire, and he told her he loved her.

"Me too, Love."

"Wait a second. I'll have a car to pick you up at your office. Five o'clock?"

She hesitated. "Well, if you want to, but I don't mind driving."

"I mind. See you then."

Logan thought Ann would be jealous of Page, but the little girl embraced Page as one more person to love her just as she had opened her arms to Logan. The three of them stood by Saturday morning while the surgeon removed the thin gauze from Ann's face and handed the child a mirror.

She stared at herself and looked at Nelson. "Is this me, now?"

"It's you, and you're beautiful," Nelson told her.

"Not quite," Dr. Mack said. "That side will soon be exactly the same color as the other side."

"It's really me?" she asked Nelson again. As stunned as she, he sat on the side of her bed and hugged her. He wouldn't have imagined that she would be so pretty.

The surgeon gave Nelson instructions for Miss Dodd and discharged Ann. Nelson and Page gathered the toys, books, cassettes and other things Nelson had bought her, packed her things and left the sanatorium with Logan and an ecstatic Ann dancing between them.

The three adults had their first taste of Kentucky Fried chicken, because that was what Ann wanted to eat.

"We'd better head home, Logan," Nelson said. "Thanks for the hospitality and moral support."

After belting Ann in the back seat, Nelson walked around to the front passenger door and looked down at Page. "The more I'm with you, the more I never want to be away from you. Give that some thought, will you?"

She took his hand and brushed the back of it against her cheek. "I have."

His heart kicked over like a trip-hammer nearly knocking him off balance. "Did you think I hadn't?" she asked.

He braced his palms on the roof of the car, trapping her between himself and the vehicle, and leaned down until his lips touched hers and he felt her body, warm, pliant and for him alone.

"It's broad daylight, and we're on the street," she said, pushing him away.

"Yeah. That and Ann are what stopped me."

"You coming to see me soon," Ann asked them when they were leaving the group home.

"You're part of my life now, Ann," Nelson said. "You can always count of me."

She hugged the two of them. "Nobody will be mean to me any more," she said and, as she waved them good bye, her smile warmed him like rays of sunlight.

He took Page's hand and walked with her to his car. As he got in, he said, "Somebody left her on the steps of the group home when she was a couple of days old. If only that man or woman could see her now! You know, I changed her life, but she changed mine more."

"How so?"

"She brought home to me the extent of my enormous blessings. A comfortable home, parents and a brother who loved me. And now... Imagine, being able to give someone a new life. It's...I'm humbled."

"She loves you."

"I know. And it's mutual."

It was time he told Page that he was Slim Wisdom. She'd been annoyed at one of his strips and maybe he'd do some more that she wouldn't like, but she deserved to know. And then, he'd... He'd cross that bridge when he got to it.

"Where've you been, darling? Mother's out of her mind. Two whole weeks, and I've——"

"Mama, back up, will you? You knew I was going on a trip, though I admit I didn't say to where. When I got back home, I called every one of your phone numbers, but you didn't answer any of them. Then I called your secretary and learned that you were investigating something or somebody in Mexico."

"Now, dear, don't be so exacting. I was on a fact-finding trip. Unfortunately, it's something we congress people have to do in order to legislate."

Yeah. Sure, she thought but she didn't say. "What did you decide about the next election?"

"What's there to decide, darling? The people are pleased with my work, and I'm going to make a run for it. I hope I may count on your vote."

Page laughed. She couldn't hold it back. Her mother's public persona was in full swing and nothing short of victory in November would slow it down. Maybe then, she'd have her mother back. But Millie could switch personas as easily as the wind switched directions.

"You didn't tell me where you were going, dear? Did you have a nice young man with you?"

She hadn't been expecting that one. Gathering grit for whatever comeback she got, she said, "I was with someone special, Mama, and I didn't tell you where I was going, because he made the trip a surprise."

"I uh...I see. Where did he take you?"

"On a cruise to the Bahamas and neighboring islands. First class all the way. If you come visit me, I'll introduce you to him."

Millie's long silences didn't fool her. She knew that in matters of romance, her mother remained old fashioned and disapproved of casual affairs. "You love him?"

"Yes, Ma'am. I love him."

"Well. Well. He must be superman. I'd begun to think I wouldn't live to see it. You bring him here to see me. You hear?"

"I will, if I can catch up with you," she said, getting some of her own. "Bye for now."

"Wait a minute. I'm going to Ghana Wednesday afternoon, but I'll be back Monday morning."

"You're going on vacation, or what?"

"Now, dear, you know the price of cocoa has been rising for months, and I have a big candy factory in my district, so I have to see what's what over there?"

"But Mama, what can you do about it?"

"I can protect my constituents."

In West Africa? Page stared at the telephone for seconds after she hung up. "I guess that's that."

Thursday morning, Phyllis dropped a copy of *The Maryland Journal* on Page's desk. "Girl, just look at that. I cracked up. Slim is da bomb!"

Page grabbed the paper and stared at the cartoon strip and the caricature of her mother on Millie-Cat's face, as the feline took off in the air with nothing to propel her but inline skates on each paw and a long scarf trailing behind her.

Odessa-Cat complained to Quigley, "That little alley strumpet isn't satisfied with the Toms here in Cat Alley. She's gotta go prowling clear out of the country. I could wring her neck."

Quigley looked at his friend and former lover, closed his eyes and licked his lips. "Your eyes have gone green, Odessa-Cat, but you're wasting good hate. Millie-Cat hasn't been in heat in twenty years. All she'll get for this trip is a reality check."

Soothed, Odessa-Cat stretched and purred. "If you ever run for president of Cat Alley, Quigley, I'm voting for you."

Page pitched the newspaper into the refuse basket and swore aloud. If she ever got her hands on that...that miserable person, she'd...

"Didn't you think it was funny, Page? Slim's got his finger square on the political pulse of this country. I think he's...Page, what's the matter? Why're you looking at me like that? What did I say?"

"Every time you open your mouth, I see your big toe."

"What? Well, kiss my grits. I never in my life! Page, Honey, you sure you're all right?"

"No, I'm not. See you tomorrow," she said, closed her computer, got her briefcase and went home.

She couldn't blame the reporters and comedians for taking shots at her mother; it was their job. Besides, politicians were fair game. If only her mother wouldn't do such outrageous things in order to stay in the limelight. She wouldn't be surprised if Millie went bungie jumping in a corset and old fashioned bloomers to call attention to gender inequality and, of course, to herself. Oh, Lord, how she wished her mother would just be a normal mother. A doctor, yes. A congresswoman, yes. President of the United States, if that's what she wanted. But a normal mother.

She had no taste for lunch, so she forced down an apple, took out her laptop computer and tried to work on her story. She answered the phone thinking she'd hear her boss' voice.

"Hi, Sweetheart. What're you doing home this time of day? You okay?"

"Hi. I'm working on a piece for this week's edition."

"Whoa. I'm not sure I've ever had this frosty a greeting from you. What's bothering you?"

"Oh, Hon. I'm glad you called. I really am. But I'm so mad right now, I couldn't be civil to Dick Clark and Ed McMahon if they showed up here with one of their big money checks."

"What happened?"

"Why are these vultures always picking on...m...on women. I get so sick of that damned Quigley, I could spit."

"What? You let yourself get this upset about a cartoon that doesn't have anything to do with you? That's the silliest thing I ever heard."

"Silly? "Did you call me silly? Is that what you said?"

"Now, look. You're just looking for a fight."

"You insult me, and when I object, you say I'm look-ing for a fight. How dare you make light of me?"

"Page, Honey, for heaven's sake, don't be childish!"

"Childish?" Bang. She slammed the phone into its cradle, and for the next fifteen minutes, her tears soaked her shirt. Christmas was only days away and with her mother likely to take off on another junket, she'd proba-bly have to spend it alone. She made a cup of tea and curled up in a big over-stuffed chair contemplating what she'd done. Never had she hung up on anyone. Anger and remorse battled for priority, and she shuddered at the thought that he might not forgive her for it. She clutched her chest at the frightening tumble of her heart. Then the doorbell rang, and she wrestled with the impulse to ignore it and with an urge to be in his arms, for she didn't doubt that he'd come to have it out with her.

He rang again. "Open up, Page. I'm not leaving here until you do."

She slipped the chain and opened it. "You knew I'd be here, didn't you?" he said. "What got into you?"

She stared up at him, looking for...she didn't know what. A sign of the sweetness he always gave her, maybe, but she didn't deserve it. "Come on in. I'm... I'm sorry I hung up on you, but I'm still mad at you for calling me silly and childish."

With both hands on her waist and his gaze locked in hers, he said, "I didn't come here to rehash that scene."

"Why'd you come?"

"Because I love you and you love me, and this is too precious to allow an argument about something like that to get between us."

"But I'm still——"

He interrupted her. "You're not mad at me anymore than I'm angry with you. We were both wrong." He searched her face. "You've been crying? Page, baby, don't you have any faith in us? In me?"

His hands stroked her back and folded her to him in a gentle caress. "What we feel for each other can't be destroyed so easily."

"I...It was an awful feeling. Suddenly, I didn't have you any longer."

"Shhh, Sweetheart. In a world of cyclones, this wasn't even a breeze."

She wanted him to stop talking, to wrap her to him and let her feel him, taste him. She raised her arms to his shoulders and lifted her parted lips for his tongue, and he gazed down at her until his body jerked and his hot male magnetism sucked her into his aura, mesmerizing her and firing her libido until she wanted to scream at him: Do something to me. Touch me. Kiss me. Hold me. Get inside of me.

"I told you there was no turning back, and there isn't." Then he plunged into her mouth, dipping, seeking, tasting and anointing.

She imprisoned him with her loving tongue, dueling frantically with his own until, at last, he fastened her hips to him and bulged against her. Weakened with the desire that plowed through her and settled in her loins, she slumped against him. Then, he lifted her into his arms and took her to bed where, together, they made the earth stand still.

Later, as he held her, he thought about his life and gave thanks for it, even the empty years, for without them, he might not have appreciated how precious she was.

Chapter Eleven

Nelson waited in the reception room of the group home while Ms. Dodd signed the permission for him to take Ann for a drive, their fourth excursion together. He drove down Old Mills Road, as he'd done previously, parked and walked with her through the thicket to the edge of Lake Linganore. Squirrels darted in their path and when Ann knelt to play with one, he stood still and watched her while she stroked his fur. Nelson couldn't believe what his eyes saw. Maybe he was bewitched. Or was it simply more of the strange power of Mystic Ridge?

They sat on a bench facing the lake, because she loved the view, and the squirrels played at her feet while she squealed with delight. She wanted to know about his childhood and he gave her an edited version of it. The hour passed quickly, and he hated to take her back so soon; those minutes with the little girl brought him a new kind of happiness. Her face had healed and true to the surgeon's promise, she'd become a beautiful child. He stopped at a roadside restaurant and bought them each a double cone of caramel ice cream.

"Right on time, Mr. Pettiford," Miss Dodd said when they returned. "Punctuality counts for a lot here." Ann hugged him goodbye and asked him when she'd see him again.

"Over the holidays for sure," he said, not realizing that the child might have her own agenda for Christmas.

"I'm going to ask Santa Claus to bring you something," she told him and hugged him goodbye.

He planned to celebrate Christmas with his brother as usual, because he assumed Page would want to spend it, or at least part of it, with her mother.

"I assume you'll spend tomorrow with your mother, but how about going with me this afternoon to see Ann. It's Christmas Eve, and I want to take her gifts."

"Wonderful. I have something for her too."

"She won't come out," Ms. Dodd told them. "She says she doesn't want to see you."

He supposed his face showed his disbelief. "That's impossible. I haven't seen or spoken with her since I left her here in this room three days ago. What happened?"

"Well, she asked if she could spend Christmas day with you at your house, and I told her the rules forbade it. Your taking her to the hospital for surgery and caring for her later in the sanatorium was special, but otherwise the children have to stay here."

He sent his fingers ruthlessly through his hair. "Granted. But why is she mad with me?"

"She thinks you didn't want her to visit you. I tried to talk to her and tell her it was a group-home ordinance, but she wouldn't listen. She's pouted and been...well, just plain bad ever since."

"I see. Would you please take these to her? We'll wait."

Miss Dodd returned with the gifts a few minutes later. "She said she didn't want them, and she wouldn't let me leave them with her. I just can't figure out what's come over her. She's always been such a sweet, obedient child."

"Maybe if we mail them to her and don't put our names on them, she'll accept them. It's Christmas, and I don't care who she thinks gave them to her as long as she gets them," Page said.

He walked from one end of the reception room to the other and back, his right hand gripping the back of his neck. "But how?" Why hadn't he thought of it? He snapped his finger. "The post office is still open. We can get Solomon to bring them in the morning." He turned to Miss Dodd. "She doesn't have to know who sent the gifts. Santa Claus could bring them. I just want her to have a wonderful Christmas."

"You're a good man, Mr. Pettiford. She sure won't learn it from me."

"She'll get them, but I don't feel good about it," he told Page as they left the post office.

"She loves you, Nelson and she's hurt, but she'll get over that as soon as she misses you."

"I hope you're right. I... poor thing. She's had such a difficult life. If only... No point in iffin. We'll drop by my place first and then yours to get our bags, and head for Baltimore. Logan's roasting a goose."

Logan greeted them in his white apron and chef's hat. "Why don't I just put your bag in Nelson's room?" he asked Page. "Then you two won't have to be tipping around in the dark knocking things over and waking me up."

Nelson glared at Logan in a chilly reprimand. "I know you pride yourself in saying what you think, so I advise you to do something about your mind. You embarrassed Page."

"He did?" Page asked.

Nelson glanced toward her and his eyes widened. Whatever he'd expected, it wasn't the wide grin and wicked glint he saw in her eyes. He threw up his hands. "Oh, you two! Do whatever you want."

After a feast of oyster stew, roast goose, wild rice, fluted cremini mushrooms, turnip greens, corn muffins and brandy-alexander pie, they strolled along Charles Street for a few blocks enjoying the lighted trees and myriad other seasonal decorations.

"Don't you have a girl?" Page asked Logan when they returned home. "I hate to think of you alone, especially at Christmas time."

"It's been almost two years," he said, "but the loss is still so fresh that I can't reach out just yet, but I'm making progress. Having you with us this Christmas takes away some of the loneliness for me, and I know I don't have to speak for my brother. Isn't it time you two made this permanent?"

It didn't surprise Nelson that she looked directly into his eyes then quickly away. When they got back, he'd tell her about Quigley, though he knew she'd spout fire, but he hoped she'd get over it quickly, because his work was his life.

"You'll be the first to know," Nelson said.

"I'm glad to hear it," Logan replied. He dimmed the lights of the ceiling high Christmas tree, and put on a CD of carols. "Let's open our presents."

Logan received an elegant briefcase from his brother to replace the one Nelson claimed disgraced the name

Pettiford. Page gave him an audio note taker with a ninety minute tape capacity. Her gift to Nelson was a bound set of Mozart's music for wind instruments, a CD of Paul Robeson ballads and an album of Fats Waller's complete recordings. Logan's gift to Page was an album of photographs from Nelson's childhood, and he had a set of fishing gear for Nelson.

Page unwrapped the bottle of perfume Nelson handed her and stared at him. "How did you know this is what I wear?"

He pointed to his eyes. "I had occasion to observe."

"Ahem," Logan said, clearing his throat. "Leave something to my imagination, Brother."

Nelson couldn't help laughing. "Oh, I did. Believe me, I did." He put his hand in the pocket of his jacket, pulled out a small parcel and handed it to Page.

"You said you'd been thinking about it," he said, as she stared in awe at the diamond solitaire. He knelt on one knee. "Will you wear it and will you marry me. You know how I love you and can't stand being without you."

Her face betrayed her bewilderment, and she shook her head as though afraid to believe her ears. "You're asking me to marry you?"

He nodded, unable to speak, for fear his heart would fly out of his chest.

Stars danced in her eyes and the smile on her face seemed to light up the room."Oh, Hon," she said, slipping to her knees in from of him, "Yes. Yes. Yes." She wrapped her arms around him, and he had to fight back the tears.

After a few minutes, she nibbled at her lower lip, and he knew he could expect an audacious word or act. She stood and looked down at him.

"Oh dear, I said yes, and you didn't make me a single promise. A girl's suppose to work this for all it's worth." She turned to Logan. "Isn't that right?"

Logan's face bore a look of pure joy. "There's still time; he hasn't put the ring on your finger."

She looked at Nelson with raised eyebrows, her expression prodding; she waited.

"I'll love you as long as I breathe. I'll take care of you and be a good father to our children." He thought for a minute. "Oh yes, and I'll take you to Tahiti on our honeymoon."

"Nobody's supposed to know that but..." Her bottom lip dropped. "You're kidding!" She held out her left hand. "Put it on before you decide you can't afford that trip."

He slipped the ring on her finger and sealed their commitment with his lips pressed to hers.

"I'm turning in. See you in the morning," Logan said.

Nelson sat in the big chair and patted his knee. "You're so far away."

She came to him, gliding along in slow motion it seemed to him—though she was only a few steps away—and sat on his knee. He slipped his arms around her and held her tight to his body.

"If anybody had told me a year ago, that I'd be sitting here Christmas Eve night with my future wife in my arms, I wouldn't have believed one word of it." With a smile that made his heart sing, she raised her face for the loving he needed to give her.

After lunch, Christmas day, he called Miss Dodd. "Did Ann get her gifts?" he asked after they greeted each other.

"Oh, yes indeed. Mr. Whitfield brought them around ten this morning, and she danced and laughed and hugged him. But Mr. Pettiford, I'm afraid she thinks the presents were from Mr. Whitfield."

"I don't mind that so long as she has them. I thought I'd stop by this afternoon."

"Uh, maybe not. After she saw the toys and played with them a little bit, she sank right back into that sad, distant way she acted before her plastic surgery. I don't know what to do."

"What about the social worker?"

Her snort surprised him. "Ann can't stand her, and I'm not enamored of the woman. Tell you what. I'll get the Board's approval and bring her to your place for a visit on my day off, if it's all right with you."

"Wonderful. Just let me know when."

The child's behavior worried him. If he could have celebrated Christmas with her for only a few minutes, he could have relished more his new status as a man about to be married to the woman he adored.

He met Mr. Whitfield at his gate the next morning, Tuesday, and asked him about Ann. "She's a beautiful child, so sweet, but I thought there was something sad about her."

"Yeah. Well, thanks for getting those presents to her on time."

"My pleasure. Here's your papers and your mail. Plenty of it today." Whitfield tipped his hat, adjusted his bag and continued his rounds.

Nelson went through *The Washington Post* first, then *The Maryland Journal*. He'd told himself that he'd leave women alone for a while, since Page got out of joint when he made fun of them, but he couldn't pass this up: Millie Shipley's antics were front page news again. In the name of Kings, what could she find in South Africa at Christmas time after just coming back from Ghana, when the cost of travel was at its peak, that she had to know in order to draft legislation or vote intelligently on a bill? He sketched Millie-Cat purring up to a proud male lion, she with the face of Millie Shipley and he the personification of Thabo Mbeki, South Africa's president.

"I guess Millie-Cat thinks she's too good for us toms here in Cat Alley, not that we're missing anything," Quigley said to Odessa-Cat.

"Not to worry, Quigley, my dear, the big lion's in for a surprise. All Millie-Cat wants is to get her picture taken with him so she can come back here and show it to us. The hussy is frigid," Odessa-Cat said, swished her tail and raised it to its full height. "The little strumpet will do anything to get noticed."

Quigley licked his paws and yawned. "And to think, I used to fantasize about the little wench." Nelson touched it up, drove to the post office and mailed it.

The next evening, speaking by phone, he and Page agreed to eat dinner together at his house. "I'll cook," he said. Little did he dream how much he would regret the idea.

"I hope you don't get shook up about this one," Phyllis said to Page that morning as she, handed her *The Maryland Journal*. "This strip just blew my mind. Face, it Girl, Quigley is inspired genius."

She looked at it, closed her eyes and counted to ten. "I'm not going to react," she told herself, knowing that Phyllis watched her. If Mama wants to make a fool of herself, it's no skin off my teeth. Though boiling inside, she draped her face in serenity, pushed the paper back to Phyllis and went on with her work.

That evening, Page rang the bell at Nelson's gate at the same time as he appeared around the house racing to let her in. Her breath seemed to stall in her throat as he swung it open, gazed down at her and grinned before picking her up and swinging her around.

"Hi. You're early. I'm just getting the stuff together."

His lips brushed her lightly, but she didn't care, for she knew there was more to come. Much more. "My watch crawled along so slowly," she said, "that I figured something was wrong with it."

In the dusk of evening, their laughter mingled as they wrapped an arm around each other's waist and strolled to the house.

"Make yourself at home while I do this," he said as he whisked egg whites. "It is your home after all," he added.

She studied the paintings and drawings in the wide hall that had the appearance of a gallery. Jacob Lawrence, Doris Price, John Biggers, Elizabeth Catlett and Romare Bearden, the greats among contemporary African-American artists, were represented. Nelson was obviously a man with fine artistic taste and the means to indulge it. Through a doorway, she saw a base fiddle leaning against the wall. Curious, she walked in to examine it and gasped aloud. There, on a large easel was a drawing of Quigley in color. She stepped closer and saw on the draft board a Quigley cartoon in progress.

Her fingers trembled as she reached out to touch it but snatched back her hand as chills shook her and she nearly convulsed in pain. But then anger took over and she had to deal with her jagged breathing and the furor that churned in her. She charged back into the hallway and got her coat.

"Where're you going?"

"Home. This was all a mistake." She slammed out of the door, slipped the lock on the gate, got in her car and went home. How dare he make a fool of her Mother!

Nelson turned off the stove, dumped the uncooked food into the garbage disposal, got a beer and went into his living room to sort things out. She hadn't thought enough of him to explain, and he wasn't going to crawl on his knees and beg. Loving a woman didn't mean you had to be her door mat. Out of habit, he flipped on the TV. Several reporters and cameramen at Ronald Reagan

International Airport in Washington caught his attention. Then he saw her.

"What do you fellows want from me? I gave up Christmas with my only child, my Page, so I could make the trip while congress was in recess. I tried to do what's right, and you...you snoops try to make me out a criminal, to turn my efforts to cement relations between our two countries into a calamity, a cause célébre. I'll bet a quarter of the congress went off on fact-finding missions this season, but you pick on me." She tossed her head and walked on. "Go do your dirt somewhere else."

He lunged forward. Why hadn't he noticed it before? Those eyes and that voice. Carbon copies. Millie Shipley was Page Sutherland's mother, and he was in trouble. He sank into the sofa. What a mess!

After a sleepless night, he got in his car and drove all morning trying to think, his one hope being she hadn't given him back his ring. Shortly after noon, he drove to Page's apartment.

"Please open the door, Page. I'm not leaving until you do." She cracked the door and he walked past her before she could ask him to come in.

"Why didn't you tell me she's your Mother?"

"Why didn't you tell me you were Quigley...I mean Slim Wisdom. I hate that cartoon. Do you hear me? I detest it."

"Political cartoons are my livelihood. How would it look if I took stock of every off-the-wall thing in Washington, and ignored Dr. Shipley, when she's one of the most conspicuous actors on Capitol Hill? She's never once written me and complained."

"You're not even sorry you made a fool of her, are you?

"I made a fool of her? If she didn't do all these crazy things... Look, I didn't come here to argue. One of us had to make the first move, and I'm making it. I'm sorry if you're hurt."

"You could at least promise not to do it again."

He stared at her. "You're asking the impossible. You want me to forfeit my impartiality, the thing that gives me authority as a political commentator. You can't ask that of me."

"You're saying no?"

"Yes, and I won't ever change."

She walked to the front door and opened it. "I'm sorry. You don't know how sorry I am."

He didn't pause, but walked out as quickly as he could. Pain shot through him, but he'd get over it. He walked into his house and heard the phone in his office ringing.

"Mr. Pettiford, this is Miss Dodd. Have you seen Ann?"

"Have I seen... You don't know where she is?"

"No. I took eight of the children to the library this morning, and I thought she was with us when we got on the bus to come back, but she was nowhere. I'm out of my mind. I've called the sheriff, and all he said was `don't worry, we'll find her.'"

It didn't take a genius to realize the child had run away. "I'll do what I can to find her. Here's my cell phone number. Please call me if you learn anything. Miss Dodd, that child is precious to me."

"I know that, Mr. Pettiford. I'll stay in touch."

He hung up and dialed Page's number. "Baby, I know you're upset with me, but I need you. Ann's missing." He explained what he knew.

"My Lord, she's run away."

"That's what I think. I'll be by your place in half an hour."

"I'll be ready."

Nearly ten hours, and she hadn't been found. His belly pinched and squeezed him, empty for want of lunch, dinner and water, but he couldn't think of food and drink. He looked over at Page as he retraced one more place they'd already searched. "Do you want me to get you something to eat?"

She shook her head. "I'm not hungry. Do you think she's been kidnapped?"

"No. She ran away. I'm sure of it. Oh, heck, I must be getting addled; I meant to turn into Boyers Mill Road. Out here on Old Mills Road is the last place I'd expect to..." He heard a staccato noise that appeared to come from the engine.

"Now what? I had this car tuned up a couple of days before Christmas." The engine sputtered once more, and the car came to a standstill."

"Just what we need."

They got out of the car, and he lifted the hood to examine the engine. "I'm sorry you have to spend New Year's Eve this way, but I... I don't know what I'd do if anything happened to that child. She got next to me the first time I saw her with those sad eyes and—"

"If we weren't looking for Ann, I'd say this is a great way to spend New Years Eve," Page said. "Did you ever see such a moonlight? No wind. It's...well, if she's outside somewhere, at least she won't be in the dark, and she isn't cold." She looked around. "Hey, do you realize this is almost the exact spot where my car stalled the night we met?"

" You think... Look Honey, someone's coming. An old man walking along with a German shepherd dog. Well, it was worth a try."

"Sir, we're trying to find a little girl. She's six years old and about this high." He bent over to show the man Ann's height.

The man gazed at them for a minute. "Over this way," he said and patted the dog on the head. "Come on, boy."

They followed their guide through the thicket and suddenly, his heart did a drum roll. He'd taken Ann there on each of their outings. Why hadn't he thought of that; she loved to go there and look at the lake. They emerged from the brush to the shore of Lake Linganore and the dazzling sight of the lake, ethereal with the full moon aglow above it, and the shadow of the silvery cylinder dancing in its waters.

A gasp from Page brought him to her side. "What is it, Love?"

"It's so touching, so other worldly. Not a bit real. I..." Suddenly, she squinted at something beyond him, for her gaze had followed the old man. "Nelson! Good Lord! Look!"

He raced to where the child lay on a bed of leaves, dropped down on his knees and placed his ear to her chest.

"She only sleeping," the old man said. "She's perfectly all right."

Nelson looked first at Page, who knelt beside him and then at the old man. Then he bowed his head. "Thank God." To the old man, he said as if in after thought, "And you. How can I thank you?"

The old man half smiled. "Don't worry. You thanked the right source."

He led them back through the thicket and, as they emerged, snow flakes so thick they could hardly see ahead of themselves fell all around them but not on the three adults, the child and the dog. Nelson opened the car and laid Ann in the back seat.

"Now if I could just get this thing started," he said to Page as he went to open the hood. "I'd gladly give you a lift, sir, but I can't get this buggy to start."

The old man, shrugged and patted the big dog that stood close beside him. "Put the key back in the ignition and turn it."

Nelson's head snapped up. That was an order if he'd ever heard one, but he did it and the engine hummed. He got out of the car to thank the man and repeat his offer of a ride, but there in the brightest moonlight he'd ever witnessed, he saw only empty space. He stepped to the road and looked both ways, but saw no one. Not even a shadow.

"Who...hooo." A hooting owl. He hadn't heard one in years. He walked back and forth along Old Mills Road checking the bushes, looking for any kind of movement. Nothing. No one. He rushed to the car and looked in the back seat, certain that it had all been an illusion. But Ann lay where he'd placed her. Rubbing the back of his neck, he looked to the sky. Then he shook his head and got in the car.

"Can you beat that?" he asked Page, as he drove toward Mystic Ridge. Do you think we dreamed up that man?"

Page looked in the back seat to make certain that Ann was there and what they'd thought they experienced wasn't an apparition. "Honey, let's just be thankful that we have her and she's all right. She's still asleep." She turned to face the road. "Uh...do you believe in angels?"

"I didn't, but now I'm not so sure. What time is it?"

She looked at the iridescent hands on her watch. Five after twelve. Happy New Year, darling."

"Happy New Year, Sweetheart. I'll kiss you when we get home. Okay?"

"Okay," she said, and he let out a long breath. He handed Page his cell phone and gave her Miss Dodd's number.

"We found her, Miss Dodd and we'll be there in a few

minutes.

"Thank the Lord and hallelujah," the woman said.

Nelson drove on to Mystic Ridge, more slowly now, aware that the pain and fear he'd shared with Page as they searched the town and countryside for Ann had tightened their bonds and strengthened their love for each other. He glanced at the woman by his side and gave silent thanks.

He carried Ann in one arm, and with the other, tucked Page to his side as they entered the group home. Standing just inside the door, he made up his mind, walked over to the sofa in the reception room and sat down. Ann clung to him, her fingers gripping his arm and her eyes wide with panic.

"Can't I ever come to your house? I want to stay with you sometime."

He tucked her close to his side. "Sweetheart, if you'll agree, I'll see about making that permanent."

Wide awake now, she stared up at him. "You... you mean—"

"I'd like for you to be my little girl and live with me all the time."

"You mean adopt me and you'll be my daddy?"

He looked at Page, and her smile of agreement sealed his resolve. "That's exactly what I mean, and you'll even get a new mother."

He'd never seen such happiness as the glow of the little girl's face. "My name is going to be Ann Pettiford. Now, it's just Ann" she said, giving him a fierce hug.

Nelson took Ann's hand and walked over to the desk. "Do you have papers here for initiating adoption proceedings, Miss Dodd?"

She clasped her hands before her. "I sure do. Well, well. You don't know how happy this makes me. It's the right thing, and I'll vouch for you." She paused. "Oh dear. A little girl and you being single and all."

"That won't be for long," Page said, looking up at her husband-to-be with loving eyes. We're getting married, Miss Dodd."

Miss Dodd beamed with delight and handed Nelson the adoption papers. Bring them back soon as you can."

He took out his pen. "How about right now." He turned to Ann and winked

"I'll get it started first thing tomorrow," Miss Dodd said. "I tell you, the Lord works in mysterious ways, His wonders to perform."

"Happy New Year, Miss Dodd," they chorused.

"Yes. A Blessed New Year. And congratulations to you both." She put an arm around Ann's shoulder, and they waved good-bye.

Half an hour later, Nelson led Page into his den. "Have a seat. I'll be back in a second."

She looked around. Quigley was still there on the easel and a work in progress graced the drawing board. It was the strangest thing, but it suddenly occured to her that Quigley looked just like that cat on Old Mills Road the night she first arrived in Mystic Ridge. She was determined not to worry about the things she couldn't explain, and just accept the fact that things simply happen in Mystic.

Nelson walked in with a bottle of champagne, a bag of potato chips and a can of peanuts. "We have to settle this first. Then I'll gladly cook."

She tried to breathe, but she only panted. "What is there to say?"

"You're ashamed of your mother, and I realize that's the reason why you left Washington and came here, why you didn't tell me who she is and why you haven't taken me to meet her."

"I'm not ashamed of her."

"Then I take it you approve of her capers."

"I don't, and I...I want her to grow up."

"There you have it, Honey. You have to learn to accept her just as I had to learn to accept my height, to see its advantages and stop worrying about wisecracking characters. Your mother is a woman of singular achievements, a physician and a congresswoman, a person who makes the laws of your country. Honey, try to stop sitting in judgment on her. This is the Twenty-first century and everything has changed, including women's roles. Can you accept her for who she is?"

"I don't have a choice. When she's in her private persona, she's a loving caring mother, but when she's being her public self, she's outrageous."

He chuckled. "Personally, I like some of those wild things she does, though I have to needle her when she pushes the envelope too far."

"When we get married, are you still going to do those awful cartons about her?" she asked, pretending to pout.

He had to laugh. "Uh...yeah, and I'll bet she makes sure I get the information. We love each other, Baby," he said, pouring champagne in two long stemmed glasses. "I want to spend my life loving you, but I won't be happy without my work. Can we set the date?"

She nodded her head vigorously. "I guess you're right about Mama. She loves the limelight. She said she wanted to meet you, and I'll take you to her this weekend." He locked arms with her, and they sipped the cold champagne.

"I love you, Sweetheart."

"And I love you."

He put their glasses on the cocktail table and bent to her waiting lips, lips now starved for his sweetness. She gripped his shirt as his tongue found its home deep in her mouth and shivers raced through her. She placed his hand on her breast and he broke the kiss.

"You're not hungry?" he asked her.

"I'm hungry for you."

He picked her up, carried her to their bed and to that other world where only they had been.

S o that's what happened, believe it or not. It's true, every single word of it. I was there, I should know. Humph, humph, humph. That was some winter. Everything and everybody changed. Something special happened to Mystic Ridge ...real special. Folks say it was the snow, that it sprinkled down some kind of magic on the town. Who can say for sure? But, just remember, if you're ever in the vicinity, and your car stalls for no reason, or a rusty-colored cat crosses your path, or you hear voices that brush across your neck like a breeze and nothing seems quite like it was only moments before ...you'll know you're close. Take a chance, take that turn and pay us a visit.

Well, I best be getting on my route, folks are waiting on their mail, plenty of surprises in this old sack, I can tell you that. Hmmm, by the looks of those clouds we just might get some snow!

Happy Holidays

Solomon Whitfield

About the Authors

Leslie Esdaile—A graduate of The University of Pennslyvania Wharton Undergraduate program at Temple University's Film and Media Arts Program, Esdaile began her artistic career when she moved into fiction writing in 1996 with her debut novel *Sundance,* followed by *Slow Burn,* which earned her BET's Literary Cafe Emerging Author pick for the Philadelphia market.

Esdaile's novella, *Home for the Holidays,* is her first work for Genesis Press. She lives in Philadelphia with her family. You may contact her by e-mail at writerLE@aol.com.

Gwynne Forster—Best-selling and award-winning author of nine romance novels and three novellas, Forster holds a bachelors degree in sociology and a masters degree in economics/demography. As a demographer she is widely published.

Her first interracial romance, *Against the Wind* was published by Genesis Press in November 1999. Her most recent Genesis Press romance is titled *Midnight Magic.* She was voted Author of the Year (1999) by Romance in Color. Forster makes her home in New York City and can be contacted by writing to her at P.O. Box 45, New York, NY, 10044-0045, or by e-mail at GwynneF@aol.com.

About the Authors

Carmen Green— Green holds a Bachelor of Arts degree, and has eight published titles to her credit. She made her debut onto the literary scene in 1996 with her first romance *Now or Never.* She was also named bestselling author in *Emerge* magazine. Her 1998 book *Commitments* has been picked to air as a BET television movie in spring of 2001.

A native of Buffalo, NY, Carmen makes her home in Atlanta, Georgia, with her husband and three children. Her novella, *Angel's Legacy* is her first work for Genesis Press. She can be reached by e-mail at Cgreen30@aol.com.

Monica Jackson—A registered nurse of almost twenty years, jackson makes her home in Topeka, Kansas, and is the mother of an active daughter. Her first romance novel, *Midnight Blue* was published in 1997.

Her most recent work, *Never Too Late For Love* was released in June 2000. Two of her novels have been picked for BET television movies: *Midnight Blue* (aired spring 2000) and *The Look of Love,* scheduled to air in the 2001 season. Ms. Jackson can be reached by e-mail at monica@monicajackson.com.